Deep Six
David Huff

David Huff— Ephraim, UT
ISBN: 978-0-9988003-8-7
Library of Congress Control Number: 2020924957
Title: *Deep Six*
Author: David Huff
Digital distribution | 2020.
Paperback | 2020

This is a work of fiction. The characters, names, incidents, places, and dialogue are products of the author's imagination, and are not to be construed as real.

Dedication

This book is dedicated to my brother Dennis, a man among men, who was a Submariner who lived and slept the submarine life and told me of his adventures when he would come home on leave.

"The greatest use of a life is to spend it on something that will outlast it."   — William James

"I can't sit back and fold my hands and think about the past for there are thousands of yesterdays but only one today and... Maybe a tomorrow."   — Red Skelton

"Entrenched belief is never altered by the facts." — Dick Francis

"Everything that is really great, and inspiring is created by the individual who can labor in freedom." – Albert Einstein

"Abracadabra, thus we learn the more you create, the less you earn. The less you earn, the more you're given The less you lead, the more you're driven, The more destroyed, the more they feed. The more you pay, the more they need, the more you earn, the less you keep. And now I lay me down to sleep. I pray the Lord my soul to take, if the tax-collector hasn't got it before I wake." — Ogden Nash

Other Books Written by this Author

Arizona Heat
Florida Heat
Nevada Heat
New Jersey Heat

The Medallion
The Valley of the Giants

The Counterfeit Presidential

The Plague

Chapter I

As the submarine moved through the water, at the speed of 50 knots, the mid-Atlantic ridge was the only reference point it needed to use based on the maps and charts borrowed from the U.S. Navy. The 10 man crew operated the Deep Submergence Vehicle (DSV) with precision as it made its way down through the darkness of the ocean, its front lights illuminating the way as it went deeper into the trench. The DSV's objective was to find the remains of the USS Dolphin, a nuclear Fast Attack submarine that had disappeared in or around this area about a month ago.   The USS Dolphin was one of three Sea Wolf class submarines in the Navy inventory with the capability to carry Tomahawk missiles and MK-48 torpedoes,   having a speed of 25+ knots (28+ miles per hour, 46.3+ kph) and a crew of 140 personnel, of which 14 were officers, and an enlisted crew of 126. With it having the latest state-of-the-art technology in submarine warfare, Chance could understand why the Admiral was interested in finding out what had happened to his submarine. Following the emergency signal put out by the USS Dolphin, the Thresher was looking to find its location in order to ascertain what kind of damage that had been done to the submarine that would cause the emergency signal to activate.

The Thresher was a one-of-a-kind DSV, built by Dalynn Research Enterprises, based in New London, Connecticut. It's one true ability was to go deeper and faster than anything the U.S. Navy had in its inventory of submarines. The Thresher was not your typical DSV, it was bigger and more capable of many things that were still considered classified. The technology for the Thresher was state of the art, as far as submarines went it was invisible to sonar and able to go 50 knots under water for three-month intervals. It could go deeper than any full-scale submarine in existence, in fact, that was one of its best features to date. The Navy wanted to purchase the Thresher but Chance, the captain and owner of the company that had built it, refused to sell it saying, "The Thresher is my baby and I will never part with it.   However, that being said, it's always available to the Navy if they have a need for it."   With a shake of a hand between Chance and the Navy, a gentleman's agreement was made for the use of the Thresher in emergency situations or as needed by the Navy.

When the USS Dolphin was reported missing the Navy contacted Chance to see if he could use the Thresher to locate the submarine for them. Agreeing to assist in the search for the submarine at its last known coordinates, the Thresher was able to track the emergency signal to the final resting place of the USS Dolphin.

The sonar man, the eyes and ears for the submarine, looked at his scope and called out to the captain, "I got the signal at bearing 360 degrees, 20 nautical miles in front of us."

Chance walked over to the sonar position and looked at his screen, waiting for the sonar and listening equipment to get a fix on the sound. As he and the sonar operator watched the screen intently for a couple of minutes the sonar screen lit up as it found its target. Chance called out to the submarine drivers, "All a head 20 knots."

"All a head 20 knots sir," the driver of the submarine said.

Slowing the submarine down to 20 knots was still considered fast yet was still manageable for the crew in case there were unforeseen problems that might arise. The seismic activity had been quiet in this area of the trench for the last couple of months, that being said, no one wanted to run into a new mountain that just happened to appear.

"Open the master screen; let's see what's out there," Chance ordered.

The panel, located in the front of the ship, slowly opened up and a window made of highly polished titanium revealed the darkness that was in front of them. The titanium window was made of material that was better and stronger than what was being used to protect the president when he was riding in his limousine.   The difference of this type of window was the thin opaque sheet of titanium that was being used in place of glass.   The titanium was used because of its ability to withstand the greater depths of the sea.   In fact, the deeper the submarine went the stronger the titanium window got. With the window open to view what was in front of them Chance said, "Driver, turn on all of the forward lights of the submarine. Now let's see what we found."

"All forward lights are on, captain," the driver said.

"All a head 5 knots driver," Chance said, acknowledging the driver.

"I've located the emergency signal again, now bearing 350 degrees, 5 nautical miles, sir," the sonar man said.

"Driver make changes based on sonar, all ahead slow."

"Aye captain, all ahead slow."

As the Thresher slowed to a crawl, Chance was straining to see something through the window. Being this deep the USS Dolphin could be right in front of them and it still would not be seen because of how dark it was at this depth. Very few people knew that the Thresher could go down this deep without a problem. This was one of its few hidden talents, besides its speed, that wasn't very well known yet and was one of the reasons why the Navy had wanted it so badly.

At one mile down the Thresher responded to the controls of the driver like a car on a Sunday drive. "It's right in front of us now sir," said the sonar operator, still staring intently at his screen.

Acknowledging the sonar report, the captain and the driver kept looking through the window, searching for anything that would indicate a submarine was in front of them. As Chance continued to search through the darkness the lights fell on a piece of manmade material on the ledge in front of them.

"All stop and hold this position," Chance called out.

The Thresher froze in the position it was in and waited for the next command. Taking the controls for the forward lights, Chance, using his joystick, moved the nose light in every direction staying focused on the piece of material he had seen. He moved the light slowly down the length of the ledge, moving it back and forth, up and down to see if there was anything else there.

"Move us around so that we can get a full visual of the ledge in front of us, driver,"

"Aye, aye, captain."

The driver complied and within minutes the ledge came into center screen. There, on the side of the ledge, hanging like a bait fish caught on a hook, was the major part of the hull of the USS Dolphin. The back half was gone and the only thing that even resembled a submarine was the conning tower.   The submarine was identified as the USS Dolphin by the name and number on the sail of the submarine.   "XO mark this location on the map, for future reference and drop a noise maker as well," Chance said.

"Aye, aye, Captain," replied the XO as he toggled a few switches on the master control panel.

In a few seconds you could hear the discharge of the noise maker as it left the Thresher.

"Let's see what we've found and see if we can determine what sank her.   All ahead slow, driver," Chance said.

"All ahead slow, captain."

The driver of the Thresher got closer and moved up and down the frame of the front half of the USS Dolphin.

"Look at that. All ahead stop, driver," said the XO as he stared intently through the window.

The driver stopped the Thresher as the light showed a gaping hole in the front side of the submarine where the torpedo room was located.   Chance now caught sight of what the XO was looking at. Resting there for a moment, Chance told the driver, "Activate the camera and start taking pictures of what you see."

Looking at the jagged edges, the hole in the side of the submarine looked like an explosion of sorts had occurred, with the blast coming from within the submarine. Chance thought to himself, *Something must have gone horribly wrong to have caused the submarine to explode from inside.*

He looked at the XO, "How big does that hole look?"

"I figure about twenty feet, maybe bigger," he replied.

"I concur. Take a look inside the blast hole, you'll see very little damage to the inside the torpedo room," he said, as they took the Thresher along the side of the submarine with its light on it.

The hole in the submarine was about 20 feet in diameter and the side of the submarine showed that the ragged edges were going out, away from the submarine.   This indicated to Chance, that whatever blew up the submarine had come from inside.   This confused him, how could an explosion create a blast hole this big and not affect the torpedoes that were still sitting in their cradles.

As they slowly turned the Thresher around, they started looking for the other half of the submarine, as this was the half that housed the Sea Launched Ballistic Missiles (SLBMs).

"Let's see if we can find the rest of the submarine," Chance said.

Leaving the forward half of the submarine, Chance asked sonar to start searching the area around them to locate the back half of the submarine.

"Aye, aye, captain.   Starting new search."

Within minutes, the sonar operator said, "Contact at 030 less than half a mile, sir."

The driver responded accordingly to the sonar's contact point and moved the Thresher in the direction of the sonar contact. As they went deeper both the captain and XO were peering through the window looking for more clues about the other half of the boat.

Finally, resting about 50 feet from the other half, the Thresher, again following the contact from the sonar operator, came upon the back half of the USS Dolphin resting on the bottom and found it sitting in the upright position. The SLBM hatches were still intact and nothing looked out of order from their vantage point. Moving up and down the back half of the USS Dolphin, the boat looked as though it was taking a break on the beach trying to catch its breath before going again.

"You getting pictures of this?" Chance asked the driver.

"Aye, aye sir, still taking pictures,"

"What do we do now?" The XO asked Chance.

"Get a fix on the location and mark it on the charts and drop another noise maker," he replied. "It's too deep for anyone to be interested in getting the SLBMs," he said, as he looked at the depth gauge as the digital readout that showed a little more than half a mile below the surface of the sea.

"Driver take us back home to the base," Chance said.

"Aye, aye, captain.   Headed home."

The driver closed the viewing window and made sure that it was sealed against the metal door covering. With that done, the Thresher turned its nose around and started for the surface, making sure not to hit the side of the ledge or the submarine as it made its way. Leveling off at periscope depth, Chance contacted the Navy about what they had found on the bottom of the trench and now waited for their reply.   Once the Navy had acknowledged the communique, the Thresher headed back to its home port in New London.

Later that evening Chance sat in his easy chair drinking his coffee and watching a little TV. Frustrated with what was on TV, he turned it off and started reading a book. His wife, Helen, was doing some sewing on a blanket for their new grand baby which was due in six months. Their daughter had been excited to tell them the news that she was having a baby, and they were excited to be grandparents for the first time. Chance was happy about being a grandpa but not too excited about feeling his youth slipping away. He shrugged off the thought, thinking he was too young to worry about getting old.

Since the startup of his company he had earned a reputation of being an honest engineer with radical ideas when it came to designing new technology for submarines. Because of his unconventional way of thinking and his habit of speaking his mind, there was a lot of push back, not only from the Navy, but also from his competitors. Nevertheless, he was able to make great strides by bypassing the conventional way of thinking, causing the Navy and his competition to take notice when they saw how versatile his submarines were in their tactical operations. In fact, some of his competitors were wanting him to come to work for them, at which point he would just smile and walk away. He liked being his own boss and knew he was killing the competition with new technology.

The times Chance enjoyed most was when he was inside his submarine, roaming the oceans looking for new animals and or new scientific information to share with the world. In his younger years he had served in the U.S. Navy aboard submarines as a sonar technician. After getting out he used his GI bill to pay for his college in an aerodynamic engineering program. His reasoning was simple for his choice of aerodynamic research and that was airplanes fly in an ocean of air, he naturally thought this seemed to be same for submarines under the water. The propulsion system of course would be different, that problem was solved for underwater travel for the time being using nuclear energy.

He had met Helen at college during his second year at Caltech. She was studying human behavior in her master's program and he was working on building a prototype submersible robot that operated on radio frequency instead of long cables being hooked onto a robot. They met at the library while studying at the same table. For Chance, she was the most beautiful girl he had ever seen and taking an opportunity he asked her what she was studying. They hit it off quickly when they started talking about how long man could be inside a small sphere and not go crazy. His contention was nine months inside the womb was long enough for anybody not to go crazy. She laughed at this, "How long were you under the water in the submarine?"

"Three to six months, which is to long for anybody in their right mind."

She laughed at his remark, "I betcha it was a crowded down there for those three to six months wasn't it?"

Smiling, he nodded at her, and from that point on he would be in her life forever as far as he was concerned. After a whirlwind courtship, they were married six months later in a beautiful old chapel in San Diego and set up home in some married housing near the campus. They stayed there until he received an internship with one of the engineering companies in the Silicon Valley during his junior summer. Helen was able to get a job working as a human behaviorist for one of the smaller companies in Silicon Valley in their human resources division.

For them life was good, and fun being married with no kids, and living in California was a dream come true for both of them. They traveled all over California during school breaks and vacations from work, seeing all that California had to offer. It was a grand experience for both of them.

When school was over Chance took a job in Groton, Connecticut to work in the shipyards, working for one of the contractors that was working for the Navy. He was involved in developing better engineering processes and better corrosion control maintenance for the ships while at sea. Trying to solve the issue of saltwater corrosion on metal was the biggest problem the Navy faced when it came to metal fatigue on their ships. Chance was able to get in on the research and development of new types of metals for ship building and apply it on the smaller ships for the Navy. Working on his own time at home, he came up with a combination of metal alloys that could resist the saltwater corrosion longer and better than what the Navy had been using. He showed what he had created to his bosses and they dismissed the idea out of hand, because it came from a junior engineer thinking he knew more than the senior engineers. Frustrated by this, he left the company and decided to go out on his own. After getting some financial backing from the banks, and with the promise of a new contract from the Navy, he started his own company. He hired his own engineers that would work with him solely, coming up with better material that could withstand the saltwater corrosion problem for the Navy's ships. In about a year the solution was found, and the U.S. Navy bought the idea and started using the new types of metal for the building of their ships from that point on.

With his financial backing secure, he was now able to concentrate on his dream of building a submarine that could go faster and deeper that anyone thought possible. The Thresher, named after the original submarine, was an answer to his dream. The Thresher was resurrected by Chance and given an opportunity to live once again and leave a better legacy. The corporate secrets used to build his submarine were given to the U.S. Navy for future development on their submarines, but for him, the Thresher was his, and only his, to use as he saw fit.

As he sat there reading his book Helen came over to him, "So what do you think?"

she said, showing him her newest attempt at being a grandmother.

The baby blanket was almost complete and already Helen was thinking of matching burp clothes and more for the new baby. Chance smiled, "That looks pretty good."

Helen was all about being a grandmother and was always calling their daughter to check on her.   He realized that it was him that was having a hard time accepting the fact that he was old enough to be a grandfather.   Not that he minded it so much, he just wondered where all of the time had gone from being newlyweds to nearly dead people in his mind. Being prematurely gray since his thirties, this was just another step to getting old or putting another nail in his coffin. As time went by, he was slowly warming up to the idea even if it was too soon for his liking.

As he was thinking about all of this and looking at the new baby blanket, the phone rang and brought him back to the here and now. Picking up the phone on the second ring he answered it. On the other end of the phone was Admiral Richards. Chance recognized his voice, "Why the phone call so late in the evening Admiral?"

"So sorry to call you at this hour but we need to see you in the morning if possible," the Admiral requested.

"Would nine a.m. work for you tomorrow?" Chance replied, knowing he would have to leave early to beat the rush hour traffic as everybody headed to work.

"That would be fine. See you then."

After hanging up the phone, he sat there and wondered why the Admiral needed to see him so early in the morning. Oh well, he thought to himself, he would know the answer soon enough.

The following morning, Chance was at the Admiral's office around 8:50 a.m. waiting to be admitted into his office. Sitting there in a chair he watched the secretary do her typing and other office work. He closed his eyes for a minute to catch up on his sleep.

The sound of the Admiral opening his door startled him. The Admiral walked over to where he was seated, "Did we wake you?" asked the Admiral smiling.

Catching him unawares, and having caught him off guard, he was brought back to reality, "I was trying to remember what it was like to work before I became rich and famous not having to ever work again," he said, smiling at the Admiral.

"It must be rough having six Saturdays and one Sunday every week."

Chance stood up from the chair he had been sitting in and shook hands with the Admiral, "It's rough, but someone has to do it."

"Let me know how rough it is will you," he said, as they walked into his office and closed the door behind them.

"Well, what brings me here so early to see you this morning?"

"First of all, we appreciate you finding the USS Dolphin and giving us some pictures showing us what you found down there."

By then the intercom buzzed, the Admiral walked over to his desk, sat down, and answered it, "Commander Jones is here, "said his secretary.

"Good, have him come in."

The door opened and a man walked in that Chance new very well. He had worked with him on the new submarine technology that he had created for the Navy a few years back. It was Commander Anthony Jones of Navy Intelligence. As he walked in, Chance stood up and shook his hand, "Tony, I haven't seen you in what, two years now?"

"It seems longer to me since our last encounter," Tony replied.

"Why, you've gained a little weight, you must have gotten married," Chance said, tapping him on the belly with his hand. "Let me guess, you married Susan, the blonde that used to work in your office."

"No, as a matter of fact, she got away. I'm a confirmed bachelor now, it's a dirty job but someone had to do it and this is the results from that fatal decision. I'm not sure there's a cure I can live with that makes me want to change it though."

They all laughed at the remark as Tony sat down next to him. By now both men looked at the Admiral, wondering what it was that brought both of them here together and waited for the Admiral to start the conversation. Not knowing where to start, the Admiral was at a loss for words in order to start the conversation. Chance, seeing this, broke the silence in the air, "So what brings us all together that is so important for us to compare our battle scars."

"We want you to go back down and get some more detailed pictures of the USS Dolphin, especially around the blast area inside the ship, if possible. We need to find out why she blew up and what caused her to sink so fast. We lost over 90 men that day and we need to know if it was sabotage or mechanical error that caused her to sink," the Admiral said, intensely.

Tony was nodding his head in agreement with what the Admiral was saying, "I need to go down with you the next time to get a good look at what happened. I need to make sure that it wasn't sabotage."

"Not a problem, I understand. When do you want to go?" Chance said.

"As soon as possible if not sooner than that," Tony replied smiling.

Chance sat there thinking about seeing the USS Dolphin laying there in the dark waters, "Not a very fitting end to a fighting ship is it?"

Tony and the Admiral nodded their heads in unison at Chance's remarks. "We need to know what happened to her and why it happened," the Admiral added.

The Admiral then handed the pictures of the USS Dolphin that Chance had taken to Tony, so he could see for himself the damage that had been done to the submarine. After looking at them for a minute Tony handed them back to the Admiral, shaking his head.

"One more thing, we want to see if we can raise her back up from the bottom of the trench and get the missiles and crew off of her," said the Admiral.

This statement caught Chance off guard. But as he thought about it for a minute, he began to run some scenarios of deep-water salvage through his mind. "It can be done, but is it worth the time or money to do it?"

"Regardless of the time or money, we still need to try and raise her if possible. This is vitally important to the Navy, so it doesn't happen again. The real question is, can you support us in this?" asked the Admiral.

"I'm not sure I can but give me a day to try and figure out the math and the logistics for it," Chance said.

"Good, then I'll have Tony go with you to assist you in this."

Chance looked at the Admiral with a serious look on his face, "I don't know if that's safe for Tony. You know, my wife can really cook a good meal and there's a possibility that Tony might not survive the ordeal."

"I'll take my chances. Oh, the things I do for my country," Tony said, laughing.

"Well, why don't you follow me to my office, so we can get started working on your requests?" Chance said.

As both men left the Admirals office Tony asked, "So tell me, how many kids do you have now?"

"I have one. She's married now and she's about to have a baby, which will be our first grandchild."

"You poor man, you are so old. Do you want me to get you a walker grandpa so you can get to your submarine?" Tony laughed.

"Keep it up, wise guy. I may just leave you at the USS Dolphin."

Chapter II

When they arrived back at Chance's office, Chance went directly to his computer to start running some mathematical equations. Tony walked over to the map case on the other side of his office that held all the charts and retrieved the one's that they would need to start the equations needed for dealing with the underwater currents. Between the two of them they started trying to sort out the best way to raise the USS Dolphin from the bottom of the ocean.

Some of the problems with high order salvage consisted of raising the submarine without attracting attention from the prying eyes of the world, namely Russia or China. The other concern was the unpredictable weather pattern for that part of the ocean, not to mention the depth that they were trying to raise the submarine from. Any one of these issues could make or break the salvage operation and determine whether it was   successful or a giant loss of money and time.

The goal of going after the submarine would be to raise it using Chance's state of the art technology with just the two pieces that it was already in. This would require the Thresher, with a crew of deep-sea salvage experts and divers, on hand plus having maintenance ships on station above them, acting as if they were doing Navel rescue exercises.   This would go on for an undetermined amount of time until it was decided if the submarine could be raised or not.   Unlike the U.S. recovery operation, code named Azorian, where they attempted to raise a Russian submarine known as K-129 from the bottom of the western Pacific ocean, the depths where the USS Dolphin lay were greater than what anybody had ever tried before. That being said, some of the lessons learned from operation Azorian would still benefit the goal of retrieving the USS Dolphin in these very extreme conditions.

As Chance went through some mathematical calculations regarding the depth that the USS Dolphin was sitting at, the reality of what the Admiral wanted was starting to sink in. From his calculations, it would require at least two teams of divers, six each, to close all of the hatches on the submarine, then fill the submarine with oxygen to start raising it from the bottom of the ocean. At this depth, the submarine could literally be crushed by the force of the sea water against the hull. In fact, Chance was surprised that it was still in two pieces, which he considered very lucky. Raising the submarine would be a painstakingly slow process of lifting and waiting then lifting again, little by little until it was at a depth where it could have an air collar put around it to continue raising it from the bottom. The air collar would have to be put on in increments at key points around the submarine. The sheer size of the floating collar would be problematic, to say the least, and then how to get it wrapped around the submarine pieces without damaging the pieces further, would require new material, as well, to meet the weight problems of the collar and the submarine combined.

The full length of the fast attack submarine was 362 feet long. The two broken halves of the USS Dolphin measured approximately 120 feet for the front half and approximately 240 feet for the back half. This would require a collar big enough to wrap around the two pieces separately and then attach the cables underneath the submarine to the other side of the collar, thereby cradling it as they raised it to the surface. Once it was brought up to the surface the maintenance ships would take control of that part of the operation. Once that half had been secured they would then be able to detach the collar from the one piece and then send it back down to be put around the other part of the submarine that was still laying on the ocean floor waiting to be picked up.

Chance stayed at the office until 6:00 p.m. running numbers and computer simulations, trying to find a way to raise the submarine from the bottom without killing anybody and his budget in the process. Tony could see the frustration and stress on Chance's face as he continued working on the computer. He checked his watch, "Hey, about we take a break and go get something to eat."

"Yeah, I guess it's about that time isn't it? I didn't realize it was so late," Chance said after looking at his own watch.

After closing the shop, they headed to Chance's house for the evening. Helen had dinner already prepared and was just waiting on them to show up when they got there. Afterwards Tony and Chance headed into the den where they relaxed watching some TV. When the news was over, after saying goodbye and thanking Helen for a wonderful dinner, Tony excused himself and headed home to get some sleep.

Chance, for the most part, was lost in his own world of math trying to come up with a solution for the problem at hand. For the next couple of days he would be working and then reworking his formulas and computer algorithms trying to find a solution to do the impossible.   On the third day of running the computer and checking his theories and equations, Chance finally came up with a feasible plan. He then called the Admiral's office to set up a meeting. In the meantime, he started to prepare visual aids to help get his idea across to the Admiral and whoever else would be with him at the meeting.

Bright and early the next morning in the Admiral's office Chance explained his theory on how to raise the submarine halves from the bottom of the ocean. Explaining his ideas to the Admiral and the others in his conference room took about an hour of show and tell. He explained the process of inflating the halves of the submarine by using its own air tanks and then filling the interior with air, as well, in order to lift it off the bottom to secure the cables of the air collar under the sections and then slowly raising the submarine all the way to the surface. He further explained that someone topside would need to be monitoring the air inside the submarine halves to ensure that the halves wouldn't implode because of the outside pressure. Once it was on the surface, one of the floating dry docks would bring the halves back to port so it could be examined and possibly torn apart to determine the cause of the submarine's demise.

"What are we looking at for cost of raising the submarine halves?" asked one of the men at the conference table.

"The cost of doing this will be expensive due to the location of the submarine and the manpower needed to complete the work. The divers would be in two teams at first and then four teams for the final portion of raising it. Each team would have to have a deep-water diving exosuit in order to withstand the depths that they will be working at. The saturation divers will need to stay down on the bottom for at least a week to seal the ship in order to pump air into the submarine. My Thresher can transport the air tanks to the submarine to fill it with enough air to start the process." Chance continued, "The air collars will have to be pressurized according to the depths needed to maintain constant air pressure to raise the vessel halves. This will require bleed valves and air hoses to feed the collars in order to maintain the pressure while raising and lowering accordingly. We're talking a cradle big enough to handle the weight of the submarine and deal with the currents under the ocean. The cradle will take at least four ships, one on each corner to stabilize the load with one ship controlling the air flow and pressure for each corner to raise the submarine halves. Each corner where the cables are attached will require a team to closely monitor the raising of the halves with direct communication to the command ship acting as the eyes for any problems that they might incur along the way. Once the submarine is close to the surface another team will guide the submarine onto the floating dry docks. The surface ships will be there to assist in this part of the operation once the submarine halves are close enough to the surface. The ships will stabilize the halves in order to secure them inside the floating dry docks." Showing another slide, Chance kept talking. "All of this is risky, but I believe it can be done if we are careful when we do it. As this hasn't been done before there will be a steep learning curve involved in all of this. I think that we should be able to complete the operation inside six weeks if all goes well," Chance said, at the close of his briefing.

The Admiral thanked him for the briefing and asked him to leave the room while the rest of them discussed Chance's ideas of going after the submarine. With that, Chance left the room and waited outside in the Admiral's office for the rest of the briefing to be completed. The Admiral watched as Chance left the room and waited for a minute to let what Chance had said settle in their minds. He looked at the other people surrounding the table, "Well what do you think about all of this?"

"Is it worth the effort and cost to go after the submarine?" asked one of the people seated at the table.

"I believe it is important to find out what happened to the Dolphin. Until we can determine if it was sabotage or a mechanical problem, we have to assume the other submarines like it are in the same situation as the Dolphin was before it sank," another said.

The Admiral sat and listened intently to the points each side made. He knew the final decision would be his to make and after another thirty minutes of discussion the Admiral ended the meeting,

"Gentlemen, I believe that we have examined all of our options, and I believe I have enough to make a decision."

He stood up, shaking all of their hands as each of them left the conference room. Waiting until everyone was gone, he walked back from the conference table and sat at his desk, his mind was busy going over the pros and cons of their discussion. Once he was certain of his decision, he opened his office door and upon doing so Chance stood up.   The Admiral asked Chance to come in and had him close the door behind him. After he sat down the Admiral asked, "Is this feasible what you're suggesting Chance?"

"I believe it can be done, sir," he said, knowing that everything he had learned was on the line.

"Well, I agree with you. I think we need to know what happened out there to the Dolphin and we need to make sure it was a mechanical failure and not sabotage. And the only way to know for certain is to it get that submarine back on land to look at it."

"I agree, sir."

"How long will it take to get the teams together to start?"

"About a week, maybe less. The long pole in the tent is having the Navy get its ships together to support us when we're ready to move into that phase of the operation."

"Let me look into what we got going on and that will give you time to organize your assets to start."

"Yes sir, I'll start right away."

"For our sake, I hope this works."

"Yes sir, so do I.   And if it doesn't, we still have the pictures, we can use those to determine where we go from here."

Chapter III

Over the next few days, using a checklist, Chance gathered all of the people and equipment necessary together to set up the operation to go after the submarine. While this was going on, he also focused on getting the divers fitted for their exosuits for their dives down to the sunken wreck.

One of the new toys he had designed earlier was a new exosuit that could go all the way to the bottom of the ocean and still be attached to the front deck of the Thresher. This would be how Chance would test the suit, it would be like being on a ride going through a tunnel down into the darkness with just what the ship's lights would show you. This required modifying the Thresher to be able to carry him to the bottom and back up again. Having a special attachment hooked to the Thresher would allow Chance to breathe air from the submarine until he returned back to the surface.

When work started on the USS Dolphin, the divers would ride inside the Thresher and would use a special chamber to enter and exit the submarine. As it was, the exosuit was made of the same material that the Thresher was made of. Chance was going to be the first to test it underwater at that depth. This was to make certain that the suit would actually work the way it was meant to. All of the divers that were picked for this job were doubtful as to whether or not this exosuit would be able to withstand the pressure of being down that deep. That being said, if Chance was willing to be the guinea pig on the first test to work out the kinks, they would be willing to do the same when it came their turn. All of the men that were being used in this mission were qualified to operate any of his equipment in all phases of the operation, so there would be no training involved which meant that there would be no down time. It would be a point and shoot to the bottom and set up the equipment for raising the submarine.

One of the divers working with Chance, assisted him with the exosuit checklist by helping him try it on and making the necessary adjustments to the suit to accommodate his size and capabilities. The suit came apart at the waist and then would be latched down with bolts and locking keys around the bottom half of the suit. A hoist was then used to lift him and the suit into the pool which was followed by some heavy duty exercises in order to get the feel of the suit and what it could or couldn't do. Chance was able to tweak and peak the suit on some of the things that the suit wouldn't allow him to do after the pool exercise.

The exosuit was basically designed like the space suit the astronauts wear in space. The difference was, on the back of the suit was a propulsion unit that would allow the diver to move faster inside and outside the submarine halves. The suit came with lights attached on the chest and helmet area, allowing the diver to see through the darkness of the water. Along with the lights, there was also a camera attached to the helmet so that the specialist inside the Thresher would be able to see what the diver was seeing. The hydraulic system inside the exosuit would allow the diver to lift things that would be impossible for one person to do, allowing him to accomplish the work of up to three men at a time. Just like the astronauts, the divers will be constantly monitored by a health specialist inside the Thresher, with full communication abilities to each of the divers. Having this mobility with the exosuit was perfect for this kind of operation. To be able to move through the submarine and close the hatches as needed would allow the air to be pumped into the closed areas of the hull, allowing the submarine to lift off the bottom in order to attach the collar.

At the end of three days, Chance had all of his equipment checked out and loaded aboard the Thresher, including all four of the exosuits, which had been tested and were ready to go, as well. He himself had taken two of the exosuits down into the darkness of the trench twice with no problems. In fact, after seeing what the exosuit could do, some of the men wanted to try it on its first real mission when it came to working on the submarine. The problem with this kind of operation is that there would always be concerns with the amount of oxygen and time spent on the bottom in the exosuit. To be effective, the diver would have to be in the exosuit for at least an hour each time to even begin to accomplish his portion of the mission. One of the other perks inside the exosuit was an oxygen filter system which would allow the diver to stay down longer than normal. The four relief divers would sit inside the Thresher waiting for their turn to start working, changing out periodically with the other divers when their time was done.

The Thresher would sit on the bottom, being used as a platform for the divers as they moved back and forth from the wreckage to the Thresher in their exosuits. Once their working air was depleted, the exhausted diver would return to the Thresher, exit their suit while the empty air tanks were refilled again. While this was taking place, a new diver would climb into the exosuit and once secured, would exit the Thresher to start his part of the job. Each of the four divers would leave, two at a time, in 30-minute increments so that there was never a safety issue.

The deep-sea recovery vehicles that Chance had used to check out the Thresher on its maiden voyage would be used as anchors on each corner of the collar with their own power sources working in unison. The DSV's were controlled by foot pedals operated by the person inside the DSV. Thereby allowing the operator's hands to be free to do the work that would be required outside the vehicle. This ability would allow complete control over the pieces of the submarine from floating away in the currents and would actually control the ascent to the surface. A controlled float would ensure that the stress on the frame of the submarine pieces would be minimal, at least that was the idea anyway.

The next phase of the operation would be to have the Navy work in conjunction with Chance's DSVs, having their ships placed above the USS Dolphin. Once they were in position, they would lower their cables to the collars that were to cradle the submarine halves at the specified depth. The cables from the Navy's ships would then be attached onto the collar by the deep-sea vehicles with their robotic hands to bring that portion of the submarine up to the surface. When this was completed the submarine halves would be towed and placed onto the two floating dry docks. Once the halves were secured on the partially submerged dry dock and the tarps were in place over them, the air collars and the cradle could be removed to reduce the clutter on the floating dry dock. The next step would be to raise the dry dock and the submarine out of the water and drain any extra water from the submarine halves, allowing them to dry out. At this point, the floating dry docks would return to port and await the explosive ordinance disposal and NCIS teams to go through the halves of the submarine, looking for any signs of sabotage. Once the submarine was cleared then other teams would be sent in to recover bodies of the crew members that were still trapped inside. The next team would come in and recover the cruise and the ballistic missiles and the torpedoes, if possible, for reuse in other submarines. All of this would require time to figure out the best procedures and updating, and if necessary, all of Chance's mathematical equations, in order to minimize any more damage to the halves of the submarine.

With everything in place from Chance's perspective, now it would be on the Navy to bring their ships and support equipment to the site for the rest of the job. The Navy would bring in their support only after Chance's team was finished with their tasks. Chance was hoping that the ballast tanks on the USS Dolphin could be repaired so they could be filled with air in order to assist in raising the USS Dolphin to the surface, thereby taking some stress off of the cables.

By the end of the week Chance had a time line/schedule set up for the steps that needed to be accomplished first before the Navy could come in to do their part of the operation. With the Admiral's permission to begin, Chance brought his people in to explain what they would be doing. Chance pointed to the white board, "Okay, listen up people, here's phase one of the plan to raise the USS Dolphin. Step one will be to seal all of the cracks in the hull of both halves of the submarine, especially, the ballast tanks. Step two will be to seal all of the hatches inside the submarine to make them watertight. The third step will be to blow air into the hatches and ballast tanks. We will be using, if possible, the existing air way system of the submarine to do this. If that doesn't work, we may have to drill holes into the submarine to fill it with air."

Chance moved another white board over to reveal phase two of the operation and continued, "Once the submarine is off of the sea floor the divers will wrap a collar around the submarine pieces and slowly inflate the collars with air. This will increase the buoyancy of the submarine half, enabling it to rise to the surface. Once the collar is wrapped around the submarine halves with the cables cradling the submarine inside the collar, the deep sea vehicles will attach cables to the collar. The lead weights will be placed on the collar's hookup points to control the rate of ascent to the surface and help control the direction of the collar. The lead weights will be dropped as needed as the halves are raised to the surface.

"At about 1000 feet the deep sea vehicles will hook the surface ship cables to the collar where they will take over raising the submarine to the surface. At this point the deep sea vehicles will be the eyes and voice for the surface ships to guide the submarine in its movements.

"Once we have the submarine on the surface, the floating dry dock will move into position and two of the surface ships will guide the cables, hooked to the collars, through the dry dock platform and pull the submarine onto the platform."

Looking at the crew sitting before him he asked, "Is there any questions about what we're doing?"

"How long are we allowed to be in the exosuit?" one of the divers asked.

"I figure about one to two hours each and then it will be time to let one of the other divers have a crack at it."

"How are we going to weld down there at that depth?" another diver asked.

"That's a tough question, I'm thinking it should be the same at 1000 feet as it is at one mile down. All of the equipment will be brought down on a lead sled, so to speak, via the Thresher and will be set up next to the submarine half in order to have the cables and rod down there to do the job. The hardest part will be to weld through the outer shell of the submarine. Granted, we can only fix what we can see, so I know there is a chance that we'll have unknown leaks to weld once we are able to move the half we're working on. They should be easy to see with the air escaping from the hull. We'll work on one piece at a time and then move onto the next piece, that is, once we get the collar around the piece of submarine we just sealed. Do you have any other questions?"

The men looked at each other and then back at Chance. With no further questions he closed the meeting. "We should be ready to go tomorrow morning, in the Thresher, about eight a.m. So, make sure you get plenty of rest tonight."

After the meeting the lead diver walked up to Chance, "Are you sure this is going to work?"

"We'll know for sure, hopefully, within the next week or two," Chance said, with a smile.

"I guess we will," the diver replied, as he nodded his head and walked away, knowing that Chance wouldn't have said otherwise.

The rest of the night was used by Chance to double check the Thresher, the lead sled, and then the exosuit platform setup inside the Thresher. The sled that the welder would sit on would have to be taken in pieces to the bottom, attached to the back of the Thresher. Then a couple of divers would need to set up the platform for the welder and rods which would be needed for the divers to use. Because of the depth, the divers would be required to wear the exosuits longer than normal in order to get the platform set up. Chance had had the diver's practice in the pool ahead of time, hoping that it would help the construction of the platform go faster. Once the platform was in place and stabilized, the welder would come down piggyback, encased in a protective shell, to prevent it from imploding from the depth at which it would be required to work at. While one of the divers was waiting for his turn to go out to work on the submarine, he would monitor the welder on board the Thresher. The divers would work in pairs using the buddy system for safety purposes. The other pair of divers would be setting up the collar for the part of the submarine they were working on. Each tank of air for the collar, would be set up to attach to the other tanks of air in a locking mechanism with eye bolts holding the tanks in place. This way the tanks could be moved and placed wherever needed and be made to fit the length of the submarine as required. There would be a steel netting connected to the air tanks to run underneath the body of the submarine, holding the submarine in place as it was being raised. The netting would have mesh material in between the steel cables to catch whatever comes off from the submarine as it is being raised from the bottom. With the collar connected by eye bolts, the surface team would be able to disconnect the air tanks via the eye bolts to allow the submarine to pass onto the floating dry dock without too much hassle.

With a plan of action set to go, all that was required now was the implementation of the plan. After checking the weather charts for the days ahead, Chance found no big storms on the horizon for the time frame that they were planning to start. By the next morning the team of divers were in place and waiting to head down to the submarine to start work. It was decided that the first shift would build the platform and the second shift would place the welder onto the platform. The third shift would actually start working on the submarine to seal it off so the air could be pumped through to the sealed hatches.

Another team on the surface would start connecting the air tanks that would be used by the collar. And then sink it down to the bottom by having lead weights placed outside the empty air tanks. Once the collar was in place around the submarine, the lead weights would be dropped, as needed, a little at a time, to be able to move the collar to where it was needed to secure the submarine. The team that was working with the air tanks would be larger than the ones working on the leaks in the submarine. The collar would be slowly guided down to the bottom by the deep sea vehicles.

Electronic marker beacons would be set up on the bottom by the first set of divers to guide the deep sea vehicles down to where the submarine was resting on the bottom. A second set of beacons would be used as a reference to where to put the collar in place around the submarine once it was floating. Once the collar was in place it would be pulled under the floating submarine. The air tanks would lose their weights and be filled with air from the Thresher. Once the collar was secured around the submarine, it would sit inside and would be ready to float to the surface intact. The lead weights would be retrieved from the bottom and brought back to the surface to be used once again for the second part of the submarine, using the air tanks again as well.

After doing another check on all the equipment that they would be using, Chance had the crew take the Thresher to the coordinates where the USS Dolphin lay on the sea bottom. As it arrived to where the USS Dolphin lay, the Thresher moved along side of the half they would be working on. Once the Thresher was secured and lying next to the submarine half, Chance left the bridge with one of the divers and went to where the exosuits were located. After getting himself situated inside the exosuit, he made sure, with the help of the second man, that the suit was sealed properly before stepping into the escape chamber. He now waited for the other diver to suit up before exiting the Thresher. Taking his first steps inside the exosuit he remembered to turn on the lights on his suit before moving on. As you could guess, the area surrounding the

Thresher was pitch black. Chance had the XO turn on all of the Thresher's outside lights so he could have a frame of reference to help him find his way around.

The first job was to unhook the platform from the back of the Thresher and place it next to the submarine. This took quite a bit of time and before Chance and his partner knew it, it was time for a change of divers. Having only placed the basic frame down on the seabed it would be the next team of divers to build upon what they had accomplished. Hopefully, it wouldn't take quite so long.

Making their way back to the Thresher and finding the hatch, Chance and his teammate opened the outside door and entered into the submarine.   Once they were inside the chamber the air pressure was turned on and the water inside the chamber slowly drained out. With the water completely removed they opened the chamber door that led into the Thresher.   The other divers met them and assisted them out of their suits and began refilling the oxygen tanks. Chance, being completely exhausted, needed help getting out of his suit. Once this was done, he called the XO to have one of the other divers come down and help the two divers that were getting ready to go out. The extra diver showed up just in time to assist the second diver into the suit and take Chance's place.   Once this was done, Chance made his way to the main deck of the Thresher.   From here he could see that the transfer was complete, and the air tanks had been refilled. The second set of divers proceeded to pick up where Chance and his partner had left off. Sitting in the sonar man's chair he was able to rest and watch all that was going on without being in the way.

As he sat there for a minute trying to catch his breath and regain some of his strength, one of the other divers came over and congratulated him for being the first man to work on the bottom of the ocean at this depth.   Chance smiled at the comment but being too tired all he could muster was, "Thank you."

At this point Chance was too tired to make any kind of statement or something more of it. He just sat there feeling his strength slowly starting to come back.   Using a towel, he wiped the sweat from off his forehead he thought to himself, *"Maybe I am getting to old for this kind of adventure anymore grandpa."* He laughed to himself, *"It may be true, but I'll never tell anyone, especially Helen."*

In a few moments he was feeling better and stood up to check on the progress of the other divers working on the platform. Setting up the platform was tedious at best, but necessary, as it was the first step in a chain of events to raise the submarine from the bottom of the sea. It would take three teams of divers to finish the work on the platform. After the platform was in place the next step was to place the transponders next to the submarine so that the deep sea diving vehicles could find their way to the exact spot next to the submarine. The third step was to set up some lights on the bottom so the divers could see and move around easier.   Once this was all completed the divers could see the submarine in its entirety.   All in all, this took approximately three days to set up. In all of this time the lights started attracting different kinds of fish and other strange looking creatures, fortunately the bigger fish left them alone.

Each of the divers that went out to work on the wreckage were pretty worn out by the time their shift was over.   And after three days of work, the platform for the welder was in place as was the transponders and lights. The Thresher went back to the surface to have the welder put on its bow cargo rack and tied down to the platform. The welder would be placed on the lead sled by a team of divers. Once it was in place the divers would start looking for the rips and tears on the submarine so they could be welded shut to keep the ocean water from coming in.

After making its way to the bottom again, the Thresher delivered the welder in its waterproof case to the platform.   With a built-in air pocket, the divers were able to move welder through the water with ease and place it on the lead sled within an hour. Once the welder was in place on the sled, the air pocket was released from inside the shell, allowing it to settle onto the sled, and the combined weight of the sled and the welder made it immovable.   The next step was connecting the cables to the welder for the divers to start the welding process. The idea of using one welder proved to be a problem, simply because if there were any problems with the single welder it would slow down the work. Because of this, Chance decided to locate another underwater welding machine and transfer it down to the bottom. He then had his men place it next to the first welder on a separate platform. This ate up some of their time but Chance knew it would pay off and was necessary over the long haul.

As the crew of divers went to work on the submarine half, from inside the Thresher you could see the welding flashes through the viewing window. It would look like a low light that would appear and be gone within seconds, to reappear for a few more seconds. With both welders working, the divers were like ants crawling all over the submarine half, looking for anything that looked like it could be a leak. It took a couple of weeks before the divers were ready for the next step.

The Thresher headed back to the surface to pick up a new set of divers that were rested and ready to go, leaving the worn out divers topside for a couple of days to recover from their work on the sea bottom. The exosuits allowed the divers to recover faster during their rest periods, due to the fact that the environment inside the suit was considered to be the same as if they were on shore. After dropping off the divers, the Thresher was fitted with air tanks that would be used to fill the submarine half that they were working on. The new set of divers ran hoses from the air tanks to the submarine half, connecting them to the adapters that had been welded onto the submarine getting it ready to be filled with air.

After the submarine had been checked a second time for any leaks, now came the job of filling it with air. Purging the water out of the submarine would be a major task. Slowly filling the submarine with air and at the same time draining the sea water out of it without cracking the hull of the submarine would be a time-consuming task. Once the submarine half was full of air and floating the divers would be able to work underneath the submarine looking for more leaks. This, in and of itself, would be a major undertaking and would be probably the most dangerous part of the job. As the air was pumped into the submarine the divers stood by looking for air bubbles escaping from the submarine so that they could weld it closed. Being able to weld the underside of the submarine was a bit tricky. Only one welding machine would be used, as the other diver now became the safety man, making sure all was right and safe for the diver doing the welding on the submarine. This took another three weeks before all of the welding was complete under the submarine.

With air now inside the submarine, it started to float about four feet off of the sea bottom, allowing the diver to crawl underneath and do another visual check to see if the welds held and look for any other leaks. Each time a leak was welded the submarine would get easier to move into any position the diver needed it to be in.

Chance already had the other team of divers working on getting the air collar ready to move to the bottom where the submarine was floating just above the sea bottom, while still being tied down by cables to keep it from moving with the current. From the Thresher the whole area where the work was taking place looked like something that you would see in an outer space movie. In which you see the one or two people moving around outside the spaceship doing their work, floating above the earth oblivious to anything else around them.

On the fifth week the collar was placed next to the floating submarine half. With more air being pumped into the submarine this allowed it to raise a little higher, allowing the collar to be placed beneath it with the open end and then slide the collar into place. With the submarine encircled by the collar the open end was closed to complete the circle, thus the submarine half was completely protected inside the collar from any outside interference . At this juncture, the weights were removed from the collars and the safety netting and steel cables, crisscrossing the collars, were raised and attached into place allowing the divers to lock down the submarine into the carriage created by the air collars. The divers made sure that the submarine half was cradled for its ride to the surface.

When the deep sea vehicles were in place the rest of the weights were removed. With the deep sea vehicles controlling the ascent, the first part of the submarine was slowly guided to the surface. At about one thousand feet the ascent was stopped while the cables from the surface ships were connected to the air collar. From here the deep sea vehicle operators would then monitor the rest of the ascension of the submarine. Once it was on the surface the tricky part would be to place the submarine half into the floating dry dock platform. The Navy divers were already in place to remove the eye bolts that were connecting the air collars together, thus creating an opening for the submarine to float past the collars. The divers, working with the crew of the floating dry dock, hooked the cables onto the deck of the submarine half once the submarine had been righted, holding it into place and allowing the floating dry dock to come underneath the submarine and scoop it up onto its own cradle. With the submarine half in place on the floating dry dock, it now became Navy property once again to be taken to the nearest port. After it was secured, they covered it with a tarp to keep it from being seen by the satellites that were always looking for something new to report.

After the Navy took control off the submarine half, the opening of the floating collar was closed and was readied to be lowered once more. The floating dry dock took the submarine half to the Navy shipyard in Groton, Connecticut. Once it was secured in a dry dock, they started working on the first half of the USS Dolphin, investigating the damage that had been inflicted upon it.

Knowing that there was a strong possibility that there would be bodies of some of the sailors aboard, trapped inside some of the compartments, the Navy Medical Examiners (ME) would be the first to go in and remove anything human remains inside for identification and then notify the next of kin for burial. The ME had a small group of ambulances, waiting on the dock to take the bodies of the sailors to the morgue to be examined, looking for anything unusual as to the cause of death besides loss of air.

The next step was to remove the cruise missiles and the SLBMs from the submarine and examine them for water damage and corrosion. Each missile was contained in its own watertight compartment inside the submarine. This meant that the missiles had been hopefully protected from the outside elements as they sat there on the bottom of the ocean for the last couple of months. Fortunately, this would mean little, if any, damage was done to the missiles, therefore not allowing them to be used elsewhere. The following step would be to remove the Mk-48 torpedoes from the rear of the submarine for use in other submarines, as well. Each of these steps would take time and all of this depended on the results from the in-depth examination of the weapon systems to be carried out first.

While all of this was going on, the divers that were below were now re-configuring the equipment for the next part of their job. Each of the divers were preparing the front half of the USS Dolphin to be raised just like the back half. The deep sea vehicles went back to the bottom to pick the lead weights that had transponders attached to them in order to find them and bring them to the surface to be reused on the air collars. At this point the lead sled had to be torn down and re-positioned closer to the front half of the submarine that was hanging on a ledge above the sea bottom. After looking at the ledge it was determined to be big enough to hold the welder without the sled sliding off. The divers set up the lead sled once more and began again welding the holes and cracks on the front half of the submarine. Because of the angle of the submarine, and how it sat on the ledge, the air collar would have to be modified to fit the submarine without it dropping off onto the bottom. Using air filled balloons inside the blast opening they were able to raise the submarine halfway into an upright position, allowing the air collar to be placed around it without too much difficulty. After the collar was in place the weights used to lower the collar down to the submarine were dropped. With the collar in place, the carriage for the submarine was locked into position and the front half of the submarine was raised just like the back half. Two weeks later, with another floating dry dock waiting on the surface to be loaded, like the back half, the front half of the submarine was taken to Groton, Connecticut to be examined as well. This time all of the research and development guys would be there to look at the gaping hole adjacent to the torpedo room to carefully examine the blast area.

The lead sled and the welders along with the transponders and lights were dismantled and returned to the surface to be stored away for the next time they would be needed. Once everything was done, Chance was pleasantly surprised that the whole operation went off without a hitch. He knew that it was the professional work done by the divers and crew members of the Thresher that had made the difference. Knowing this he released them all and gave them some comp time with extra pay for their hard work, courtesy of the U.S. Navy for raising the submarine from the bottom

Chapter IV

The job for Chance was over at this point and now it became a matter of curiosity to him as to what happened to the submarine and why it sank like it did. It would take weeks, maybe months, to determine the cause as well as the damage done to the key components aboard it. Chance was happy to take some time off while he waited for the answers that were forthcoming from the investigation. In the meantime, the Navy put out a safety warning for the submarines that were operating on both sides of the continent to be careful about their mission procedures and to start double checking their torpedoes for anything unusual, mainly as a matter of precaution.

With both halves of the USS Dolphin in dry dock, the investigation teams went to work looking for anything unusual that would indicate what had caused the explosion. The MEs started their grim task of cataloging any unusual discrepancies found with the bodies of the dead sailors that had been trapped inside. Most of them had died due to oxygen starvation when the submarine broke in two, causing a major power failure to the oxygen system of the boat. For the sailors that survived the explosion and the splitting of the submarine, it was only a matter of time before they would die also. The telltale signs were there on the bodies, especially the bloodshot eyes and or spots on the whites of the eyes of the victims. The sailors would start feeling the effects of the lack of oxygen with headaches, blueish skin, and then feeling like fainting. Because the bodies were in self-contained compartments, some of the bodies never decomposed, in a sense, they were in suspended animation.

As the MEs went from the back half of the submarine to the front half of the submarine to continue their investigation the damage to the bodies became more apparent. In the torpedo room, due to the explosion on the side of the submarine which had created a gapping whole, the animals in the sea were able to get to the bodies that had been caught there and destroy any evidence of their deaths. The

MEs continued to make their way into the other hatches that were closed or sealed by the sailors during the time of the explosion. It was there they found that some of the sailors had been shot through the head at point blank range. This information was sent to the Admiral and then sent to Tony Jones's office in the Navel Intel department.   After receiving this information, Tony contacted the Admiral, "Admiral, I've looked over the preliminary medical reports from the USS Dolphin and I recommend that NCIS start a background investigation on all of the crew members of the submarine."

"What makes you say that?"

"The reports indicate that some of the men were murdered by someone aboard the submarine."

"Well if that's the case I concur, we need to find out who is responsible for this and did they die onboard the submarine, as well. I'm concerned that there might be more saboteurs aboard our other submarines. The problem is how do we go about finding them if they are? This has become a major investigation, whatever you need, just ask.   I need you to take the lead on this investigation, Tony.   This is a matter of top priority and needs to be solved, no matter what it takes."

"Yes, sir.   I agree and I'll start today," Tony said, as he set the phone back into its cradle.

Tony sat there at his desk thinking about his conversation with the Admiral and according to the Admiral, this just became a case of sabotage and murder on the USS Dolphin.   The first thing Tony did was to initiate background checks on every sailor who was assigned to the submarine fleet. It had to be done quietly so as not to alarm any of the men or women being investigated or, for that matter, any other interested parties.   He realized that the background checks would be time consuming, only because there were no survivors or witnesses to the destruction of the USS Dolphin. He would also have to play this investigation close to the chest and not let anybody know of it unless it was absolutely imperative that they needed to know.

Everybody that had anything to do with submarines now became suspects in the destruction of the USS Dolphin and the murder of over 125 people aboard the submarine. This was to include the builders and engineers and all the other people involved in the development of this submarine. This was a race against time for the lives on board the other submarines and a national security issue for our country, as well. Tony was very much aware of all of this and the sleepless nights were about to begin for him and his team of investigators.

Tony had always wanted to be in the Navy ever since he was a young man. His dad had been a career sailor onboard one of the carriers as a cook. When he would come home, he would talk about all of the places he'd seen and always brought him home something special. When the Navy ships would come into the San Diego Naval Base harbor, especially after a long tour, he and his mom, along with   the other families, would be there waiting for the sailors to disembark the ship to meet their loved ones. Tony knew from then on that he wanted to be on one of those ships. Always going somewhere and doing something, he wanted to be part of the adventure of what lay out there on the ocean and the rest of the world. After high school he had been accepted into the Naval Academy where he had completed his schooling. He then went on to be trained as a Surface Warfare Officer on board a destroyer. He liked chasing the proverbial mouse under the ocean as the cat. His career had followed the traditional career path. He had served two tours on board a ship, had been selected to teach as a Warfare Tactics Officer at the school for newly commissioned officers, and had gone to Naval Post- graduate School to earn his masters degree. As his career was moving in the right direction, while instructing at the Warfare Tactics course he was involved in an automobile accident that ended his career being onboard a ship for any length of time. Being forced to change his career path, he crossed over into the Navy Intelligence arena where he completed his five months of training in the Naval Intelligence Officer Basic Course, which covered strategic intelligence, counterintelligence, and war strategy. To him he was still looking for the proverbial mouse, but in a different way, and on a bigger scale. At his rank of commander, he became a supervisor in the collection, analysis, and dissemination of intelligence information, critical to his command's mission. While assigned to Washington DC, he had proved himself capable of handling even the most critical Intel in a rather unique way. His understanding of naval tactics in sea warfare had given him the capability to see almost, in a three-dimensional way, the battlefield, involving surface ships and submarines. The Admiral, seeing this in his reports, picked him to work on his staff as an Intel Officer and as a Surface Warfare Analyst.

Tony enjoyed working for the Admiral. He considered the Admiral a forward-thinking officer, who knew his way around the politics of Washington D.C. and also knew how to get what he needed in order to get the job done without ruffling feathers along the way. This was a talent that Tony had learned by watching him and it wasn't lost in his chain of command above him as well as below him. He was thought to be a firm but fair leader and his subordinates and his superiors respected him for it.

This incident with the USS Dolphin, would be Tony's biggest challenge to date and the Admiral was counting on him to find the weak link in the chain of evidence that would break the case wide open and put things right for the Navy. Tony's team would consist of two NCIS agents, Jim Davis and Ted Kelly, these two agents were veterans with over ten years of experience, each having served tours on submarines and other ships in the past. They were both familiar with submarine operations and quite comfortable in working with Tony.

The first part of the job would be to do background checks on all of the people assigned to the USS Dolphin. They would concentrate on these people, while the Navy would look at the rest of the submarine crews that were serving on other subs.

Tony handed the crew lists to Davis and Kelly who in turn divided the names up according to who was on board and who was at port the day the Dolphin went down. It was decided that Davis would investigate the names of the crew that were onboard the submarine that day and that Kelly would do the same with the names of those that were on port call. Tony decided that he would take the maintenance logs for the last time the Dolphin was in for a refit or maintenance to review. The USS Dolphin would be on her normal patrol for six months at a time, and at end of her tour she would go into port for her normal scheduled maintenance and upgrades. All three men were busy looking for something out of the ordinary in the records of the personnel and maintenance logs. They continued to scour the records for the rest of the week. Finding nothing out of place, they then went and did a more in depth look at any of the records that piqued their interest. Upon closer inspection, they found that a couple of the personnel onboard the submarine had some kind of financial problems and had been counseled about their spending habits. The supervisors of the maintenance teams, made up of the other crew members, were dealing with infighting and disrespecting the leadership onboard the submarine during their tour of duty. According to the logs, it had been sort of worked out. The maintenance logs that were found onboard the submarine, indicated that there was work being done in the control room, forward of the sail of the submarine. Although the pictures of the USS Dolphin showed the gaping hole on the starboard side of the ship, the main force of the blast entailed the bottom third of the submarine where the torpedoes were stored.   The control room would have suffered damage to its compartment as well, just from the blast. With the location of the blast hole being in that part of the submarine, and with a hole that size, there would be no way possible to save the submarine.

As Tony was looking at the photos of the back half of the submarine on the bottom of the ocean, something caught his eye. The problem was, he wasn't sure what he was looking at. Pinning the first photo of the submarine to the white board, he started looking at the front half of the submarine resting on the ledge. Pinning the second picture to the white board as well, he pushed them together and then stepped back and continued looking at the pictures. "Hey, Davis and Kelly, come over and take a look at the pictures of the submarine."

Both Kelly and Davis dropped what they were doing and came over and looked at the pictures.

"What do you see?" Tony asked.

As both agents looked at the pictures for a moment, Kelly said, "All I see is the two pieces of the submarine laying there."

"Me too boss," Davis agreed.

"Look at the base of the submarine. Do you notice a slight upward bend in the wreckage?"

"I think I see it, but I don't get it," said Kelly

"I don't see it at all," Davis said.

Using his finger to follow the outline of the submarine, Tony showed an upward bend of the submarine at the base of both pieces that had been raised from the bottom of the sea. "C'mon, we need to go to see the submarine," Tony said.

All of them rode in Tony's car, and headed to the shipyard where the submarine lay. After getting permission to enter from with the security guard at the gate, they continued on to where the submarine was located. Tony went to look for the lead investigator in his office while Kelly and Davis went to see the submarine themselves. Tony found the lead investigator sitting at his desk, talking on the phone, so he waited patiently for the phone call to end. As the investigator hung up the phone, Tony laid the pictures on his desk. The investigator picked up the pictures of the submarine, "Tell me what you see in these pictures?" Tony asked.

The investigator looked at the pictures and studied them for a moment before answering. "I don't see anything, what are you trying to show me?" the investigator asked, perplexed.

This time Tony, once again using his index finger, followed the bottom of the submarine showing the upward turn of the keel of the hull, "Do you see it now?"

The investigator took the pictures from Tony, this time looking closer at the pictures. All of a sudden, he saw what Tony was trying to show him, "Well I'll be damned, why didn't I see that before."

"You see it too then, now that I pointed it out to you?"

"Man, you've got good eyes to pick that up."

Getting on the phone, he called his team of investigators into the office. Davis and Kelly also came in with them. The two agents found a place in the back of the room, to sit down to watch and listen. Once seated, the lead investigator introduced Tony to his team before turning the floor over to him to speak. Tony began by sharing the photos with the team, "If you look really close you can see the upward bend of the submarine in these two pictures. At first, I thought it was just the submarine going through the final stages of settling on the bottom, but the front half looked the same way as you see here. However, the difference is, the front half never made it to the bottom. This submarine was hit by a small torpedo before it sank, just big enough to seal its fate before sinking to the bottom."

Now the team of investigators were scrutinizing the pictures that were being passed around. Tony continued, "The blast from the submarine was caused by something onboard. But the real damage was done by the torpedo from under the belly of the submarine. Both of these actions would have been enough to sink the submarine.

The question is, what kind of torpedo would be powerful enough to do this?"

"Now it all makes sense. While looking at the base of the submarine, I noticed an upward bend in the titanium metal running along the length of the submarine half," one of the team members stated.

"This submarine was destroyed by a torpedo that only used its blast as a way to cripple the submarine. The explosion onboard the submarine was after the fact, which sealed the fate of the Dolphin," Tony said, after he gathered all of his pictures back.

Davis and Kelly stood up and walked over to where Tony was standing as the lead investigator was talking to his team. "We need to find more evidence leaning towards a new type of torpedo that was used to cripple this submarine, it isn't much to go on, but we've done more with less before. We need to get smart on this one as quick as we can," said the lead investigator.

As he finished, the team hustled back out into the area where the pieces of the Dolphin lay.   They were now looking for any kind of sign of damage done by the torpedo which was used to cripple the submarine.

Tony waited until the team of investigators were out before talking to the lead investigator again, after taking a seat, "I think what happened was the Dolphin was attacked by another submarine and the bomb, or whatever it was onboard her, was made to look like the blast destroyed the submarine from inside, causing it to sink. With it being on the bottom, the submarine should have been crushed beyond recognition and would have remained a mystery forever. What kept the submarine intact, was a blessing from above so that we could find it. The bad guys were not expecting anything to survive the depths of the ocean, especially something as big as the USS Dolphin."

The lead investigator was shaking his head in agreement while Tony continued, "We're now dealing with a saboteur and an organized attack on the Dolphin from a foreign power. I need to advise the Admiral about this new information," Tony said, as he quickly got up to leave.

As Tony left the office, Kelly and Davis caught up with him at the car, "What do you want us to do boss?" Kelly asked.

"Stay here and see if you can find anything to confirm what we've found, alright? Davis, you start digging into the files of the dock workers who were assigned to do work on the Dolphin."

"Will do, sir."

"Let me know if you find anything. I'll expect to see you guys tomorrow morning. I've got a meeting to go to," Tony said.

Upon arriving at the Admiral's office, the next day, Tony told his secretary that he needed to see the Admiral and that it was important. The secretary walked into the Admiral's office and let him know that Tony was waiting to see him. Within a minute the Admiral came out of his office motioning for Tony to come in. After seating himself in the chair opposite Tony, the Admiral told his secretary "No interruptions till I tell you otherwise."

The secretary nodded her head and left the Admirals office, closing the door behind her. The Admiral looked at Tony, "So, what have you learned about the Dolphin?"

"We think she was sunk by a torpedo, sir. The blast hole was supposed to cover up the torpedo strike in case the submarine survived and was found."

The Admiral looked at him for a moment, taking in what Tony had said. "Are you sure of this?"

"I ran it by the engineers and the inspectors yesterday and they're in agreement with what I'm saying. Whoever has done this has come up with a new kind of torpedo and tried to use it against the Dolphin. I'm beginning to think someone planted a bomb on the inside of the super structure of the submarine, setting it to go off at a certain time or depth. It means that somebody in the work crew is in league with a foreign power to destroy our submarines and make it look like an accident."

The Admiral just sat there taking all of this in, after a moment he said, "Murdered sailors and torpedo's with new technology, this is not good news at all. We need to find out who the worker or workers are and stop this before we lose any more of our subs."

"I agree with you, sir.   One of my people is now going over all of the records and backgrounds of the workers who had anything to do with the maintenance on the Dolphin. I hope to have something soon."

"Is there anymore I can do for you at this time?"

"As a matter of fact, I would like to get Chance on board with this so we can go back down to where we found the submarine and look around the area to see if anything else turns up. I could also use two more people for the background checks, just to hurry up the investigation, if possible."

"Consider it done for the extra help and I'll get a hold of Chance to see if he can assist us with this. Is there anything else you can think of that you might need?"

"No sir, I think that should cover it for right now."

"Well then, I'll let you know when I get in touch with Chance and let you two set up a time to go fishing again."

"Thank you, sir, for your time, I'll keep you posted," Tony said, as he stood up to leave the Admiral's office.

Once Tony left, the Admiral called out to his secretary, "Get Chance on the phone for me, will you."

In ten minutes, the call was over, and Chance was calling Tony from his office for a dive time meeting.

When Tony got back to his office a recorded message was waiting for him from Chance, "If you got the money, I've got the time to go fishing. Call me when you get this."

Tony quickly called back, "I need to meet with you ASAP, can you come over now?"

"I'll be over in 20 minutes and I'll bring a pizza with me."

"Fair enough, I'll see you soon."

Tony, realizing the rules of the game had changed, decided to start carrying his weapon, a Glock 19, 9MM. Pulling it from his top drawer after taking his coat off and putting his shoulder holster on, he tucked the gun into the holster and the two extra clips in the magazine holder for added insurance. Chance, being true to his word, was there in twenty minutes with a pizza and both of the men sat down and started eating the pizza. In between bites, Tony explained what he wanted to do, as far as going back down into the area where the sub had been found, in a sense, going back to the scene of the crime for further investigation.

"Not a problem, anything to help the Navy once again. When do you want to go?" Chance asked.

"How soon can we go?"

"How about tomorrow morning, is that soon enough for you?"

"That'll be fine, what do I need to bring?"

"Just yourself.   What are we looking for?"

"Anything that doesn't look like it belongs on the bottom of the ocean from the wreckage of the submarine. Maybe we can find a clue as to what happened to the Dolphin on her final run."

"Looking for a needle in a haystack, are we?"

"About sums it all up."

"I'll be waiting for you, don't be late."

After finishing the pizza Chance got up, "Next time, you buy the pizza."

"Fair enough," Tony replied, as he left to get into his car.

As he sat there thinking about all that had transpired, he now was beginning to think that he was becoming paranoid about the USS Dolphin.   And as the old saying goes, 'Just because you think they're after you doesn't mean they're not.'   Shaking his head, he chuckled to himself as he looked over his shoulder.

Chapter V

Early the next morning, Chance and Tony, along with the crew of the Thresher, were ready to go back to the site where the Dolphin had been found. Slipping under the waters of the Atlantic Ocean after clearing the harbor, they set out into the dark abyss of the trench of the Atlantic Ocean. Chance checked his coordinates on his computer and the map making sure that everything lined up. "It shouldn't take too long to find the spot where the Dolphin lay on the bottom."

"I'm hoping to find something that isn't part of our submarine down here, something that may be from a foreign nation. Can I take a look at your map of the ocean floor where the Dolphin was found?" asked Tony.

Looking at the maps on the navigation table, Chance handed him the latest map of the ocean floor. Tony started looking over the topography on the map for anything that might indicate a place where another submarine may have been hidden. He was looking over the area where they found the front of the Dolphin on the ledge, as well as any crevasses that might hold some of the debris from the encounter. "We need to look this over pretty thoroughly, if we can, and then scan the rest of the area below it," he said, pointing at a spot on the undersea map.

Chance took a look at the spot on the map, "I'll get us there easy enough. Driver make it so," he said as he gave the new coordinates to the driver.

Within an hour the submarine driver notified Chance, "We're over the area now and have begun our descent to the ocean floor."

The Thresher responded to the submarine driver quickly and its smooth descent to the bottom was uneventful. Once the depth was reached, Chance ordered the viewing window to be opened with lights on so they could see what lay before them.

"Tony, we're here," Chance said, looking at the map to make sure.

Tony walked up to the window of the submarine and started looking for any debris that might indicate that a battle of some sort had occurred here.   As the Thresher moved slowly across the top of the ridge, just above where the front half of the Dolphin had laid, the team used their sonar to ping the area. At one point they had a return from the sonar, so they went in the direction of the return to check it out, only to find it was a rock outcropping made up of lead deposits. Resuming their original search, they went down the side of the mountain, crisscrossing the face of the cliff, searching for anything out of the ordinary. After an hour of searching they were finally getting close to the bottom part of the cliff. Using the same pattern, they came across some wreckage that appeared to be part of the Dolphin.   After taking a picture of the sight and the pieces they had found, one of the crew used the robotic claws to sift through the remains of what they had found. Most of the pieces were too small to indicate anything of value as to what Tony was looking for. Continuing on in their search along the base of the cliff, they came upon some more wreckage that was different from what they had found earlier. Chance ordered the driver to get closer to the debris for a better look. Using the cameras to take pictures, Tony asked, "Can we bring some of this stuff back with us? I would like to do a metallurgic test on the pieces."

"Shouldn't be a problem, all we need to do is hang onto it as we head to the surface."

Carefully maneuvering the submarine closer to the debris, using one of the robotic hands they grabbed a hold of one of the bigger pieces.   As the Thresher turned away from the cliff, one of the other observers said, "Skipper, I think there may be some other stuff over there in the three o'clock position."

Chance and Tony headed over to look at what the observer was pointing at.

"Driver, head in that direction, will you."

"Aye, Aye skipper."

As they got closer to the area that the observer had pointed out, the search light from the Thresher rested upon another piece of debris.   Tony's eyes got big, "What's that, out there!?"

Chance, hearing the excitement in Tony's voice, called out, "All ahead slow, driver.   Let's see if we can get close enough to get a picture of it in case, we can't grab it," he said, as he now saw what Tony was looking at.

On the face of the wall of the cliff, about six feet from the bottom, was a piece of debris sticking out of the rock. After taking a few pictures of the object, they began trying to recover it with the one claw that was still available. Finding that the piece was lodged loosely in the rock, they dug from the bottom of the ledge to loosen it even more. With the piece of metal barely hanging off of the rock, they were able to retrieve it from the cliff face easy enough to hang onto it. The debris was long and narrow and had some writing on it that wasn't English. Using the claw to secure it, they continued to where the back half of the Dolphin had rested on the bottom. The search continued for approximately two more hours, going from one end of the canyon to the other, searching for anything that would indicate that there were other players in the area at the time the Dolphin went down. Unable to find anything else they headed back to the surface and then to the port with both pieces of debris firmly held in place by the robotic claws of the Thresher. Having one of the divers retrieve the debris from the claws, Chance helped pull it from the water then handed it over to Tony. "I hope this helps."

"So, do I. Thank you for the trip," he said as they shook hands, "If you will, please send the bill to the Admiral." Tony said, as he took the debris and headed out to his car.

"Not to worry, I sent it to him before we left," Chance said, laughing.

"Smart man, now I know why you're my friend," Tony said, smiling.

Driving back to the base at Groton, Tony pulled into his parking spot, got out of his car and walked into his office. Kelly and Davis were already there sitting at their desks and drinking their coffee, as they went over the files of some of the workers at the dock. Still not finding anything of interest, they kept going through the records and calling the financial institutions as part of their background checks on some of the personnel that piqued their interest. The good news was that the two people, the Admiral had promised, were already in place and working on the background checks.

When Tony got to his desk he asked, "Were there any phone calls for me that were urgent or needed action on before I head out to the crime lab?"

"Yeah, the Admiral called to see if things were going good on our end of the investigation," Davis said.

"What did you tell him?"

"I told him we're still working the background checks on all of the personnel that were assigned to the Dolphin and the work crew on the dock. I told him that we were slowly, but surely getting there."

"Did he seem satisfied with your answer?"

"He did and wished us good hunting."

"Okay, I'm outta here for the rest of the day. I'll see you guys tomorrow a.m. sharp."

With that, he closed the door behind him and was gone. He got back into his car and headed down the street to the engineering section of the crime lab for a breakdown on the metal that had been retrieved by the Thresher near the sight of the submarine. Arriving at the front door he met the lead engineer of the investigation as he was coming in also. He handed him the two large pieces of metal that he found on the bottom of the ocean, "What do you make of these?"

The engineer took them and looked them over. "Where did you find these?"

"The bigger piece was found sticking out of the rock wall, near the area where we found the Dolphin lying on the ledge. The smaller piece was found on the ocean floor not too far from the cliffs."

The engineer listening to him, looked at him as if he was telling a joke, but thought better of it and went back to looking at the metal in his hands. He looked at it once more, "This isn't anything we've built here in the United States. The markings on the side indicate a foreign country designed this. Let me keep them for a day and I'll tell you where they came from as soon as I can, alright with you?"

"I need to know as soon as you can tell me about it. We think this is what sank the Dolphin."

"I'll have my team stop everything until we figure this piece out for you. Good enough?"

"That'll do. Remember, as soon as you can, let me know. No matter what time it is, call me."

"We'll get on it right away."

"Thanks, I'll be waiting for your call."

With that, Tony went directly to the Admiral's office to let him know what they had found near the crash site of the Dolphin. "Keep me posted on what you find out," the Admiral said.

"As soon as I find out, you'll be the next to know."

He looked at his watch and realized that it was already six p.m. Regular quitting time.   He drove home to his place and changed out of his uniform and into some regular clothes and went out to his favorite restaurant for dinner. As he sat in the booth waiting to order his dinner. A young lady came over to the table. "Is this seat taken?" she asked.

"No it's not, would you like to join me for dinner?" he said, as he stood up to let her inside the booth, as he tried to remember where he had seen her before. Her hair was black, and her green eyes sparkled when she smiled. She stood about 5 foot six inches tall and was what would be considered petite.

"Sorry to be so pushy.   I've seen you in here before and always by yourself."

"No, not at all.   It's nice to have someone to talk to.   This is my favorite place to eat, the steak is really good here. In fact, I've never had a bad meal here yet."

"That is saying something.   Me, I like their shrimp salad," she said, as the waiter set two glasses of water on the table.

"Are you ready to order?" the waiter asked, as he pulled out his pad and pencil.

Looking at his guest, "You first," he said.

"I'll have your shrimp salad with some red wine," she replied, now looking at Tony, waiting for him to order.

"I'll have a New York steak, medium rare with the vegetable of the day. And I also would like some German beer as well, to wash it all down."

Looking at her for a minute, Tony remembered he hadn't asked her name or gave his name to her. "I guess I should introduce myself, my name is . . .,"

"Your name is Tony, you're in the Navy and you work at Groton Shipyard," she said, as she smiled at him.

"You have me at a disadvantage, just who are you anyway?" he asked wondering how she knew so much about him already.

"My name is Ann and I work as the Admiral's secretary," she said, smiling at him.

Hearing her place of work as the Admirals secretary all of it fit together now. Tony realized where he had seen her before now and was very apologetic about not recognizing her. "I must apologize for my ignorance in not recognizing you," he replied a little red in the face.

"I must admit most men would notice me before the Admiral, but you were not even aware I was there. You know what that can do a young lady and her frail self-esteem?" she said, smiling at Tony.

"Oh, heaven forbid that I would cause such an issue to have to be dealt with. What can I do to make up to you?"

"Well, having dinner with me is a good start, what do you think?"

"I can't think of a better way to start to heal your self-esteem," Tony said, smiling at her.

By then the food was brought to their table, and the rest of the evening was spent talking and getting to know each other as they ate. In fact, both of them stayed the whole night at the restaurant until closing, and then went over to a small coffee shop for some coffee as a nightcap. Realizing the time, and that it was late, both of them decided that it was time to call it a night so that they would be ready for the next day. Feeling comfortable with each other Ann asked, "Would you like to come over to my place for some more coffee?"

"I would love to, but like you I have a busy day as well tomorrow," he said, as he kissed her.

"Oops, there goes my frail self-esteem again," she said, as she kissed him back.

"I can see this self-esteem issue is going to require some homework on both of our parts."

"When do we start working on it?" she asked, as she fluttered her green eyes at him.

"How about tomorrow evening let's say about seven o'clock your place."

"You know what, my self-esteem is starting to feel better already. Here's my address and phone number," she said, as she kissed him again before giving him the slip of paper with her information on it.

Tony was excited that Ann was beautiful and was something special. Best of all is that she liked him just as much as he liked her.

Not wanting to go home and wanting to savor this time with her, he forced himself to say goodnight before kissing her again, "Till tomorrow evening then?"

He drove home in a daze, and couldn't remember how he got back to his apartment.   This was the best evening he'd had in a long time.

The next morning Tony got the call he had been waiting for from the lead engineer.   He quickly got dressed and left his apartment to drive over to his office where the lead engineer was waiting for him when he arrived. Seeing the engineer sitting there Tony motioned for him to come into the conference room. "What did you find out?" asked Tony.

"Well, we found out plenty.   First of all, the writing on one of the metal pieces is Russian and the metal make up is from Russia, as well. That is when things get interesting.   This was used by one of the Soviet's allies."

"What do you mean, Soviet's allies?"

"According to what we know from the metal and our own Intel, this weapon is a brand-new system being sold throughout the Soviet Bloc nations and the Middle East.   The markings on this piece are Russian but underneath the Russian writing is Iranian instructions."

"Well, that does make it more interesting, doesn't it?" he said, as he took one of the pieces and held it in his hand, looking at the writing.

With that, Tony stopped the briefing for a moment, and called out, "Kelly, Davis, get in here for a second, I need you two to hear this."

Reiterating what he had already said, the lead engineer finished his brief and stood there for a moment. Both Kelly and Davis sat there taking in everything that had been said.

"So, where do we go from here?" asked Davis.

"That's for somebody else at a higher pay grade than ours to decide. Although, I have my own ideas about what to do and how to handle this particular situation.   However, that being said, I will let the higher powers decide for themselves," Tony replied.

With this new information, the background investigation took on a more urgent need to find out the five W's, that is, Who, What, When, Where and Why.   Having some of the W's answered, the other W's now became more pertinent to know.   The bad guys involved in this were a foreign entity with a capability of doing serious damage to our nation's national security and to our war fighting capability.

Later that day, at his briefing with the Admiral, Tony suggested, "I think with this new information, we should be planning to bring in our submarines, one at a time, and thoroughly inspect them to see if we can find any other bombs."

The Admiral continued to listen to Tony, "I believe that the blast hole on the side of the submarine was a separate attack, it's obvious that the blast would have been enough to sink the Dolphin. That being said, how do we account for the fragments of the torpedo found where the Dolphin was recovered. I believe that someone here, at the yard, attached an explosive device to the submarine while it was being refitted and the Dolphin might have been at the wrong place at the wrong time when it was disabled by the torpedo."

"I agree, we need to tell the skippers of each submarine, that there's a possibility of a bomb planted on their vessel and that the indications are that it would be near the torpedo room. They need to go through their boats and see what they can find onboard."

"In either case, as it stands, given the evidence, the submarine would have been lost, no matter what. What we need to do now, is make certain that there isn't an explosive device on any of the other submarines. I'm not sure what to think yet about this new torpedo. We don't have enough information yet to determine what it did to the Dolphin."

"I'll get the word out to the skippers and have them start bringing them into port for a more thorough check. We can't let whoever sabotaged the ships know that we are aware of their tricks. We need time to find out who did this without raising any suspicion on our part. Maybe we can use some of the other ports that have the capability to examine the submarines elsewhere, that way we would be able to keep it under our hats. I'll get my XO to run a check on which ports are available to do this."

"I don't know how many of our subs are involved in this. I'm hoping just on this side of the ocean, but to be sure we probably need to check them all out."

The Admiral nodded, "Better to be safe than be sorry on this. Keep me informed on anything else. Right now, I've got some phone calls to make."

After leaving his meeting with the Admiral, Tony stopped at Ann's desk and mouthed the words seven o'clock tonight. Ann nodded her head and smiled at him as he left to go back to his office. As he got into his car, Kelly called, "We found something on one of the dock workers that might be of interest to you."

"I'm on my way, I'll be there in five minutes."

When Tony got to the parking lot, Kelly and Davis were outside waiting for him.   As he got out of his car he asked, "So what did you find?"

"In our digging around, we came across an individual by the name of John Graham, who just went through a divorce and lost his house and kids from it.   After doing a further background check on him, we found that he had been busted by the local police for a DUI not to long ago," Kelly said.

"We decided to contact the local police and after showing them his picture, they had one of their Vice detectives come and talk to us. According to them, to make things worse for the guy, he has been spotted hanging around a known dealer who happens to be considered a radical member of the Mosque in Groton.   Evidently, while the guy is high on drugs, the dealer's indoctrinating him into the religion of Allah," Davis added.

"That's very interesting isn't it? Do we have enough to bust the guy, or should we wait for more to nail his friends to?"

Davis looked at Kelly, "I get a feeling that there's more going on here than just the indoctrination of our dock worker.   According to the detectives, John spends a lot of time down at the Mosque.   If possible, if there is anything else going on, we need to nail the whole group on this one.   Let's follow John and see where it leads us and then after a week or two, we can decide what to do then."

"I agree with him on this one, no use getting one when we can nail all of them," said Kelly.

"Fair enough, we still have the other two researching the records on the others, so tail this guy and see where it leads us.   Just remember, our time is limited to find the other ships that may have been sabotaged," Tony said, as they walked into the office.

Kelly and Davis picked up their coats, holstered their weapons and headed out the door to their car so they could get started on the stakeout.   Kelly made sure that they brought the dock worker's personnel file with them to get a better profile on John. While they were sitting near his house, Kelly started reading out loud from

John's file to Davis, while he monitored the house with his binoculars.

"According to his file, John was an electronics specialist by trade who has been working for the Navy for approximately ten years. He had been assigned as part of a team that would go in and update the electronics on board the ships and submarines after returning from their tour of duty.   Because of his clearance, all he needed was his badge and he had access to any of the ships without being questioned by any of the crew."

"Wow, I can't believe this guy still had a clearance after getting busted for DUI," Davis exclaimed.

"Yeah, usually they pull their clearance and do another background check before they allow them to have their clearance and their job back.   And that could take months."

What Kelly and Davis didn't know was that John had gotten married after high school and was going to college to become an electronics engineer, he had two years of college left when he found out that his wife was pregnant. Choosing to work instead of continuing to go to college, he took a job as an electronics specialist in order to support his family.   After the birth of their baby, his wife was continually sick and became addicted to alcohol and prescription drugs brought on by her postpartum depression. She now started to stay in the bedroom all day long and hide there till John came home from work. In the process, it left him to raise the child on his own and take care of his needs, as well.   When their second child was born, it was determined that the baby was born with fetal alcohol syndrome as a consequence of his wife's continued drinking while she was pregnant.   John was pretty exhausted from carrying the whole family on his back without support from his wife. Having had enough of the stress of trying to make his marriage work, he went to see a lawyer. He wanted to know if he could get a divorce from his wife on the grounds of incompatibility, due to the neglect of their children and drug abuse. The attorney sent one of his investigators to look into John's allegations about his wife. The investigator gathered all he could to prove that John was right, pictures, statements from the neighbors and such. Presenting them to the lawyer, the lawyer started drawing up the paperwork to start the proceedings.

Later on in the week, one night after dropping off the children at a babysitter, and while his wife was passed out in their apartment, he went out drinking with his work buddies.   As he was driving home after being at the bar with his friends, he was pulled over for DUI. For him, this was the final straw. Knowing that his job was on the line, the uncertainty of the future, and with his marriage falling apart, and not knowing where to turn, he decided that he hadn't anything to lose and turned to drugs to help him get through the bad choices he had made in his life.

Finding the drugs was easy for John, being near a large Naval base with the night life there for the Navy personnel to blow off steam once they hit port. It was only a matter of time before he knew where to look for them. One of the dealers, who had sold him the drugs, had a friend that was looking for someone who worked on the base that could give him access to the shipyard.   The dealer, introduced John to his friend who would give him free drugs and a sympathetic shoulder to cry on, slowly gaining his trust and friendship.

In only a short time John was hooked bad on the drugs, and it was only a matter of time before the new friend started asking him for little favors.   At first, it was the badge that he wore when he was on the base, just to see what it looked like. Once when John was high sitting in the corner of the friend's apartment, the friend took a picture of his badge for his own use. After a little while, the friend started asking where John worked on the base and when he worked, always with a promise of free drugs for his information. Occasionally, he would buy something for John, like a new watch or just give him money for nothing. This had been going on for about six months before the friend had a plan put together to have him ride with John onto the base so that he could see for himself where John actually did his job.   Upon hearing this request from his friend, John balked at this, but with the promise of free drugs he finally agreed to take him.

The friend, having seen the submarines at a distance, all lined up next to each other in their berths, started talking to some of his extremist friends about a plan to sink one of the submarines. At first the idea of sinking it at its berth was considered, but that was given up because the Navy would just raise the submarine where it lay and fix it and then return it to sea duty. Their next plan they had come up with was to plant a bomb aboard the submarine and have it blow up while at sea, using John as their way of getting it on board the boat. They all liked this plan, but the problem they were up against was whether John could get away with putting it on board without being caught. Because of his erratic behavior when John was around them, the only thing that would settle him down was more drugs.   He was considered the weak link in their plan and yet the most important part of their plan. The leader of the group thought that maybe one of them could get aboard with a counterfeit badge to assist John with planting the bomb.   This was considered risky, yet most likely possible if done at night while there wasn't so much traffic on the docks.   Knowing that John would balk at doing this, they decided in order for John to do his part they would have to come up with a plan where he wouldn't realize that he was bringing a bomb on board the submarine.   It was decided that when John showed up again for his fix, his friend would approach him about putting a gag gift on board the submarine.

The next day John's friend approach him, "Hey John, what would you think if we pulled a surprise for the crew aboard one of the submarines you're working on while they're out at sea?"

"What do you mean?" replied John.

"How about we plant a gag gift where no one can see it until it goes off?"

"I can't do that, because if I get caught, I could lose my job over it."

"Well, if you don't want to help, I'll just have to find someone else, and no more free drugs for you.   It's up to you, my friend."

Not wanting to lose his source of drugs, John readily agreed to do it. The friend smiled and promised to give him extra drugs because, as a friend, that's what you do. The rest of the night John was on a trip, without ever leaving the room. The next morning when he was sober, his friend handed him a box, "Don't look inside it. The reason is, I want it to be a surprise for the whole submarine when they are out at sea.   I need you to put it somewhere where it can't be found.

"No problem, I know just where to put it out of sight."

Over time, as John went from ship to ship and submarine to submarine updating the electronics, he would leave the boxes aboard the ships and submarines, placing them out of sight and away from prying eyes.   This went on for six months before John's friend decided he'd done enough for him.   At the end of all of this his friend stopped coming to the Mosque and the free drugs started drying up. John couldn't understand why his friend wasn't coming around anymore and when he did show up, he acted as if he didn't know John.   The last time John went looking for a fix from his friend, he got beat up by him and some others in the alley way next to the Mosque.   Laying in the alley crying, he picked himself up and went back to his apartment.   John still had his job and that was all he had, his wife and kids had moved out of their apartment because she couldn't get any more money for her habits from him. At night he was all alone in his apartment with nothing to show for his life, except for mistakes, drugs, and the one person he thought was his friend was now gone.

By now, everybody that worked with him noticed that something was wrong. Not wanting to get him fired, they covered up for his mistakes, making up excuses for him because of his wife and kids having left him.   By now, John was being carried by everybody on his team.   In the morning he would come in and start working on board the ship and eventually fall asleep in the corner of the area he had been working.   His team would let him sleep, leaving him alone to deal with his mess in his own way.   What his co-workers didn't realize was that John was coming down hard from the drugs that he couldn't get anymore. At times his coworkers could hear John scream as he was going through withdrawals.

Davis and Kelly followed John for the next week, watching to see what he did.   One night after John got off work, they followed him to the Mosque where he met his friend and watched him try to get drugs from him.   Kelly and Davis left their car, deciding to see if they could get a closer look.   They made their way across the street to the market that was still open.   It was at this time that Kelly noticed that the man that John was talking to was of Middle Eastern descent.   He nudged Davis to take out his cell phone and take pictures of the two of them.   Davis, acting as if he was calling someone, started taking pictures of John and his friend.   When they got back to their car, Kelly called Tony with this information, "I think we've found a connection to the bombing of the Dolphin. Davis will be emailing you some pictures of John Graham's friend that he met at the Mosque. Would you please run a facial recognition on him and a background check as well?"

"Well, the local police should have all the information on all of the patrons that frequent the Mosque. Let me give them a call to see if they recognize the individual in the photo. I'll get back with you as soon as possible with the information, sit tight for a minute," Tony said, as he got up from the couch in Ann's apartment.

Walking into her bedroom, he called his contact in the local police department and then sent the pictures to him. A few minutes later, after receiving the photos the police confirmed who the person was. Tony called Kelly back, "The man you asked about was not considered a threat, although that doesn't mean anything. He could be a sleeper for all we know. Keep an eye on the guy and see who his friends are."

"Will do and we'll get pictures of them, as well," Kelly said.

Tony came out from Ann's bedroom and sat down next to her. Ann could see his mind working on this new information via the phone call. She reached over and kissed him on his cheek and went to check on dinner. As he thought about the phone call from Kelly, he decided to follow up with the Admiral to make sure he was aware of what had transpired. Again, going into the bedroom, he dialed the Admiral, "Sorry to disturb you so late at night, but we have a man that's a dock worker, who has connections to some people at the local Mosque that are of Middle Eastern descent. I'm having my men tail the dock worker to see where it leads. Should I check with the FBI on this, just to see if they know anything?"

"Good idea let's do that. That way we might be able to share information on this with them and maybe they will share with us what they have," the Admiral replied.

"Right, I'll get right on that tomorrow morning, sir."

With his job done for the evening he found Ann setting the table for dinner. Holding her from behind he kissed her neck, "By the way have I told you how beautiful you are?"

"I don't think so, but you can keep on telling me. You know how fragile my self-esteem is," she said, as she turned around and kissed him.

The next day Tony contacted the FBI office in New Haven asking to speak in with the lead agent in charge. After explaining why, he was calling the agent replied, "It would be easier if I met you at your office tomorrow, about one p.m."

"That works for me, I'll be waiting for you," Tony said.

Tony called Kelly and Davis, who were still on a stakeout, to let them know about the meeting with the FBI the following day at one o'clock, and that he would like them to be there with the pictures that they had taken of John Graham and the men he was with at the Mosque.

When the next day rolled around, all of Tony's team were in place when the FBI agents showed up. The Senior agent introduced himself as agent Smith and his partner agent Jones. Kelly and Davis smiled at their introduction. The Senior agent saw them smile, "Try living it. It's really hard to be taken serious when your name is Smith and your partner's name is Jones," he continued on, "So, what do you have for us this fine afternoon?"

Tony introduced agents Kelly and Davis as NCIS personnel assigned to work with him on the sinking of the USS Dolphin. Tony continued, "We think there was some sabotage on the submarine that caused it to sink. I had Kelly and Davis stake out the dock worker, John Graham, who met up with a guy that was of Middle Eastern descent at the local Mosque located in Groton."

Turning out the lights, they showed the pictures of the men that the worker had met the night before. Kelly continued to brief the FBI agents about what they had seen while they were staking out John.

"John wanted to get some drugs from the Middle Eastern guy, but he refused to give him any. When John wouldn't take no for an answer, some of the guy's friends showed up to get rid of him. Here are some pictures of his friends."

The FBI agents looked at each picture and studied each face, looking at one another every so often. Tony could tell something was going on between them and after five minutes he asked, "So, do you recognize any of these people?"

The senior agent looked at Tony, as if in deep thought, "Do you guys have a SCIF (Sensitive Compartmentation Information Facility) here."

Tony pointed to the steel door, walked over to it and opened it for the men to walk into another room that was secured from listening devices. After everyone was in the room, Tony secured the door, and asked again, "So, tell us what we are up against here."

"We have been tracking at least two of these men you have pictures of. They've been known sympathizers with ISIS, and we picked up on them about two months ago, during a routine background check. Two of the men, who are supposedly the leaders, have claimed refugee status, but they have both traveled to the Middle East in the last year or so since we began checking their backgrounds. They haven't done anything to warrant them being considered a threat to our country other than being on our watch list, for right now," agent Smith said.

"Looks like they're dealing drugs to at least one person that we know of. Isn't that enough to pull them in for questioning?" Davis asked.

"We could, but we would have to release them right afterwards because we have no real proof," Jones said.

"With what you have on the submarine going down and these guys showing up on your radar, I'm not surprised by it at all. If I were you, I would bring the worker in and start asking him questions, especially, if he works on the ships when they're in dock," Smith said.

"We already planned on doing that later today, in fact, right after we're done here," Tony said.

"If you'll keep us in the loop, we'll do likewise as well," Smith said, as they got up to leave.

"Don't be to surprised if they're involved in this," said Jones.

As the FBI agents left the building, Tony had Kelly and Davis head out to go pick up John Graham. They went to his work area first and found out he was home on sick leave. Heading there next, they arrived at his apartment about 20 minutes later. "I'll take the back door," Kelly said.

Kelly quickly made his way to the back side of the apartment. Waiting a few minutes for Kelly to be in place, Davis proceeded to knock on the door. Hearing the knock on the door, John looked through the peep hole and didn't recognize the man standing on the other side. He cracked the door open a little, "Who are you?" John asked.

Davis showed his badge and identified himself as NCIS. John, realizing he was in trouble, immediately tried to shut the door. Seeing this, Davis lunged at the door, but to late. John took off running through the apartment to the open window and went down the fire escape to get away. Davis was finally able to bust down the door and follow him to the window which lead to the fire escape. Unable to stop him, Davis called out to Kelly, "He's coming your way." He then quickly closed the window and locked it just in case John might double back to his apartment. He made his way out of the apartment to meet Kelly and help him capture John.

"Alright!" Kelly yelled out, as he started looking for John.

Kelly could see John coming down the fire escape and moved in closer to the building, waiting patiently for him. John, seeing Kelly below, waiting there to catch him, realized that he had no other choice but to keep going down the fire escape. Kelly grabbed John just as he came down off the ladder and threw him to the ground, knocking the wind out of him, and held him there until Davis arrived. After catching his breath, Davis looked at Kelly, "Next time you get to go through the front door, and I'll wait outside in the back."

"It's a good thing you didn't have to chase him, we would've had to call an ambulance because you had a heart attack."

"Boy, you ain't a kiddin. I guess I better start working out again."

After they cuffed John, they picked him up and took him back to their car for transport to their office.

Once they arrived back at the office, they placed John into one of the interrogation rooms and locked his hands to the table, he just sat there with his eyes closed, mumbling to himself, "Don't say anything about anything."

Tony watched all of this through the two-way mirror and shook his head at what he saw. After an hour of being inside the room by himself, John started screaming at his reflection in the two-way mirror and started hitting his head on the table. To John, this felt better than the pain he was feeling from the withdrawals. Seeing blood start to appear on his forehead, Kelly and Davis came in and restrained him so that he couldn't move or hurt himself anymore. After 20 minutes of trying to free himself, he was exhausted and having no more strength, he was ready to settle down. Panting like a dog and sweating profusely, he stopped trying to break free from his restraints. All three men were watching from behind the two-way mirror and couldn't believe what they were seeing. A shell of a man strung out on drugs, and coming down real hard from the effects thereof, and then finally passing out. Kelly and Davis had to go into the room and check on him to see if he was still breathing. At one point, John threw up, barely missing Davis.

Tony had Kelly call an ambulance to come get John and take him to the hospital. The medics, having seen cases like this before, strapped John to the gurney before transporting him to the hospital. While John was still passed out the nurses put IV drip lines into his veins to keep him hydrated. The nurses, talking amongst themselves, declared that they had never seen anything this bad before. They carefully continued to keep an eye on John as he lay in the bed, making sure that he was as comfortable as could be, considering that he was restrained to his bed with both of his hands hand cuffed to the bed rails. A guard was posted outside his room to help the doctors and nurses if needed.

Tony felt frustrated, knowing that it would take days for John to be able to answer any questions from anybody. Days that they couldn't afford to waste, waiting for something to blowup, or for that matter, for John to regain consciousness. It was a real test of patience, with the implication, that the longer he was out, the more people could end up dying.

Tony contacted the Admiral one more time and arranged to meet with him at his office. Once they were behind closed doors, he told the Admiral about what the FBI agents had told them in their meeting about the men that they had under surveillance at the Mosque. He also informed him about the civilian dock worker they had brought in for questioning, hoping to ask him some questions about the Dolphin and if he knew anything about it. Unfortunately, the dock worker was now in the hospital going through withdrawals from the drugs he had been taking. "The problem is that we don't know when we'll be able to interrogate him."

"Well, at least we know what ships and submarines our dock worker has worked on."

Tony nodded his head. "I've already got my men looking at all of the ships and submarines that the worker and his team had been refurbishing in order to get an idea of what ships to bring into port for security checks. We're still not sure that the worker did anything wrong.   My hunch is that he's the one that planted the bombs."

"You say some of the ships are still here in dry dock?" The Admiral asked.

"Yes, there still being worked on for other repairs. These vessels will be easy to search, simply by having the bomb dogs go through the ship. I took the liberty to ask the Army and the Air force if they could loan their dog teams to us in order to speed things up."

"Good call.   If there's any grumbling from our sister services, let me know and I'll take care of it."

Later the next day, after getting a list of each ship that John and his team had worked on, Tony and the two NCIS agents began the work of looking for the bombs in earnest. Between the three of them, they each took explosive detection dogs with their handlers to each of the ships that had been identified.   Once the ships were clear of all personnel the handlers and their dogs went to work looking for the bombs.   Tony and the two agents stood on the dock waiting to find out if any bombs were found.   Not knowing where to start, the handlers and their dogs had to search each ship from stem to stern. They moved quickly through each corridor and cubby hole, looking for anything out of the ordinary that was disguised to look ordinary. They worked in two teams, each team started at one end of the ship, working in opposite directions and meeting in the middle. The dog handlers hit pay dirt on the second run through on the first ship. The dog was able to find the package lying next to the hull behind some empty lockers inside the engine compartment of the ship.   Once the bomb was found, they cleared the area around the ship of its workers and waited for the bomb squad to come in and disarm it.

Upon hearing that the dog teams had found a bomb, Tony called the Admiral, "We hit pay dirt."

"I'll be right down," the Admiral said, as he grabbed his hat and headed out the door.

The bomb squad, in full gear, went up the gang plank into the ship, to find a nervous crewman watching over the bomb. After they dismissed the crewman, much to his relief, they carefully diffused the bomb and carried it off of the ship inside a lead box. The bomb squad supervisor looked at the bomb and identified the telltale signs of the builder of the bomb. "This has the markings of a type of bomb built in the Middle East by ISIS.   It's considered very crude in that the bomb builder uses local materials or whatever they can find, to build it.   It's considered very effective, in that it's very easy to build and what it can destroy.   One more thing, this bomb was set to go off when the bow of the ship reached a certain angle in the water. See the mercury switches here, any kind of movement, one way or the other in either direction, would have detonated the bomb. I gotta tell you that whoever put this together knew what he was doing."

Tony stood there listening to the bomb squad supervisor and watched as they gathered up their equipment and moved on to the next ship where they waited to see if another bomb would be located.

The Admiral had arrived just in time, to hear the last part of what the bomb squad supervisor was saying to Tony and watched him take his team and move on to the next ship.

The bomb dog handlers were getting ready to walk up the plank when Tony and the Admiral reached the ship.   They stood there watching the dogs work from one end of the ship to the other on the top deck before going below to continue their search.   At this point, Tony told the Admiral, "Following our list, accordingly, we have a total of six ships that our friend has worked on, that's not including the two ships out on patrol. So far, we've found one bomb, and we're still looking for the others here in the shipyard. I have Davis and Kelly working on the other four ships as we speak."

"Good work Tony.   We should call the FBI and see if they can pick up the suspects."

"Yes sir, I'm already on it."

Within minutes, one of the dog handlers came up on top of the deck and signaled for the bomb squad to come aboard. When the leader of the bomb squad met the dog handler, he told them where the package was located and then proceeded to show them the way. Once the bomb had been located by the bomb squad, the dog and the handler left the ship.   After five tense minutes, the bomb squad came back up on deck, carrying a lead lined box very carefully.   As they reached the bottom of the gang plank two other men in bomb suits took the lead box and carried the bomb over to containment vessel and gently placed the package inside it.

The bomb squad members were busy trying go from ship to ship in their bomb disposal suits, which made climbing in and out of the ships just about impossible to do. You could see that the men inside were sweating due to the heat and physical exertion needed to keep searching for the bombs.   The suits that the men were wearing were set up with a fan inside, so that the helmet screen would stay clear, and a communication system, so that they could talk to each other as they worked together on a bomb. The suit would protect the bomb specialist if the bombs were not to big, otherwise the suit was useless. Tony watched from a distance as the team of men worked together diffusing the bomb and brought it to the containment trailer.

As they went from ship to ship, the bomb dogs had found a total of six bombs that needed to be removed. The bomb disposal team was pretty busy getting rid of the bombs and getting the container out to a safe distance to detonate the bombs they had found. There were two ships, that the maintenance team had worked on, that had already left port. In this case the dog handlers and their dogs were flown out by helicopter, with another helicopter bringing bomb disposal personnel to the ships. Once the ships had been identified as being worked on by the maintenance team, the ships were required to sit stationary in the water, leastwise until they could be checked out.   Finding bombs aboard each one of the ships, the bomb disposal team gently brought the bombs to the aft section of the main deck and dropped them overboard away from the ships. After few minutes, a giant plume of water erupted from the surface before settling back to normal again.   After all of the ships that the maintenance team had worked on were checked out, the only bomb that had detonated was the one aboard the USS Dolphin.

Tony reported back to the Admiral, "We found all of the bombs that were aboard the ships and submarines. That being said, it would behoove us to check the other ships, as well, to be sure."

"I concur, I'll set it up and we'll need other units to come here to assist in the security checks."

"We got lucky with only losing one submarine in all of this."

"Not lucky for the crew's families on the Dolphin. Don't get me wrong, it could have been worse, but it's still bad. What about the worker, is he still in the hospital recovering from the drugs?"

"The last time we checked on him he was still in bad shape from the drugs, and the withdrawals were taking their toll on him. The doctors are keeping an eye on him for right now and will let us know when we can come and visit him when he comes to."

"Very well, please let me know what you find out when he comes to.   By the way, you and your team did good.   I'll make sure all of you get recognized for your work."

"Thank you, I'll pass it on to the guys.   I wish we could have found the bomb aboard the Dolphin before it was too late."

There was a pause from the Admiral for just a second before he replied, "I wish the same thing, myself. The good news for us is that it's only a few letters that have to be written instead of eight ships crews."

"Yes, sir."

Tony met Ann at her apartment, feeling very tired from the stress he felt as they looked for the bombs. And yet pleased with finding all of the bombs that had been placed on the ships. Sitting on the couch and drinking a beer, he watched the TV as Ann changed into something more comfortable. While he waited for her, Tony leaned his head back against the couch and closed his eyes. "So where would you like to go out for dinner tonight?" she called out to him from her bedroom.

Not getting any answer, she came out to see him asleep on the couch. Coming over to where he was, she reached over and kissed him. Tony smiled from being kissed and continued sleeping. Seeing that Tony was out for the night, Ann smiled and quietly went and got a blanket and pillow for him to use. She had heard from the Admiral about what Tony and his team of agents had accomplished in finding the bombs. With him stretched out on the couch she whispered, "Go ahead and sleep my hero, you've earned it," as she went into the kitchen to prepare something for herself to eat.

Chapter VI

Special Agents Smith and Jones had taken over for Davis and Kelly while they went and searched for the bombs. The attempted bombing of the ships would fall under Navy security and yet would also fall under the purview of the FBI because it was a terrorist attack on American soil. They continued watching from where Kelly and Davis had been staked out, located inside an apartment building across the street from the apartment that the terrorists were living in. As part of their stakeout the agents were using a telephoto lens on their camera to take pictures of the men as they came and went from their apartment. They then sent the pictures to the FBI headquarters to run them through a facial recognition software computer. In the end, they were able to identify three of the men as ISIS agents with ties back to their homeland. Having their names, they searched each of their files and found that they had been trained at one of the terrorist camps that was located in the Ethiopian desert and were considered qualified in building and using explosives along with small arms operations.

It had been determined by the two FBI agents that Ahmed was identified as the leader of this cell and he was responsible for all of their living expenses and the recruiting of new members. It was he who had befriended the American worker and paid for all of his drugs and other gifts. Ahmed felt nothing but disdain and hatred for all Americans, he considered them as weak inferior people, who didn't believe in Allah. Therefore, in his eyes, they were less than human. The Americans were considered as Infidels that needed to be eradicated by all of the true believers of Allah. They were a nuisance in his goal of converting everyone to Allah. He loathed the freedoms that the Americans had, when it came to their culture. For him, it had been a real trial to remain true to his beliefs while living in this decadent country. The other two men in his terrorist cell were Abba and Abdul, both were considered true believers, but were useful only as soldiers and not as smart as he was. They were both willing to die for Allah, whereas Ahmed would choose to live to fight another day.   He was the mastermind of the cell and had been in America the longest of the three.   He was there to recruit any refugees and students to do the work of ISIS, and of course, Allah.

For the most part, the recruiting had been dismal, simply because the people from his own country he thought he could recruit had already started becoming Americanized.   They liked their TVs, cars, clothes, fast food, and especially, the way the American girls dressed. The biggest draw for them was the pornography, which was everywhere, and of course, the drugs were easier to get a hold of in America.   In America, nobody cared about anything when it came to doing what you wanted to do. For Ahmed, a true believer, he had seen it before in other cities, not only in America but in Europe, as well. He would bow down towards the east to pray for Allah to give him strength and not be tempted by America's downward spiral into hell. Ahmed was a true believer, even if the others from his country were not, he would deal with them later. But for now, he was waiting and watching the news to learn if any of the U.S. Navy ships that they had placed bombs on, were missing and or sunk.   Ahmed would confirm this with John, knowing that it would only take some more drugs to get the information out of him.   He smiled to himself, thinking that his actions would destroy, not only military weapons, but also the Americans who were on board the ships.   For his actions, he was guaranteed that his 70 virgins would be waiting for him.

Agent Smith contacted Tony, "Would you create a fake press release about one of your ships sinking while out at sea for the benefit of the terrorists? We need to have them think that they were successful in planting their bombs aboard the ships, in order to draw them out."

"How soon do you need it?"

"No later than the end of this week."

"Let me check with the Admiral before I say yes or no.   I'll get back with you as soon as I can."

Thinking it best to meet with the Admiral in his office, Tony called the Admiral's secretary to set up an appointment before driving over.   Ann was surprised that Tony was calling ahead instead of just coming in. "I missed you after I left you on the couch," she said, after checking the Admiral's calendar for openings to get with the Admiral.

"I must apologize for falling asleep on you yesterday. I got up early so that I could change my uniform and get cleaned up at my place."

By now the Admiral had arrived and was asking for his coffee and his itinerary for the day. Ann set the phone down, "Sir, Tony wanted to meet with you today, if he could be squeezed in. I have an opening at 9:45, before your ten o'clock meeting."

The Admiral nodded his approval and walked into his office to start his day.

"Can you be here at 9:45 sharp?" Ann asked Tony.

"Yes, ma'am, I can.   See you soon my precious," Tony chuckled, as he hung up the phone before Ann could respond.

Tony arrived at 9:30 and sat in the outer office talking to Ann while he waited to meet with the Admiral.   After a few minutes, the door to the Admiral's office opened and a Navy officer came out carrying an attaché case.   As he waited for the Admiral, Tony could hear him, "Tony, come on in and bring us some coffee."

Doing as he had been asked, he smiled at Ann as she handed him two cups of coffee before going in. She whispered, "Here you go, my precious."

To which he turned beet red as he walked away.

Closing the door behind him, Tony sat down in one of the chairs facing the Admiral. "Sorry to bother you, I've been asked by Agent Smith, from the FBI, to create a fake press release indicating that we lost one of our ships.   They're hoping that this will draw out all of the terrorists that were involved in the sabotaging of our ships and submarines."

Upon hearing this, the Admiral sat for a moment thinking about the request, "I understand what he wants, and why.   The question I have is, how do we get the rest of the Navy to buy off on this. Have you contacted the Public Affairs office about this request?"

"Not yet.   I wanted to get your thoughts before proceeding any further."

"I know it can be done.   The only thing I need to do is to coordinate with my bosses so that they're not taken by surprise, thinking that the press release is real.   How soon do they need this done?"

"In a couple of days, most likely.   That way they'll have the manpower in place to do what they need to do."

"Good.   That will give me enough time to clear the deck for the press release.   Once again, keep me posted so that I can tell my bosses what's going on. I'll call you once I get it all squared away."

"Thank you, sir," he said as he got up to leave.

Stepping out of the Admiral's office, he looked at Ann and mouthed the words, "I'll see you tonight."

Ann smiled at him and nodded in reply. In a few minutes the Admiral came out of his office and smiled at Ann. "You know that Tony guy, he'd be a real catch if you were so interested."

"It's funny, I was thinking the same thing when I first saw him," she said, as he reviewed his schedule for the rest of the day.

After his conversation with the Admiral, Tony obliged Agent Smith by contacting the Navy Public Affairs office with a story of a ship disappearing while on training maneuvers in the Atlantic Ocean. The article went on to say that the ship had just left Groton after being refitted.   There were only a few survivors found in the water near the site where the ship had disappeared.   As to why the ship sank is still under investigation.   The story ran on the nightly local and national news for about two days saying that the Navy was investigating the remains of the ship and talking to the survivors.

Ahmed, seeing this on the news with Abdul and Abba, went out that night to celebrate their victory against the Infidels by getting drunk and watching porno films.   Ahmed, having given himself permission to indulge in viewing the pornography and drinking, but knew he would have to pray for forgiveness because of his actions. This kind of celebrating was done mostly for Abba and Abdul. Ahmed knew that, even though they were committed to the cause, they were spiritually weak.   He was hopeful that pretty soon the U.S. Navy would be reporting more of their ships sinking or missing.

Being able to take credit for sinking the Navy ships, he would be able to go back to his country and town a hero for ISIS and make his way to become a master planner of terrorist activities in other countries. Eventually, the leaders in ISIS would see his contribution to the cause and send for him to come back home, allowing him to come back a hero for Allah and work for them.

Once the ships were destroyed by the bombs and word got out that he had masterminded it, the first thing Ahmed planned on doing when he got back home was to visit his friends and family. As he sat thinking about his glorious return to his homeland, he could see that Abba and Abdul were involved watching the porno films. They wouldn't see him leave or even miss him as he left the porno shop to go back to their apartment and pray for forgiveness and guidance from Allah. As he drove back to his apartment, he wondered if the sinking of the ships would be enough to get the attention of his leaders and garner the respect, he felt he deserved. As he opened his apartment door, he started considering bigger ideas on how to stop the Americans from taking over the world. He vowed that this time it would be closer to home for the Americans and it would be on their own soil. This time there would be more infidels dying and it would be covered in greater detail by the press. "Praise Allah," Ahmed said to himself, as he continued to pray again for inspiration on how to destroy the infidels.

Agents Smith and Jones sat at the street corner knowing that Ahmed and his two goons were inside the porno shop watching films. They were surprised to see Ahmed walk out by himself and get into his car. They followed Ahmed back to his apartment and sat in their car, watching and waiting for him to go into the apartment complex he lived in before heading back to their own apartment to continue their surveillance.

While Ahmed and his friends were out celebrating, a crew of FBI specialists had gone into Ahmed's apartment and planted bugs and small cameras, to keep tabs on the three terrorists. The FBI would know everything that Ahmed and his lackeys were planning to do before the terrorists could act on their plans. The specialists would monitor their activities from another room inside the same apartment that agents Smith and Jones had already set up for their stakeout. After checking to make sure that the cameras and the listening devices were working properly, two of the specialists would stay behind to monitor the recordings of the terrorists with their equipment that had been set up in the second room. From their apartment across the street the FBI would now start to monitor these three terrorist twenty-four hours a day.

After a few days Ahmed received a message, via his courier, from his leaders congratulating him on sinking the Navy ship and that Allah was proud of him and his team for being able to pull it off. They were now expecting greater things from him and his cell to make Allah proud of them once more. The three men and the courier were ecstatic about the message, smiling and laughing about how they had made Allah proud of their actions. Abdul grabbed Ahmed and started dancing and singing in his own tongue. At first Ahmed was annoyed by Abdul's actions but relented and started singing as well. Together all of them celebrated the first step in the demise of America. The next project would have to wait until tomorrow after the partying was over.

One of the FBI specialists was watching all of this on his video feed from the camera in the apartment. He saw everything, to include the man who was the courier. As more people came into view agents Smith and Jones started putting together a simple network of Ahmed's terrorist cell. As soon as the courier left the building, Agent Jones shadowed him till he got to his place of living. Jones watched the courier go into the apartment complex and climb the stairs to his apartment. Noting the floor and the number of the courier's apartment, he called Smith and told him where he was and the courier's address. Smith contacted his bosses, explaining what was going on in his area and asked for more people for a stake out on this new apartment complex. Within days, agents started showing up with their equipment, ready to surveil the new apartment to see who else was involved with the courier. Having two teams watching both places, made it easier to keep their eyes on all of the players without blowing their cover.

Chapter VII

NSA Intelligence Analyst Weaver looked up from his book upon hearing a notification bell from his computer, indicating that a message was being transmitted. As he opened and read the message, he could tell that it was for someone that was fluent in one of the Middle Eastern languages. He then marked it with his initials and date stamped it. The next step was to take the printout to his supervisor and put it on his desk. "This just came in from Iran. It seems as if we're starting to get more traffic from there lately," Weaver said.

"Yeah, I noticed that myself, this is the third message that we've intercepted from there in the last two weeks," Mr. Bliss replied, as he looked up from his desk.

As Bliss read the message, he decided to make a copy of it and pass it on to the CIA liaison, Ms. Snow, "This might interest you and your team," Bliss said as he handed her the message.

"Thank you, I'll let you know what we do with it for your report," she replied.

Ms. Snow looked at it then typed it into her computer and sent the message rip to the covert field offices in Iran for dissemination. The field operatives in the different intelligence compounds would look at the new information and determine if immediate action was required. If not, it would be posted on the bulletin board locally and at the compounds, as another source to review for some type of action in the near future.

Mr. Bliss, looking at the message again, realized that it had something to do with what was happening in America and sent a copy of it to the FBI liaison, with a note attached to it, "I don't know if this has anything to do with your agency, but I think you need to be made aware of this."

The FBI liaison, Mr. Greene, thanked him for the message, and then faxed the message so that it could be posted at the FBI information center for distribution. Although the message wouldn't be seen by Special Agent's Smith or Jones, the FBI was in a position now to work with the Department of Justice to start building a case against the terrorist cell operating in the metro area of Groton, Connecticut. Based upon the photos taken of the courier that were sent to facial recognition center in Virginia, the face was identified as Bashir Alabir, a known student in the Hampton city community college. He had been investigated once already as a person of interest to the FBI about a year ago. Although they didn't find anything out of the ordinary, he was not considered a threat, leastwise, until now. The investigative arm of the FBI now started looking at Bashir for anything that would indicate covert action against the United States and abroad. With the FBI ramping itself up for action against the terrorists, it was now a matter of time before something would bust loose, hopefully before anybody else got hurt.

Within minutes Special Agent Smith received all of the information about the courier, Bashir Alabir, including his background information before and after he had come to America. After reading the information on Bashir, Smith passed it on to Jones.

"Looks like we're going to earn our pay on this one," Jones commented.

Smith nodded in agreement, "At least they're giving us more manpower to cover both of them."

"So, what do we do now?"

"Well, we have a stakeout going on with three known terrorists and we're getting a stakeout set up on a courier named, Bashir. It looks to me like we need to be patient and wait and see what their next move is going to be."

"I agree, I just hope we can handle it when it starts really getting busy."

"You and me both."

Ahmed was still thinking about what he could do to create or generate a statement for ISIS that would send him back home as a hero to the cause to show them that he was a strong soldier and leader for Allah here in the United States. He was determined that these Americans would either bow to Allah or die. He thought about several different options, the first was a bomb, or maybe a biological weapon of some sort, and then maybe renting a truck, load it with explosives, and drive it through a crowded intersection before detonating it.   All of these would be good for the cause, but he needed to really give some more thought about doing something that hadn't been done before in America. He realized that this would take some time and knew he would be thinking about it for some time to come. Being startled for a moment, he heard Abdul and Abba come into the apartment bringing groceries from the market.   They went to Ahmed's room to check in with him but could see that he was deep in thought.   Not wanting to interrupt him they quietly closed the door to his room and went about cooking dinner and talking amongst themselves.   An hour later Ahmed came out of his room ready to eat dinner, with no clear plan.

The next morning when all was quiet, Ahmed woke up as usual and as he lay there in his bed his mind was still working on his next project to strike a blow against the United States. He thought about all of the friends he knew who had lost children in the war due to the predator strikes that were targeting ISIS leaders without warning, and how the hellfire missiles took the lives of the children and others. Thinking on this, he wondered if he could do something to help heal the wounds of his friends by striking a blow against the children here in America.

He sat up in bed with a start, smiling about an idea that had just come to him.   He would destroy the heart of America by destroying the rising generation of young people just as the Americans had in his country.   How to do it was the question that now lay before him. He thought about using bombs, but they would be easy to find when the police were alerted to the threat. Then his thoughts turned to using a biological weapon that would be odorless, tasteless, and would be complete in killing everyone in the vicinity of the weapon. Especially, in a closed environment.   He knew just the place to use it with the most lethal impact, and that would be the schools, where all of the kids would be during the day attending classes.   Now it was a matter of finding the right biological weapon and the equipment to use to carry out his plan.

He checked his watch and saw that it was now time for morning prayer and his roommates needed to be woken up for their daily morning ritual.   Getting out of bed, he went to wake up Abdul and Abba so they could start the day with prayer.   This was Ahmed's first responsibility every day, and he thought to himself, *"Abdul and Abba would be easy to replace when the time came, simply because they didn't have the vision of Allah or the discipline that he had."* He knew they were useful in doing what needed to be done, and they would earn their 70 virgins someday soon for Allah. He would make sure of this, before he left to go home a hero and back to his friends and family. He reminded himself to be patient with them, leastwise, now that he had to plan a death strike against the infidels. He knew he must be careful now that he had planning to do in order to teach the infidels about Allah. He didn't want the police to find out what he was doing and destroy his plan against the infidels. Yes, the lesson would be a harsh one, but sometimes that's what it takes for the learning to begin. Anyway, it was time for morning prayer to Allah and he couldn't miss that. There would be time later today to start formulating their next mission.

As the FBI agent sat listening to the bugs in Ahmed's apartment, he looked out his window and noticed that the sun was starting to rise in the eastern sky. Checking his watch and writing the time down on the surveillance sheet next to him, he saw and heard Ahmed starting to move around inside his apartment. With nothing new to report, he was now waiting for the day shift to come in and replace him so that he could go home and get some sleep so he could be back later tonight. About 30 minutes later, his replacement came in to relieve him from sitting there listening and watching the TV screens in the small room. Bringing in some hot coffee and donuts, they switched places and the day shift began. Not having anything to say except hello and goodbye as they greeted other, the ritual would begin again with a set of fresh eyes and ears to watch and hear the day's events in the lives of the terrorists who were now kneeling in prayer, facing the eastern sky. The FBI specialist laughed to himself, wondering what the terrorist would do if they knew he was watching their every move in their apartment.

Tony reported to the Admiral, "All of the packages that were placed on the ships have been recovered by EOD and the security checks on each of the ships are in the process of being completed just in case there was more than one bomb planted on the ships."

The Admiral breathed a heavy sigh of relief. "That was to close for comfort. What about the worker who had done all of this?"

"He'll recover from the drugs and everything else that goes with it."

"Have you been able to talk to him yet?"

"We're hoping to do that today. We should be able to question him about his part in it and if there was anyone else involved."

"Good, that's good.   Again, keep me posted."

"Will do sir," Tony replied as he got up from his chair and left the Admirals office, closing the door behind him.   He stopped by Ann's desk, "How about we go do something tonight,"

"Sure, why not, what do you have in mind?" she asked.

"I haven't the foggiest idea yet. How about we talk about it tonight?"

"I'll see you tonight then," she said, smiling at him.

Leaving the Admirals office, he got into his car and headed back to his office, trying to come up with something that he and Ann could do tonight.   Not coming up with anything, he decided to let it go for right now.   He opened the door to the office and called out, "Hey you guys want to go and interview our guest in the hospital to see if he can identify his friends that got him to plant the bombs?" Tony said, smiling.

"Should we wear some plastic pants when we interview him, just in case he's still sick?" Davis asked, still remembering their last meeting with John.

Kelly laughed at Davis's comment and Tony smiled, remembering the look on Davis's face wanting to get even with John, not caring that he was sick.

Chapter VIII

As Ahmed thought about the plan he was hatching to kill the American children, he wrote down a list of things that he would need to consider in determining a target. First of all, what kind of biological weapon would he use to carry out his plan, and where would he get it. Second, he would need a few containers to carry the bio-weapon in, which would be easy to find almost anywhere in a hardware store. Third, the school would have to be chosen based on the size of the student population, and the surrounding areas. Fourth, when it would be released into the school for the maximum effect would need to be considered, as well. He wrote all of this on a piece of paper, listing the materials that he would need to have in order to create the weapon. He looked over the checklist once more, making sure that he didn't miss anything. As he reviewed what was on the paper, he put a mark next to each item that he could readily find anywhere. Starting with number three, he had Abdul go on the internet to find out about the schools in the area and their locations.

With his plan in the beginning stages, he needed to contact Bashir in order to get a message to his leaders about trying to get a biological weapon brought into the United States. He figured Anthrax, or something like it, would be readily available, only because Al-Qaeda, which had morphed into ISIS, still might have some bio-weapons secretly stored in a cave somewhere in Iran or Iraq. He put on his coat and headed to the local community college to make contact with his courier. The agent seeing this, let Smith and Jones know that Ahmed was on his way out.

While he was walking through the commons area at the community college, he saw Bashir seated at a table with some of his friends from school. Ahmed sat down with the group at the table and passed a note to Bashir while shaking his hand. The school bell rang, indicating that the next hour of class had begun. The group of friends got up and left to go to class, leaving Bashir alone to read the note he had been handed. Ahmed waited patiently as Bashir read the note. "You do realize what you are asking for?" Bashir asked.

"I know and I understand. The stupid Americans will never expect this," he said, as if he had already done it.

Bashir looked into Ahmed's eyes knowing what he already had accomplished for Allah. "Let me look into it for you and I'll let you know soon."

Ahmed got up and walked back to his apartment to wait for Bashir's reply. He thought to himself, *If Allah was proud of what his follower had done already, then the answer would be yes.* He smiled to himself, knowing that the answer would be yes.

Agents Jones and Donaldson, who were watching the exchange, filmed the transaction as it took place between Ahmed and Bashir. Bashir stayed at the school, so Agent Jones followed Ahmed as he made his way back to his apartment. Before leaving, Jones asked Donaldson, "Is your team all set up, as far as bugs and cameras in Bashir's apartment?"

"Yep, we got two other agents watching his apartment right now."

"Good, let us know if you get any information from the message Ahmed gave Bashir."

"Will do, as soon as we know something."

Tony, Kelly and Davis went into the hospital and found that the guard was still standing in front of the room where John Graham was recovering from the drugs he had taken. He was still being kept in restraints for his own protection so as not to harm himself or try to get away. They walked into the room and looked at the man lying in the bed, his eyes were still closed, and his arm had an IV bottle hooked up to it to keep him hydrated. The drugs had taken their toll on him physically, he was malnourished and looked more like a bag of bones than human. As Kelly and Davis found a seat, Tony stood next to the bed, opened John's personnel file and started to read out loud about the young man before him. "Your name is John Graham and you were born on December 15, 1982. You're married with two children and you recently filed for divorce from your wife because she's addicted to pain killers and alcohol."

Hearing a man's voice, John opened his eyes and was looking at Tony, wondering, where he got his information about him and why he was in the hospital.

"Who are you and why are you here?" John asked.

"You are under investigation for the sinking of a nuclear submarine in which you planted a bomb on board, causing it to sink and killing all hands onboard."

John closed his eyes, saying nothing at first, just laid there and started crying. Seeing his reaction, Tony couldn't help but feel sorry for the man lying in the bed, his life was over, and it wasn't going to get any better from here on.

John stopped crying and looked up and for the first time realized that he couldn't move his hands as they were restrained. "I didn't know they were bombs; it was supposed to be surprises for the crews when they were out at sea. I should've known better than that. I could blame my wife and the drugs, but I realize that it was my choice, no matter what."

"Who are the guys who gave you the packages to put aboard the ships and how many were there?"

"I don't remember, the guy was supposed to be my friend. He gave me the drugs to help me and money to buy things."

Tony pulled out some pictures and showed them to John. "Are these the guys that are your friends?"

John looked at the pictures and pointed, "This one is my friend, the others were mean to me. Man, can you get me something, my insides are on fire. I need something to help me."

Tony ignored the question and continued, "How many ships did you plant the bombs on?"

"My friend wanted to surprise all of the ships I worked on. He was nice to me, he gave me what I needed and was my friend, then he went away."

By now John was dealing with the late stages of the withdrawal and the side effects were starting to show. He started throwing up again, shivering and shaking from the cold, and his body was screaming for the drugs it needed to survive.

Tony nodded at Davis to go get a nurse. He popped his head out of the hospital room door and made eye contact with the nurse, motioning for her to come in. She quickly went to the room and checked the IV bottle and the needle in his arm. She noticed that the heart monitor machine was blinking red and shut it off for a minute and then turned it back on to reset the machine. She quickly grabbed a towel and started wiping the sweat from John's forehead. The nurse then hit the call button, bringing another nurse into the room, "What do you need?"

"Get me 100 ccs of Demurral and an orderly to come clean up the room," said the first nurse.

The second nurse left and then came back in carrying a tray with a syringe on it. The first nurse took the syringe and stuck the needle into a sealed opening on the IV drip line, emptying the contents of the syringe into the line. Within seconds John started to relax and the sweating stopped. The nurse looked at Tony, "He should be feeling better here in a minute or two. You can only stay for a few more minutes, then he has to rest."

"I'll be brief nurse."

After a few minutes, Tony decided to continue with his questions. "How many are there that you know of?"

"Three people. The others didn't like me, only my friend liked me."

"Do you know where they live?"

"Same place as my friend."

The nurse came back in to check on her patient and seeing that Tony was still there, gave him and the others the evil eye routine about having stayed to long. Tony, seeing this, took the hint and as the nurse left they followed her out of the room.

"How the hell do you get so far down that you would end up like this?" Tony asked, after leaving John's room.

As they walked out of the hospital Davis asked, "How come they never show this side of the drug world on TV. Someone should film somebody going through detox and the physical effects it has on the body when they are really hooked on the drugs and can't get any."

Kelly thought about what Davis had said. "Don't you know that famous statement said by so many, 'Man that won't happen to me, I can control it and I can leave it when I want to.' "

Tony chuckled and said to the others, "Tell that to John, he'll believe you."

As Tony left the hospital he realized, that for all practical purposes, his interrogation with John was over and that now it became a matter for the FBI to take over and run the show to catch the terrorists.

Tony decided to call the Admiral and let him know where everything lay on this investigation. Ann answered the phone and instantly knew by his voice it was Tony, "Hey sailor, looking for a good time," she said, half laughing.

"As a matter of fact, I am.   What do you have in mind beautiful?"

"Why don't you come around tonight and I'll show you," She said enticing him with her voice.

"Be still my beating heart.   I'll be there around seven.   Now, I really need to talk to the Admiral."

"Well, I never," she said, acting hurt.

Once the Admiral picked up the phone Tony informed him, "Sir, as far as I can tell, John was the only American that was used by the terrorists to try and destroy the Navy ships in dry dock."

"That's good news.   Do you have any more leads to follow on this?"

"I need to talk to the FBI and see what they've come up with. That being said, I think from the Navy's point of view, we can consider this case closed."

"Check with the FBI and see where and what they're doing about it and we'll go from there."

"Will do sir.   I'll let you know what I find out."

"Hey Tony, you and your team did a good job in finding the terrorists and the worker who planted the bombs."

"Thank you, sir, I'll pass it onto the team. I just wish we could have done more before the USS Dolphin was gone, sir."

"Me too, but the good news is, we saved a lot of people by finding the bombs onboard the other ships and submarines before anyone else had to die."

"Yes sir, we did do that for sure."

"Let me know what you find out from the FBI and again, good job Tony and good night."

"Good night, sir."

As Tony hung up the phone, he thought to himself, *"For having done such a good job, how come I feel like a failure? I wonder if this is what is meant by a hollow victory?"*

After he arrived back at his office, he told Kelly and Davis about the comment the Admiral had said and congratulated them on doing a fine job catching John and finding the terrorist cell. Both Kelly and Davis seemed pleased with themselves for doing their job, but both of them could see that Tony was not all that excited about having done the job and about closing it out.

"Hey, what's up boss?" Kelly asked Tony.

Tony looked at his men, wondering if he should say anything. "I feel like we did the hard work of finding the weak link in the chain and we saved a lot of lives onboard the other ships.   It's just that I feel that we should have done more before it got this far."

"What more could we have done? We had no indication of anything being wrong before the Dolphin was brought up from the bottom," Davis responded.

"Besides, it was you that caught the slight curve of the submarine indicating that a torpedo was used against it," Kelly added.

"I guess you're right about that."

"It would've been good to be proactive, however, that being said, where would we have looked to find the bad guys?   Maybe, if we had more resources or more personnel to work with, we could be more forward thinking in finding the bad guys.   The sad part of our jobs is, that we have to wait and see before we can act upon anything.   It's just the nature of the beast," Kelly added, as Davis shook his head in agreement.

"We'll always be behind the curve when it comes to fighting the bad guys and it's not because we aren't trying," Davis stated.

Tony thought about what Kelly and Davis said and after a minute he realized that what they had said was true. "Time to get back to work guys," he said, as he smiled indicating that their words were true.

Tony picked up the phone and called Smith at the FBI office to find out if anything had shaken lose about the terrorists. The secretary answered the phone, "Agents Smith and Jones are not in the building right now.   Can I take a message for them?"

After he identified himself, Tony said, "Have either one of them give me a call when they are available."

"I will be glad to pass on the message to them," the secretary said.

Looking at his watch, he was making sure that he wasn't going to miss out on meeting Ann tonight. "I'm done for the night, why don't you two knock it off for the night as well and I'll see you two tomorrow morning," he said, as he left the office.

Davis looked at Kelly, "You know that secretary the Admiral has is quite a looker."

"I know what you mean, it's a good thing she's on our side," he replied.

"Should we tell our boss that she's clean?"

"Naw, I think he already knows it; don't you think?" both men chuckled at the last remark as they closed the door behind them headed out into the night.

Tony arrived at Ann's apartment and knocked on her front door. When she opened it, all Tony could do was stare at Ann as she reached for him and pulled him into her apartment by his tie.

NSA Intelligence analyst Weaver once again picked up the printout from the printer at his desk and looked at it before marking it with his initials and date stamped it....

Once again, the message would be sent to the CIA field offices in Iran The field agents would compare the first message with this new one, especially coming back to Iran, and this would pique the curiosity of the teams in the field. Why two messages coming and going from the same two places? Why now? There was no increase in communication chatter lately. What are our terrorist friends up to now?

The lead CIA agent, whose job it was to watch over Iran and Iraq, decided to start looking into the communiques that were starting to come in from the field. He assigned one of his agents to go and check it out. This would be the first step to start the ball rolling to find out what was going on. The second step would be taken once there was more information to go on. But for now the second message was enough to start with.

Ms. Snow's interest was now piqued about what was going on, especially with the second message coming from America, *"What does our enemy have in mind to do now?"* As she sat and thought about it, she wished she was a field agent doing the investigation. Her job was, to say the least, slightly boring, just passing the information along to her bosses. That being said, she was happy to know that she was at least doing her part and hopefully making a difference in doing her job.   Moving the information forward to the next level she thought, *"Who knows, maybe it may save someone's life.   Aw, who am I kidding, nothing like that ever happens around here or to me."*

Chapter IX

Agents Smith and Jones were seated by the windows in a room directly across from Ahmed's apartment building, each of them looking through their binoculars, watching and waiting for something to happen. Smith thought to himself that somehow, seeing a stakeout portrayed on TV or a movie, wasn't all that exciting in real life. But it was, as he thought, a necessary part of the job in catching the bad guys. It had been a long night, Smith looked at his watch and saw that it was already midnight. The three suspects had retired for the evening, giving the agents, who had been watching and listening, a chance for a break. Scanning the apartment across the way and seeing no indications of movement, Smith allowed everyone to go outside onto the balcony to stretch their legs and breath in some fresh air.

Agent Smith also stood up to relieve the soreness in his muscles, he started thinking about his earlier conversation with Tony and his interview with John Graham. About how much of a wreck the young man was and also all the trouble he was in. According to Tony, John had identified one of the terrorists as his friend, who had given him the drugs and the bombs to put aboard the ships. Accordingly, Agent Smith knew they had enough to bring them all in and possibly hold them for terrorist activities. Deciding against this, as he wanted the whole setup, including the ones that were in Iran, not just the small fish in the pond.

The ringing of his cell phone brought him back to the here and now. He looked at his cell phone and saw that the call was from Agent Donaldson on the other stakeout watching the movements of Bashir. Smith answered, "Smith here, what's up?"

"Just to let you know, Bashir just left his apartment and may be heading your way to visit your guys over there."

"Thanks for the heads up Donny, we'll be in touch if needed. Put a tail on Bashir, just to be sure."

"Already done, he's being followed by Reynolds right now."

"That's good, I'll let you know if he comes this way."

Reynolds made sure that he was at least two cars back as he tailed Bashir on his motorcycle as he drove through the streets. Bashir rode through the town, being careful not to break any laws, so as not to attract any undue attention from the local police, being especially careful to obey the speed limits and the signs of the road. He made his way over to Ahmed's place. He parked his bike out front and went inside and climbed the stairs to Ahmed's floor. Reynolds waited outside about a half a block up and watched for Bashir, wondering how long it would be before he came out of Ahmed's apartment. By now all of the agents were back on the job, watching and listening for the two men to start talking.

Bashir was excited to let Ahmed know that he had received a message from Iran. And was more excited about him receiving permission to proceed with his plans. He wanted to make sure that Ahmed was able to act on it quickly. When he arrived at Ahmed's place, he knocked on the door to the apartment and waited impatiently for one of the three to open it. Bashir was hoping it would be Ahmed, not one of the others living there. When Ahmed did open the door, Bashir was relieved that it was him. He walked in and sat down, waiting for him to be fully a wake so he could read the message that he had brought with him. Waiting a minute, he smiled and handed the message over to Ahmed, who started to read it. Within seconds, Ahmed's face broke into a smile, grabbing Bashir he started talking excitedly about it. Bashir was just as excited as Ahmed was, and was talking just as quick as he could, as well. Finally, both of them settled down and were sitting on the couch, "What are you going to do now?" Bashir asked.

Feeling happy about being approved for his idea, Ahmed told him, "Today, we plan our biggest strike against the infidels and when it is done, we will be heroes and our countrymen will honor us in song and with great tales of bravery."

"What are you going to do to bring this about, oh great one?"

"We're going to attack the infidels on their own soil and destroy hundreds of them in one quick action."

"How is this possible?"

"We will attack their children and destroy their will to fight against Allah by poisoning them with a bad disease. You see, the message says that the weapon I want to use is on its way here through Mexico and it will arrive in a week. That will give us time to plan our next steps in order to carry it out."

Bashir was excited to be part of something so big that would have such grave circumstances for the infidels. "What can I do to help in this great cause?" he asked Ahmed.

"Just be patient and quiet about this message, do you understand?"

"Yes, I do. I will guard this secret with my life."

"That is good for now. Go home and act as if nothing has changed. I will contact you when it is time for you to be there."

"Allahu Akbar, my friend."

"Yes, Allahu Akbar."

Both of them hugged each other before Bashir left the apartment. As Bashir came down the stairs, Reynolds was there, watching him as he came out of the apartment complex and got on his bike to go back to his apartment.

Upon hearing this new plan, Agent Smith and the others went cold inside. Smith quickly called Donny about the late-night visit from Bashir. "I need you to follow Bashir extra close, no matter what happens. We need to find out, if possible, the connection to Bashir and the communication point of contact, where it is and who it is."

Smith then called his superiors that night and informed them about the latest information recorded by the linguist. After hearing from Smith, the midnight fires started to burn in alphabet row near Washington D.C. The Department of Defense would be brought in on this, as well. Their part was uncertain at this time, but they needed to be ready and standing by, just in case.

The first step was to find out what kind of weapon was coming through Mexico to the United States. The second step would be to identify the couriers and their points of contact in Mexico and America, then destroy the package and the men who were bringing it into the country. This would require ICE (Immigration and Customs Enforcement), along with the Border Patrol, working with the FBI to intercept the package.

Over a thousand miles away, a package was being prepared In Iran to be used against the United States and it had to be wrapped in a self-contained, airtight case, for transfer. This package would need to be hand delivered by trusted personnel, to ensure its arrival in

America. The man responsible for the package being made safe to transport was Dr. Salaam, he was a chemist trained in America, and at one time worked with the CIA. He'd been in charge of producing the anthrax disease for his country. He had worked in Afghanistan in a secret laboratory, in one of the caves, to create enough anthrax for Al-Qaeda to use against Iraqi soldiers during their border war and then was re-purposed against the Americans during Desert Storm. Once the Americans found out what he had done in making more of the disease, the manhunt was on as they searched for him. He barely made it out of Afghanistan carrying some of what he had created with him before the U.S. forces overran his compound and destroyed it. Dr. Salaam made sure the package was ready for the move with a smile on his face, knowing what he had created would kill hundreds of Americans. Thinking it ironic that the same people who trained him would now see and feel the impact of what he had learned. The two couriers who were taking the package to America had pledged their allegiance to Allah and were ready to go to America with the intent of getting the package there or die trying to do it.

The trip would be uneventful for the two men. The first leg of their journey would be to fly to Columbia on fake passports. They would then catch a connecting flight from Columbia to Mexico City. Then would travel by car to the border that separated Mexico and the United States. The two couriers would pay the standard fee to be escorted into Arizona, passing through the openings in the fence or tunnel that led to Nogales. Then onto Tucson where they would be picked up by friends. From there they would go by bus to the east coast to Connecticut and deliver the package to Ahmed. The two men would stay with Ahmed to work with him to complete the job. They carried with them the special instructions, detailing how to control the biological weapon safely until it was ready to be used on the targets.

Ahmed was concerned that it would take time to get the package from Iran to him. The time and distance was a key factor in getting the package to Connecticut. He knew anything along the way could happen to terminate his planned mission. The Americans could get lucky and find the package anywhere along the route that the two couriers were taking. Or they could accidentally lose the package, or it could bust open before its intended use.   Ahmed tried to put all these thoughts out of his head by saying if Allah wills it then it will be okay.

Agent Smith knew that finding the package and the two couriers coming into America, would be like finding a needle in a haystack. There was a chance they could be found if they took commercial transportation anywhere along their route to Connecticut. His bosses had put out a nationwide BOLO on the two couriers, however, that being said, they had no idea of what they looked like or where they would show up.   Not having this information made it damn near impossible to find or follow them. Maybe with a little luck, they would find them somewhere along the way.   As Smith thought about this, he prayed that his luck would hold out long enough for the two people to be found before it was too late.   He knew that the easiest way into America was through Mexico, crossing over into Arizona, and or Texas, and that was as good as any place to start. He contacted his counterparts down in Phoenix to let them know to be expecting two Middle Eastern men who were carrying a package with them into America. They, in turn, contacted the Border Patrol about the possibility of two Middle Eastern men sneaking in through Mexico on their way to Connecticut.

In order to oversee this operation, David Smith became the point of contact from the Phoenix office.   He had already seen the BOLO that was put out on the couriers and passed the notice on to Lucas and Miguel, "Would you guys be interested in looking for these two guys?"

Miguel and Lucas nodded their heads in unison at the question, "When do we start?"

"Right now, as far as I'm concerned. When can you two be ready to go?"

"We'll be ready in five minutes," Lucas replied.

"Let's get going then, you're burning daylight," Smith said.

Miguel and Lucas went out to their truck, loaded it and went to top off their gas tank.   They grabbed some food to eat at the gas stop, got in and drove to Nogales.   After checking with the Border Patrol chief in the Nogales station, they headed out into the desert, to where the known trails were that the illegals would use to come into the U.S.   Lucas and Miguel would coordinate with the other Border

Patrol agents already down there and supplement their ranks with themselves, covering areas that their regular manning wouldn't allow. Miguel and Lucas were working for the FBI as a special unit on special cases that went above and beyond the border patrol duties that Lucas had become familiar with.   Lucas knew this area like the back of his hand after serving at the Nogales station for four years prior to being picked up by the FBI for this special duty assignment. For Miguel, it brought back memories from a previous case he and Lucas had worked in this area a while back.

After finding a place to park their truck, Lucas and Miguel got out and walked over to a ridge. Using their binoculars, they scanned the desert floor, looking for any kind of movement that would indicate illegals trying to cross the border. Most of the illegals would wait for darkness before trying to cross the desert into Arizona where a truck was waiting for them on the American side of the border. They did it this way because darkness, hopefully, would cover their movements and it was cooler at night to travel.   There were many stories of people getting lost in the desert and dying due to the heat and the lack of water. The problem for Lucas and Miguel and the other Border Patrol agents was to find the illegals before they got to their transportation and disappeared into the night.

As Miguel and Lucas sat watching from the ridge Miguel asked Lucas about Amanda, "So what's up with her?"

"Awww, she wasn't ready to settle down with one guy just yet."

"I'm sorry to hear that."

"Yeah me too, it's okay though I found another girl that lives in Glendale and already has kids and a husband.   All I got to do is get rid of the husband and I'm home free, what do you think?"

"Is her name Marissa by any chance?"

"Why, how did you know?" Lucas said laughing.

"Funny, I thought she had better taste than to date a Border Patrol kind of guy."

"She kept saying that her husband wasn't living the kind of life she has always wanted, especially like the Border Patrol agents live. Fast cars, lots of money, and trips to places that no one has ever heard of."

By now Miguel was starting to laugh at Lucas, "You should be so lucky to find someone like Marissa."

"Yeah, I know you're right.   By the way, does she have a sister?"

"No, but I can hook you up with her brother if you like."

"Oh, you are such a friend, indeed."

Both of them were laughing so hard they had to wipe the tears from their eyes. Lucas knew that Miguel was the best friend he ever had, and he knew that Miguel felt the same way about him.   They'd only been working together for a short amount of time and through their adventures each of them had saved the other one's life several times already.   Forming a bond through all of this made them two of the best agents working this part of the country.

By now it was 8:30 at night and the human traffic was starting to make their way to the border. As the night wore on, the infrared binoculars that Lucas was using picked up some heat signatures heading towards them through the darkness. The coyotes were being very careful with the illegals that they were trying to help cross the desert tonight.   Among the mules were two men who stayed to themselves and spoke only to each other, as needed. The illegals didn't understand anything that was being said by their escorts to these two men. All of them knew that they were from another country and therefore they were not to be trusted.   They could see that the two men were not treated the same way they were being treated. Which to them, was another reason not to like them. This preferential treatment the two men got from the coyotes, meant they didn't have to carry any drugs or clothing or food with them. This was done by the others trying to cross into the U.S. They carried everything for the two guys, except for one package that the two men carried themselves. These two men took turns sleeping, so that one of them was always awake to keep an eye on the package. The illegals knew that the two men had guns as well, and seeing this, they knew not to ask what the package contained.   For all they knew, it could get them killed for being curious. They were more interested in getting to America to find and live the American dream for themselves.   Besides, it wasn't their business to ask anyway. That night, as the illegals made their way to the fence that separated the two countries, they waited for the coyotes to say it was safe for them to cross over.   When the group was in place, the coyotes signaled with their radios and flashlights as they waited for the proper response from their compadres on the other side of the border.

Miguel and Lucas sat there watching all of this using their infrared scopes. They had called in their position, letting the other agents know that some illegals were trying to cross over the border in their area and would need backup to catch them all. As the Border Patrol agents moved in through the darkness, they waited at specific points to catch the illegals. Miguel and Lucas had positioned themselves in front of the illegals and waited for them just on this side of the border. The coyotes not knowing they were being watched, were being careful about making sure everything was good to go and safe for their guests. The coyotes, having received the proper reply from their counterparts on other side of the border, proceeded to move the illegals across.

Miguel moved their truck closer to the wire fence and when the illegals were about to cross, he turned on his lights from the headache bar which lit up the place, catching all of them in the light. The two terrorists, who were caught in the lights as well, pulled their guns and tried to shoot out the lights on the truck. Shooting wildly, they missed the lights completely. With the reports of gunfire filling the night, all of the agents pulled their weapons and started looking for the shooters in the crowd of illegals. The illegals, hearing the gun fire, scattered in all directions, leaving the two shooters in the lights of the truck. Standing to the side of the truck, behind the lights, Miguel and Lucas returned fire, killing both of the men as they stood there in the light. Once the area was clear of the shooters, both Lucas and Miguel went down to where the two men lay on the ground. The other agents started rounding up the other illegals and started herding them over towards the lights of the other pickups that had been waiting, to be processed by the INS. The coyotes, seeing the lights of the truck come on, took off immediately and were long gone, back into the darkness, getting ready for their next trip in the near future. Once everything settled down, Miguel and Lucas searched the bodies of the two men they had killed. In their search they found a package. Lucas set it aside as they continued their search. Lucas looked at the two bodies lying on the ground, "Hey, Miguel, take a look at these guys."

Miguel stopped what he was doing and walked over, "What about them?"

"These aren't your typical illegals, Miguel."

Miguel looked a little closer and stepped back, "I wonder if these are the two everybody is concerned about. You know, on that BOLO that was put out?"

"Could be, here's the package I found with one of the bodies."

"I've a bad feeling about this buddy; I think we need to call our boss over to look at the package before we get ourselves in trouble with it."

Lucas called the night shift supervisor to let him know about what they'd found.

"Hey boss, you know that BOLO that was put out about the two men yesterday?"

"Yeah, what about it?"

"Well, I think we found the guys."

"I'll be right out, don't touch anything."

"Will do boss," replied Lucas.

Within minutes, the supervisor showed up along with two vans. The supervisor walked over to where Lucas and Miguel were standing near the bodies. Looking closer at the bodies he signaled the driver of one of the two vans to come over. The driver, wearing a hazmat suit, came over and checked the two bodies of the men with a sniffer. Getting an audible alarm from the sensor he looked at the supervisor, "You need to clear the area while we do our checks,"

Using his radio, he called out to the other agents to vacate the area. Lucas heard the orders. "Boss before we leave, they had a package with them and it's over there next to the second body."

The hazmat guy, hearing this called for his team to get a container from the van and bring it over to where the second body was located. Finding the package still intact, they put it inside a container that sat in a small box inside their van and left. After being photographed and fingerprinted by the other part of the Hazmat team, the bodies of the two men were put in body bags, loaded into their van and drove off following the other van, for further tests.

Realizing the two dead men were not from South America, and were from parts unknown, the interrogators started talking to the illegals about the two dead men. After about an hour, all they knew for certain was that nobody had anything to do with two men and that they stayed to themselves the whole trip. Realizing nobody was going to talk, they kept the illegals there until Hazmat said they could be released, pending what the package contained in it.

The Hazmat team got back to their office in minimum time with a police escort.   A team of chemists and doctors were waiting for the package to be delivered to them.   When it arrived, everybody was dressed in white Hazmat suits, waiting patiently for the box that contained the package. One of the lead chemists, carefully put the container into a self-contained glass room that was big enough for one person to operate the controls.   On the other side of the glass room, there were two sliding doors to protect the others as they watched the chemist that went into the room.

Automatically the blowers turned on and the lead chemist put his hands into gloves that he would use to open the container and then the package.   Every precaution was being used, just in case it was a bio-hazard. The chemist unhooked the clasps of the container that held the package, and with his right gloved hand, reached into the open container and pulled the package out of it.   Setting the package in a glass container on the table, he then closed the top of the Hazmat container.   The chemist moved the glass box containing the package onto a cart that could be moved to another self-contained area inside the lab.   The initial room sensors that were set up to go off in case of a leak remained quiet, indicating that there had been no leaks in the big Hazmat container.   Having the original package sealed inside the other room, the chemist opened the door to take out the Hazmat container.   A second chemist came in and they both went into the glass room and started testing the package to see what it contained inside.   The people watching all of this included, Lucas, Miguel, and other agents from the FBI, ICE, and DHS.   Each of them waiting, all wanting to know, if they had been lucky to catch the two couriers from Iran.

All the while, as the chemists worked on the package in the self-contained environment, facial recognition was working overtime to identify the two dead men.   A DNA scan was also being done, as well, to confirm who they were and where they came from.   All of this was happening as everybody held their breath, hoping and praying, that they had found the couriers with the biological weapon, and if so what to do now with the terrorist cell in Connecticut.

Agent David Smith, in the Phoenix office, was standing by, waiting to hear any news about what had been determined by the Hazmat team and the other tests that were being run, i.e., facial recognition and DNA.

Agent Smith and Jones, in Connecticut, were also standing by, anxiously waiting for the news to come out about who the two men were that were killed in Arizona and the package that they had brought with them.   Smith, checked his watch, realizing that it was past midnight, was on his third cup of coffee and Jones was finishing his fourth, knew that it was going to be a long night as they waited for the news.

As the chemists worked on opening the package, an alarm went off notifying everyone in the building, that a bio-hazard had been detected. The first chemist, hearing the alarm, looked at the second chemist who reached over and shut it off. The whole building was locked down and each of the people watching the chemists knew that only a thin piece of Plexiglas separated them from this weapon. They now knew they had a real bio-hazard in their self-contained glass room. The chemists were now determined to find out what kind of bio-hazard it was. Carefully opening the plastic seal from around the glass containers inside the package, they saw that it was in a powder form and that its color was white.   The chemists look at each other, and speaking through their head pieces, determined that it must be anthrax in a powder form. Calling the leader of the Hazmat team, they communicated that there was, indeed, a bio-hazard in the package and that, from all appearances, it was anthrax. Only with further testing could it be confirmed without any doubt. But for all practical purposes, they got the couriers and the package before it was delivered to Ahmed and his terrorist cell in Connecticut.   With the news, all of the people standing outside the glass room, were relieved to have found the bio-weapon and stopped the couriers before delivery.   The chemists took a sample of the anthrax and it was rushed to another self-contained room for more analysis. This sample would be compared to other samples that had been collected over the years. After a few days, the analysis was complete and it was confirmed that the new sample was a stronger strain, never before seen. Although it was similar, in some characteristics, to what had been identified as coming from Iran before, this new sample was far more deadlier than what they had seen previously.   Because of all of the labs that operated independently in the Middle East now the FBI would have to have their biochemists look for certain identifiers to indicate where it was made and by whom.

Each team lead from the FBI compared what they had with the samples from all over the world. Each sample has its own signature indicating who made it and where it came from. In this case, the white powder was basically built the same way that identified Dr. Salaam as the creator of this strain.

When the news reached FBI agents Smith and Jones, that they had intercepted the couriers, both men sat down said a thank you prayer to Heavenly Father for his help. The question now was, what to do with Ahmed and his cronies, and how to get to the Iranian chemist and take him out of the picture so this doesn't happen again.

By now the Intel community was starting to marshal their people together to answer the call of the attempted use of a bio-weapon here on American soil. At a meeting that had been called by the FBI, all of the alphabets, including department of defense, were present. The chemist who had analyzed the package spoke about this new strain of anthrax being stronger than the typical strain they had previously seen, yet very similar in appearance to the sample they had from Iran. This caused quite a stir in the group of people sitting and listening to him speak. The typical questions were, <u>who</u> had been assisting Iran in the development of this new strain, <u>where</u> was it being done, and <u>when</u> was it completed? The <u>why</u> and the <u>what</u> was already known by simply watching the tensions that were getting worse between Israel and her allies, against the Muslim world in the Middle East.   Once the chemist completed his portion of the meeting he sat down. The Director of the CIA stood up, "I think we all know what this means to all of us and the impact it will have on the free world. I propose we send a team in to find the location and any information that would help us in destroying the place where it's being made."

Everybody around the table agreed with the Director of the CIA's thoughts on what to do. The CIA Director continued speaking, "I also believe it is imperative we let Israel know what we have found out as well."

With all in agreement for the proposed actions, it now became a situation of logistics for setting up the mission to Iran.   Israel, upon hearing the news, even offered to send in some of their people to assist in the search to find out where the anthrax was being made. The final solution was to take the offer of help from Israel and the CIA would also send one of their field operatives in, as well, to find the place where the anthrax was being made and stored. The Navy offered to give the Intel team a ride to the drop off and pick up point. The Air Force offered airlift support to take in the military troops and get them out once the complex had been found and destroyed.

With all of the basics of the mission worked out, the Intel mission was set to go in a few days. The Admiral, who had been present at the first meeting with the Intel community, contacted Chance to see about the use his submarine, Thresher, as a taxi to take the team in and pick them up once they had completed their mission.   Chance jumped at the opportunity to help, "Ready whenever you are," he said.

The Israelis and the CIA sent their people to the U.S. to meet up with Chance for their ride from Groton to the Caspian Sea.   As the men sat around waiting to leave, Chance checked one more time to make sure that they had the latest Intel on the weather reports. Finding that nothing had changed, they proceeded to board the Thresher and made their way to the drop off point north of Tehran.

Chapter X

Richard Dean looked at his watch while he sat dozing on the fold out bunk aboard the submarine that had been contracted to take him and his team into the Caspian Sea. Arriving at the drop off point, he was now waiting for the sun to go down so that his team could leave the Thresher to do a recon on a supposed bio-weapons compound in Iran. The satellite photos they had obtained could not see the entire compound because of the camouflage used by the Iranians to conceal it, or for that matter what was underground. Their job was to confirm the location and presence of this compound, why it existed, and how extensive it was. Simple enough, if you knew where to look for it. Fortunately, or unfortunately, depending on how you looked at it, this mission was extremely dangerous, considering all they had to do was go in and get the information and get out in one piece. Only three men were chosen for this mission, Richard Dean was from the CIA and knew the language, having had years of experience working in the Middle East, not only as one of the Embassy personnel, he had also worked Humint (Human Intelligence) in clandestine operations all over Iran. Ben Carson and David Riddle were also selected to go with him. Both of these men were Mossad agents on loan from Israel assigned to work on this mission. Both of them had been trained extensively for this type of mission and had proved themselves quite capable of breaking into anything that was supposed to be impenetrable. They were also fluent in the local languages of the area and considered deadly assassins in their work as agents.

Chance came into the sleeping quarters where the men sat waiting to go. They all looked up when he said, "Ready in five minutes."

Richard looked at Ben and David and then back at Chance, "Were ready when you are."

Five minutes later, Chance raised the Thresher to the surface near the town of Chalus, located on the Caspian Sea. The town that Richard and his team were looking for was Marzanabad, which is in between Tehran and Chalus. Shahid Bahonar, the microbial bomb plant, was supposedly located on a mountain top nearby Marzanabad. With their help, the Russians had assisted the Iranians in setting up a plant to develop four types of bio-weapons for their use. Along with these four bio-weapons, four more were also created and as confirmed by Western Intelligence. These eight bio-weapons were the following:

- Anthrax, originally this bacterium was developed by the United States during World War II and through espionage was obtained by the Soviet Union, which has long mastered the production. Russian scientists have helped the Iranians to produce anthrax.
- Encephalitis, the blueprint of this virus, Venezuelan Equine Encephalitis, was provided by Venezuelan President Hugo Chavez in an agreement two years ago with the Islamic regime.
- Yellow grain, developed with the help of North Korea but named "yellow grain" by the Iranians, has no smell and upon impact will destroy the body's defensive system. Victims would have a hard time walking or breathing within hours and slowly their digestive systems would be destroyed, likely followed by death within 48 hours.
- SARS
- Ebola
- Cholera
- Smallpox, Iran, with North Korea's help, has genetically altered the smallpox virus that makes current vaccinations useless against it.
- The Plague

"Yellow Grain" is similar to "Yellow Rain," which the then-Soviet Union allegedly provided to North Vietnam and Laos to use against U.S. backed rebels that lived in the highlands of Viet Nam and Thailand.

Richard knew all too well that this could be a suicide mission if they were discovered by the Iranians. He could also see the political ramifications if their capture made the newspapers and the press. After making sure again, that their equipment was squared away for the tenth time, Richard and his team followed Chance to the deck of the Thresher and loaded all of their equipment into the three small rubber rafts. Chance looked at Richard, "I'll wait for two weeks, if you're not back by then, I will assume you're not coming back."

"You know what they say about assuming anything?"

Both men laughed at Richard's remark. After shaking hands, Richard and his team made their way to where their rafts were tied and waiting for them. Chance watched as the team silently went into the water. Each man had a small raft to pull behind them as they made their way to the shore. Each raft contained backpacks with sensors for bio-weapons leaks, cameras for photographing anything they found while they reconned the area of the microbial plant, and food rations to eat while they were out in the field. Their purpose was to see how extensive the plant had become. Hopefully, they could get pictures and other data to find out what other bio-weapons were being created and be able to report it.

As they slowly made their way to the shoreline, they stopped to make sure the coast was clear before proceeding to unload their equipment and put on their backpacks. After burying their rafts to hide them, the team started their hike to recon the plant. It would be rough going, climbing the mountain to the top, carrying their equipment on their backs, especially in the dark. Richard took the lead and the other two followed all dressed in the traditional garb for the area. Their main concern at this point, was not to be seen or heard as they made their way to the mountains. Using their compass and GPS coordinates, they found a trail that they could follow from Chalus that would take them in the direction of the city of Marzanabad. Upon reaching Marzanabad they would need to climb and cross over the mountain in order to find the right mountain top where the compound was located and confirmed by their GPS coordinates. Richard and the team would hike the distance of 30 miles across the mountains to get to the compound, this would be accomplished by walking at night and laying low in the day to avoid detection. About a mile out from Chalus they stumbled upon a trail to follow, that led from Chalus to Marzanabad allowing them to save time as they walked in the dark. Using the trail they would be able to cover the distance in minimum time, without breaking an ankle or leg which was a concern if they had to climb the mountains in the dark.

One of their major concerns was the security around the Shahid Bahonar compound. It had been reported that all personnel that entered the compound were searched and disarmed by the security forces protecting the complex. To make matters worse, in order to protect the compound from air strikes, the Iranians had installed anti-aircraft missiles and gun batteries around the perimeter. Some of these anti-aircraft defenses had been identified from the satellite photos, compliments of the Air Force. The Iranians had also expanded the size of the main research facility by building a self-contained lab underground, where most of the bio-weapon testing was being carried out. Their expansion was not only in the research area, but also included new housing for the lab workers, which was currently under construction, and a small hospital to take care of the people working there. All of this had to be verified by the team for future action.

As the team made their way to Marzanabad, Richard was looking for the roads that would allow easy transport of military personnel to and from the compound and marked his map accordingly. Along the way, he took pictures of the roads and the bridges that could be destroyed by using planted bombs or even missiles to hinder the security forces of the compound. Ben and David were looking for a landing zone (LZ) that would allow a team of soldier's easy access to launch a mission from the LZ to the compound and back again, with little resistance. All of this was done to stop the building of bio-weapons that would be used against Israel and her allies. This recon information was vital and necessary in order to maintain a balance of power in the Middle East so that Israel could co-exist in a highly volatile environment.

After doing a recon of the area, they continued on with their hike, making their way to their first stop as the sun was beginning to rise. Checking their map coordinates to see where they were, in relation to the compound, they stopped for the day and decided to find some shelter in the nearby rock outcropping which was about 100 yards off the trail. After looking over the area, they found a place that offered protection from the sun and the elements, allowing them to rest and catch their breath. Once again, they again checked their equipment to make sure nothing had happened to it since they started their hike. Using their Sat phone, Richard called their handler to let him know that all was well and where they were. Once they were settled, Ben and David closed their eyes to sleep while Richard kept guard. Ben would relieve Richard in two hours, so he could get some sleep, as well.   Staying out of sight on the mountain was a bit tricky since the local people would be using the mountains to feed their sheep and goats and could possibly discover them by accident. If this occurred, the team would have to decide how to handle the situation right then and there.   Hopefully, it would not end up with them being discovered or them having to kill someone.   As it was, they weren't bothered by anyone.   Once they were all rested, they brought out some of their food rations to eat.   It would be a cold camp so as not to attract the locals with a cooking fire. "I don't know about you guys, but I could never get used to eating MRE's. Especially, without heating them up," Richard said, as he ate the meatloaf cold from its container.

Ben looked at Richard, "I know what you mean, but it's better than nothing.   In our training they put us out in the desert with just a knife and they told us we'll pick you up at the rendezvous point in a week."

"Don't you believe him, it was only for three days, with water," David added, smiling.

"Hey, it's my story," Ben replied.

"And here I thought you guys were snake eaters like our Special Forces guys," Richard said, smiling.

"Oh, but we are," both chuckled and said it at the same time.

When they were finished, they carefully buried their trash so it wouldn't be found after they left.

It took two more uneventful days to make their way to the city of Marzanabad. Sticking to the mountain trails instead of the road, they continued to use the city as their reference point to find the bio-weapons compound.   Using their GPS and compass, they headed in the direction of where they thought the compound should be.   Even with the GPS coordinates and the satellite photos showing the layout of the surrounding area of the compound, they all agreed that it would take another day of searching to be able to find the compound.

After another day of traveling, they found the compound nestled near the top of the mountain.   As they rested just below the ridge of the mountain, Richard used his binoculars to describe the compound while Ben and David reviewed the sat photos.   The photos were correct in showing the building and construction that was being done inside the compound. They watched from their perch as the construction workers would come in and leave at a certain time of the day from their jobs. By day five, Ben had come up with an idea of blending in as construction workers in order to gain access to the compound. That way they could take pictures and find a secure place to set up their bio-weapon sensing equipment. The idea was to get into the compound with the workers, stay the night and leave the next day in the afternoon, after the work shift ended. The question now was how to get the equipment past the guards without being caught. It was suggested by Ben, that before they went into the compound, they should bury the equipment next to the fence line and retrieve it once they were inside the compound. After completing their mission, they would re-bury the equipment and retrieve it before leaving the area. All of them were hoping it would be easy in and easy out, for the three of them.

With their faces covered, no one would recognize them as anything other than common workers. On day five of their mission, they made their move, blending in as construction workers. After getting their work assignments for the day, they headed with the others to their assigned area in the compound to start work. Their job was to level the ground in preparation for the foundations of the new buildings to be built.

The two positive things working in their favor was that there were no guards posted in the work areas and no head counts were being done at the beginning and end of the shifts for the workers. This allowed Ben and David to scout the surrounding areas within the compound without being detected. Richard would be the cover for them when they would take off to scout for places to hide at night when the construction work was shut down for the evening. On the sixth day, they stayed back and hid in some heavy equipment that was being used to haul rock and dirt to the work sites. They sat in the back of one of the rock haulers and waited for it to get dark so they could start their recon of the area. Once the sun went down, they were able to move around the compound and collect their buried equipment without being seen while the guards were in place watching over the main buildings, specifically the entrances. The three of them watched and waited in the shadows for the right time to sneak into the guarded buildings. This would be the hardest part of their mission, as the chances of being discovered an caught were high. It was decided that one of them would have to create a diversion to draw the guards away from their posts. The next step of their plan would entail all three of them wearing guard uniforms so that they could get access to the buildings inside the compound. Looking for the guards' barracks was first on their list of getting the needed uniforms to wear.   Finding it was easy, as it was the only building with lights on at night.   All three men headed over to the building and under the cover of darkness watched the coming and goings of the soldiers. They carefully moved nearer the building, staying in the shadows away from the lights and waited for the right time to make their move.   As they watched, one of the soldiers' was carrying some boxes from the back of the truck to take inside the building.   Ben and David, looked at each other and nodded before walking over to the truck and asking the soldier if he needed any help with bringing the boxes into the building. He gladly accepted their help, to which David and Ben each grabbed a box and carried them inside. They set their boxes down in the center of the room as the soldier smiled and thanked them for their help.   Offering him a cigarette, Ben and David started a conversation with the soldier as they looked around the room, trying to size up the challenge of finding uniforms. The room for the soldiers was like the old buildings used for military basic training, they were open bay barracks with lockers for each one of the guards set against the wall. Each locker would have uniforms hanging inside.   Once the soldier finished smoking his cigarette, he left the room to take the truck back.

Ben and David started going through the lockers to find uniforms that would fit them. They found three uniforms and headed out of the barracks, carrying them over their shoulders to where Richard was waiting inside the rock hauler.   While Ben and David had been going after the uniforms, Richard started drawing a layout of the compound, depicting each building and where the power generators were located.   He also identified where the camouflaged anti-aircraft missiles were located on the perimeter of the compound and the ground radar systems for each of the missile batteries, for future reference.

Quickly changing into the uniforms, they had found, they made their way back to the buildings that were being guarded.   Carrying a couple of the boxes that they had helped load into the barracks, they approached the first building.   Richard had a clipboard with papers on it and met the guard at the door, briefly explaining to him that the boxes of supplies were to be brought into the building for the bathrooms. "You can't believe how much trouble these chemists are when they don't have toilet paper to use when they are on the throne," Richard complained.

"They have become westernized and soft because they think that they are important, that's for sure," replied the guard.

All of them laughed at the comment from the guard as he examined what was inside the boxes and let them pass. Richard grabbed a roll of toilet paper and handed it to the guard, "It never hurts to take care of one of your own."

With that, Richard led the way into the building and headed to the stairway that led down to the basement floor. When he got to the door, he opened it carefully and stood guard while Ben and David made their way into the laboratory to start their search. Finding a room that was self-contained inside the laboratory, they started looking into what was being stored inside the room. As they went through one of the desks near the door that opened into the containment area, they found a notebook. Ben started going through the notebook and realized that it had the times and dates of the testing done inside the containment unit. He started taking pictures of the pages in the notebook, as well as the interior of the laboratory itself. David began searching the other rooms down the corridor, looking for unlocked doors. Reading the title on one of the doors, he realized he was looking at the office door for one of the main chemists that was involved in the development of the bio-weapons. He jimmied the lock on the door and got into the office. Once he was inside, he found a laptop computer sitting on the desk. Looking it over carefully, he tried to open the computer by using a login password. Unable crack the password, he looked under the desk and inside the drawers of the desk, hoping to find something with the password written on it. Finally, finding a slip of paper taped to the inside the top drawer with words on it, he tried the first word that was written on the paper, thinking that it might be the password to open the computer. Fortunately, the computer recognized the password and it gave him access to the hard drive. He pulled out his thumb drive and began downloading the information. When the download was complete, he put the thumb drive back into his pocket, closed out the computer, and left the room untouched.

At this point, Ben and David had all they needed and were ready to leave the building.   They found Richard and all three of them made their way back to the entrance of the building, opened the door, visited with the guard once more and walked out into the night. They did this with each building they came to, carrying a box to the building and going in to check out the layout and take pictures of what was inside the laboratories. In some cases, they took empty bottles with them and took samples of what they thought might be of value, as possible evidence thinking that it might be something important. Carefully packing them inside their robes to take them out to be tested at a later date.

When the night was done, they had been able to enter into each of guarded buildings, using their equipment as they went along, to obtain Intel.   One of the benefits of having access to the buildings was being able to retrieve samples and download the hard drives from each of the computers that they had gained access to.   After changing out of the uniforms they buried them, along with their equipment, so that they couldn't be found.   Then they waited for the morning shift to show and slowly worked themselves back into the group, working and waiting for the shift to be over so they could leave the compound with the other workers. They waited for nightfall before picking up their equipment and leaving the area.

Having completed their mission, they made their way back down the mountain using the same trail that led back to Chalus, so they could meet up with Chance to leave Iran.   As the men were returning to the pickup point Richard was happy that all had gone as planned in getting the information they had retrieved from the compound.   David and Ben were happy about being part of the mission and being able to get away with it.   As they made their way down the road, back to outskirts of Chalus, they were careful to stay out of the main part of the city, so as not to attract any attention to themselves.   Ben and David were walking in front of Richard, when a truck, driving too fast, almost hit them.   Richard grabbed both of them, pulling them out of the way just in time before the truck stopped.   When Ben and David got over the shock of almost being hit by the truck, the driver started cussing at them for being in the road.   At first Ben and David let it go, but the driver wouldn't let it pass. As the two walked away from truck, the angry man started following them down the road.   By now, the man was in their face and at this point, both Ben and David recognized him as a wanted criminal in Israel for a bombing that killed some civilians and two soldiers in Tel Aviv. After they had confirmed their suspicions about the wanted man, Ben and David stopped walking away. They stood there looking at the guy, who now started to realize that he was no longer in control of the situation. Realizing that he had overloaded his backside with his mouth, he walked back to his truck and drove off, leaving Ben and David trying to catch up to him.   At this point, Richard, who had been watching the reaction of Ben and David asked, "Why are you two acting this way with this guy?"

"That man is wanted in Israel for the murder of some civilians and two soldiers in my country. They were killed in a bomb blast in Tel Aviv last summer," David replied.

Richard knew that these two Mossad men wanted to take this guy out for what he had done in Israel.   Knowing, that now was as good a time as any to take him out, he asked, "So, how do you want to handle this?"

"We track him down and kill him," Ben replied.

"What can I do to help?" Richard asked, knowing it would be useless to argue about it.

Ben smiled at him, surprised that he wanted to be part of this. "First, we need to find him again and follow him to a place where he won't be missed for a couple of days. The town is small, and we know what the truck looks like. So, if we find the truck, we'll find him," David added.

"Shall we start then?" Ben asked.

"We've only two days to do this.   Do you think we can find him before we need to get back to the rendezvous point with the submarine?" Richard asked.

Ben and David both looked at each other. "We can try."

"Alright, let's go and find the arrogant bastard before we have to leave," Richard said.

As the three of them headed back down the street in the direction the man had driven, they started looking for the white truck.   The first thought David and Ben had, was that the man was pompous and concluded that he must be important around Chalus. Maybe he was a businessman or somebody in the political hierarchy in the town.

All of them were sure that he would park his truck out in the open, on a street nearby.   After crossing the street, they headed into the market area of Chalus, mingling with the crowd of people who were trying to sell their goods to the locals who were buying what they needed for dinner and anything else that was necessary.   Richard sat back and watched as Ben and David searched for the man in the crowd.   Not finding him in the marketplace, they moved on to the next street.   As they made their way down the street, each of them were aware that they were headed in the direction of the business district part of town.   Due to the size of the town, they figured that he had to be nearby, he couldn't be that far away from where they were looking for him.   As they walked past some of the smaller businesses, they eventually found themselves in the center of town where the bank was.   They walked toward the bank, and there in front of it was the white truck.   All three of them stood in the shadow of a nearby tree as they tried to figure out their next move. As they moved towards the bank, they found an alley not too far from where the truck was parked.   Hiding in the dark recesses in the alleyway, the three of them sat and waited for the man to come out of the bank to get into his truck.   After waiting for an hour, the man came out and drove away.   Ben and David walked into the bank and went to the teller. "Can you tell us who the man is that just drove off in the white truck?"

The teller looked at Ben and David, not sure what to say, "Why do you want to know about him?"

"The man dropped his wallet and we would like to give it back to him.   Every time we get close, he leaves just before we can give it back to him." David said, as he pulled out his own wallet to show the teller. The teller looked at David and the wallet, "His name is Achmed and lives not too far down the street, above his own business."

"What kind of business is it?" Ben asked.

"It is an import export business, about two blocks down the street on the right side," said the teller.

"Thank you, may Allah bless you," replied Ben, as they left the bank.

Richard had been waiting outside of the bank for the other two to return.   Upon seeing them, he motioned for them to come over to where he was. "Hey, I just saw our truck go down the street and park over there on the right-hand side."

"According to what the bank teller told us that must be his business," Ben said.

David nodded, "Let's go check it out."

All three of them started walking down the street to go after the truck, looking for anybody posing as a lookout that would alert the owner of the business. They saw one man sitting in front of the store, drinking coffee and reading a newspaper, as they got closer to the building. Ben, seeing the guy, nudged David and nodded in that direction. All three of the men stopped and went into the alley next to the building to watch the man seated in front of the business. Ben whispered, "The man sitting in front of the store is a guard. We need to take him out quietly."

Richard, not wanting to miss any of the action volunteered, "I'll take care of him, while you go get your man."

As they waited for the closed sign to be put up in the window several men had come into the business and from the looks of it they weren't there to buy anything from the store. Ben pulled out his camera and started taking pictures of the customers coming and going from the business, just in case any of the people would prove interesting to Israeli intelligence back in Israel.

When the closed sign finally went up in the front of the store, Ben and David made their way to the back of the building and started to climb the outside stairway to the second floor. Seeing that the two men were midway to the door on the second floor, Richard walked over to where the man had been sitting in front of the store with his right hand covered by his clothing. He nonchalantly walked up behind the man and shot him in the head with his gun that had a silencer on it. Carefully, grabbing the man before he fell to the ground, he picked him up and carried him into the store. He locked the door behind him and slowly started working his way through the store looking for others. Finding that no one else was around, he went back outside and signaled Ben and David that they were clear to proceed.

When Ben and David got to the top of the stairs, they waited and listened through the door to see if they could hear the men talking inside. As they looked through the window, they saw Achmed get up, walk over to a desk and pull out a map and begin marking it with red X's on different parts of the map. By now, the other men who had been listening to Achmed, shook their heads no and point at another spot on the map. Achmed looked at the man that was saying no and crossed out one of the marks on the map, changing it to where the man wanted it. This made the man happy and he smiled at Achmed, patting him on the back. Achmed then pulled out a box from below the table, placed it on top of it and opened it. Inside the box was an electronic device that Achmed wanted to show the man. Using his cell phone, he called the electronic device, causing it to light up. The others in the group were impressed by what they saw. Ben and David recognized the electronic device as a detonator that could be triggered by a cell phone by calling a certain number.

By now, Ben and David had seen enough of what the conversation was about between the men. They pulled their handguns and rushed through the door, forcing the four men up against the wall. Richard came from behind David and Ben and grabbed the map and the electronic device. After looking at the map, Richard gave David the map, who recognized that it was a map of the city of Jerusalem. The marked areas on the map were considered holy sites to the Jews and highly trafficked areas by Christians, coming from all over the world to see the places where Jesus had walked and taught. By all appearances, these men were planning to bomb Jerusalem, fortunately, they were still in the planning stages. As Richard held his gun on them, Ben and David searched the house for anything that would be used for making bombs. In their search they found some papers that had names of people who were part of their network and where they were located. After they had finished searching, they found the wiring, black powder, and the lead pipes in Achmed's garage. As Ben and David were debating about what they were going to do, Richard came over, still watching the men and said, "I've an idea that you might like. I need one of you to bring the truck into the garage."

"Okay, I'll move it around to the garage," said David.

Once David had parked the truck in the garage, he helped Ben and Richard move the men downstairs to the garage. Using a back entrance to the garage, made it easy to place them into the garage without being seen by any of the locals.

"I need you to tie their hands behind their backs and put them into the truck, making sure the ones in the cab have their seat belts on," Richard told Ben and David.

When this was done, Richard asked, "Do either one of you know how to build a bomb with the equipment that you found in the garage?"

Ben and David smiled, nodding their heads yes, "Give us about 30 minutes."

In less than 30 minutes they had wired two pipe bombs together with one electronic detonator and Ben stood there watching David place both of the bombs under the seats of the truck where the men now sat.   By now, the two men in the cab, knew what was going to happen to them and were struggling to get out of the truck. Richard, who was watching them used his own gun to butt stroke both of the men until they quit struggling.   Ben, watching all of this, looked at the two men, "I don't understand what you're afraid of. You thought nothing about killing the people in Tel Aviv last summer.   In fact, I bet you were congratulated for being a hero for killing defenseless Jews."

Achmed, now realizing who these two men were, started to struggle again, this time knowing what was going to happen. "Quit fighting to free yourself and think about the seventy virgins waiting for you," David said, as he connected the wires to the electronic detonator.

Richard looked at Achmed, "With your luck you'll get old men or old ladies."

As he continued assisting David gather all of the bomb making material and placing it around the truck, with most of it going into the bed of the truck. The men in the bed of the truck started to cry, begging to be freed.   Once the charges were set, all three of the men walked out of the building and went across the street to make the phone call to detonate the bombs.   Once they dialed the number, they set the phone down on the ground and walked away. Within seconds, there was an explosion that rocked the neighborhood, taking out Achmed's building and two adjoining buildings, as well. As they headed out of town, away from the smoke and debris flying in the air, they could hear the sirens responding to the blast.   All three of them smiled, knowing that there would be two less bomb makers that would cause pain for innocent people in the world.

Having accomplished their mission and taking out a wanted bomber and his associates, they headed to the designated spot to be picked up. Being a day early, all three of them decided to go back and visit the market square to sit down and watch the people buying and selling their wares. Every once in a while, they would hear people talking about the explosion and the death of the owner of the store. As they listened, the rumor was that someone from Al-Qaeda had come in and killed him. Another rumor was that two men had something to do with it, according to the local bank teller. Fortunately, the teller couldn't remember what they looked like. That being said, the bank teller was reluctant to give a good description of the two men because they were so honest in wanting to return the dead man's wallet. With no real clues to go on, the only thing the police could agree on was that they had killed themselves while trying to make a bomb. Ben and David smiled, knowing they had gotten away with it and the added bonus of having new information about the whole operation. As the end of the final day arrived and at the prearranged time, they headed out into the water to be picked up.

At the correct time in the middle of the night, the Thresher rose to the surface and the three men began swimming out to the submarine. They were met halfway in their swim by the crew. The only witness was a drunken old man, who was sitting on the beach almost passed out, and couldn't believe his eyes when the Thresher surfaced like a sea monster, threatening the people on the shore. He hid behind some boulders for the rest of the night. The following day the old man went to report what he had seen the night before, but because he was known to be an old drunk, no one took him seriously.

Once everyone was aboard, Chance let the submarine sink back into the Caspian Sea and within minutes it was as if they had never been there. Within three days, Richards team was back on solid ground in the Intel office at Groton shipyard in Connecticut. The information they had brought back was being evaluated for any Intel that could be used by the Navy and others in the alphabet. It would take a week or two to figure out what was good and what was considered useless. In the meantime, Ben and David returned to their regular work areas with the news about the death of the man involved in the bombing that had occurred in Tel Aviv last summer. After being debriefed, they waited for their next assignment.

The Israeli Intel section went to work, looking at the photos that Ben had taken outside the import export business building, trying to identify the men and women that entered the business. Richard went back to the consulate to continue being an analyst for the state department. Both the US and Israel shared the information that had been gained from the work of the team, amongst themselves, in the hope it would serve both their purposes in dealing with the bio-weapon threat.

Once the information collected by Richard and the Israelis was dissected and analyzed by the Intel community, the questions of who what and where, had been answered. They now had proof that the Russians were helping the Iranians and also getting help from our enemies i.e., North Korea and Venezuela, in their development of the bio-weapons. From the downloaded computer hard drive, it was now known that the work was further along than anybody thought. The Iranians had found a way to deliver the bio-weapons in bombs and missiles, to anywhere in the Middle East and were working on a delivery system that could reach Europe and the U. S., as well. The bio-weapon threat was real and had to be stopped before it could be used against anyone else.

With this newfound knowledge it now became imperative that the bio-weapon compound be destroyed to stop the development of any more bio-weapons. The question was, who was going to do it; the U.S. was hesitant about getting involved simply because they didn't want their image of being the peace maker to be tarnished in front of the world. As it was, the Israelis had already offered to help by sending in a team to take care of the problem. As the President thought about the image of the U.S., If they were to destroy the compound in Iran, the questions were, what would the political fallout be for him and his administration? However, in the final analysis, the world image be damned, he remembered that it was a U.S. submarine that had been destroyed, killing all of the crew onboard. Evan though Israel had offered to go in and destroy the compound, the President knew that they had to do something, simply because it almost happened to the American people on U.S. soil. The President of the U.S. had decided to let the Department of Defense have free reign on the United States' response to the attempted bio-weapon release in the U.S. With that, the Special Operations units from the Army and the Navy, began training for their specific missions.   It would take a month for the teams to prepare for their mission. The Delta team would be used to destroy the compound and the Seals would be used for payback against the sinking of the USS Dolphin.   Each team practiced their special skills with absolute certainty so that they would be able to do what was required of them when the time came. The fact was that the Department of Defense was excited to be able to be part of the operation to destroy the compound, not only for the threat it posed, but also because Russia and other countries were involved in helping the Iranians. This would make each of these countries reconsider helping Iran plus give each of Iran's friends a black eye in front of the whole world.

Chapter XI

Agents Smith and Jones reported to their supervisors about their stroke of good luck at finding the couriers and the bio-weapon as they tried crossing the border of Arizona before any damage was done. They were both pretty sure that their supervisors had already heard the news from other sources. That being said, it was still good news and appreciated by their supervisors. Everybody was feeling pretty good about having the bio-weapon intercepted at the border, stopping a major terrorist attack. The two agents were now anxious to find a way to bring charges against Ahmed and his friends and lock them up forever, never to see the light of day again.

When they got back to the FBI office, the three agents were talking amongst themselves, trying to figure out their next move. Smith and Jones had just received the file on Dr. Salaam and, according to the file, the doctor had attended the University of Utah for his medical schooling with a minor in chemistry. When he returned home to Iran, he practiced medicine in Tehran and taught chemistry at the local university. One night, while he was teaching, his wife and kids decided to visit her parents and while they were there they were killed by the Americans using one of their Predator drones, firing a Hellfire missile at a known terrorist headquarters that was located in the village. His wife and kids were killed in the attack and were considered collateral damage in the report that was filed. After he had recovered from the loss of his family, the doctor offered his services to Saddam Hussein to build biological weapons for his country.

"Talk about bad luck! Losing his family that way. I kind of understand why he's doing what he's doing," said Smith, as he finished reading the file.

"I guess he thinks that by killing innocent people in our country it will make up for the loss of his family," Jones added.

Reynolds, who had been listening to the conversation, was deep in thought, he knew all too well how the doctor felt. His brother had been killed by a vehicle IED (Improvised Explosive Device), while he had been on patrol with his unit in Iraq. "The way I see it, we have two options here: One - we can arrest the terrorist cell right now or two - we can go after the doctor and maybe save more lives."

Both Smith and Jones started thinking about what Reynolds had brought up.

"You may be on to something there. Why settle for the small fish when we can have the bigger fish as well?" replied Smith.

Jones nodded his head in agreement, "In for the penny, in for the pound, as they say."

As all three of them sat there thinking about how to go about accomplishing this.   Reynolds came up with another thought, "Why don't we have someone or somebodies, impersonate the couriers that are bringing in the anthrax and let them go through the act of taking out their targets."

"Yeah, by doing this, maybe we can lure Dr. Salaam out into the open and nail him, plus his network as well.   Not only in Iran, but all along the path that they used to get into the United States."

"Maybe we could nail the cartel that helped in the movement of the two couriers. That way we may be able to shut down the network in its entirety," Jones added.

After coming up with a plan, Agents Smith and Jones pushed it up the chain of command to get their opinions on it. Within days, the powers that be, came back with a message of, "Let's do it."

Upon receiving the go ahead, the question now was, who could they get to act as the couriers and deliver the package to Ahmed and his friends, that could speak the language, look like they were from the Middle East, and knew the places in Iran that ISIS was known to frequent, in order to carry it off.   With these requirements in mind, the FBI reached out to the CIA in this endeavor.   With their assistance, two men were found who had been trained by the CIA and who were of Middle Eastern descent, that could play the part of the couriers. It took a day to make contact with the two men who were located in one of their field stations in Iran.   A helicopter was sent to pick them up and deliver them to a U.S. military base, where they were taken by a C-130 cargo plane to Germany and from there to America.   While they were on the plane, the two men were prepped for their mission so that no time would be lost in getting them up to speed. They were ready to go when they arrived at Langley Air Force Base in Virginia, two days later.

Upon arriving at Langley Air Force Base, FBI Agents Smith and Jones met and briefed the men on the latest developments about their target. As Jones drove the car to Reagan International Airport, Smith told them, "One of our agents was able to crack the code that Bashir was using when he sent his messages to his superiors."

Both of the CIA men looked surprised that someone had been able to break the code and yet didn't say a word.

Smith continued, "Because we were able to crack the code, here are the two coded passwords that you will need to get in good with Ahmed and his terrorist cell."

Handing each of them a slip of paper with the passwords on it, both men looked at the paper and then handed them back to Smith. "The name for this operation is Karma and you will be known as Simon and Simon. Easy to remember, but effective for this operation. Just to let you know, that for the duration of Karma, all of the Intel agencies, including ours, are doing their part in assisting in the take down of the Iranian network in America."

The Department of Defense is currently training a Seal team and Delta Force to go into Iran and do a search and destroy of the Anthrax repository, along with taking out all of the chemists who had anything to do with the development of the Anthrax bio-weapon," Jones added.

"The Navy and the Army are working together as one team to make this happen. The Air Force will fly the Delta Force into a Forward Operating Base, operated jointly by the Army and the Marines in Afghanistan as the staging area for the final push into Iran. The Seals will arrive by water through another route," Smith said.

"The CIA and NSA will work together to gather the Intel that will be needed for the teams to go in and take out the labs and the personnel involved. As the proverbial saying goes, the bad guys have awakened the sleeping giant who always had one eye already open."

Simon and Simon continued listening to the agent and in between the agent taking a breath asked, "So where are we headed to now?"

"Oh yeah, I almost forgot. Here is your itinerary for your flight to Nogales. When you get to Nogales, you will be met by a Border

Patrol supervisor who will give you a package to be delivered to the leader of the terrorist cell," Jones added, making sure they knew what to expect when they got to Phoenix and Nogales. "Besides picking up the package, you will terminate the connection that was used to bring the terrorists into the country. This will make them think twice about aiding the terrorists the next go around."

By this time, they were at the airport terminal drop off. All of them got out of the car and shook hands as both men walked into the airport. Once Simon and Simon entered the airport they were met by a airport security officer who escorted them past the security checks and then directed them to their gate for their flight to Phoenix. Within an hour both men were on board a flight headed to Phoenix and from there a short hop to Nogales, Arizona. As they were getting off the plane they were met by one of the Border Patrol supervisors who gave them a package similar to the one that had been recovered by the Border Patrol agents the night they intercepted the two couriers. The difference was, the white powder was a fake anthrax that would still have the same effect as Anthrax, but was not lethal. This was to fool Ahmed and the other terrorists into thinking that it was still the real thing that they were dealing with. The physical reactions would be the same, yet it would only last a couple of days and then be gone out of the human body, with no ill effects from that point on.

Chapter XII

Simon and Simon had worked together in the past on several different operations. They knew who each other was and had a good working relationship that would be useful to have in the near future. Their real names were Dan Adams and John Quincy. Both of them were college graduates and had served in the US Army as Rangers and linguists before being approached by the CIA for use in one of their field stations in Iran. Both had the right temperament for working in the desert under intense conditions and had proven themselves in combat during the war in Iraq.

Now that they were stateside and had been briefed by the FBI and had picked up the package from the Border Patrol, they were ready to start their mission. The first place they went after being dropped off was to a McDonalds and a Burger King to have a traditional meal from America. Both men still had their long hair and thick beards, playing the parts of being couriers from Iran. The people that were there in Burger King kept watching them while they sat and ate their meals.

Pretending not to notice, Dan asked John, "What's this I hear that you got married to your favorite goat?" Thinking it would be funny for those that were around them listening and watching them.

"Yeah, she was the love of my life. I sure do miss her," John replied, smiling.

"Well I've got kids now, you ought to see them jump around their mom. You want to see the pictures?" Dan asked, reaching for his wallet.

"Don't remind me, I already miss my Gertrude."

"Yeah, I know what you mean, I miss my Madge as well," pretending to wipe a tear from his eyes.

Both of them laughed at their conversation, knowing full well that the people hearing it were now wondering who these two men were and should they be allowed in public.

When they were finished with their meal, they went to their hotel and stayed there until they met their contact. After getting the key to their room, they walked down the hall and opened the door. They looked around their room, "Be it ever so humble, there's no place like home." John said, sarcastically.

"It's still better than what we were living in, in the sandbox."

After staying in the cheap hotel in Nogales for a couple of days, one of the Border Patrol agents, dressed in civilian clothes, brought news to them that it was the Monterrey Cartel that had been paid to do the job of bringing the terrorists into the U.S. and that they could be found in a room above the Maria's Cantina on the other side of the border. With this information, Dan and John, waited until it was dark before making their way over the border, looking for the cantina where the cartel was located on the Mexican side of Nogales. Once they found the cantina they walked into the bar. As they stood there they could see that the cartel people were seated around the tables, drinking and waiting for their next opportunity to make money by taking people or drugs over the border. Dan approached the leader of the cartel men, "Do you know anyone that would be willing to be a guide to take me and my friend here, over the border? We are willing to pay."

As he lay the money on the table to pay for their help, the leader of the group, seeing the money, quickly started to reach for it. Dan stopped him, "You'll get the money when we get across the border."

After hearing this, the leader smiled. "Please forgive my manners, it has been a long day for me and my compadres," he said, with his eyes still on the money.

He stood up and walked over to the bar and spoke to one of his men, "These two gringos are wanting to cross over the border." Looking at Dan and John, he smiled and continued talking to the man, "We need to find out if they are carrying drugs or maybe some kids to sell in the big cities on the other side of the border."

The man he was talking to replied, "Maybe we should kill them now and take whatever they have and keep it for ourselves," he smiled, as he looked at Dan.

"Patience my friend patience. All good things come to those who wait. I need to setup a border crossing and maybe en-route we will relieve them of their cargo and sell it ourselves."

"As you wish," his friend replied.

Having finished the conversation with his friend the cartel leader came back to where Dan was standing, "It will take a couple of hours to organize passage for you and your friend to cross the border."

"Where should we meet you?"

"We will meet you here at the cantina.   We will have everything arranged for you the next time we meet."

Within hours the plan was put into place to transport Dan and John across the border.   Later the next day they met the leader for the last time when he took them to the men that would be their guides to take them across. Dan and John walked with the group leader to the house where the meet would take place. When all of the men were gathered together, the leader introduced Dan and John to their guides. At this time the leader sat down and waited for the money Dan had promised to pay him.   Dan reached into his pouch and pulled part of the money out and laid it on the table. He reached into his pouch a second time, pulling a gun out and shot the leader in the chest with two quick shots.   The leader fell backwards and died with a surprised look on his face. John had his gun out with a silencer attached and shot the two guides while they were trying to escape.   The other men sitting at the table were also shot as they tried to use their weapons.   At this point, Dan and John went through the house, going room to room, searching for any others that might be hiding.   Finding no one else in the house, Dan picked up the money from off the table and put it back into his pouch and blew out the candle on the table. Both of them went to the door.   Dan opened it slowly, looking both ways for anybody that wasn't supposed to be there. Smelling smoke and seeing the burning end of a cigarette in the shadows across the street, he nodded to John to let him know that there was someone outside waiting for them. Dan closed the door quietly and locked it. John went into the back area of the house and finding another door, he looked out into the darkness and waited to see if someone was there as well. Not seeing any indication that anybody was waiting for them, they both left the house and went back to the original meeting place at the bar where they had made their first contact with the group. Upon entering the cantina, they went into the back of the bar looking for the leader's associates. Especially, the man that had been at the bar talking to the cartel leader. Once they entered the back area, Dan, saw the man that the leader had spoken to at the bar before the meeting had been set up. He was sitting at the table with his friends. When he saw both Dan and John coming towards him, he stood up and pulled his gun and raised it to fire. Dan seeing it first, fired while the man was still raising his gun, hitting him in the chest. All of the others started to get up and move out of the way and were shot as they tried to escape, leaving only one man alive to tell the story.

"Next time you let a terrorist across our border you'll get worse, comprende señor?" John said, as he looked at the man lying on the floor bleeding from a leg wound.

Unable to move, the man lay on the floor looking for something to protect himself and not finding anything. Dan, seeing the man trying to get away, shot him once again in the other leg. This time causing him to cry out from the pain.

Seeing him unable to move, Dan said, "I guess you'll remember what my partner told you?"

Dan and John looked over the main floor of the cantina, looking for other men that might shoot them as they left. The people in the cantina who had been watching all of this happen, sat back down and continued on with their own interests that had brought them out tonight.

As they walked out of the cantina, Dan pulled the money out of his pouch and placed it on the counter by the cashier. "Sorry about the mess, this should take care of it."

The cashier grabbed the money not saying a word and went back to work. By now it was time to head back to the American side of the border.

Once they were back on American soil their next step was to get on board the Greyhound bus and ride for the next two days to Connecticut to meet with Ahmed and his team. The trip was uneventful and downright boring with plenty of time to sleep on the bus. Seeing the country by bus made them both realize how much they had missed being in America. Best of all, was that there was no desert to look at the further east they traveled. Every time they stopped the two of them would head to a McDonalds or Burger King for something to eat. By the end of two days they were so sick of eating hamburgers and french fries that they decided to try chicken.

Chapter XIII

When they arrived in Connecticut, Dan called the phone number that had been listed as a contact in the paperwork from Dr. Salaam. As they waited at the bus terminal, they were met by Bashir waving at them to make sure he had gotten their attention. Both Dan and John had to tell Bashir to settle down and to start acting as an adult. After exchanging the pleasantries and the code words to each other, Bashir took them to meet Ahmed.

As they were driving to Ahmed's place, Bashir started asking questions. "So how is our mother country?"

"It has gotten better since ISIS is winning the war against the infidels," Dan replied.

"That is good news indeed. I hope to impress the leaders with our next task."

"No doubt we will accomplish that with what we brought with us," John said, as he patted the container holding the bio-weapon.

Bashir smiled at the remark, "No doubt in my mind either. Our leader will be pleased with our efforts and see even when we are surrounded by infidels, we can still serve Allah."

"That is good," Dan said.

"I trust all is ready for what we have brought with us?" John asked.

"Once we received word that you were on your way, we made all of the arrangements for the handling of the package," Bashir said.

"That is good news, we do not want to have an accident before we accomplish our mission here do, we?" Dan said.

"We have everything ready for the security of the package, not to worry everything is ready. We have been waiting anxiously for your arrival." Bashir replied, excitedly.

With that, the conversation ceased with the exception of Bashir pointing out different buildings and other points of interest, one of which was the local porno shop down in the worst part of town.

"This is where most of the young and old people go to view men and women that are naked as they have sex. It is truly a decadent society here, it has been hard for our people not adapt to their ways here," Bashir said as he pointed it out.

Simon and Simon looked at each other and smiled, "You truly are strong to withstand these kinds of temptations. Praise Allah for your strength," Dan said.

This comment made Bashir proud and he smiled at the recognition of being strong, as he continued to drive to Ahmed's place.   When they arrived at Ahmed's apartment complex, Bashir jumped out of the car and grabbing their luggage he excitedly showed them the way to Ahmed's apartment.   He was beside himself trying to be helpful and was almost becoming a pest with his antics of trying to impress the two men.   Both John and Dan were almost laughing from his antics, but to remain in character they let him continue.

Bashir knocked on the apartment door. After a few minutes Ahmed opened the door to let them in. Ahmed turned out to be a gracious host by having something for them to eat and place where they could rest from their trip. Bashir, once seeing that all was well said, "A thousand pardons, but I need to be excused so I can report that you two have arrived."

"I need to report in as well to our leader, may I go with you?" Dan said, seizing the opportunity.

"Yes, please do. Follow me and I will show you the way that we communicate to our leaders when we report in."

Dan followed Bashir out of the apartment back to his place, in order to report to the leader of the arrival of the couriers.   As Bashir set up the computer to report in, Dan watched with interest as he contacted their leader to confirm the arrival of the two men with the package.   After Bashir reported in, Dan said, "I need to report to Dr. Salaam about having successfully arrived in Connecticut and see if there are any instructions, we need to be aware of."

Bashir let Dan sit down in front of the computer to file his report and find out if there was anything new.   He quietly watched from behind Dan as he went about reporting in. At this point Dan looked at Bashir with a distrustful eye, "I need to be alone to talk to the doctor. You see, very few people know where he is located, this is for his own safety. And I don't like people looking over my shoulder at what I am reporting on."

Bashir, realizing that Dan was a little upset, backed away so as not to be in the way.

"A thousand pardons for intruding master. I will be in the other room so as not to bother you."

"I will let you know when I am ready to go back to the apartment."

Bashir nodded his head as he bowed when he left the room.   Dan heard the door close behind him and found himself alone in the room with the computer.   He did a quick scan round the room to make sure that he wasn't being watched and then started looking for the IP address to the leader's computer so that he could copy and send it to Agent Smith.   After a few minutes he was able to find the IP address and quickly wrote it down. He was now able to begin searching the computer hard drive for all of the email traffic and anything else of importance.   Using a thumb drive, he proceeded to download all of what was on the hard drive.   He pocketed the thumb drive, finished his email to Dr. Salaam and waited a few minutes for an answer.   He checked his watch and realized the time difference between countries; therefore he probably wouldn't get a reply until the next day. He then closed out of the computer before opening the door to allow Bashir back into the room.

Dan looked at Bashir, "According to the good doctor, you are to assist us in the delivery of the weapon when it comes time."

Bashir smiled and was ecstatic over the opportunity to serve in helping so many infidels to meet their maker. "I would be honored with this chance to prove my loyalty to Allah. What is it that you would have me do?"

"When the time is right, I will let you know when you are needed. Until then, keep going to school and try not to stand out amongst your friends."

As Dan and Bashir left the apartment and went back to Ahmed's place, everything was set up for the next step.   When they arrived at Ahmed's place John and Dan brought out the package they had for Ahmed and placing it in a sterile container they put it away in the closet for safe keeping to avoid any accidents.

Now it came time to start putting together a list of targets that they would be using the super Anthrax against. Over the next couple of days, Ahmed drove Dan and John around, showing them possible targets of interest that the super Anthrax powder could be used on. By the end of the second day, they had finished visiting the possible targets and headed back to Ahmed's apartment to review the list. After evaluating each of the targets on their list, they categorized all of them based on the amount of people that would be affected. The first, or primary target from the list would be the elementary schools in the surrounding areas. The second target would be a sporting event where people would congregate in mass to cheer on their teams. The third target could be a mall of some sort and the fourth target could possibly be a church and its congregation as they met on Sunday to worship. Ahmed's overall plan was to instill fear in the general public by hitting more than one target. This would require two teams working in sync with each other. As the military jargon would say, it was a target rich environment with plenty to choose from. It now became a matter of choosing a target or targets that would have the most casualties in the shortest amount of time. All of the possible targets were good for mass casualties, but to be the most effective, the best area to spread the super Anthrax in, had to be a closed environment, where it could do the most damage. John and Dan looked over the possible targets by themselves, as Ahmed sat close by listening to them work through the pros and cons of each target. They needed Ahmed to tell them the shortest routes they would need to take so that the Anthrax could be used to do more damage elsewhere, thus creating panic in all of the areas infected with the bio-weapon.

It was determined, that because of their familiarity with this hybrid bio-weapon, Dan and John would be the leaders of each team, with specific targets for each of them. Dan's team would include, Ahmed and one of his lackeys. John's team would include Bashir and the other lackey from Ahmed's terrorist cell. After looking at the maps of the area, they found that the easiest targets were close to an interstate or a major cross street, allowing easy access and escape. Each target would have to be hit at the same time, and fortunately, they were all within a five-mile radius of each other. Thereby, each team would have an escape route nearby so they could make a clean getaway to go after the other targets, as time would permit.

Dan and John, looking at the map, thought the elementary school would be a good target as there was a mall nearby to hit, as well.

Both of the places had a closed ventilation system that could be easily opened up to plant the super Anthrax inside the air conditioning or heating systems from the outside. Dressed as workman, they could easily access the ventilation system on the roof to load the super Anthrax into it.   By the time anyone realized what was happening, it would be to late as everybody would be feeling the effects of the super Anthrax, and all would be dead in days.   The first symptoms could be one or more of the following, sore throat, fever, achy muscles, a cough, fatigue, chills and vomiting, like having a cold or flu.   If the powder came in contact with a break in the skin it would form a small blister, with surrounding swelling that turns into an ulcer with a black center. After the kids are exposed to the super Anthrax, the school would call the parents to come and get their children and take them home, thereby infecting the parents and the rest of the family.

Ahmed smiled at the prospect of inflicting mass casualties with more than one target to go after. Allah would be pleased with this, knowing his servants would be killing so many infidels and, if necessary, dying in the process in order to have 72 virgins waiting for them on the other side.   Having figured out their targets, the next step was to decide when to strike them. The first target for Dan's team would be the elementary school.   This would require the team to go in during the night and set up the bio-weapon along with the electronic timers to release the super Anthrax into the ventilation system.   Once this was done, the next target would be the mall, and it would be done after they were finished setting up the bio-weapon inside the school. The mall was chosen simply because it always seemed to be crowded with people shopping.

John's team found another elementary school as their primary target on the other side of town.   Their second target would be a church nearby that held preschool classes during the day.   Each target had their own issues that needed to be reviewed by the assigned team in order to make the plan work. All of this would need to be worked out to minimize any complications that might arise as they put the super Anthrax into the ventilation systems.

Each team would take pictures of their targets for a thorough review, in order to determine what equipment, they would need, as well as how much time it would take to set things up.   At this point, their only concern would be to activate the release of the bio-weapon without attracting attention. They also did a practice run leaving the school and going to the mall, to see how much time it would take to get to the next target and leave the area, using the best possible route without creating a scene. Dan and John had decided to use timers to delay the dispersal of the Anthrax so that the teams could get away without having to deal with local law enforcement agencies as they showed up.

Each package of the super Anthrax would be set up so it could be attached to the inside of the air intake ducts, using duct tape and magnets to hold it in place. When the timers were activated, the bio-weapon package would create a small explosion, thereby releasing the white powder into the air ducts which would carry the powder into ventilation system of the school, dispersing it into each classroom, affecting all the adults and children inside. The damage done would be extensive and thorough for everyone inside the school.

The next step for the six men would be to have an escape plan to leave the country without being caught.

"When we travel, it would be best if we did so in pairs to avoid having the ear marks of a mass exodus," Ahmed suggested.

"I know this is standard protocol in your training at the camps back home, but for myself and Dan, we have our own way of getting home," John said.

"We plan on leaving the next day after the bio-weapon is released. But in order to protect us, that is all you need to know," Dan added, as he and John left the apartment. Leaving the other four to figure out their own way back to Iran.

When they were away from the others, Dan and John went to contact their handlers about the targets they had chosen.

The other four terrorists began looking at their options of leaving the country, one thought was to fly out of the country or maybe drive to the Mexican border via a car rental, or better yet, they thought they might head to Canada with their visas, then back to Iran from there. All of the options were given considerable thought. In the end, they decided that driving to Mexico wasn't a good choice, simply because they could be picked up by any law enforcement agency along the way. The best they could come up with was a combination of the two ideas.

Ahmed, being in charge of the group stated, "Bashir and I will drive to Canada, then take a flight home to Iran. I think it is best that you two drive to New York and fly to Europe and then on to Iran."

"Where do you plan on meeting after we get back to Iran?" Bashir asked.

"We will meet a week after we get back home at the Mosque in Tehran," Ahmed replied.

This pleased the other two men, and they could barely contain their excitement as they were eager to leave this country and go back home to be with their families. Ahmed smiled, seeing how the other two were reacting, knowing full well that if anybody was to get caught it would be them.

Once everything was planned out, it was decided that the date for using the bioweapon would be on a Friday, ahead of a three-day weekend. The sales in the mall would be ramping up and the kids would be in school, ready for the break. As they looked at the calendar, it was decided that it would be on Presidents Day, to further inflame the people with anger and hurt. This date would be forever in the minds of the people who were the survivors of the bio-weapon, as well as the rest of the country.

The school chosen was George Bush Elementary school, at the crossroads of I-95, State Route 1 and Route 184. This would give the first team more than one option to choose from to travel without any issues and would cause the law enforcement to guess which route they had taken to get away, thereby delaying any actions to find them. The other target would be the Seagate Mall, located on State Route 12 north off of I-95. With these targets identified, then came the task of building a timer to use in order to dispense the Anthrax powder. There would be four timers built using burner phones that would ignite the small amount of black powder needed to release the Anthrax into the air ducts. Using the burner phones enabled the teams to be far enough away so they wouldn't be considered as the ones that had set off the Anthrax. Dan and John reconfigured the burner phones to operate as detonators after they were bought by Ahmed. Ahmed being curious, asked, "I'm curious, can you show me how the burner phones work?"

Having all the others gather around, Dan opened the burner phone and explained, "Okay, here is the small charge of black powder that is taped to the back of the phone. You'll notice that the wire is connected to the charge on one end and the other end is connected directly to the phone.   All we do now is punch in the phone number and as you do so, it sends an electrical charge to the powder, causing a small explosion which will be strong enough to open the containers, allowing the Anthrax to escape."

"Are there any other questions?" John asked, looking at the others in the room.

Being satisfied, Ahmed smiled, "Allah be praised."

Once the burner phones were all configured, it was now time to load the bio-weapon into the duct systems, without being noticed. This would have to be done at night to avoid being seen by anyone, especially law enforcement.   They decided to put everything into place Thursday night.   By Friday morning, the teams would be out of sight and gone. In order to put the bioweapons in place, each team would be dressed as maintenance workers doing their jobs, without interfering with the normal daily operations of each building.

In order to make sure their cover was good, Ahmed rented two white vans and posted the magnetic placards, identifying the truck as ACME Air Conditioning and Ventilation Specialists. Ladders would be mounted on the outside of the vans, on rails, for easy access. With the vans, they could transport all of the tools they would need to accomplish setting up the bio-weapons.   The bio-weapons would be disguised in lunch boxes so that the workers could take them into their work area without anybody being the wiser for it.

As all of the preparations were completed one by one, getting closer to Thursday, both of the teams were excited and already to go by Wednesday.   After everything was completed, Dan said, "I think that now is the time for all of us to prepare ourselves for the mission by taking some time to ourselves and think about what each of our parts are."

Everybody agreed and each member found a place to meditate and pray for guidance and strength to carry out their assigned duties. John asked Ahmed and Bashir, "Do you have the tickets for your flights and car rentals?   I need you to make sure that everything is in order so that there's no confusion."

Ahmed produced the airline tickets and handed them over to John, "We have them already."

"Let me see them for a minute," Dan said.

Ahmed handed them over to Dan with a curious look on his face, wondering why he wanted to see them.   Sensing that Ahmed was curious, as was Bashir, Dan explained, "I just want to make sure that everything is in order."

After scanning the tickets, Dan returned them to Ahmed. Unbeknownst to Ahmed, as Dan scanned the tickets, he verified the flights and times for each of the four men, just in case they got away.

As the four continued to meditate, Dan and John decided to go over the finer details of the plans.   They found a place where they would not be bothered by anyone and went through each step of the plan, looking for any weaknesses in it.

When they were done meditating, Ahmed and Bashir went out to verify that the rental vans had everything that they needed and that all was in order.   The others continued to meditate by themselves, seeking the higher light of Allah, as they prepared themselves for the mission.

Dan and John decided to walk in the park nearby to clear their heads and talk to each other about the plan. Leaving everyone to their duties and themselves, Dan and John left for the park. Once they were clear of Ahmed's apartment complex they stopped and looked behind them to make sure that they weren't being followed.

"Were you able to write everything down for our friends?" Dan asked John.

"I have it here in my pocket, ready and waiting to be dropped."

Dan, looked at his watch, "It's about time, let's go ahead and make our drop to let them know what's going on."

"I know there will be someone there, but I'll be damned if I can catch them.   They really got it over our people when it comes to doing a stake out."

John had written out the plan with the time and place of attack on a piece of paper to be dropped off at a preassigned place for the FBI to pick up. As they sat down on the bench near some shaded trees, the drop was made by John, placing the note under a rock in the flower bed near the trees. The rock was hollow inside, like one that you can buy at a hardware store for looks, if you were so inclined to do so. Across the other side of the walkway was a woman dressed in a jogging suit, sitting on a bench with her dog and reading a book in the sunlight.   Without raising her head, she watched John place the note under the rock, as Dan continued sitting on the bench, making sure nobody noticed what was going on. They continued to sit there for a few minutes more before getting up and heading back to Ahmed's apartment. As they got up from the bench, she continued reading until both men were out of sight. When she stood up, she accidentally dropped the leash and the dog took off running towards the trees where John and Dan had been seated. The lady chased her dog over to where the bench was, and when she finally caught up with him, she sat down on the same bench trying to catch her breath. She did a brief scan of the area to make sure no one was watching. She reached under the rock and pulled the note out from under it and placed it inside her fanny pack. Then taking her dog by the leash, got up and walked to her car which was located near the entrance of the park and drove off. She drove to a nearby sidewalk cafe, parked her car and found a table outside to sit at. A waiter came over and handed her a menu to order from,

"Can you please bring me a cup of coffee while I look at the menu?"

"Yes, ma'am, I'll be right back with it."

After looking over the menu for a few minutes, she laid it back down on the table with the note inside. The waiter soon returned with her coffee and took her order. While she sat there drinking her coffee, she waited to see if there was a reply to the note to go back under the rock.

As she was waiting for the waiter to return with her order, he was in the back of the cafe sending the information on the note over a secure phone to the FBI. After the note was reviewed at the FBI office, they then faxed the message over to Agents Smith and Jones. Everyone in the chain of command realized that it was a travel itinerary for the terrorists on how they would be leaving the country after the Anthrax was dispersed. The information was for other agents at other locations that were nearby the airports so they could be set up and waiting for the terrorists as they tried to leave the country.

The waiter received a confirmation back that the office had received the note and that there was no reply needed. In a few minutes the waiter came out with her sandwich and the bill. As she looked over her bill, the waiter whispered to her, "No reply is needed."

Nodding her head in agreement she finished her meal and left the cafe. She went back to her car and drove home to change her clothes and drop her dog off before heading back to the FBI office.

Chapter XIV

Agents Smith and Jones read the note that John and Dan had dropped off with the information on it. They called their superiors to inform them that it was a go for the bio-weapon to be used. Their superiors contacted each of the other government players and participants that would be involved in tracking down the terrorists when the time came to do so. The state police would be watching the highways and the state routes that the terrorists planned on using. Airport security would be on high alert if by chance they made their way to the airports. The IP address that Dan was able to get off of Bashir's computer had been traced and tracked all the way back to Iran. In the process, they were able to locate Dr. Salaam and his associates in their laboratory compound. The Delta Team had their orders and were standing by, having already been inserted into Iran under cover of darkness, ready and waiting for the go code to destroy the lab and the doctors. The Seal Team was standing by with their equipment, in a submarine that was resting on the bottom of the Persian Gulf along the Straits of Hormuz, near Bandar Abbas, the Iranian naval base, home to 12 Iranian submarines bought from Russia.

The Delta Team was sent in to set up a laser sight, as a backup, on the building that housed the laboratory so the U.S. Air force could fly in a pair of B-1 Bombers with several JSOWs (Joint Stand Off Weapon) and launch them on the GPS coordinates. Once the JSOW hit the target, the Delta Team would go in and make sure Dr. Salaam was either dead or bring him out of Iran and interrogate him to get what other information he may have had that would be useful to America, and then terminate him with prejudice.

The Seal Team's job was to plant modified magnetic limpet mines on each of the hulls of the Iranian warships that they could find in the harbor, in order to sink them as they made their way out to sea. The modified mines were twice as powerful as the original limpet mine used in WWII, using new technology in the explosives. They were configured with a small, time delay fuse, which would detonate the mine after the ship had sailed a certain distance. This was done so that it was more likely to sink in deep water, hopefully, out of the reach of easy salvage, making it harder to find out what had caused them to sink. A team of Seals would also be sent in to plant the same type of bomb that was used to sink the USS Dolphin on the Iranian submarines. This was done by having the Seal Team get onboard the submarines and place the bombs in the same area near the torpedo room. This was the most dangerous part of the mission for the Seal Team, however that being said, the Seals wanted payback for the crew of the Dolphin. In order to get onboard they had to create a diversion by using a chemical gas leak that would force all personnel, in and around the submarines to evacuate, allowing the Seals access to the submarines. In the end, the USS Dolphin would have the last laugh. All of this was to occur on Thursday night while the terrorist was setting up the anthrax on each of their targets.

When Dan and John had returned from the park, they were clear in their minds about how the operation would go. They found a private place and went and knelt on their rugs, facing East, as was the custom of all Muslims, and stayed there until it was time to go to bed.

The next couple of days were filled with excitement and anxiousness, knowing what they were about to do. In order to control their feelings, all of them decided to take some time off and go sightseeing. It was at this time that Ahmed boasted about how he and his team used an American worker to help sabotage a submarine and other Navy ships.

Dan and John listened with interest as all four of them bragged about how stupid the American worker was. "Truly Allah has smiled upon you and your team for accomplishing such a dangerous mission," Dan said smiling, knowing he wanted to kill them all right then and there.

Ahmed and the others smiled at receiving such high praise from two men who would bring word back to Iran and their leaders.

When Thursday night rolled around, Dan and Ahmed, took their team in one of the vans and John and Bashir, went in the other white van, each of them heading towards their targets. Dan and Ahmed went to the school at about 8:00 pm and undid the straps holding the ladders on the van. Dan kept hold of the package containing the super Anthrax while Ahmed and Abdul placed the ladders against the building where the air conditioning units sat. Dan carried the package cautiously up the ladder to the top of the roof. Finding the duct for air running into the building, he had Ahmed carefully cut a square hole in the duct close to the roof that would be hard to find. Dan then carefully removed the container holding the bio-weapon and gingerly placed the bio-weapon on another piece of sheet metal that had been modified to replace what Ahmed had cut out. He then taped the bio-weapon onto the sheet metal and then riveted the sheet metal piece back into place inside the duct, then sealed it with putty. They were done. While Abdul kept watch, to make sure no one saw them, they quickly made their way down the ladders and loaded them up again on the van and were gone inside two hours.

When John's team arrived at the mall, they went inside and found their way to the mechanical room where the air conditioning controls were located next to the ducts which controlled the air coming in from the outside. Looking at the schematics, they found the duct that pushed the air from the outside into the system and then into the mall. They proceeded to cut a hole and attach their bio-weapon in the same manner as did Dan and his team. With the primary targets completed, they moved on to their secondary targets. When the bio-weapons were in place at all of the locations, each team showed back up at the apartment. By 11:00 pm everyone was totally exhausted and happy to be done with each part of their job.

Dan and John decided to celebrate their good fortune with the terrorists for a job well done. At this point, to show their appreciation for all of the hard work each team member had done to make their mission a success, they brought out some nonalcoholic beer. Ahmed and Bashir were ecstatic with the nonalcoholic beer and opened their bottles and started drinking. The other two grabbed theirs and proceeded to do the same. John and Dan did, likewise, enjoying the time of celebration, but for different reasons. After the second round, everybody headed off to find a place to sleep. For some reason, known only to John and Dan, the four terrorists were having a hard time staying awake as they celebrated completing their mission. Ahmed was the last one to fall asleep, boasting, "What we have accomplished tonight will be our statement to the infidels that they will either bow to Allah or die."

The next morning, John and Dan were wide awake, waiting for each of the four Iranians, who were still drugged from the non-alcoholic beer, to wake up and start the process of using the burner phones to activate the timers so that the anthrax powder could be dispersed. Dan, checked his watch and could see that it was 9:00 am and that the school was in full session with teachers in their classrooms and the office staff was doing their part to keep the school running. The mall was just opening its doors to allow the early birds access to the sales that were going on for Presidents Day weekend. Along with the early birds, were the mall walkers who came in to walk their miles inside the mall for exercise. At 10:00 am Dan and John were set to call the cell phones and trigger the Anthrax to do its deadly job. By now, the others were awake, packed and ready to leave the apartment and head to the different airports and then onto Iran.

Dan and John were ready to make the phone calls from the burner phones to release the Anthrax into the ventilation systems of the school and the mall. They stood outside the apartment complex when they started dialing the numbers to activate the packages. Ahmed, Bashir, Abdul and Abba were watching from the window of the Ahmed's apartment. When the phones indicated that the Anthrax powder had been released, Ahmed and Bashir were surprised that they could hear a small bang inside the apartment. Within seconds Bashir noticed a white cloud of mist floating inside the apartment. "Ahmed! Look, at the white powder!"

Ahmed was coughing, trying to catch his breath and could see white powder all over the place. "What is going on!?" he yelled out.

By now, the white powder was starting to do its magic on all four of the men inside the apartment. Ahmed fell to the floor, his mind racing, he was trying to understand what had gone wrong. Why would there be anthrax inside the apartment? Who did this to them and why? Could it be that they were meant to die because it was part of the plan from their leaders? All of these questions raced through his mind as he realized that he had been betrayed by his leadership in Iran.

"We are dying, we've been betrayed!" Ahmed said.

Bashir, having heard Ahmed's words, started yelling, "I don't understand. What happened!?"

The other two tried to get out of the apartment but the door was locked from the outside. Being unable to open the door they were overtaken by the fumes and passed out near the door.

John and Dan made their way up to the apartment and opened the door and saw the four terrorists lying on the floor. They both had gas masks on as they went into the apartment and dragged each of the four men out into the fresh air of the hallway. Ahmed and Bashir were the first to recover and were happy to see that John and Dan had come in to rescue the team. Ahmed knew that even if he had died, he had served Allah well and that the 72 virgins were his. By now the police had arrived and had started taking the four men out of the apartment building. A Hazmat team, dressed in their white suits, started moving the four terrorists into the big self-contained van. Dan and John stood there, with guns in their hands, watching the Hazmat crew do their work. The news reporters were busily getting set up to do their reporting about what was going on. Ahmed could hear one of the reporters saying that the four Iranian terrorists had been captured by the FBI in an apparent mission to use a bio-weapon to take out two elementary schools, a church, and a nearby mall. It was only then that he realized that John and Dan were agents working for the FBI and that he had been used by them. John and Dan walked over to Ahmed and his friends. He leaned over and said in Arabic, "How's it feel to know you're going to die for nothing by the same type of weapon that you were going to use on those innocent kids in school?" John asked, "Oh, by the way, Dan, as a joke, had planted one of his own fake anthrax packages inside the apartment."

"You're lucky, you will recover from this shortly and then you're going to prison until you die. Don't worry, you won't have to wait to long." Dan said.

Ahmed thought for a moment inside his pain addled brain, only realizing that he would die for nothing. Ahmed looked into the eyes of both Dan and John and could see the hatred in their eyes towards him. He had been played by the foolish Americans, tricked by the infidels, and now was being sent to prison for his actions. The biggest disgrace would be having his face and the others on television with the Americans laughing at him, for having failed in their mission. Being angry after finding out they had been used, Ahmed spit on Dan and yelled, "You traitorous pig!"

Dan, wiped the spit off of his face and decked Ahmed, hitting him in the face, breaking his nose. One of the police officers who had witnessed the incident, picked Ahmed up, "Mind your step, these sidewalks can really be treacherous. I hate to see you fall again," smiling as he said it.

While the terrorists had been passed out from the date rape drug that had been planted in their beer the night before, John and Dan called the Hazmat team to let them know where the fake bio-weapons were located in the duct work at the four places identified by the terrorists. The team quietly removed the faux bio-weapons and put them in a self-contained box and shipped them back to the Hazmat building, where they would be destroyed. The schools and the mall had been unaware of just how close it could have been if the real Anthrax had been used.

The next few days were a blur to the four terrorists, all they knew was that they were being held without bail in Federal lockup. This was announced during their arraignment after being moved to and from the courthouse by the US Marshals. Coincidentally, every time they were moved, they were required to wear bullet proof vests to protect them from being shot. As they were being moved, there was always the cameras taking pictures and reporters continually asking questions of how they felt. The defense attorneys, who were compelled to come in to talk to them, were trying to come up with some sort of defense for each of them, but to no effect.

By now the effects of the fake anthrax were starting to wear off of the four men and it was only now that they started understanding what was going on. The lawyers really didn't have much of a defense, due to the FBI's wiretaps and videotapes for the last three months of the defendant's lives. They knew, by all accounts, that they would be sent to a maximum-security prison either at Guantanamo Bay or, most likely, Florence Colorado for the rest of their lives. The four had to be housed in the same cell in solitary confinement from the general population of the jail, and were allowed one hour each day to be outside their cell when the general population was back in their cells, so that they wouldn't be beat up or killed by the other inmates while they were awaiting their trial in court. Ahmed thought it interesting that the American legal system did so much to protect them from being killed, when in their country, if you did something wrong the Sharia law was the answer to everything. Here, these infidels were doing everything they could to make sure that the due process of law was being followed, even though they were known to be guilty of trying to kill the same infidels. These infidels were foolish for putting so much into their laws when the answer to the crime was simple and that answer was death for their attempt to kill the same infidels that were now following the rules of law to ensure a fair trial.

With all the evidence they had against them, along with the testimonies by John and Dan that was to include them bragging about their part in sinking a US Navy submarine and trying to destroy other Navy ships, they knew there was no way they would ever be free. After about a week of waiting for a decision from the court, Ahmed had asked if Bashir would do an honor killing on him so that he would die as a martyr for his cause.   In their attempt, the surveillance cameras alerted the guards as to what was going on. The guards rushed into their cell and stopped Bashir from making that happen. Because of this, all four of the defendants were separated and in their own cells for their own good.

In the cell next to the Ahmed there was another man sitting in the corner, not saying anything at all. Ahmed looked at the figure and thought to himself that the guy looked familiar from a distance. After being in the jail cell for two weeks, sitting and waiting, the man in the cell next to him was called out by the guard who was opening his cell door. The guard said to the man, "Time to testify, John."

When the man stood up and started walking towards the guard, Ahmed recognized the guy as the one they had used for planting the presents on board the ships. Ahmed called out to him, yelling, "John, tell them we had nothing to do with planting the bombs on the ships and submarine. Tell them it was all your doing."

John stopped, looked at Ahmed and thought for a moment, "Ahmed, I'm going to hell for what I did for you and you are too. The only good thing about all of this is that I get to testify against you and your friends. When I get to hell, I'll tell Lucifer that he can expect four more souls, compliments of me doing the right thing for the right reasons. Who knows, maybe you might be going there ahead of me, waiting for me in hell."

With that, John turned and walked out of the cell following the guard.

Ahmed stood there for a moment, not knowing what to say, as the rest of the terrorists listened to John, as well. Ahmed looked at his friends, not saying a word, sat down and thought about what John had said to him. He had never thought about death like this before. He had wanted to die a glorious death, knowing that he had done his part for Allah. Ahmed was now realizing for the first time that he was a failure and that there would not be 72 virgins waiting for him. No honor, no celebration, no nothing, for him and his friends, just death waiting for them some time off in the distant future. Where was the honor in this kind of life, knowing that he had failed? As far as he could tell, there was none. His life meant nothing to anybody here in the western world or even in his own country. Death without a purpose is a life wasted for nothing, taking up space and nobody caring. Breathing air that someone else would have made better use of. It would have been better not to have been born than to live a life or die without a purpose. Ahmed was starting to lose his mind and didn't know it yet, knowing that he would be known as a failure by his own people's standards and beliefs. He realized that even though the infidels were doing their part to keep him alive, he knew that death was the only answer for him. Death was the only answer to cover his own shame for being a failure. The longer he sat in the jail cell, the more his mind started to come apart, knowing that he had failed and was still alive. Bashir and the others watched as their leader slowly went mad. As they continued watching this unfold before them, they wondered if it would happen to them as well. However, for them, it was never about living or dying for Allah. It was about being strong, even in their own temptations and weaknesses living in a westernized world. They had tasted another life in a different place and were found weak in not being able to live by the law of Allah. The things they detested about the western culture had already taken hold of them in their weakness. The way the women wore their clothes and walked around by themselves or with each other, was a temptation that would have been covered in chadors or robes. The easiness of finding pornography and the accessibility of television and alcohol made it easy to overpower the teachings of Allah and had already started taking their toll on the friends of Ahmed. The men who were weak would always have had Allah to protect them from themselves, or so they thought. The only problem for the friends of Ahmed, was that to embrace Allah you did it willingly, having the right desire to serve him, out of love not fear, and not with blind faith, but with your eyes open to Allah's glories, that were not seen, only hoped for. A religion to be followed in word only, would or could not, give the strength to the weak or simple minded, to survive the temptations in any part of the world, the weak minded would always fail.

When the court was finished, and the four Iranians were sitting in their jail cells, Dan and John stopped in to visit them. Dan looked at Ahmed first and saw that his nose was crooked, "Does your nose feel better or does it still hurt?"

Ahmed looked at Dan and sneered at him from his bed.

"How does it feel knowing you failed your mission and what's worse is that there are no virgins waiting for you?" John asked.

The question sent Ahmed off in a terrible rant, yelling at both of the infidels about being lower than pig crap on the earth. Dan and John looked at him and laughed loud and hard at his expense. Which just infuriated Ahmed that much more. It was Bashir who called out to the two men, "Please to leave Ahmed alone, can't you see he is sick and losing his mind?"

Dan looked at Ahmed and could see that he was past being sensible. "Couldn't happen to a better failure," John laughed at Dan's reply as they walked out of the jail.

In the background they could hear Ahmed screaming and yelling to be killed so that he wouldn't have to live with knowing that he had failed and was a failure. Even knowing that he had destroyed a submarine, killing its crew, he would not be remembered for this, but for having failed his last mission.

Chapter XV

Meanwhile, on the other side of the world, the Delta Team had been dispatched to go into Iran and was making their way up a mountain overlooking the compound where Dr. Salaam worked in his laboratory. Once they made it to the top, they assembled the laser guidance system and focused the beam precisely on the fuel tanks of the compound and a second laser beam on the main building where Dr. Salaam's office was. The B-1 bombers would come in and drop the JSOWs on the targets that were highlighted by the lasers. This would allow the JSOWs to follow their glide paths to each point lit up by the lasers. Now it was a matter of time for the B-1s to show up after the team had reported in that they were set up and operational. Once their message was confirmed, two of the Delta Team members would stay on the mountain, babysitting the laser hardware, while the others of the team made their way to the compound.

At a given signal, a pair of B-1 bombers came flying in low and fast across the desert, well below the radar coverage, being masked by the mountains around them. The two men monitoring the laser systems checked in with the B-1 pilots, confirming visual contact with them as they made their final approach closing in on the compound. At this point, the two men contacted the rest of their team, "Show time."

The team lead confirmed, "Ready and waiting."

About half a mile from the compound both the pilots and co-pilots pulled back on the yokes of their planes and pulled up into the sun as the bombers screamed for altitude. The weapons bay doors opened with two JSOWs falling out of the belly of each aircraft. As the bombers were flying away, the first two JSOWs found the laser markers that pointed into the compound and the main building, following the laser beam, both bombs hit their targets within five feet of laser image. The first blast knocked out the fuel tanks that supplied power to all of the buildings inside the compound, to include the main building, which contained the laboratory chambers inside.   The second set of JSOWs that had been launched hit the military barracks where the soldiers stayed. With all of the explosions going on, the Iranian soldiers were unable to regroup to launch a counter attack on the Delta team members and were cut down as they left their burning barracks by two of the Delta Team members waiting for them.   On the next run the B-1s dropped their third pair of JSOWs, taking out the radar system used for the anti-aircraft missile defense system, rendering the missiles useless. The second JSOW took out the main power plant, located on the north end of the compound. Dr. Salaam, upon hearing the explosion of the fuel tanks, went to his window and looked out to see where the explosions had occurred.   As he watched the fireball rise in the sky, he stood there looking through the window, wondering what had caused the blast. The second blast, which happened just seconds apart from the first, took out the office building in the center of the compound. Dr. Salaam and the people inside the building never knew what hit them. The doctor was thrown to the floor by the blast, he picked himself up and staggered through the debris, making his way out of the building.   When he reached the compound fence, he stood there watching the building he had just been in, in flames. He could see that the frame of the building was now all twisted metal and rubble, where there used to be walls was now open space engulfed in fire. He saw his co-workers, that hadn't been killed in the first blast, start making their way out of the rubble and smoke. They slowly made their way to where Dr. Salaam was standing.   He could see that some of them were shell shocked and weren't aware that their clothing was on fire.   Racing over to help them, he was able to extinguish the fires and assisted them to the fence to get away from the blast zone and the fires.

Most of the survivors sat down against the fence, still in a state of shock.   As he watched the fire, he soon realized that all of his work was being burned up by the fire or blown apart from the blast. He couldn't believe that 25 years worth of work was destroyed in a matter of seconds and there was no way to save any of it.   The initial blast took out the part of the building that could be seen above ground.   As the fires continued burning, the chemicals that were stored in the basement came in contact with the flames and started to explode.   The ones that were still trying to get out of the building were killed instantly by the secondary explosions. The survivors that were near the fence could hear the screams of the ones that were caught in the blasts. Dr. Salaam could do nothing but stand and watch because of the chemicals that were escaping from the basement and the intense heat from the fires.

Having already cut holes in the fence, the Delta Force team was in place, waiting to see if they could find their quarry, Dr. Salaam. Each Delta team member had a picture of him and were now looking for the doctor.   Holding the picture of the doctor up against each of the survivors, they slowly and methodically made their way through all of them.   If their face didn't match that of the picture, they were tied to the fence, their picture taken and then sent by cell phone to be reviewed by facial recognition software at NSA.   From there the results would determine the final action that would be taken. The doctor was finally located and once it was confirmed that it was him, the team lead dragged him further down the fence line where others of his team were standing guard, watching over the rest of the team as they made their rounds searching the compound for possible intelligence information.   The doctor, still in shock, was forced to lay face down as one of the Delta Force soldiers put his foot in the center of his back to keep him from escaping.

By now the Iranian military, having heard the explosions, decided to go check out what was going on at the compound. The two Delta Force members that were on the mountain could see the dust from the trucks that were carrying the Iranian soldiers to the compound.   They immediately called the team lead, "Bowshot, this is Archangel, you have unfriendly's coming in your direction."

The radio man, hearing the transmission from Archangel, confirmed the message and advised the team lead. Upon hearing the message, the team lead signaled his men, "People we got company coming, get ready," he then turned and looked at the comm guy, "Contact Mother Hen and tell her that we need some chicks to come help us."

Switching frequencies, the radio man contacted the AWACS bird, circling over neutral territory, and asked for some air support against the approaching trucks.   The controller aboard the AWACS contacted the two F-35 pilots flying nearby the compound, "Rooster one and two, you are requested to lay some eggs on the approaching trucks for Bowshot."

The two F-35 Joint Strike Fighters saw the trucks traveling down the dirt road bringing the soldiers to the compound. "Mother Hen, this is Rooster one, we have contact with a column of trucks. Request permission to engage."

"Rooster one, this is Mother Hen, you are cleared to engage."

Getting clearance to engage, the lead aircraft fired his heat seeker missiles at the first truck carrying the soldiers. The other trucks in the column attempted to take evasive action but were unable to because the second F-35 took out the last truck in the caravan using a heat seeker missile. The lead truck and the last truck in the column never knew what happened as the heat seeking missiles locked on to the heat signature of the trucks. The soldiers in the two trucks went flying through the air from the explosions, landing in the brush next to the road. There were pieces of soldiers lying all around the ground, parts of arms, legs, and torsos were everywhere. Both trucks were on fire and smoking from the attack, as they sat dead in their tracks. The soldiers that were wounded were helped by the soldiers that were still able to move around. Out of fifty troops that were in the back of the transports, only three was left standing with others lying on the ground wounded and or dying. The Iranian officer in charge of the caravan, sitting in his jeep, called his headquarters, "We're under attack! Send some air support!"

The first F-35, having circled around, came in and dropped two 500-pound bombs on the burning trucks, leaving the area completely lifeless, with two smoking craters in the ground as he flew away. As the F-35s continued circling above the chemical compound, they were searching for signs of a military presence that had been dispatched by the Iranian army.

"Mother Hen, this is Bowshot, tell your chicks, well done and thanks."

"Bowshot, this is Mother Hen, anything else we can do for you?"

"Not at this time, over."

The two F-35s circled one last time as they started climbing to a higher altitude after being contacted by Mother Hen that they were cleared to return to base. Within minutes, Mother Hen called out, "Rooster One and Rooster Two disregard last order, we have two guests that weren't invited and are trying to crash the party. Bearing 180 degrees from Mother Hen."

"Roger that, we got 'em, Mother Hen.   Are we cleared to engage?"

"Don't fire until fired upon, Rooster One."

"Roger wilco."

The Iranians dispatched two fighters to do a flyover over the compound. One of the pilots reported that the compound was on fire and people were lying on the ground with an unknown military force present. On their second pass, the Migs-31s came in low, strafing the Delta force personnel inside the compound, forcing the Delta team to take cover.   As the two Migs circled around to make another strafing run and were lining up on the men below, the lead Mig-31 was blown out of the sky, falling onto the compound fence line, spreading burning fuel all around the area and creating a black plume of smoke that rose into the air. The second Mig-31 pulled up automatically and headed into the sky, looking for anything on his onboard radar that would indicate the location of the enemy.   With the sun in his eyes and not having radar contact, the Mig pilot was unable to see his opponent's location. Receiving a warning tone in his helmet, he looked at his radar screen and caught a glimpse of the fighter on it.   Having found the target, the pilot turned to fight the unknown aircraft. With the F-35 already in the sun, the Air Force pilot turned off his gun and went directly to re-engage the heat seeking missiles switch.

Waiting for the Mig-31 to come into his cross hairs. Rooster Two, finally got the lock on tone he was waiting for in his helmet and fired his missile at the Mig-31.   The pilot of the Mig was in full afterburner and headed straight up, knowing that if he didn't get enough altitude, he would be a sitting duck against his opponent. As he was looking around, he heard the lock on tone from inside his helmet, he quickly banked right to avoid being hit by the missile. As he was banking right, he saw the first missile on his left as it went past him.   Coming around, Rooster One saw the Mig banking to the right and waited for a good tone to fire.   Unaware that there were two hostiles in the area, the Mig pilot came around to line up on Rooster Two intent on taking him out.   Rooster One, finally getting a lock on tone, fired his second missile at the Mig, The Mig pilot, heard the lock on tone in his helmet and for the first time realized that there were two hostiles he was up against.   Caught by surprise, he tried to bank right once more but to no avail, the heat seeker had a good tone on the Mig-31, and even with all the banking and jinking, the Mig couldn't shake the missile. The missile corrected itself from the Mig banking right and came around from behind and hit the engine of the Mig, destroying the back half of the aircraft. The pilot was able to eject from the Mig and after popping his shoot, rode the parachute to the ground, still searching the sky above him, never knowing what or who had shot him down.

The Delta team leader, seeing the parachute and a man hanging from it, sent two of his men to recover the pilot. He turned around and looked at the man lying on the ground next to him and had him stand up. He took the picture that he had been given from his vest pocket and verified that it was Dr. Salaam. Once this had been confirmed, he started asking him questions, "How many more of these compounds are there?"

Dr. Salaam, still in a state of shock, didn't understand what the team leader was asking. The team leader asked again, "Are there any more compounds like this around here?"

This time, hearing what he was being asked answered, "No more compounds."

"Where did you get your technology to build the bio-weapons, doctor?"

"We made them from scratch, from samples we received from Russia, North Korea, and other countries."

"Where is the bio-weapons compound in Iraq?"

"In one of the old palaces built by Saddam Hussein while he was in power, located near the outskirts of Baghdad."

"Where in Baghdad is it located?"

"I do not know; I've never been there."

"Do you have any more bio-weapons here in Iran?"

"No, you blew up our only stockpile of bio-weapons, except for what is in the bunkers that are located on the north side of the compound."

"What about the missiles that carry the bio-weapons?"

"They are located inside the bunkers as well, near the power plant."

With all of the team leader's questions answered by the doctor and having no more to ask, the team leader pulled his gun out and shot the Dr. Salaam through the forehead and left his body lying on the ground. He then ordered his men to kill the others that had survived the building being blown up. He now looked at his men to make sure they were ready and called for the choppers to come in to take them out. As the helicopters were coming into the landing zone the two men that had been sent out to get the downed pilot, came running up to their team lead half carrying the pilot. "What do we do with him?" One of the men asked.

Within minutes the helicopters could be heard coming in to extract the Delta Force team out of Iran. The team lead, not wanting to leave any clues as to what had happened at the compound, handcuffed the pilot and had him loaded into one of the helicopters. As the two F-35s flew top cover, the HH-60 helicopters left Iranian airspace, being escorted by Apache helicopters.   Once they were all finally airborne and on their way back to their own compound in Afghanistan, the team lead realized that there were no injuries to report and with Dr. Salaam having been terminated with prejudice, as well as the other chemists and their assistants, he smiled to himself for having completed the mission without losing any of his team.   He also knew that, for all practical purposes, the Iranian government was out of business when it came to manufacturing more bio-weapons, that is until the other nations with the same goals as Iran would start to help them rebuild it again. This time, it would take a few more years to do it, and a more brains to create the missing information from scratch.

The bunkers that were located on the north end of the compound were left to the Israelis to take out. This would occur in the near future by Mossad, with the help of the CIA who had provided the Intel for them to use. With the report from Delta Force, the Israeli's would be setting up a search to find Iraq's bio-weapons compound near Baghdad.

Out in the desert at the U.S. Embassy Richard read the after-action reports that had been generated by the Department of Defense and smiled knowing that he had been part of it.

Chapter XVI

The submarine slowly raised itself off the floor of the gulf of Oman Straight and leveled off when it reached the depth of 60 feet below the surface. The submarine's commander raised the periscope and did a complete sweep around the area. Seeing nothing, he gave the command, "Take us down to 100 feet."

"Aye, aye, captain, 100 feet."

In a few minutes the submarine had leveled off at 100 feet. At this depth the submarine was able to stay submerged and remain unnoticed by the harbor security patrol boats. Upon hearing the helmsman's report, the commander gave the signal for the Seal Team to start exiting out of the escape hatch of the submarine. At this depth the Seals, with their air tanks on, could leave the submarine without killing themselves.   The Seals quietly made their way to the submarines and surface ships that were docked in the harbor at Bandar-e-Abbas. Each Seal brought with them six limpet mines with timers set up to delay the mines going off before they sailed into deeper water. Each of them placed their magnetic mines on the hull of each of the surface ships. The 12 submarines that were berthed there in the port were boarded by teams of two Seals. Waiting patiently, the Seals wearing gas masks, were able to board the submarines by causing a chemical gas distraction using sulfur and methane, which cleared the guards that were posted on the submarines. With the decks cleared, they were then able to go in and plant their bombs in and around the torpedo room. Once they were done and the air cleared, the guards returned back to their posts not knowing what had caused it. After having completed their part of the mission, each Seal returned to the prearranged meeting place and dived to where the submarine was and crawled back into the escape tube of the submarine.

Once everyone was accounted for, the submarine commander quietly let the submarine sink deeper into the water of the harbor, guiding it slowly back out into the open water of the Strait of

Hormuz.   While they had been submerged in the harbor, two decoys had been placed strategically by the Seal team earlier, close to the opening of the harbor.   They were placed there to create noise on the sonar equipment of the patrol boats that protected the harbor.   The commander turned on the decoys by a remote switch. The Iranian Navy patrol boat commanders, not knowing what it was and thinking they were under attack, immediately contacted the Harbor Master.   Realizing that the ships in the port would be sitting ducks during an attack, the Harbor Master alerted the ships captains of an impending attack and had them fire up their engines to get them safely out of the harbor.

As the Iranian ships made their way through the harbor and into open water, the limpet mines that were attached to the ships started blowing up, sinking all of their surface ships that were able to leave the harbor.   The Iranian submarines slowly moved through the harbor and into open water, diving as they went. Their underwater explosions could be heard on the sonar and other listening devices aboard the American submarine. With each explosion the XO marked his note pad to count them. Within an hour, two thirds of the Iranian Navy lay on the bottom of the gulf in the deeper part of the channel, never returning to the surface again, simply because the gulf was too deep to salvage any of the ships that had been sunk. The final count by the XO was 15 surface ships sunk and 12 submarines sunk. Of the 15 surface ships that sank, five of the ships were frigates, two brand new destroyers, two missile boats, one helicopter carrier, five fast attack craft.   Of the submarines that were destroyed, ten of them were Kilo class submarines, one Nahang-1, and the Ghadir midget submarine. By all estimates, approximately 1000 to 1200 men were lost at sea trying to keep the ships out of harm's way.   As the American submarine slowly headed out to deeper water, the Iranian patrol boats found the unmarked noise makers.   After closer inspection, they could see Russian and Iranian instructions written on the side of the casing.

At the United Nations Building a protest was filed by the Iranian and the Russian governments against the United States, Great Britain, and Israel for attacking Iran, destroying their Navy, and their medical compound. Of course, all of the nations that Iran had filed against denied knowing anything about what had happened. The worst of it was, there was no proof that any nation had done it, except Russia and Iran. Thus, leaving Iran totally frustrated by the whole mess. Unbeknownst to the world, Iran would not get the technical support needed for rebuilding their bio-weapons program from their allies, for fear their own brain pool would be wiped out as well, in a similar style attack.

The final nail in the coffin for Iran, was when the United States and Israel brought forward at the United Nations conference, undeniable proof of Iran's involvement with Russia in the development of Anthrax and other bio-weapons for military use that were being developed in that same medical compound, that somehow mysteriously had been destroyed. The Iranian representative to the United Nations was silent, knowing that if he confirmed or denied the accusations by the US and Israel, the world of public opinion would be against Iran and their allies.

Russia reacted by sabre rattling a little, by flying their bomber missions closer to the American border near Alaska and along the east coasts. They also had their Intel ships sail closer to the shores of America, doing the same thing to American allies as well, to show they were not afraid of America and her friends. That being said, nobody wanted to start World War III over Iran or the Middle East, knowing that no super power would win the war, even if one side went nuclear in which case, the other side would retaliate in kind as well. This would end in a proverbial stalemate, sometimes known as a cold war, between the two superpowers. The U.S. and Russia knew that this was another move in a game of chess being played by them, trying to win the game in subtle moves on the chessboard of the world by using fanatics from third world countries to pull the trigger. With the news coverage of the terrorists in court, and with what had happened in Iran, as far as their Navy ships being sunk and the bio-weapons compound being destroyed, the Iranians were strangely quiet about all of the world press they had been receiving lately. And when asked about what had happened to their facilities for developing medicine, they refused to answer any questions about it. Within days their security forces were looking for the spy that had caused the sinking of their Navy.

As Iran's Ayatollah contemplated all that had happened in his country over the last three months, he tallied everything up and then called the Prime Minister in to ask him some questions about all of what had transpired. The Prime Minister knocked on the door and waited to be allowed to come in.

From inside he heard the Ayatollah call out, "Enter."

"You sent for me, Marja?"

"Are you aware of what has happened to our country lately?"

"Yes, I am, Marja," the Prime Minister answered quietly.

"What are you planning to do about it?"

"We must redouble our efforts to attack America and her allies, to teach them a lesson."

"And, what about our Navy?"

"We must rebuild using our resources and buy what we can from our friends."

"Have you started on this endeavor?"

"Yes, we have. We will be building a better facility that will be built completely underground, so that no one will know that it exists."

"Will our friends help us in this?"

"I'm sure they will once everything quiets down," the Prime Minister said confidently.

"Very good, you may leave."

"Yes Marja."

After the Prime Minister left, the Ayatollah called for one of his chief officers to come in. Upon arriving the officer asked, "What is it you wish, Marja?"

"I want you to keep an eye on our friend the Prime Minister and make sure he's doing his job. If he doesn't you know what to do. We cannot afford any more of this kind of embarrassment to our country."

"Yes, Marja, I understand," he then turned away to go find the Prime Minister.

When the Prime Minister left the palace, he knew that he was in trouble and on borrowed time. He knew that he must do everything in his power to rebuild what had been destroyed. He remembered what had happened to his predecessor who he had replaced, the man did not take it seriously enough to make things right according to the Marja. He was replaced and no one knows where he disappeared to. Calling on the members of his cabinet for an emergency meeting to get things started, he was determined not to disappoint or disappear into the night.

151

Chapter XVII

Tony was still thinking about the piece of metal that they had found near the USS Dolphin at the bottom of the ocean. The fact that it was of Russian origin and that they used it to build torpedoes for the Iranian Navy, wasn't a surprise and was considered normal under any kind of situation. The United States had been assisting Israel by selling military hardware and the latest technology to their government in order to level the playing field in the Middle East, even before Nixon took office.   As the old saying goes 'War is good business for the buyers and sellers of the merchandise'. The problem is, that the other countries that did business with our adversary's weren't too particular about who they sold to. Lunatics who embrace war for power and control of their country at any cost, are always dangerous not only to themselves but to everyone around them.

Tony had a piece of a torpedo that was developed in Russia with Iranian writing on it, the question on his mind was what to do about it.   From what he knew, Iran was out of the loop when it came to bio-weapons, leastwise, that's what Tony got from the newspapers and the news networks. The problem was, aside from Iran, how many other countries had this same capability to sneak up on a submarine and launch a torpedo on a unsuspecting US Navy submarine and cripple it.

He quickly glanced again through the final reports on the USS Dolphin incident that had been prepared by the investigation team and submitted to him and the Admiral.   Their conclusion suggested that, although the damage was minimal, it should be a primary concern that the Dolphin didn't know it was even being tracked, or for that matter, being shot at.   He wondered, *"Did someone have a stealthier submarine than we did, or maybe was it just a lucky shot for the bad guys?"* Tony wanted to know the answer to those questions and needed to know it quickly.   He realized that if the enemy had this kind of technology that it would change everything when it came to underwater warfare for the United States. He decided to take the report home so that he would have more time to digest the information and maybe come up with answers for his meeting tomorrow with the Admiral.

The next afternoon found Tony getting ready to meet the Admiral once again to discuss the final report for the USS Dolphin incident. He knew that the Admiral would have questions and he hoped he had the answers. Ann led Tony into the Admiral's office, bringing in a cup of coffee for the Admiral with her. The Admiral was on the phone at his desk and motioned for Tony to sit down. Tony nodded and took a seat, waiting for the Admiral to finish his call. After hanging up the phone, the Admiral looked at Tony and smiled, "What's going on that you're here bothering me again?"

"Have you had a chance to look at the final report yet?"

"Oh, that's right. We did have a meeting scheduled this afternoon, didn't we?"

"Yes, sir. I've been researching the piece of metal from the torpedo we found near the Dolphin."

"Yes, I remember. What about it?"

"I was thinking about how an enemy submarine could get so close to the Dolphin without being seen or heard and then launch a torpedo at it, without the skipper of the ship knowing about it?"

"What are you suggesting Tony? the Admiral asked, as he considered his question.

"I'm thinking, the bad guys have come up with a new type of technology that we haven't seen before. I don't think that it was a lucky shot that caused the Dolphin to sink, sir."

The Admiral thought about this for a minute, and slowly thought out loud, "I wonder if that could be true. What have you found so far?"

"Nothing really, sir. Just a hunch, my gut tells me we need to look into this a little closer. I think we need to go back over the final damage reports on the Dolphin to re-evaluate their conclusions."

"You know, I've heard some rumors that the Russians have come up with a new submarine that's considered invisible to sonar and any listening devices. Let me make a few calls to my Navy counterpart on the west coast and see what they might know. I should be able to tell you something shortly.   My secretary will call you as soon as I find out anything."

"Okay, I'll wait for your call.   In the meantime, I'll keep checking into my sources, as well."

"That works. Until then, good hunting and let me know if you find anything."

"Thank you for your time, sir."

As Tony left the Admiral's office, he leaned over and kissed Ann on the cheek.   "Am I going to see you tonight?" she asked.

"I'm afraid not.   This submarine incident has got me over a barrel right now.   Maybe if it's not too late I can come over later tonight."

"Come on over no matter what time it is. I'll be waiting."

"It's a date."

As he left the office and was sitting in his car, he wondered what he was going to check on and who with.   With all of the resources available to him, he didn't know where to start on this one. He had already gone through the damage reports sitting on his desk and really didn't know how to make heads or tails of all of it.   He needed to find someone, with a high enough clearance and the proper engineering background, to re-evaluate the final report. Maybe looking at it with a fresh set of eyes and a different perspective, they might be able to pick up on something that he or the investigating team had missed.

As he started up his car, the first thought that came to him about who he might talk to that would understand any of the damage reports, would be his friend Chance. He decided to give him a call as he drove back to his office.   Fortunately, he caught him while he was still at his office, "Hey Chance, this is Tony, can I come over and see you about these damage reports on the Dolphin?"

"Come on over, I'll be ready for those reports when you get here. Actually, why don't you plan on having dinner with us, that way we can go over the reports then?"

"Depends on what you're having," he replied with a chuckle.

"I'm thinking we're having steak with a chaser of cake afterwards."

"That sounds great.   About thirty minutes okay?"

"Fair enough, let me call my wife to let her know and I'll see you then."

After ending the call, Tony wondered if Chance would be able to decipher these reports for him, he would just have to wait and see. Even if Chance couldn't find anything, it would be a opportunity to get together with his friends and have some good home cooking from Helen, and boy could she cook.

After dinner was done and all the pleasantries were said about dinner, both Chance and Tony headed into the den. As they sat down, Tony explained, "What I'm thinking is, that there was another submarine with some kind of new technology, that could get close enough to damage the Dolphin, causing her to sink. I believe the Dolphin was already crippled by the torpedo that we found a piece of, before she exploded. I'm not sure of the sequence of events in any of this.   All I know for sure, is that a submarine went down."

"What makes you say that?" Chance asked, as he sat and listened.

"I'm not really sure about this, but I think the Dolphin was attacked by a submarine that was, how you say, stealthier than anything we have seen before." Handing the reports to Chance for his review of the data, he continued, "I believe the hole in the submarine may have happened after the Dolphin had started sinking."

"Oh really," Chance said, as he started scanning the reports.

"I don't know, just a feeling in the middle of my gut keeps nagging me about the way we found the torpedo."

"What do you want me to do?"

"I can't make heads or tails of these damage reports and I need you to look at them and try and make sense of them for me. I know I'm asking you for a big favor, but something tells me that the Dolphin was attacked by another submarine that the skipper of the Dolphin wasn't even aware of, until it was too late.

"There's a rumor out there about a submarine that has new technology that makes the submarine stealthier than anyone knows about."

Tony's words caught Chance by surprise and got him thinking about what might be going on and who was behind it. Tony continued, "Granted, the explosion in the front of the submarine was enough to sink the Dolphin, however, that being said, I think that occurred after the fact of being attacked and crippled by another submarine."

"I've got to tell you, what you've told me has me concerned. You realize that this will change all of submarine warfare, right?"

"Yes, I've thought about that myself and I agree.   That's why I need you to go through these reports and give me your professional opinion. I know I'm asking for a lot, but I need you to review and confirm or deny my theory about this," Tony replied.

Chance continued scanning through the reports, "I'll need some time to go through all of this material. What are we looking at for a time frame, Tony?"

"I've already talked to the Admiral about my thoughts on what happened, and he said he would check with his sources to see what they had to say.   That all being said, the Admiral just said he was making it a top priority and would get back with me as soon as possible.   I figure it will take him a week to get some kind of answer."

"A week then, is that what you're saying?"

"That's the best I can give you on this. I would like to tell the Admiral something about this in my next meeting."

"Let me take a look at the reports and I'll get back to you soon as I can.   If I find anything out of the ordinary, it may be sooner than a week."

Tony looked at Chance as he let out a sigh of relief which he picked up on and chuckled, "You really believe that there is some kind of new technology out there?"

"I don't know what to think on this Chance, but we can't just let it go without checking.   I don't know if I'm right or wrong, all I know is I've got a gut feeling on this one."

"Well, let me look into these reports.   Maybe, just maybe, I'll be able to find something in the reports that confirms your feelings on this."

"Thanks Chance, I know I'm asking a lot on this. That being said, at least I can sleep a little better knowing you had a look into the reports."

After the discussion had ended, Helen came into the den, "Do either of you have any room for some of my home-made apple pie for dessert?"

Tony looked at Chance, "Yes ma'am, that sounds good! I believe I do have some room left for some of your pie. Could you maybe put a scoop of ice cream with it?"

"Yes, I think we just might have some in the freezer," she replied, and then looked at Chance.

"I know I do, besides, what's one more lap around the track for me?   Can I have a scoop of ice cream to?" Chance added.

"I think I have just enough ice cream for Tony, I don't know if there will be enough for you to," she chuckled.

"Do you mean we're going to have to fight over it?"   Tony asked, smiling.

"So, how bad did you want these reports looked over?   What's it worth to you?"

"Okay, you win.   Dirty, real dirty," Tony laughed.

After they were finished with their dessert, Tony looked at his watch and realized that it was later than he thought. "Wow look how late it is, I must be off.   It's been a wonderful evening, thank you for having me over and for your excellent pie, Helen.   Even though I didn't get any ice cream."   To which everyone laughed. Chance walked with Tony out to his car. When they reached his car Chance said, "I should know something about what your concerns are, hopefully, in the next few days."

"That'll be fine.   In one way, I hope I'm wrong in all of this."

"And if you're not? What then?"

"I guess we'll cross that bridge when we get to it."

"Well, until then, good night."

"Good night, Chance."

As Tony drove away into the night, Chance started thinking about his concerns dealing with a new invisible submarine with silent torpedoes and such.   He chuckled at the idea of a submarine with a cloaking device that could move through the water like a spaceship moves through space. Kind of like a Bird of Prey from Star Trek. As he shook his head, he wondered if it could be possible for such a thing to be created, knowing that his Thresher was capable of everything that he was thinking about.

Tony looked at his watch again and remembered what Ann had said about coming over. He picked up his phone, "Ann it's Tony, is it too late come over?"

"No, by all means come on over. I've got the popcorn all buttered and a movie we can watch."

"Oh good. What's the name of the movie?"

"Pride and Prejudice.   It's the latest version."

"Oh, be still my beating heart. My favorite movie," Tony said, after a long pause.

"It was either that or Rambo, I wanted you to be able to get in touch with your feminine side" she said, with a chuckle.

"Just my luck.   Now, my self-esteem is under attack. See you in a few."

Chapter XVIII

Bright and early the next day, Chance had already started going over the damage reports, and as he did so he would write down his thoughts on a piece of paper to either agree with the findings or put a question mark next to their conclusions in the report.   At the end of his second day of reading the reports, his findings were evenly stacked, with each half showing either correct findings or questions about their findings.   After doing another check on the areas that he had concerns about, he wasn't sure what to make of them. The reports showed some kind of anomaly dealing with the way the spine of the submarine had been bent and yet the damage was superficial. It was like somebody being slapped in the face, but you didn't see it happen all you could see was the red mark where the person had been hit. It was obvious, but at the same time, there was no physical damage done, or so it appeared.

When Tony got to his office the next morning, he was feeling a little sluggish after getting in late the night before.   He grabbed another cup of coffee, hoping that it would wake him up so he could function the rest of the day.   The two NCIS agents, Davis and Kelly, watched their boss as he went to get his second cup of coffee. "You have a long night sir?" Kelly asked, with a smile.

"Is it that obvious?"

"Ain't love grand." Davis chuckled.

Tony made his way back to his desk and sat down to go through his email traffic.   As there wasn't anything that needed his immediate attention, he decided to go to the lead investigators office to ask him some questions about the final report on the Dolphin incident.   He picked up the phone and dialed the lead investigator's number. "Hi, this is Commander Jones, I was wondering if you had time for me to come over and visit with you about your final report on the USS Dolphin?"   Tony said, when the lead investigator answered the phone.

"By all means.   What's your schedule look like?"

"I'm pretty much open all day."

"Okay, how 'bout we meet in half an hour?

"Works for me.   I'll see you in a few then."

When it was time to go, Tony took his coffee with him and drove over to meet with the investigator.   When he got there the investigator was already waiting for him and led him into his office.

As he sat down Tony asked, "In all of your investigation, did you happen to come across the captain's log?"

"Yes, it was found in the captain's quarters, among all the debris. We were finally able to dry it out and fortunately, were able to read it" replied the lead investigator.

"Can I review it for myself?"

Tony watched as the investigator rummaged through his desk and thought to himself, *"And I thought I was the only one that couldn't find anything on my desk,"* he chuckled.   The investigator eventually found the notebook that cataloged all of the things that were found by the engineers while they were completing their evaluations of the submarine.   He held it up in his hand and smiled, showing it to Tony.   He then opened the notebook up and started going through the pages, looking for the location of the Captains log. Finding it, he got up and walked over to a filing cabinet, pulled the middle drawer open and reached in and grabbed the Captain's personal logbook. He returned to his desk and handed the Captain's log to Tony, "It's in pretty good shape for being under the water. Fortunately, we found a way to dry out the logbook by using the old microwave oven. It's pretty tedious to do because it has to be done page by page. After signing for the logbook, Tony headed back to his office to read it and try to find some clue that would prove his theory about what had happened in the last few moments of the submarine.

Grabbing another cup of coffee and making himself comfortable, he started skimming through the pages, beginning with the last couple days in the logbook.   On one of the pages he came across something that caught his eye. It seemed that there had been a problem with the acoustic systems aboard the submarine. In fact, it was mentioned two or three times in the captain's log, and it seemed to get worse in the final days of the Dolphin. The captain stated that the issues were of unknown origin and would last for about an hour and then disappear. It seemed that the skipper had his radar man go through diagnostics on all of his equipment every time the acoustics would start acting up.   Being unable to find anything that was causing the problem, he wrote it down as a glitch in the equipment to be fixed on the next refit.

As Tony pondered on the Captain's log, he wondered if maybe the captain was picking something up but not knowing what it was and had considered it to be a malfunction of the equipment. As he pondered on this thought, he was tempted to call Chance and let him read the log.   Maybe the equipment was picking up something that hadn't been observed before, leastwise, till now. Maybe it was an acoustical signature that was unrecognizable because it was different from all of the cataloged sounds that were stored on the submarine. Maybe the new submarine had a totally different sound signature due its propulsion system. Maybe it wasn't powered by diesel or a nuclear reactor. Maybe the Russians had found a new power source to use and were testing it against the Dolphin to see if it could detect it. If that was the case, it would change the balance of power in the grand scheme of things.   As he leaned back in his chair and took a sip of his coffee, he thought, *Too many questions, not enough answers.*

Tony went back to the lead engineer's office and showed him the captain's log, "Do you have any idea about what the captain was dealing with when it came to the acoustic issues he was having onboard the Dolphin?"

When the engineer saw Tony's concern he replied, "I'm not sure, let me look on my computer.   It's usually part of our investigation to check the electronics, to see if there was anything that would indicate any kind of problems."

He went over to his computer to find the appropriate file that had the submarine's electronic test results.   As he pulled up the report on the computer, he found that what was left of the acoustics on board the submarine was in pretty bad shape, simply because it had been on the bottom for so long. The engineer that had evaluated the electronics, had stated in the report that all of the acoustic systems and the sonar had been fried from the sea water that got inside that portion of the submarine.   Tony thought about this for a moment, "Is it possible that the electronics was fried before the water got to it?"

The engineer looked at the report, "Well, let me take a quick look here. According to what he's written, there is no indication one way or the other. Let's call the man who did the evaluation on the equipment."

With that he picked up the phone and called the engineer to come over. About fifteen minutes later the engineer showed up at the lead engineer's office. "You wanted to see me?" Bill asked.

"As a matter of fact, we did. Can you tell by the wiring on the submarine if the electronics were fried before or after the water got to it?" the lead engineer asked.

"Funny you should mention that, I wondered about that myself. I've always thought that fried wiring would react differently when it's touched by water. The wiring aboard the Dolphin looked like it was cooked before the water got to it."

"What would cause the wiring on the submarine to fry its electronic systems?" Tony asked.

"In this case, it could be an overload on the system from within the submarine, however, the fuses would blow first before the electronics would be destroyed. Or maybe an overload of the acoustics from outside the submarine, something similar to a very powerful signal that could electronically jam the listening systems. In that case, it would fry the acoustics. It would make the submarine blind and deaf in the water and basically helpless."

"Could the submarine recover from that type of jamming or frying?" Tony asked.

"It's hard to say, it depends on how quick they were able to replace the boxes with the right equipment and re-tune the system. If it was a phased array jamming, or in other words, jamming multiple frequencies at the same time, it wouldn't make a difference to the acoustics. The submarine would still be deaf and blind in the water, no matter how many backup systems you have on board."

"Is it possible to build a system like that on a submarine?" asked the lead engineer.

"Yes, I think so. We have been testing something like this for quite some time now, in hopes of being able to put it on board our submarines."

"How about the Russians being able to do the same thing on board their submarines?" asked the lead engineer.

"Yes, but only on the more modern submarines in their inventory. The weight of the system is the number one reason we haven't put it on our submarines as of yet."

"How far are we away from doing it ourselves for our submarines?" asked Tony.

"At least a year, maybe two, depending how fast our technology grows."

Both Tony and the lead engineer looked at each other, thinking about the implications of what Bill had said.

"With what you've said, I'm wondering if the Russians are ahead of us in this race of technology." Tony stated.

"I wonder if that's the case. Well Bill, you've been very helpful. Thank you for your time."

"You're welcome," as he got up to leave, he asked Tony, "Would you be interested seeing what we've been testing, once we get it set up?"

"Yes, that would be great.   Please let me know when and where, and I'll try to be there."

"Fair enough," Bill said as he left to go back to his office.

"If what Bill says is correct, we have just opened a can of worms that I don't think we can close."   Tony said, as he and the engineer watched Bill leave.

"I pray that Bill is wrong on this one."

Chapter XIX

After getting back to his office, Tony called Chance and got his voice mail and after hearing the beep he left a message, "Hey Chance, I've just come across some new information about the USS Dolphin and it may have something to do with her sinking. I need to meet with you as soon as possible."

As he ended the call, he sat there trying to decide whether to tell the Admiral about what he had learned from his discussion with the electronics engineer regarding the USS Dolphin. After thinking on it, he decided to wait until he had better information to offer the Admiral in order to make a better decision about the submarine fleet. Tony didn't want to come off as a conspiracy nut in front of the Admiral, leastwise, not until he had something more tangible to prove his conspiracy theories. At this point, everything was still in the air as to what happened to the USS Dolphin. Only time would tell if there were any connections to what he thought and what really happened.

In order to gather more information to support his theory, his next stop would be to the Intelligence section where the SigInt (Signals Intelligence) personnel would be listening for anything out of the ordinary in communication chatter from countries of interest that was picked up on the day the Dolphin went down.   After that, his next stop would be to check with the radio people operating the ELF (Extra Low Frequency) system to see if they had picked up anything of value on the day the Dolphin went missing.   That all being said, it would all have to wait till tomorrow before he could make the phone calls to arrange a meeting with the right people. For tonight, the best he could hope for was a visit with Chance, not only to tell him what he had learned, but also to learn what he had gotten from the reports.

As he sat at his desk, Tony checked his phone messages, wondering what he was going to do now.   Chance had called back and left a message, "Sorry I missed your call. How about we get together tomorrow morning around 8:00? Unfortunately, that's the only time I have available to get together and discuss the report with you. If I don't hear from you, I'll assume it's a go. Okay then, hope to talk to you tomorrow."

After hearing Chance's message, Tony looked at his watch and decided there was nothing more that could be done tonight. He picked up the phone again and called Ann to see what she was doing. "Hi beautiful, what's up?"

"I'm just checking my self-esteem and thinking about you."

"I hope their good thoughts. I was just wondering if you wanted to get together tonight for dinner?"

"Your favorite place?"

"Doesn't have to be. We could go somewhere else."

"I've a better idea, why don't you pick up some steaks and bring them to my place and we'll cook them here."

"Oh, okay. What about dessert?"

"I think I can come up with something."

"Sounds like a plan. I'll pick up the steaks and be right over."

"Okay, love. See you soon."

Hearing her reply, he sat there thinking about that word 'love'. He had been so busy with all that was going on and just spending time with her that it never crossed his mind about his feelings for her. He smiled to himself, thinking about all the time they had been spending together and how much it meant to him to have someone he could go to and be able to be himself around. Still smiling and a little nervous, he realized that he felt the same way as she did. With those thoughts lingering in his mind, he got up from his desk and closed up shop. He looked around and realized how empty the place had become since Davis and Kelly had gone back to their office after having closed out their portion of the investigation with the capture of the terrorists.

The next morning Tony met with Chance and told him about what he had learned about the submarine acoustics, "There's a possibility that the acoustic's wiring systems were fried before the water got to them. I'm thinking that the bad guys have a jump on us in using a jammer of sorts to make the submarine deaf."

Chance thought about what Tony had said and before adding his thoughts, he shuffled through one of the damage reports, skimming through the pages, looking for a specific paragraph. Upon finding it, Chance read the paragraph to Tony, "The hull of the submarine had become pliable due to something that had broken down the molecular structure of the hull, causing the metal of the hull to lose its structural integrity, something akin to metal fatigue. With this change in the hull, it would make the submarine prone to the inward pressure brought about by the depth of the water surrounding the hull."

Tony sat and listened to what Chance had read aloud to him, trying to figure out what it meant. He looked at Chance, "What does that all mean?"

"It means that someone has found a way to use ultrasonic weapons underwater to destroy the hulls of submarines. And with the barrage jamming on the acoustics system, including sonar, it renders the submarine useless in the water and susceptible to water pressure, crushing the hull of the submarine in very little water, even at depths we consider safe for submarines.   It's like packing a one two punch, you knock the fighter senseless by taking out their sensors, then you hit them with an ultrasonic device to destroy the hull of the ship, thereby causing it to rupture and sink. In the Dolphin's case, evidently the ultrasonic weapon wasn't strong enough to rupture the hull. I'm thinking they used a torpedo to destroy the submarine, hoping that it would hide the new weapon."

"Who would have that kind of technology?"

"Not sure at this point.   However, that being said, we have been trying to harness an ultrasonic weapon of our own for the last couple of years ourselves."

"It looks as if someone has beaten us to it. Who would have that kind of technology available?"

"I'm figuring the Russians, or the Chinese have come up with it, and maybe decided to test it on one of our submarines."

"That's a pretty bold move on their part, don't you think?"

"Pretty gutsy, I would say. We need to find out who did it and where it is, so we can either destroy it or steal it from them."

With that Chance called his secretary, "Cancel all of my meetings for the day and if anyone should ask, tell them something has come up and it can't be helped."

"We need to see the Admiral pronto, I take it?"   Tony asked.

"This changes everything when it comes to fighting underwater. Our submarine fleet is useless until we have the same capability or are at least able to destroy their capability."

Tony and Chance drove to the Admiral's office and told Ann that they needed to see the Admiral immediately.   She looked at Tony and Chance and could see that they were serious. Before she got up from her desk, she wrote a message down on a piece of paper to hand to the Admiral. She then got up from her desk and walked into the Admiral's office and waited for a break in the meeting that he was having.   The Admiral, seeing his secretary standing there, paused for a moment so that she could give him a note saying that Tony and Chance were outside and that it was urgent that they speak with him. The Admiral raised his eyes toward his secretary and nodded to her. After a minute he came out of his office and saw Tony and Chance standing there, "You brought reinforcements, did you?" he said looking at Tony.

Tony smiled, "First of all, I apologize for interrupting your meeting.   However, we both feel that this is important for you to hear. We have found out something new about what had happened to the Dolphin, sir."

"We think the Dolphin may have been destroyed by a new weapon that renders the submarine deaf and blind in the water.   Then, while it is in this state, a different kind of weapon, using ultrasonics, destroys the hull of the submarine, causing it to sink, even in shallow water," Chance said.

The Admiral stood there listening, "Now it all makes sense. Some of our Intel says that our bad guy friends have been experimenting on a new technology that, supposedly, would change the undersea battles for all involved. Give me a minute to break up the meeting and I'll be right back."

The Admiral then looked at his secretary, "Call Jimmy over in the Intel shop and have him come over, stat."

After five minutes of waiting, the men filed out of the Admirals office and headed out the door.   By now Jimmy was on his way to the Admiral's office, wondering what was so important.

After having everybody come into his office and being seated, the Admiral turned the time over to Chance and Tony to let them explain what they had learned about the sinking of the USS Dolphin.

Tony started off, "First of all, after reviewing the photos of the hull of the USS Dolphin, I noticed that there was a crease that ran the length of the submarine. After doing some more checking, I contacted Chance and had him look over the reports to get his opinion as to what might have happened."

"After going over the findings of the investigating team, some questions have come up that indicated that there was more going on than previously thought," Chance added.

After they explained the details of what they had found out through their own investigation, Tony and Chance sat there waiting for either Jimmy or the Admiral to say something. At this point, Jimmy looked at the Admiral, nodded his head and smiled.

"Jimmy, why don't you go ahead and share your thoughts about what you have learned since the Dolphin sank," said the Admiral.

"You two are absolutely correct on your assumptions and I'm impressed that you found out about it. At one hour past midnight on the 30th of January, the ELF picked up a burst of energy coming from the direction of the USS Dolphin, or at least where we think she was. After the burst of energy, we never heard from the Dolphin again, leastwise, until Chance here, found her lying on the bottom of the sea. Right after the burst, we heard another sound that we didn't recognize, simply because it had never been recorded before. After some analysis, we figured it was some kind of weapon that could create sound waves in the water, strong enough to render the Dolphin useless," Jimmy said.

The Admiral waited for this new information to sink in before speaking. "And you guys have stumbled upon a new weapon, that not only destroys our submarines and surface ships, but changes the playing field for all of us in the submarine business."

Tony looked at Chance, who in turn looked at the Admiral.   The look on Chance's face said it all, without saying a word, the question was, *What do we do now?"*

"The first thing we need to do is find out who did this to the Dolphin and either destroy the technology or steal it from them, preferably the latter of the two options," the Admiral said.

"We're all in agreement in this. The question is, where do we go from here?" Jimmy said.

"Go back down to where the Dolphin was and look around for anything that'll give us a clue as to who did this. There has to be something down there that will tell us something. Chance, we need you on this one.   Can you help us, or better yet, will you help us?"

"Count me in on this one.   I have only one request, and that is, we need to make sure no other sound signature was picked up in the same area where the Dolphin went down. If there was, we need to put that information into my computer on board the Thresher, just in case we find it."

The Admiral looked at Jimmy, "Was there any other signature or noise besides the Dolphin down there?"

"We picked up a faint signal that we couldn't identify, that may be the signature of the attacking submarine. The problem is, it's one we've never heard before. In other words, we've never heard it before or since."

"Can you get me a copy of it so I can load it up into my acoustics computer and have it, just in case?   Besides, maybe we can track the signal to where it came from and find its resting place," Chance replied.

"I'll bring a copy of it to you in about an hour, will that work?" Jimmy asked.

"That'll be fine."

With that, Jimmy left the meeting.   As the Admiral and the other two left his office, he looked at Chance and Tony, "I know I don't need to tell you that this is very important and there's lot at risk. You need to find this new weapon before it takes out another one of our subs."

Tony looked at the Admiral, understanding the gravity of the situation.   "We'll find it, and if necessary, destroy it."

"Good enough for me, good luck on your hunting."

Both Chance and Tony left the building. "I hope we can find this submarine before it finds us," Chance said, as they rode back together.

"You and me both. That being said, my moneys on you."

"Thanks for the vote of confidence."

When Chance got back to his office, he called the crew of his submarine and had them meet him at the dock so they could get the Thresher ready for another dive. True to his word, Jimmy showed up within the hour with the thumb drive, having the sound bites to be downloaded onto the Thresher's computer. After the sound bites were loaded, he checked the computer to verify that the signals were loaded correctly. Jimmy looked at Tony and Chance after he finished checking the computer, "Everything checks out fine, your good to go.   Good hunting and bring us back a big fish."

Tony laughed, "We'll do our best not to disappoint you on that."

As Tony watched Jimmy leave, he looked at Chance, "It seems to me that the home team is counting on us in this one, what do you think?"

"You get that impression too, I thought it was just me feeling that way."

Both of them laughed at the statement and continued helping to load boxes onto the Thresher. Tony looked at all of the boxes that were being carried onboard.   "What's in all these boxes?"

"These boxes are carrying extra backup parts; in case we lose our acoustics going against the submarine that took out the Dolphin."

"Good thinking, I guess that's why they pay you the big bucks."

Chance nodded and smiled, "Sometimes that's not enough."

"Amen, brother, Amen."

With the submarine prepped and ready to go, Tony and Chance climbed aboard the Thresher to begin their search for the other submarine. As they headed back to where the Dolphin was last known to be working, Chance guided the Thresher into the area and turned on all of the sensors, looking for the unknown submarine. Using the faint signal Jimmy had provided them, they now began fishing for the enemy.   This was the tedious part of the job, looking for a needle in the haystack or maybe a better analogy, would be looking for a single goldfish in the ocean and not knowing where to look for it. As the hours wore on, the Thresher approached the area where the remains of the Dolphin were found. Using this as a reference point, Chance started using a different pattern to comb the area.   From there they circled the area in ever widening circles, as they looked for the faint signal. Both Tony and Chance were watching the sensors, hoping to catch something that would be similar to the faint signal that was loaded onto the shipboard computer. On one pass they thought they had found the signal, but after viewing the area it was found to be and underwater chimney giving off its plume of smoke and heat. Chance marked the area for later exploration, telling Tony that this was a one of a kind find for the science community who studied the animal life around the opening of the heat and gas.

As they continued their search, they were still unable to find anything. After ten hours of looking, Chance decided to call off the search and head back to base. Having had no luck in finding anything the first day, they continued their search for two more days in different areas east of the crash site. All the while, still finding nothing that even came close to the signal they were looking for. Finally, realizing that after three days there was nothing out there to track, Chance looked at Tony, "Well, what do you think, should we continue or call it off?"

"I don't know what to do at this point; it could be we're looking in the wrong area. With that being said, I don't know where the right area is."

Chance nodded his head in agreement, "Let's head back and check with Jimmy to see if any new information has been found since we started on this adventure."

When they pulled up to the pier and tied off the Thresher, both Tony and Chance headed to Chance's office to check for any messages and make a phone call to the Admiral.

As they listened to the messages Chance had received, there was one message from the Admiral. Something about some new information that dealt with another submarine sinking. Chance picked up the phone and gave the Admiral a call, "It's Chance, I got your message.   What's up?"

"When can you two come by my office?" the Admiral asked,

"We can be there in 20 minutes."

"That'll be fine, I'll be waiting for you."

When they arrived at the Admiral's office, they walked in and saw that the only light on was in his office and that Ann had already gone home for the day.   As they made their way into his office, they could see that he was studying an undersea map of the Atlantic ridge. The Admiral, surprised by their appearance, stood up to greet them. After asking Tony to close the door to the office, he sat back down, "We found out that another submarine was sunk. Fortunately, this time it was a Soviet sub. Our Intel guys picked up the same signal just before the submarine sank. The Russians are doing a sweep of the area, trying to find their submarine. So far, not so good. I'm thinking, from the looks of it, that it's too deep for them to locate. According to our Intel, we think the submarine went down somewhere in this area of the North American Basin," pointing at the map with his finger.

Chance looked at the map where the Admiral was pointing, "I know that area. If I remember correctly, they'll never find their submarine, it's too deep for anything they have searching for it."

"Do you think you can find it in your submarine?"

"I'm not sure, that area's pretty deep and on top of that, it's also known for its mountainous terrain and seismic activity. It may take some time to find it, and that's with no guarantee that we will find it."

"I guess we need to decide how much time we want to spend looking for the submarine," the Admiral stated.

Tony sat and listened to the two of them talk, "I suggest we get Jimmy back here to see if he can triangulate the signal to further define the search area for us."

The both of them thought that might be a good idea and grinned at Tony, "Sometimes it takes someone to think outside the box to find our way," said Chance.

The Admiral put in the call to Jimmy, "Do you think that with the noise of the signal you could get a more accurate location on the whereabouts of the Soviet submarine?"

"I'm not sure. Let me check into it and I'll call you back."

Thirty minutes later the Admiral's phone rang, he picked it up and listened to the voice on the other end. After listening intently for the duration of the call, the Admiral finally said, "Thank you for checking again."

He hung up the phone and looked at Tony and Chance, "That was Jimmy, as you have probably already guessed. He tells me that we got what we got and that's it."

Chance thought about taking the Thresher to the last known whereabouts of the Soviet submarine, "I'll do it, but I'm not expecting to find anything out there, simply because of the terrain of the trench."

"I know you just got back, however, how soon do you think that you'd be ready to go again?" the Admiral asked.

Looking at the map again, and doing some figuring inside his head, "Should be able to start in a couple of days. You want to go along on this one Tony?" Chance asked.

"In for the penny, in for the pound," he said after getting an approving nod from the Admiral.

"Good, I'll be leaving Tuesday morning and I'll meet you where we're parked now.   Now, if you'll excuse me, I've got some work to get done before we leave."

"I'll get you a car out front in a minute to get you back to your submarine," the Admiral said.

As Chance left the Admiral's office, Tony stood there and asked the Admiral, "If we find the Soviet submarine and see that the damage is the same as was on the Dolphin, where do we go from there?"

The Admiral thought about the question for a minute before answering, "Our goal here, is to determine who is doing this, and how to stop it from becoming a real problem for all concerned. With this in mind, we'll have to cross that bridge when we get to it."

"With all due respect, sir, what happens if we need to destroy it?"

"We do what we got to do.   Fortunately, we now know that it isn't the Russians doing this."

"Yes, sir, I agree."

Tony left the Admiral's office, and as he walked outside the building feeling exhausted, and needing someone to talk to he thought about calling Ann, wondering if it would be okay if he came over.   He dialed her number and waited for her to pick up.   Upon hearing her voice on the other end, he asked, "Can I come over?"

"Sure, please do.   I haven't seen you in a day or so."   Hearing the tired in his voice she asked, "Is there anything wrong?"

"No, I'm completely exhausted with all that's going on and I just need to talk to you."

"I'm glad you thought of me. I'm here for you. You know that don't you?"

"It sure feels good to know that.   I'll be right over."

When he got to her apartment, she met him with a kiss and a hug. And looking him over, she realized that he needed a shower to clean up.   She went into the bathroom and started the shower for him and when it was ready he went in and threw out his clothes as she handed him some oversized sweatpants and tee shirt to put on when he was done.   She took his clothes and put them in the washer.   "You just be glad that the water pressure is good here so that way you won't be surprised when the water turns on for the washer," she yelled out.

Oblivious to anything else, Tony let the warm water run down his back and let all of the tension and stress melt away, going down the drain with the water.   After about 10 minutes he felt like a new man again.   When he came out of the bathroom wearing the sweatpants and tee shirt, he looked at Ann, "Do these clothes make me look fat?" he asked with a smile.

She stood there speechless and laughed at Tony, "I just love my men in sweatpants."

Tony reached for her and held her in his arms, closing his eyes he whispered, "I love you."

Ann, hearing this replied, "I love you to."

Chapter XX

Tuesday morning came way too fast for Tony as he hustled to get everything squared away to make the trip with Chance and he found himself running late. So, he gave Chance a call, "Just to let you know I'm on my way so don't leave without me."

"We're running slow this morning also, not to worry, just get here when you can."

Fifteen minutes later, Tony showed up on the dock carrying a small bag of personal belongings with him. He walked over to where Chance was supervising the loading of some boxes that were marked fragile top and bottom, onto the Thresher. After making sure that the boxes were secured, Chance was now ready to get underway.

As they pulled away from the pier, Tony and Chance stood on the sail of the Thresher while Chance gave instructions to his crew, guiding it out of the harbor. It was a busy morning at the shipyard, Chance and Tony watched the crews onboard the docked ships as they went about their duties, preparing their ships for either refitting or getting ready to leave port. In one instance, they saw a ship that was dry docked, the welders could be seen working on the hull of the ship. From their vantage point it looked like twinkling lights as the welding rod made contact with the steel hull.

As they cleared the harbor and sailed into the open waters of the Atlantic, Chance decided to keep the Thresher on top of the surface in order to make better time. Tony stood watch, looking through his binoculars, for other ships that were headed into port. He watched as the water slipped past the bow of the Thresher as it pressed forward, and every so often the nose of the submarine would catch a swell causing the water to spray, hitting him in the face. The weather was beautiful for this time of the year, not a cloud in the sky and there was a slight ocean breeze coming in off of the ocean in front of Tony and Chance as they headed out to sea.

When the Thresher cleared all of the channel markers Chance and Tony secured the hatch to the sail as they went below. As Chance was using his checklist, they began their descent into deeper waters. After 15 minutes of diving they leveled off at two thousand feet and started heading southeast into the area of the Mid-Atlantic Ridge. Chance knew that the Mid-Atlantic Ridge ran about 10,000 miles from the Arctic Ocean to the southern tip of Africa and the width of the underwater mountain range was as wide as a thousand miles in some places.

Having fed the coordinates into the navigation system, Chance gave the orders to follow the compass heading from the computer. In the meantime, he pulled out a map which showed the area they were heading too. Tony went over to the plotting table where Chance was looking at the map. He had marked their position in reference to that part of the Mid-Atlantic Ridge. Even with the maps being current and as accurate as they could be, Chance knew not to put all of his trust in them. The Mid-Atlantic range was known for its seismic activity that could change the layout of the mountains without any notice. Hence, the reason the Navy had oceanographers and cartographers working together so they could identify any changes as they occured. Chance, and everyone else onboard, knew the last thing they wanted to have was an encounter with an unknown mountain that wasn't marked on their map, while they were looking for the last known position of the Soviet submarine.

As he looked at the underwater mountain range on the map, Tony looked at Chance, "How accurate are these maps you're using?"

"As accurate as you can be for this area, barring undersea earthquakes, rockslides, and anything else that could go wrong."

"That accurate, huh." Tony said smiling.

"Well, at least since last week anyway."

Chance, looking at the map put his finger on a spot, "This is where we are headed, and this is where we are right now."

Tony looked at the different points Chance had showed him, and he could see that there was about six inches on the map between the two spots, "So how far is that in laymen terms?"

"About three hundred miles distance from where we are at now."

Tony continued looking at the undersea map showing the mountain they were headed to, "How deep are we going to go on this dive?"

"I hope not deeper that three miles.   The Thresher's okay down to that depth, but I've never taken it down past that."

The Thresher continued on its course and after two hours the sonar man called out, "Sonar contact, bearing three six zero degrees, 100 miles, coming at us captain.

"All stop, run silent, let's see who else is out here with us. What's his depth sonar?"

"One three zero, zero, sir."

"Gently take us up to fifteen hundred feet driver."

Tony watched Chance as he was looking at the map, trying to make sure they didn't hit a mountain and figuring out how to get a look at this unknown contact. Chance called out to sonar, "Bearing and range sonar."

"Three six zero degrees and eighty miles captain."

Chance looked at Tony, "See that switch over your shoulder, the red one?" Tony turned and looked over his shoulder and pointed to the red switch. "This one here?"

"Yes, that one, flip it up will you. That way we can get a signature from the unknown and feed it into our computer,and maybe be able to identify it, as to what it is and who it belongs to.   Sonar, range and bearing please."

"Three six zero and 50 miles, and he's at a depth of 500 feet, sir."

Chance looked at the map, calculated where the sonar contact was and pointed it out to Tony. "Now, let's go fishing.   Driver, rig for silent running and come around and get behind him.   If possible, we may be able to surprise our guest.   Bring us up to 1,000 feet and hold her there."

"Aye, aye, sir, coming around."

Tony stood there watching as Chance called out orders and was amazed at how quickly his men responded to him, it was like watching a well-oiled machine. Once the Thresher was level and steady, he walked over to the sonar console and watched as the unknown contact passed over them by at least 500 feet.

"Sonar range and bearing please," Chance requested, looking for an update.

"He's right above us and slowly moving away."

"XO, get me an audio recording of the contact so we can take it back with us to give to the Navy."

"Yes, sir.   Recording now."

Everybody aboard the Thresher was silent as the Kilo submarine passed over them.   In some ways it sounded like a locomotive as it went by.   After another five minutes, Chance looked at the XO, "Did you get it?"

"Yes, sir.   We got it."

"Sonar, range and bearing."

"Three six zero and two miles, heading away sir.   He's on our nose, sir."

Chance smiled at Tony, "Now comes the fun part."

By now the computer had identified the submarine as a Kilo class submarine from the Soviet Union. Chance looked at the signature from the read out and said to the driver, "Get closer, I want to look at this submarine and get some pictures."

As they got closer to the submarine, Chance had a strange look on his face and shook his head for a second. "The signature is correct for a Kilo class submarine, but it's also making other noises, as well, that aren't supposed to be there.   I believe we may have found what we're looking for."

Tony agreed with Chance, thinking that maybe they had found the submarine that caused the Dolphin to sink.

"Sonar, give me an update," Chance requested.

"Still in front of us sir, one mile dead ahead sir."

"Open front viewing window and get us closer to that submarine," Chance ordered.

Slowly the Thresher made its way closer to the Kilo submarine. The sonar man kept giving range and bearing until Chance was able to see it through the window. At this point, Chance said to his second mate, "Turn on the camera and start recording."

By now, Tony saw it as well, the submarine looked like a Kilo class submarine alright, but there was something extra sticking out of the sail that wasn't part of the original equipment for that class of submarine.   Chance grabbed a Jane's Almanac on Navy's of the World and started skimming through the pages.   He finally found a picture of the latest Kilo class submarine and compared it to what they were following.

"Tony, come look at this."

Tony went over to look at what Chance had found in the book.

"Do you see anything different in this picture and what we're following?"

Tony looked closely at the picture, and then at the submarine in front of them, "The sail looks as if it has been transplanted onto the hull of the submarine. And look, there are two bubbles, one on each side of the sail that are very pronounced, kind of hard to miss."

"Hey Second, are you getting pictures of this?"

"Yes, and video too, sir."

The acoustics computer started clicking again with new information about the sounds coming from the Kilo. When Chance heard the sounds coming from the computer he went over to view the screen. He stood there for a moment, "I believe this is the bad guy that has been causing all of our headaches lately."

Tony walked over to the view screen and stood next to Chance, watching the submarine, "Are there any markings on the submarine that identify where it comes from?"

"None that I can see for sure, I suggest we follow this Kilo around for a while maybe he'll show us where he lives. Driver put us behind him by at least 10 miles. Sonar, please let me know if he changes course or speed, or for that matter, if anything else happens."

With that, the game of cat and mouse began. The Thresher, who was invisible to sonar, followed just behind the Kilo submarine and out of hearing range. Having the video of the Kilo with its modified sail, Chance and Tony studied it, trying to determine what the bubbles were for and who owned the submarine. They decided that they had enough video and pictures to study so they closed the window and decided to just use sonar to continue to track the submarine.

With the fall of the Russian Empire, most of their military equipment was sold to other nations to those who wanted to build up their own military arsenal. When this started, the United States' only concern was the sale of nuclear weapons, specifically the land-based ICBMs (Inter Continental Ballistic Missile) and SLBMs (Sea Launched Ballistic Missiles), that the Russian submarines carried during the cold war. In order to keep them from being sold on the black market to terrorist nations, our government purchased the nuclear weapons and sent teams from the Department of Defense over to Russia to oversee the dismantling of the nuclear warheads and missiles themselves. This was done to ensure that the Middle

Eastern countries wouldn't use the nuclear material for their own purposes and build their own weapons of mass destruction to use against us or our allies. With all that being said, there was still a risk of a third world country getting a hold of one of the warheads on the black market or maybe reverse engineering one of their own to build and use. The threat was real and very plausible, Chance and Tony knew that it was important to find out who the submarine belonged to and somehow destroy it if need be.

As the Thresher moved in sync with the Kilo submarine, Chance could see that the Kilo was looking for another target to do its magic on. He watched the Kilo on the sonar scope go through its paces as it started to follow the regular routes of the shipping channel that spanned the Atlantic Ocean. From the looks of it, the Kilo was looking for a surface ship to try on for size. It found a Russian cruiser that was part of the search team looking for their lost submarine. The cruiser was searching in a zig zag pattern, trying to triangulate the search. The Kilo moved in parallel to the cruiser and set off its signal jammers and sonar burst to render the cruiser useless in detecting the Kilo submarine. Once this was accomplished, the submarine did a ninety-degree turn, heading in the direction of the cruiser and started to set up a firing solution aimed at the wounded ship. Chance, hearing the torpedo doors open on the Kilo, realized what was happening and quickly decided to do something to stop the Kilo from sinking the cruiser. "Radioman transmit a message to the cruiser warning them about the Kilo submarine. Make sure you give them the location coordinates of the Kilo, as well. Sonar, send an active sonar signal to the Kilo."

At this point Chance told the driver, "Get us out of here, away from both the cruiser and the submarine, just in case they might want to get froggy."

After moving at top speed to get away from the Kilo and reaching a distance of twenty miles, Chance said, "Driver all stop and rig for silent running, just in case."

The Kilo getting pinged, and being unable to identify where it came from, aborted its attack on the Russian cruiser and headed away from the area as fast as it could. The Russian cruiser being crippled by not having any listening capability, turned ninety degrees away from the submarine, thereby making a torpedo shot just about impossible for the Kilo to make.

Chance, stood by the sonar man, "Take us off active and go to passive listening on the Kilo."

"Aye, aye, sir."

The Thresher continued to follow the Kilo as it left the sea lanes, taking evasive maneuvers, while trying to find who it was that had pinged them. After two days the Kilo quit looking for the ghost submarine and started sailing in a straight line. After two more days of following the Kilo it appeared to be headed back to its own base. This is what Chance and Tony had been waiting for, to actually find the home base of the Kilo submarine and find out whom it belonged too.

Checking his maps and other charts, Chance called Tony over and pointed at the map with his finger, "Here's where we are and there is the Kilo we're following."

Tony looked at the map and shook his head, "Africa, of all the places in the world. Why Africa?"

"So it seems. I think we'll learn more about this submarine as we continue following it to its home port."

As the Thresher continued to follow the Kilo, Chance and Tony continued watching the sonar scope as the Kilo got closer to land, at that point they lost the submarine's signal. This threw them for a loop, trying to figure out what happened to the Kilo. "Is there any chance we can get any closer to where we lost the signal?" Tony suggested.

"How close do you want to get?" Chance said, as he looked up from the map.

"I don't know. I'm thinking that there must be some kind of underwater entrance they're using to hide the submarine."

Intrigued by the thought of an underwater tunnel, Chance looked at the driver, "All ahead slow. Second, open the window."

With the viewing window open, the Thresher moved closer at periscope depth towards the coastline, looking for anything that looked like it could be an entrance.

The Second began searching through the viewing window for signs of an underwater cave while Chance looked through his periscope for the same thing above water. In the meantime, Tony was looking at the map trying to discern where they were. Swinging the periscope around, doing a 360 check for situational awareness,

Chance yelled, "Down periscope! All stop and let her sink to 400 feet."

Tony looked at Chance with a questioning look on his face, wondering what was going on. Chance saw the look on Tony's face, "We got company."

Within minutes, the sonar operator called out, "Surface target acquired, bearing 180, distance 10 miles."

"Hopefully, they didn't see our periscope, it seems as if we have a cargo ship coming our way," Chance said.

The Thresher's driver called out, "500 feet level."

"Did you see anything that looked like a cave big enough to handle a cargo ship?" Tony asked Chance.

"I didn't see anything. Hey Second, did you see anything?" Chance asked in response to Tony's question.

"Negative, sir," the Second responded.

"Sonar, update."

"One eight zero, distance 5 miles."

Thinking for a minute, "Take us up to periscope depth. Driver, let's follow the ship to see where it goes."

"Aye, aye, sir."

The Thresher slowly came up to periscope depth. All the while the submarine crew could hear the screws of the cargo ship turning as it went over them. Waiting until the ship passed, Chance brought the Thresher back up to periscope depth again to watch what the cargo ship was going to do. Moving slowly, they followed the ship as it headed into an opening in the rocks and disappeared behind some camouflaged netting. Chance seeing this, called out, "Sonar, I need an update."

"I've lost contact, sir," the operator replied.

"Sir, I see a steel net closing up ahead," the Second called out.

"All ahead stop, hold our course. Take us down to the bottom gently," Chance responded.

After getting an update on their GPS coordinates, Chance marked the entrance to the cave on his map and fed the coordinates into the computer navigation system. He then looked at Tony, "Do you feel like a moonlight swim?"

"Why Chance, that's the best offer I've had in years, when do we go?" Tony said, smiling.

"You don't get out much, do you. We'll go out in about three hours. In the meantime, we need to get our gear ready to go and also contact the Admiral about what we have found. Driver take us out of here and get us up to 150 feet to use our radio."

"Aye, aye, sir."

The driver complied with Chance's request. In a few minutes, they contacted the Navy to let them know where they were and what they had found. The Navy replied, confirming their message and the sighting of the underwater cave. At the bottom of the message it said to standby. Within minutes, another message was received, *"A Seal team is being sent to your location. Request you meet with team in two days for pickup at the coordinates listed below. End of Message"*

After reading the message, Chance told the radio man, "Send this reply: *'Message confirmed on pickup of team and standing by new coordinates.'"*

Chance looked at Tony as he read the message, "Do you still want to go for a swim?"

"I think it would be easier if we did, just to get a layout of the base.   That way the Seal Team wouldn't be going in blind."

"I agree, let's get our gear ready and get suited up for our swim."

Within the hour both Chance and Tony were ready to go for their moonlight swim.   After they checked their communications equipment to make sure that they had contact with the Thresher, Chance had the driver take the submarine into the sea cave, up to the point where the steel net was. They used the escape chamber on the submarine to make their exit. Chance and Tony entered the water, carrying what tools they thought they might need with them. With diving lights strapped to their arms, they swam to the steel netting to see if it could be cut open and also to look for wires that might set off an alarm in case the net was being messed with. Finding none, they used an underwater torch they had brought with them to cut through the steel net to cut an opening so they could pass through. Rising to the surface on the other side of the steel net to look around.

"Man can you believe how big this cave is?" Tony asked.

"Yeah, I'm thinking we might want to use the sea scooters, before we go any farther," he replied as he looked around the interior of the cave wondering if part of it was manmade.

"You would think that they would have something to navigate with through the cave," Tony replied.

They returned to the Thresher and picked up the scooters and swapped their air tanks for full ones. Now having the scooters they re-entered the sea cave once again and moved past the hole in the steel netting they had made. Once they were on the other side they used their compasses to get their bearings before moving deeper into the cave. Uncertain as to what they would find they continued moving through the cave following the lights they had brought with them. After about fifteen minutes of swimming, Chance saw an underwater glow up ahead and signaled Tony. Using his hands, he pointed in the direction of the light and once Tony saw the glow they decided that they would follow it and check it out. When they reached the light source they found that the light was used as a marker for the submarine to find its way through the cave. When they surfaced again they could see that the cave opened up into a larger cavern that was only partially in the water. They could also see the cargo ship and the Kilo submarine berthed at the pier and men that were loading and unloading equipment from the cargo ship by a crane to be taken to the submarine. Chance signaled Tony to let him know that he wanted to get closer to the Kilo. As they moved through the water, Chance and Tony made their way to the side the Kilo. Staying hidden beneath the dock, they listened to the men talk as they worked, all of them were talking in English as they loaded more boxes onto the submarine. Chance noticed that the corporate logo on the side of the boxes depicted a Grizzly bear standing up on its back legs. After taking a picture of the corporate logo, they waited for the men to quit work. It wasn't too long before the men left for the day. Chance and Tony, seeing their opportunity to go aboard the submarine, waited another ten minutes before heading onto the submarine. They carefully set their gear aside and made their way up the gang plank to go onboard and check out what was inside. With his camera, Chance took pictures of the interior where the modifications had been made to house the new electronic equipment. While Chance was taking pictures, Tony went into the command center and looked around to see if he could find anything that would indicate who the submarine belonged to now. Seeing the Grizzly bear on some of the modified equipment inside the center, he found what he was looking for. The name of the company was,

Bear Industries, located in Angola, Africa. With this new information, Tony went back to find Chance to tell him that he had found the name of the company. When he arrived where Chance was, he could see that he had one of the electronic panels open and was doing something to the inside the panel.   He tapped him on the shoulder, "What are you doing?"

"I'm taking pictures of the inside of the panel to take back with us. Let's get topside and get a look at their base here."

After making sure the coast was clear, Tony and Chance exited the submarine and made their way around the outside of it.   Upon closer inspection, they found that the cave went another hundred yards deeper into rock. Chance saw what he had been looking for, and that was an entrance that led to the outside onto dry land via some stairs. The cave also housed buildings for supplies and sleeping quarters for the men who worked aboard the submarine. There was also a small cafeteria for the men to use when they were hungry.   As Chance continued to take pictures, Tony looked around and   thought to himself that this whole operation was pretty well self-contained for the crew and the leaders.   And depending on their supplies, they could stay here forever, and no one would be the wiser for it.

Within an hour they decided that they'd seen enough and not wanting to press their luck any further, they made their way back to where there had left their air tanks and sea scooters.   With their gear back on, they slipped quietly back into the water, slid beneath the surface and swam back to the Thresher. After they arrived back at the Thresher and got cleaned up, Chance told the driver, "Take us to the rendezvous point to pick up the Seal Team."

As the Thresher made its way to the pickup point, Chance sent the information and pictures of the underwater base to the Navy Intel center for analysis. With this new information, the Seal Team would be better prepared for whatever might occur and possibly save a life in the process.

Tony and Chance sat on the bridge of the Thresher looking at the pictures they'd taken of the submarine, trying to figure out who and what it was, as far as technology went, and if it could be reproduced by the Navy engineers back at the base. The interior shots of the Kilo showed the actual stations that managed the signals that emanated from the Kilo submarine. Hopefully, the pictures were good enough for some engineer to do something with them. Ideally, the best they could hope for, was to steal the submarine and take it back to America and reverse engineer the whole program. With that thought in mind, Chance looked at Tony, "Do you think we could steal the Kilo from the owners?"

Tony smiled, "I think it's worth a try.   Besides, what have we got to lose besides our lives?"

"Driver take us to the surface. We need to send a message to the Navy."

Taking a chance, Tony sent a message directly to the Admiral about their idea of stealing the Kilo submarine. After receiving Tony's request, the Admiral gave it some thought and passed the message to the Submarine division to be handled ASAP.   Within an hour, the Submarine Command sent a list of names of personnel that would be available for this kind of operation. He knew that the size of the crew would be barely enough to get the Kilo out of the harbor, but also knew that it would be worth it, just to have the technology aboard it. With the protection of the Seal Team, it would make it easier to pull off the theft. The Admiral called the Submarine Command and got the ball rolling for the crew members to show up along with the Seals. With the addition of a submarine crew and the Seals, it took a day longer for the rendezvous with the Thresher to occur. The extra day proved to be no problem; the Kilo never left port while the Thresher kept watch at the entrance of the sea cave with its long distance sonar equipment.

Taking a chance, the Thresher left from guarding the sea cave to go meet the submarine that was bringing the crew and the Seal Team.   They rendezvoused with the submarine at night making it more secure from the passing satellites and ships that would be curious as to what was going on.

Once the men were boarded onto the Thresher and everyone was settled in for the trip, the trip back to the underwater sea cave was uncomfortable, to say the least.   The quarters were slightly cramped with the maintenance techs and the Seals jammed together inside the Thresher, along with the regular crew. None the less, nobody complained to loudly. In fact, Tony asked Chance, "Have you given any thought about building a bigger submarine?"

"Now that you mention it, it might be a good idea.   By the way, when was the last time you took a shower?" Chance laughed.

"I believe it was last week, but I'm thinking that it isn't just me that needs one."

Once they were underway, Chance got on the PA system, "Attention, this is the captain, I don't know if you've noticed, but we have some extra people onboard," waiting for the laughter to stop, he continued "We are heading back to the cave to steal a submarine. The submarine we are going after happens to be the one that was responsible for sinking the USS Dolphin and a Soviet submarine, as well. Hence, the reason for picking up the Seal team and the extra crew. Our job is to take them to the submarine so that they can commandeer it and bring it home. Hopefully, it should only be a matter of hours before we're back on post, sitting in front of the cave."

After hearing Chance's message, everyone onboard seemed to settle down and come together with the idea of taking the Kilo, no matter how uncomfortable it was aboard the Thresher.

Within six hours the Thresher was sitting in front of the underwater sea entrance to the cave. All of the extra submarine crew were dressed in swimming trunks and air tanks, each having a bag attached to their waist carrying a gun in case they needed them. The Seals had their own equipment and sea scooters, to lead the way. One of the sailors for the submarine crew was to take a container filled with the sailor's clothes so that they would be able to change into uniforms once they were on board the Kilo. Part of the crew for the submarine was made up of a couple of electronic technicians, whose job was to go over the specialized equipment for the Navy once they were onboard the submarine and, on their way, back to port. Each member of the two groups had a specific job that they were to do. The main job for the Seals was to provide security for the crew while they got onboard the Kilo to hijack it. All of this would require surprise, in order to get away with it. If they couldn't, the backup plan was to sink the Kilo where she was tied to the pier and then blow up the cave entrance to the sea.

When everyone was ready to begin, the Seal Team would be the first to leave in order to secure the area around the Kilo. Once word was received by the Seals that the area was secure, then the submarine crew would leave the Thresher and make their way through the cave to the Kilo. When they were onboard, the crew would take control of her and take her out into the open water to be escorted back to the Groton shipyard to be analyzed. All in all, it would take a week for the Kilo to get to Groton to be tied up to the pier, that is, if no one was chasing them.

The Seals waited for darkness before they left the Thresher to better conceal themselves in the water as they to cut the steel net that was blocking the entrance to where the submarine was. The Seal's team leader moved his men out in two teams of six. One team would secure the Kilo and the other team would secure the base, while placing charges at the entrances of the cave and killing anyone who tried to stop them.   The Seals carefully made their way through the tunnel and surfaced underneath the pier next to the Kilo. One of the Seal's saw two men that were standing guard over the Kilo. He crawled onto the submarine and slowly made his way towards the two guards. Using his gun, with a silencer on it, he killed both of them. The Seal, with help from one of his teammates, carefully moved the bodies and slowly slid them into the water where his teammates took the bodies and tied them to one of the posts of the pier.

Four of the Seals then went into the Kilo to secure it just in case someone was inside. They then stayed onboard as the other two reported to the team leader that the submarine was secure, and they could call for the new crew to come through the cave to take the submarine. With that being accomplished, the two seals went to the opening of the cave and placed bombs at the entrance. The second team placed charges around each of the buildings that housed the communications system and personnel. The fuel storage area was set up to explode with C4 charges on timers.

All of this was done in about 30 minutes, start to finish. Now it came time to load the new crew on board the Kilo and quickly move the submarine from its berth. The new crew, led by Chance and Tony, were able to board the Kilo inside two minutes. As the crew went through the startup procedures, the Seals were positioned at different locations to protect the crew aboard the Kilo, in case someone heard the engines start up. All was quiet until they started up the submarine's engines. The original crew, upon hearing the submarine's engines come to life, headed out the door of their building trying to figure out what was going on. The Seals, watching the building, detonated the bombs they had planted, leaving most of the men dead as they tried to leave the building. The survivors of the blast were killed by the Seals as they stood up after being knocked down. The communications building was the next to explode, and it went up in a ball of fire. You could see the radio antenna on the building from the Kilo as it fell into the water in the middle of the explosion. The Seals had also planted bombs at the land entrance to the cave, waiting for the local soldiers to come through. As they did, the Seals cut them down with a barrage of bullets and finally blew up the entrance which sealed it with the rock and debris from the blast. Now the only way out for the Seals, was by submarine or by swimming back to the Thresher. As Tony lifted the rope that was fastened to the submarine, it fell into the water, still attached to the pier. By now the submarine was ready to move. Chance was standing by on the sail and started giving orders to the crew inside as to what direction they needed to move the Kilo. The Seals made their way back to the Kilo and jumped onto the deck, crawling down one of the escape hatches on the main deck. When all of the Seals were accounted for, Chance ordered the crew to submerge the submarine. As they passed through the entrance of the cave, the Seal team lead activated the timers on the bombs that were set to blow after five minutes to seal the cave and everything else inside it forever. After clearing the entrance and getting to diving depth, the Kilo made its way out to the open sea. By now the Thresher had picked up the submarine on sonar as she was moving through the undersea tunnel. The Thresher fell in line with the Kilo and began escorting her back to Groton. The two submarines remained underwater for the next two days of their journey, with the Thresher acting as the eyes and ears for both submarines. This would give the technicians a chance to evaluate and analyze the electronics that was housed onboard the Kilo.

Chapter XXI

When word got out that the Kilo had been stolen by unknown thieves, the president of Bear Industries was livid with anger that his prize submarine was gone. And, adding salt to the wound, his secret base had been destroyed in the process. He thought that it might be one of the countries that was making a bid on his very secret technology, who didn't want to pay. He had planned to sell the Kilo's technology to the highest bidder after showing what it could do against two submarines. The two countries that were primarily interested in the submarine's technology and what it could do, were Angola and Sierra Leone, two third world countries with terrorist backing. Upon hearing that the Kilo had been stolen, the president of the company, in order to avoid embarrassment from the interested parties, offered to sell the technology for half of the asking price and the return of the Kilo submarine. This caused the Sierra Leone and Angola navies to start looking for the Kilo. Locating the Kilo would be easy, simply because the sound of the diesel engines that powered the submarine were noisy, so much so, that you could drive a train near the submarine and not hear the train as it went by. The Sierra Leone Navy was the first to find the submarine with their sonar. After finding the Kilo they began pacing it in a parallel pursuit, dropping depth charges all around it in order to try and raise it to the surface.

With depth charges exploding all around them, sounding like sledgehammers hitting the hull of the Kilo, Chance, his crew and the electronics technicians aboard the Kilo, were highly motivated to get the special equipment to work. You could say their lives depended on it. They had started to get some idea of how to run the special equipment onboard, but without a sure knowledge of the operation, it was a guess as what to do first. Fortunately, one of the crew members found a technical orders/instructions book to assist them with this. In order to buy some time, the Kilo dived down into the deeper parts of the ocean while the two technicians tried to figure out the sequence, or steps, to bring the system alive. For everyone onboard the Kilo, the experience of being bombed by depth charges was their first encounter of this type of submarine warfare, which they had only seen in the old war movies. The Kilo was a holdover from the cold war, being old and Russian made, it had all of the crew, even the nonbelievers, praying. The repeated concussions from the blast of the depth charges on the hull of the submarine was taking a toll on the old Kilo. The crew were busy running up and down the submarine trying to seal up the leaks that had started to appear since the depth charging had started. Even the Seals were nervous as they were trying help the submarine to stay afloat.

"I wish we were aboard the Thresher right now," Chance said, as he helped Tony fix the leaks that were nearby.

"You and everybody else onboard. Whose idea was this anyway," Tony said, with a smile.

"From what I hear, I think it was a couple of idiots," Chance replied, as he grabbed the headphones to the radio to make contact with the Thresher.

"Thresher, this is Chance. We a need some help down here. Can you do something to get this tin can off our back?"

"Roger that Captain, we'll see what we can do," the Second replied.

The Thresher, carrying no weapons at all, could only do one thing and that was to start actively pinging the Sierra Leone patrol boat with its sonar. By doing this they were hoping to draw it away from the Kilo, thereby giving it a chance to get away. As the Thresher led the Sierra Leone ship away from the Kilo, it started to move around the ship to disorient the sonar receivers aboard it, causing it to completely stop in order to regain a good lock on what they thought was the Kilo. Because of this, the depth charging stopped, allowing the Kilo to survive. By now the technicians, reading the technical orders, figured out what to do. They called Chance on the sub phone, "We figured out how to make it work! What do you want us to do now?"

"Standby for a second before turning on the system," Chance told the techs.

Chance then called the Thresher over an open radio frequency, "Get yourselves away from the patrol boat and shut down your acoustics and sonar. You have five minutes to comply."

Upon hearing the radio message, the Second yelled out, "Shut down the acoustics and sonar and get us the hell out of here!"

Hoping the message got through, Chance asked the technicians aboard the Kilo, to start up the jammers. As they went through the steps the lights dimmed aboard the Kilo when the first pulse left the submarine. Watching their sonar screen, to see if the patrol boat was hit by the pulse of energy, they waited to see what would happen next.   Chance, taking a risk, took the submarine up to three hundred feet from the surface, and placed the Kilo right up next to the patrol boat. The patrol boat was dead in the water without any sonar or acoustics, she was blind and deaf. Chance called down to the technicians, "It worked."

The two techs congratulated themselves for figuring out the sequence of steps for using the jammer system. Their apparent victory was short lived because the sonar man called out, "We have an unknown surface contact coming in our direction, range twenty miles at three six zero."

Tony was the first to get to the sonar station.   Seeing the target closing in fast, he yelled out to Chance, "We got to go down deep, now!"

As the ship continued to bear down on the Kilo, Chance, acting on what Tony had yelled to him about the new threat, told the driver to initiate an emergency crash dive. Diving the Kilo down deep to its maximum depth of about eight hundred feet in order to get away from the destroyer.   Receiving the echo returns from the submarine, the destroyer started launching their own depth charges against the Kilo. Still diving for deeper water, the depth charges barely missed the tail section of the Kilo as she continued her dive.   Getting rattled and rolled, Chance called the technicians, "Can we do it again with the jammers?"

Their reply was, "Negative, we need some time to build up the power again to get the pulse strong enough to be effective."

"How much time are we talking here?"

"We're not sure. We haven't figured that part out yet."

Chance looked at Tony, "Enough is enough, I need you to go to the Torpedo room and lock and load a couple of torpedoes for me. See if you can find someone that can help you."

"I'm on my way," Tony said, as he stepped through the hatch, headed to the forward section of the Kilo.

Chance made a call over the PA system aboard the Kilo, "I'm looking for anybody who has experience with torpedoes to meet in the torpedo room immediately."

By the time Tony found his way to the torpedo room, two other men were already there to lend a hand. Tony looked at the both of them, "You know more than I do, I'll follow your lead."

The three of them grabbed a sling, wrapped it around one of the torpedoes and rolled it onto the ramp and pushed it towards one of the tubes that was now open, then placed the torpedo into the tube and closed the hatch behind it, sealing it with air.   One of the men found the lever to open the outer torpedo doors to the Kilo, when the outer doors were open the red light lit up on the console to show they were ready to fire. Chance saw the red light on his own console light up, as well.

"Sonar, where's our target?"

"She's at zero nine zero, 5 miles from us. It seems that she lost us."

"Very well. Driver, take us to 200 feet, nice and easy and turn us around."

He then turned the Kilo 90 degrees to face the oncoming destroyer.   Chance then began to work up a firing solution on the destroyer using the onboard computer to go after it.

Tony and the other two men loaded another torpedo into the tube next to the one they had just set up. When the second light came on, indicating that another torpedo was at the ready, Chance called the torpedo room on the sub phone, "Tony, I need you up here to assist."

"I'll be right there," Tony replied.

When Tony arrived at the control room, Chance was working on the targeting computer to get the final solution on the destroyer.   It was at this time that the destroyer picked up the Kilo again and was making its way towards it.   The distance of the destroyer was closing fast and the skipper of the destroyer, knowing that the Kilo class submarine was for shallow seas only, had his men re-calibrate the depth charges to sink to 300 meters before exploding.

Chance had to act fast in order to survive the next barrage of depth charges. The two torpedoes were fed the coordinates of the destroyer from the computer to the guidance system on the 71MKE TV electric homing torpedoes, which had the capability of active homing sonar. Chance waited for Tony to read the range data to him to get maximum kill capability on the destroyer. Waiting for the input from the computer, Chance had his hand on the button to fire the torpedoes as Tony continued to read the range and azimuth to him.

Once the computer lit up on the screen to show a good lock on the destroyer, Chance fired both torpedoes at once. It was at this time that Tony clicked the stopwatch on and waited to hear the explosions.

"Driver take us deep," Chance ordered.

The alarms went off onboard the destroyer while their sonar man was yelling, "Two torpedoes at zero, zero degrees, a thousand yards and closing." Letting the skipper and the crew know that torpedoes had been launched against them. The skipper ordered the weapons officer to launch noise makers in hopes of drawing the torpedoes away from the ship. As they tried to jam the torpedoes sensors, and move away from their path, the first torpedo slipped by him while the second torpedo had a good lock on the destroyer as she moved to get away.   The torpedo countered the move, hitting the middle of the ship and broke the back of the destroyer into two pieces. The first torpedo, still controlled by the sonar aboard the Kilo, was fed the new coordinates, turned around and hit the front half of the destroyer, breaking it in two, as well. The destroyer sank in five minutes.   Hearing the explosions, the crew reacted wildly, knowing they had sunk a destroyer using a Russian submarine, operated by Americans, to do it.   The Kilo came up to the surface to verify that the destroyer had been sunk.   Chance and Tony were on the sail with binoculars, looking for survivors through all of the debris. Not finding any, Chance looked at Tony, "Score one for the good guys this time."

"It's about time."

The sonar room called up to Chance, "We have a surface ship on radar, coming from bearing one eight zero, speed 20 knots, range 5 miles, closing fast."

Chance grabbed the binoculars and started scanning in the direction where the surface ship was coming from. Within minutes, he was able to see the ship as it fired flares into the sky. Realizing it was the Thresher, he breathed a sigh of relief, as did Tony.   As they waited for the Thresher to come along side of the Kilo, Chance's second in command pop up through the sail, "Looks like you've been busy skipper."

"You don't know the half of it," Chance replied.

As the crew aboard the Kilo were talking amongst themselves, the Seal team leader asked, "I know this has been fun but I'd like to transfer my team over to the Thresher just in case you guys attract anyone else?"

"I thought you guys were tough," replied Chance, smiling at the leader.

"We are. But this is crazy, and I have to tell you when we can't shoot back at the enemy it's no fun."

"I see your point," agreed Tony.

Within 15 minutes the Seal team was ready to transfer over to the Thresher while some of the Thresher's crew came aboard the Kilo.

After making the exchange of men, Chance continued to take the Kilo into the shipyard in Groton, Connecticut for final analysis. Until they were in US waters, the submarine would stay submerged and then come to the surface as it entered into port. All of this would occur after dark to ensure that no one would panic at seeing a Russian submarine appear all of a sudden. The Thresher would run point for the Kilo, letting the Navy know that the Kilo was in American hands and would be coming in at night and not to fire on it. Once they had made contact with the Navy brass, they obliged by offering an armed escort for the Kilo. As agreed, upon, once on the surface, the Navy would escort the Kilo submarine into a closed off area of the port and put it into a covered berth.

The trip to Groton, Connecticut was uneventful and was a learning experience for the crew aboard the submarine as they started learning the secrets of the Kilo as she begrudgingly yielded all of them up to the crew and Chance. The technicians finally figured out the procedures for using the jammers that had been used by the Kilo on the Dolphin. From that point on, the crew would be used to help figure out the day to day operations of the Kilo submarine. Some of the men, including the techs, aboard the Kilo were surprised at some of the tube technology from the fifties that had been modified to work at the turn of the century. Once it was fully manned, the Kilo would be taken out for numerous shakedown cruises at night to see what she could do and compare that to our own submarine's capabilities. The lessons learned from the exercises would be incorporated into new submarine tactics to use against the Kilo class submarines if the need should arise. The submarine crew would be assigned to the Kilo for quite a while, leastwise, until the evaluation and testing was complete.

The torpedoes would be taken apart and reversed engineered, once they were on land, as would the new jamming system that was incorporated onto the Kilo submarine. The combat computer used in the plotting and tracking of multiple targets would be analyzed for its weaknesses and strengths, as well. Then the new knowledge would be compared and used against the US submarines in a mock game of cat and mouse under the sea. The Kilo was considered a gold mine of new information for the US Navy, simply because it was their first time of having one that was seaworthy and actually fully functional. The new combat tactics, gleaned from the Kilo, would be incorporated into new training for the crews aboard the American submarines and surface ships in their anti-submarine warfare training.

Chapter XXII

It was about ten o'clock pm when Chance brought the Kilo to the surface. Opening the hatch to the sail, he could see the lights of the shipyard not too far off in the distance. As he continued looking around, he could see two American destroyers on each side of the Kilo. Tony stood there watching the destroyers blinking their signal lights at the Kilo.

"I wonder what they're asking us. I never did get the hang of reading signal lights," Tony said.

"I have to admit that I never learned how to use them either. Maybe someone on our crew knows how," Chance replied.

Chance called for one of the crewmen to come up and answer the signal lights from the destroyers. After responding back to the destroyers, the lights of the destroyers turned on in order to secure the Kilo. Once everything was secured, the destroyers threw ropes over to the submarine to assist in guiding the Kilo into its berth. After the Kilo was secured under the covered pier, a group of men and women were waiting to go aboard the submarine in order to start the testing and evaluation to learn all they could about the Kilo submarine and the new technology that was aboard her.

Chance and Tony waited for the others to come aboard to do their thing before they left the submarine. The Admiral was waiting for them on the pier as they came down the ramp. Saluting first, then shaking hands, "I hear you had some fun out there on the high seas."

"I'm never going to book another cruise with these guys ever again," Chance said.

"The movie really sucked!" Tony added.

"I don't blame you one bit," the Admiral said as he laughed, "How 'bout we get together after you guys get some rest and get cleaned up."

"Sounds good to us, we'll see you soon," Tony said.

Tony and Chance got a ride back to Chances office, complements of the Navy, so that Tony could get his car to go home. Tony pull out his phone and called Ann and waited for her to pick up the phone, a sleepy voice answered on the other end. "Hello, this had better be my Tony."

"It is, and I'm wondering if you would be up for a late-night visit?"

"I don't know if that's wise, this late at night. You know I have to get up early just to be presentable for the day."

"I'll take my chances, especially after sinking a destroyer and blowing up a secret submarine base in Africa, and that's only after we stole a submarine. I can't tell you anymore because the rest of it is classified," he said, laughing.

"Well in that case, I may have to torture you to get the rest of the information then. Come on over and I'll put a pot of coffee on for us," she said, laughing as well.

Within the next couple of days, everyone aboard the Kilo had been debriefed as to what they had learned about the submarine. With the exception of Chance and Tony, everyone would be assigned to work on the Kilo as part of a special operation.

The next step for the Navy Intel personnel was to locate whoever had sanctioned the sinking of the submarines and bring them to trial. Then if necessary, go after Bear Industries and dismantle the business one piece at a time. This would involve the FBI and the CIA working together one more time with DOD. After doing some research, they learned that the Bear Industries headquarters was located in Germany and had offices throughout Africa and Latin America. They were ranked as number five on Forbes list of the top 100 companies in the world worth over ten billion dollars. They were involved with electronics technology development, agribusiness, aerospace design, and mining operations throughout the world. Each of these areas was strong enough to stand on their own as a separate company, yet with the financial backing of the corporate headquarters, they were considered heavyweights in the business areas they played in.

Upon further investigation, it was determined that the lead money making company for Bear Industries was their electronics division. The most lucrative part of this division was their new research and development area. This part of the business had hired the most powerful electronic engineering minds from all over the world, with the one thought of having the capability to invent or create new technology that was on the leading edge and beyond. Countries throughout the world were always being courted for their money to invest in new technology. And each country was treated very well in their return on their investments from Bear Industries. The research and development demands came from countries coming up with a need and then asking them to come up with a solution to their idea or problem.

According to the briefs for each of the countries they were courting, Bear Industries had a 90 percent success rate in meeting the needs of their customers. Hence, money was made by Bear Industries and their customers were always happy with the solutions from the newfound technology, created just for them. Because of their success, the electronics technology division had been contacted by a third world country to develop a new technology to help in their civil war against their enemy, who had been involved in using their navy against them. They were looking for a way to disable the ships that were giving them problems. They had the money; they just needed the technology. Being intimidated by the enemy's military strength, the leaders of the country decided to counteract the threat by buying new technology from Bear Industries. Hopefully, this would neutralize the worst navy threat to them, which was their submarines. The submarines were being used as a way to sink their oil ships and keep them from moving their cargo to the countries that were buying it.

Part of the field testing was to show the customer that the new technology worked and the only way to do that was to test it against a known military force that was considered invincible, hence the U.S. and the Russian Navy. After seeing the success against these navy submarines, Bear Industry's president got greedy and decided to put it out there on the market to sell to the highest bidder. The original country was now being pushed to pay more for what they had contracted Bear Industries to buy. Once North Korea and Venezuela saw the results of the field test, they became interested in the new technology as were China, Syria, Hamas, ISIS, and even some of the drug cartels, for moving drugs into the United States. Each country or organization was willing to pay millions of dollars for this new weapon that could bring the biggest navies in the world to their knees.

The USS Dolphin was the first example of what the new technology could do. The torpedo from the Kilo broke her back, and as she sank, the bomb that had been placed aboard her exploded, sealing her fate forever. Being blind and deaf just made it all the worse for her crew and the submarine as the blast flooded her forward compartments, sealing her fate forever. The Soviet submarine, was again, just an example to reinforce the capability of the new technology to perspective buyers that were interested in getting their hands on it for their own reasons.

The president of Bear Industries knew he was stepping into an unknown arena with selling to the highest bidder like this. But the temptation to sell it this way would help offset the losses over the first half of the year, which only a few people inside the corporate headquarters knew about. Nobody, except a few accountants inside the company, knew that Bear Industries was hemorrhaging money to offset their other business ventures that had turned into money pits. To the president, it was about staying alive, and he would do anything to make it happen, even if it was illegal. The careless spending was brought about by overextending their company in just about every area they were involved with. Especially, their aerospace department, having lost out to Lockheed on a multi-million-dollar contract to build new aircraft for the U.S. Air Force and the U.S. Navy. Add on top of that, the countries they were doing business with started defaulting on their payments to the company. It had been a risk just to do business, but with the loss of the aerospace contract as it was, it was the proverbial last nail in the coffin. They had no other choice but to deal with these countries and it proved to be their worst nightmare, times ten.

Now that the US Intelligence had the new technology from the Kilo, it was just a matter of time before Bear Industries would be found out and the world would watch as they would slowly die a miserable death. The corporate president, seeing what was happening to his business, was trying to buy time so that he could take some of the money he had embezzled and go to a new country and live out his days in relative comfort, away from the eyes of the world looking for him. In his mind, the money he had taken was his golden parachute and severance pay, all wrapped into one tidy package. The president, realizing that there was no way out, had planned a meeting in South America in order to justify flying his

Lear jet to Brazil, simply because it has no extradition agreement with the United States. He had planned on landing at one of the smaller airports and have a guide waiting for him to take him into the back country to get away from it all. The president had seen the demise of Bear Industries and had started siphoning money to pay for a new house in the middle of nowhere so that he could live in comfort. He had found a new girlfriend on a previous trip and planned on leaving his wife and kids behind, so that he could share his money and time with the new girl. The president felt he was ready to leave the world he had help create, and with a cool 65 million dollars, he would be just fine for the rest of his life in hiding.

The first signs that Bear Industries was faltering in its business dealing would take six months to figure out. By then the president would be gone and considered lost. With the company president gone, having embezzled 65 million dollars, the chairman of the board and the major stockholders started realizing the financial jam they were in. To offset the crises, they would need to start selling their stock before it was too late just to break even. For the stockholders, Bear Industries was breathing its last breath as it went under. All of the businesses that had operated under Bear Industries were being sold off, one piece at a time, at half their value. The lives of the people and their families that made up the companies were considered collateral damage to the board of directors as each of them struggled to survive. While all of this was going on, the president had already landed in Brazil and was now lost in the jungle.

Now that the Intel community saw that Bear Industries was going under, the FBI stepped in and started looking into their financial records as the CIA was looking into the companies that had been operating throughout the world. The FBI found out, through the financial reports, what had happened to the company. The records showed that the president had embezzled 65 million dollars and was responsible for selling off the company's assets in a bid to recover their losses. These records were forwarded to Germany so that they could take action against Bear Industries. Interpol was now actively pursuing all of the head stockholders, checking their backgrounds for anything that was illegal according to the laws in Germany and the other countries they had been operating in.

The president of Bear Industries was now wanted for misappropriation of funds, amongst other charges, by Interpol. Needless to say, the United States and Russia were now looking for him, as well, for destruction of military equipment and the murder of their submarine crews. The real question was, who was going to find him first and get the first crack at him for what he had done. All the while, the president sat in a chair on his patio, drinking his orange juice and eating breakfast with his blonde girlfriend and some other girls, lounging around the pool. Deep down inside, the president knew his days were numbered and it was only a matter of time before he would be found and either killed or brought to trial. In his mind, he hoped he would be killed rather than face the music for what he had done. It would be less embarrassing for him than having to face the world and his wife and children for his crimes and sit in prison for the rest of his life. And as he thought about this, his girlfriend reached over and started rubbing his forehead to ease the stress in his face. He looked up and smiled at the young lady sitting next to him and let all of his thoughts disappear. Until then, the president would enjoy his new life with his new friends in the local government and here on the patio. There would be time later to deal with the realities of life, as they came, knowing full well that they would.

Chapter XXIII

With the Kilo submarine under lock and key and hidden in a place that doesn't exist, except on a need to know basis, Tony was able to take a couple of days off to spend time with Ann and recover from being in the hijacking business and working with the FBI trying to find the president of Bear Industries. He and Ann were able to drive up to the Appalachian Mountains to do some hiking.   Being out in the fresh air was just what the doctor ordered for both of them.

On his first day back to the office, there was a message waiting for him from the Admiral, wanting to see him as soon as possible. Not knowing what to expect, he rushed right over.   Tony went into the outer office where Ann was sitting doing some typing, "Hi beautiful, where did you get that tan?" he chuckled.

"I'll never tell. But it was fun." she replied, smiling.

"The Admiral sent for me."

Upon hearing his voice, the Admiral yelled out, "Is that you Tony? Get yourself in here."

"You wanted to see me, sir?" Tony said, as he walked into his office, noticing the two men in suits that were seated around the conference table.

"Yes, I do, as a matter of fact.   I want to introduce to you to these gentlemen."

Tony, still standing, walked with the Admiral over to where the men were sitting.

"Tony, this is Special Agents Smith and Jones," the Admiral said, smiling.

Tony recognized the two agents, "Why, haven't we met before?"

Both Smith and Jones stood up to shake Tony's hand, "Hey, I hear you're pretty good at stealing submarines," Smith said, with a chuckle.

"It's legal until you get caught.   Besides, I need to have a skill I can use when I get out of the Navy," Tony said laughing.

With the formalities over, the Admiral offered a seat to Tony and the others around the conference table. As he sat down the Admiral buzzed Ann to come in, "Can you get us four coffees please."

In a few minutes the secretary came back in and placed the tray of coffee in the middle of the table and as she did, so she winked at Tony.   To which Tony almost turned red.

"Thank you, would you please make sure that we're not disturbed," the Admiral said, as she left the room.

As the door to the Admiral's office closed, the Admiral started, "First of all, what you did getting that submarine back to us was a masterful piece of work. These two agents have a proposition for you to hear. I would like you to listen and see if you would be interested in what they have to offer."

Smith stood up at this point and walked over to turn the video machine on and turn off the lights in the room. As he sat down the picture of a man came up on the screen, "As you may already know, this is Gunther Reichman.   He's the president of Bear Industries. From what we've been able to learn, he was the mastermind behind the technology that took out the USS Dolphin and the Russian submarine. He has now taken off with 65 million dollars of his company's money and has flown the coup to South America.

"Yes, I remember, "Tony said.

"We would like you to go with us to track down Gunther and bring him back to face the law. The Admiral says that it's up to you to decide," Jones said, waiting for Tony's reply.

Tony looked over at the Admiral who then nodded yes to him, "Just when I thought life would get boring and me getting old and useless."

"You'll be acting as a liaison on loan to the FBI, in case something comes up that might need the Navy's input.   Seeing as how you've been involved in it already from the start, you're the most likely candidate for the job," the Admiral stated.

Tony sat there, in the dark room, remembering that he had worked with Agent Reagan of the FBI in their investigation of Gunther Reichman, to find out where he had gone to. His motivation in working with the FBI was because of what had happened to the USS Dolphin.

Agent Smith continued, "Not having a flight plan made, Gunther left Germany with 65 million dollars. We've been unable to find the pilot that flew him over to South America. We think that Gunther gave him, not only the Lear jet, but also one million dollars to go away, never to be found again. Evidently, the pilot has made good use of the plane and disappeared into the unknown. Probably, flying drugs or one of the cartel bosses around the country."

"The FBI will be the lead on this investigation, and you will follow their lead," the Admiral added.

"As it stands right now, we have a worldwide APB (All Points Bulletin) out searching for Gunther. Personally, I think that he's holds up somewhere, waiting for us to get tired of looking for him," Agent Smith added.

"So, when do we leave?"

"As soon as we know where he is. Agent Reagan will lead the investigation once we have a general idea of where he might be," Agent Smith replied.

"So, am I standing by for a standby?" Tony asked.

"Pretty much. Agent Reagan will be in touch with you," Agent Jones replied.

Gunther was sitting quietly on the veranda, watching the girls in the pool and enjoying his new life with his new identity and passport to go along with it. He smiled to himself, knowing that people were searching the world over for him and the money he took. He wasn't worried about it too much, it would take months maybe years, before someone would be able to connect the dots to find him. Unbeknownst to Gunther, the FBI would get their first break in the case, and it would come from a very unlikely source. A place they had never thought of.

One of Gunther's girlfriends that had been staying at his villa, eventually left to see if she could make more money on her own, had been caught in a prostitution sting in the United States. She had been picked up for solicitation in El Paso, Texas. After getting bored of living in Brazil she had made her way from South America and, hearing how good it was in America, decided to go to the United States. She worked her way there by selling drugs and being a mule for the cartel, which gave her the access she needed to get into America. When she arrived in America she found that the money she had made as a mule went faster than she thought it would, and add to the fact, she had become addicted to the drugs she was bringing over. Being hooked, had forced her into prostitution in order to survive on the streets.   Leastwise, until she could go back across the border for another load of drugs to bring into America.

One of the officers involved in the sting operation started interviewing the girls that had been arrested in order to set up police records for each of them. When it was her turn, the police officer waited while they took her photo, then one of the other officers escorted her over to his desk so he could start the paperwork.   After she was seated, the interviewing officer asked, "Alright, what's your name?"

"My name is Dannelle Batista."

"Where are you from?"

"I am from Brazil."

"What part of Brazil?"

"I'm from the area of Bahia, in the small town of Salvador."

"Besides the American dream, what brings you here?"

As the officer listened, she started telling him what brought her here.   She said that she had started in Brazil working as prostitute for a German guy that lived all by himself in the middle of the jungle. The officer taking the report now started asking more questions, "When did you start working for this guy?"

"Oh, about four months ago.   It took me a long time to make my way here."

"What part of Brazil did he live in?"

"Just over the mountain from Golania. It is hard to find unless you have a guide."

"What did this man look like?"

"Oh, he is an old man, with white hair a scar right below his left eye."

"So, about how tall is he?"

"I'd say maybe this tall," she said, holding her hand in the air above her head.

The officer looked at her and where her hand was and figured that he must be about 5'11".

"Was he fat or skinny?"

"Uh, he was fat, very fat.   I do not like him; he is mean to me and the other girls.   All he cares about is his money and sex."

"Can you guess how old he is?"

"Fifty or sixty, I do not really know."

"Where was he from?"

"I think Germany, he has this funny coo coo clock he brought with him when he left his country."

Once the officer had finished his report, he had one of the other officers take her back to the holding cell.   As he watched her leave, he got up from his desk and went to see his boss.   He knocks on the boss's door and opened it. "Hey boss, do you remember telling us about that APB we got from the FBI, about some German guy taking off to South America with some money?"

"Are you talking about the 65-million-dollar embezzlement?"

"Yeah, that's the one.   I just processed one of the prostitutes we busted, who claims that she worked for a German guy who lives in the middle of the jungle in Brazil."

The boss had heard, through one of his friends in the FBI, about this guy who had taken off to Brazil with a bunch of money to live out his life in a country that had no extradition agreement with the United States. After talking with his officer, the boss called his friend in the FBI.   "Hey Buck, this is Riley.   Do you remember when you were telling me about a German guy that embezzled 65 million dollars and went to South America?"

"Yeah, I remember that.   What about it?"

"Well, one of my officer's was processing a prostitute that was picked up in a sting.   She claims that she worked for a German guy in Brazil."

"Do you think she's telling the truth?"

"I'm not sure.   However, I don't think she had a reason to lie about it."

"Do you still have her?"

"Yes, she's in lock up right now."

"Can you keep her there until tomorrow?   I can be there in the morning."

"I don't think that will be a problem.   I don't think she has anywhere to go."

Agent Buchanan came over the next day about 10:00 in the morning, with some pictures of the guy for the prostitute to look at and to check out her story.   After he checked in with his friend,

Riley, he was taken to an interrogation room to wait for the prostitute who had been locked up for the night.   The prostitute was soon brought into the room and seated. The officer that had brought Dannelle into the room introduced her to the FBI agent and then moved to one of the corners in the room in case he was needed.

The agent introduced himself to Dannelle, "Hi, I'm Agent Buchanan," he said, as he showed her his badge.

"What do you want from me?" she asked, nervously.

"From my understanding, you worked for a German guy when you lived in Brazil?"

"Yes, I did.   He was such a pig, always hurting the girls."

"Can you tell me about him?"

"What is in it for me if I tell you?" she asked, defiantly.

"First of all, take a look at these pictures and see if you recognize the man," he said, as he laid the pictures out on the table.

She carefully looked over all of the pictures and the picked one of them up, "This is him!" she exclaimed, as she spit on the picture.

At this point, the FBI agent got up and walked over to the officer in the corner of the room, "This is the guy that we've been looking for.   We need her in order to find him."

"Merry Christmas, she's all yours," said the officer, as he handed the agent her file. "I'll let Riley know that you're taking her."

The agent returned to the table and looked at her, "If you show us where the German lives, we'll drop all charges against you, if you promise never to come back to America and work as a prostitute or mule for the cartel."

The prostitute nodded her head in agreement, "I will be glad to show you where he lives for free ride back to Brazil."

At this point, the interview was over, and the officer escorted her back to the holding cell.

Agent Buchanan called his supervisor, letting him know what he had found out about Gunther Reichman, "I think we've found our man Gunther."

"Great! Make the deal with her and we'll go from there.   In the meantime, I'll write up the agreement to get her released into our custody," the supervisor said.

The FBI supervisor contacted his next level supervisor, Mike Reagan, and reported the news about a German living in Brazil that matched the man they had been looking for. Tony was sitting at his desk in Connecticut when the phone call came in from the FBI, "Is this Commander Anthony Jones?"

"Yes, may I ask who's calling?"

"This is Mike Reagan.   Are you ready to go look for Gunther?"

"Hi Mike, I'm ready whenever you are?"

"Well, we think we found him.   A woman has come to our attention that supposedly knows of him. Would you be interested in going with us to talk to her and find out if it's Gunther?"

"Sure, when are you leaving?"

"We're leaving on Monday at noon from Langley to go down. We'll be using one of the Air Force's Lear jets to fly down to El Paso to pick up the girl who can identify the German.   If all goes well, from there we'll go to Brazil, find him and bring him back to face charges."

"Okay, I'll meet you at Langley Base Operations."

Tony hung up the phone and rushed over to see the Admiral. When he entered the office, he asked Ann, "Is the Admiral in?"

About that time the Admiral came walking out of his office, "Yes, I thought I recognized that voice, what's up?"

"The FBI just called me, and they think they found Gunther Reichman, the man who's responsible for sinking our submarine. They want to know if I want to go with them to pick him up."

"Where's he hiding?"

"In Brazil, sir. I think we don't have any extradition agreements with Brazil, but I'd like to go down there and bring him back by any means possible."

"You're not suggesting kidnapping him, are you? That would be illegal and against international law. Because, if I was to find out that you did go down there to Brazil and kidnap the German, I would have to take some kind of action for what you had done. Well, if that's what you're suggesting, then you're going down there on your own, and make sure you fill out your TDY orders properly," the Admiral said, with a smile and then looked at Ann, "You didn't hear any of this."

"Yes, sir. I'm going down strictly as an advisor, to make sure the German is the right guy, for his own safety.   You know, now days, you can't be too careful when you're in South America. Well, I'd better hurry to get that paperwork filled out.   I'll be in touch, if I get a chance, I'll send you a postcard."

Later that night, as Tony and Ann were eating dinner at their favorite restaurant, Ann was rather quiet.   Tony sensed this, "You seem rather quiet tonight, what's wrong?"

"You know, the last time you were gone I worried about you the whole time.   And when you got back and told me about your adventures I was upset because you could have gotten yourself killed and I would have never seen you again," she replied, as the tears started running down her cheeks.

"Don't worry about me.   I'm only going down as a liaison for the Navy in case something comes up that needs the Navy's input," he said, as he took her hand and held it.

"Don't you know, I've fallen in love with you and I can't bear to be without you?"

"Well, I want you to know I've fallen in love with you too.   I would never do anything to jeopardize that in anyway."

Hearing this from Tony, she smiled, realizing that he loved her as well. After dinner was done, they went back to her apartment to be together and enjoy each other's company.   Ann didn't want to ever leave him and sat as close as she could on the couch next to Tony. For the first time in his life, Tony realized that he was not excited about leaving. He too wanted to stay by her side forever.   Being quiet and not saying anything, both of them fell asleep on the couch, happy just to be together holding each other.

The following Monday, with suitcase in hand, Tony was at Langley Base Operations, sitting in a row of chairs waiting for the FBI to show up.

At about 11:00 am, the FBI team arrived and Special Agent Mike Reagan walked over to Tony to introduce himself.   "I see that you're ready to go," Mike said, as he shook Tony's hand.

"I just hope it isn't a wild goose chase," Tony replied.

"You and me both, brother."

"Is this the team?"

"Yeah, just in case we have any problems along the way."

"What could go wrong?" Tony said, smiling.

"Yeah, what could go wrong," Mike replied.

There was a total of six people on the team, all of whom looked like the "Men in Black" characters, with their sunglasses and black suits, not saying a word. "I'm sure glad there on our side," Tony said to Mike as he looked at the six men.

"Me too. I wouldn't want to get on their bad side in any way shape or form."

Tony sat back down in his chair as Mike walked over to the operations desk to check on their flight. "Is our flight ready yet?"

The airman at the desk looked at his itinerary sheet and scrolled down the page, stopping on the information of the flight going to Texas, "It looks as if your team is cleared to Texas, actually, El Paso International Airport."

"That's the plan. Is the plane ready to board?"

"You should be able to board in about ten minutes, they should be done refueling her by then."

"Thank you for the update."

Mike turned and walked over to where Tony was seated and sat down next to him. The other part of the team stood by their luggage and patiently waited to board. As they sat and waited the ten minutes, Agent Reagan pulled out a photo of Gunther Reichman and showed it to Tony, "Just so you know, this is who we're going after."

Tony looked at the picture and started memorizing the face for future reference. Looking at the man you would never know that he was responsible for killing two submarine crews. After a couple of minutes, he handed the picture back to the agent, "You'd never know that he would be capable of killing anybody."

"Yeah, I know what you mean. I've never met, in all my time, anyone that hasn't said 'I'm innocent or they forced me to do it'."

While they were waiting to board, the pilot and co-pilot came walking over to the flight operations desk. After talking to the airman, they turned and came over to where Mike and Tony were sitting and shook hands with them, "We're ready to board the aircraft now."

"That's good news. It'll only take a few minutes to load our gear and then we'll be ready to go. Oh, by the way, this is Commander Tony Jones, and he'll be going with us on this trip."

The pilot nodded to Tony and shook his hand, "I see you're a Navy man, what's your interest in this trip? Are you a casual observer?"

"You might say that."

"Fair enough then."

The co-pilot, seeing the six men standing there, asked Agent Reagan, "What do you feed those giants?"

"Anything that doesn't move," Agent Reagan chuckled.

The pilot excused himself from the group, "If you'll excuse me, I've got to do the preflight checks before we take off."

With that the pilot and co-pilot left to go find their airplane. The pilot and co-pilot were busy doing their preflight checks, while the FBI team and Tony loaded all their gear aboard the aircraft and then boarded the Lear jet themselves. Once everybody was seated aboard the jet, the pilot started going through the startup procedures and as he did so the co-pilot would call out "Check," then repeat the step to the pilot.

Once the startup procedures were complete they taxied to the designated end of the run-way and asked for clearance from the control tower and then waited again for permission to take off. After they got clearance for their takeoff, the Lear jet started rolling down the runway in full afterburner and was airborne in half the length of the 5000-foot runway, reaching into the sky for more altitude. Upon reaching their intended cruising altitude of thirty thousand feet the jet leveled off and turned slightly into the sun headed into a southwesterly direction towards Texas.

The five and half hour flight was uneventful, and everybody was able to find something to do to keep themselves occupied. Having served a couple of tours onboard a carrier, Tony had learned how to deal with the boredom and took advantage of this time to close his eyes and doze off. All was quite onboard the jet until the pilot called over the intercom system to let them know they were on final approach to El Paso International Airport. Once they had landed, the Lear jet taxied to a separate part of the terminal that was empty. As they came to a stop in front of the terminal, the co-pilot opened the door and, with some assistance from the ground crew, lowered the steps on to the tarmac. As they made their way down the steps and into the terminal, they were met by an FBI agent, who had been waiting for them.

"Hi, I'm Agent Reagan and this is Commander Jones."

"Agent Buchanan, nice to meet you. My partner is waiting for us, in one of the security rooms. If you'll follow me, I'll introduce you to our star witness."

"That's good," Reagan said, as he turned and signaled the rest of his team to stay put.

They proceeded to walk through the airport to one of the closed rooms used by airport security. An airport security guard was posted by the door, waiting for Agent Buchanan to show his badge before he let them into the room where his partner and Dannelle were seated.

As his partner stood up, Agent Buchanan introduced him, "Agent Reagan this is my partner Agent Tyler, and this here is Dannelle Batista.   She's the one that has information on Gunther Reichman."

Mike, set down his attache case and opened it and pulled out some pictures of the German named, Gunther Reichman. He handed the photos to Dannelle, "Is this the man you were with in Brazil?"

"Yes, this is the man I know in Brazil," she said, as she nodded her head in agreement and continued looking at the pictures.

"Are you sure this is the man?" Reagan asked one more time.

"Si, this is the man," she replied, as she looked straight into Reagan's eyes.

Reagan thought for a moment, "Well, it looks as if we're on our way to Brazil then. Tony, would you get with the pilots and find out what our schedule is for the trip while I make a phone call to my bosses," Reagan said, as he got up to leave the room to make the phone call.

Agent Reagan called his office in Washington to let them know that their witness was able to identify Gunther and that they would be on their way to Brazil to pick him up.   In the meantime, Tony walked over to the pilots, "There's been a change of plans, we need to fly to Brazil now.   How long will it be before we can take off again?"

"Well, we'll need to file a flight plan, get refueled, and get something to eat for the trip.   I expect it shouldn't take more than an hour to be wheels up."

"Okay, that works.   I'll let the others know."

The captain was correct with his estimated departure time. With the plane refueled and the new flight plan filed, everything was squared away for their trip to Brazil. Just before taking off, Reagan thanked Buchanan and his partner for doing a good job. "This will mean a lot to the wives and kids of the crews that died aboard those submarines."

"I'm just thankful that we found someone that could lead us to him," Buchanan replied.

They all shook hands before boarding the aircraft with their star witness. The flight would take a little over 14 hours to fly from Texas to Brazil, with two stops along the way for fuel. Having already spent five hours on the plane just to get to El Paso, one of the team members found out that the Lear jet had a DVD player onboard and bought some DVD movies to watch along the way.

In the meantime, Mike and Tony continued to interview Dannelle for more information as to the actual location where the German was living in Brazil. Mike pulled out a map and showed it to her and asked her to point out where Gunther's house was. Dannelle studied the map for about five minutes and then pointed to a small town near Anapolis, close to the city of Brasilia.

Mike walked up to the pilot of the aircraft, "We need you to take us to Brasilia, Brazil can you do that?'

The pilot checked his flight map and looked over the layout of the airport, "It's big enough to land with no problems. Let me look into changing our flight plan."

After five minutes, the pilot came back to where Mike and Tony were sitting, "All set."

The change in flight plans made their time in the air shorter by about three hours, as the distance was not as far to Brasilia as their original destination of Rio de Janeiro. Upon landing at Brasilia, they found a hotel near the airport to spend the night at. They would start the next part of their trip into the jungles of Brazil the following day.

As the team watched the Lear jet roll down the runway and fly away into the setting sun, the feeling of being in another world took hold. Tony, never having been to South America, felt it the most. Not knowing what to expect on this new adventure he was already looking forward to being back home with Ann. As he picked up his gear, he followed the others to the waiting cabs that would take them to the hotel that they would be staying at.

215

Chapter XXIV

The first couple of days in Brasilia were spent getting the transportation, supplies, and food that they would need to go into the jungle to look for Gunther Reichman, and mainly just to rest up after the 20 hour flight from Virginia. Being in a small town, the locals were suspicious of what brought eight men and one woman into their town. None of them, with the exception of the girl who was a local, looked like they fit the profile of being tourists. Once they had found the transportation they needed, they left at midnight so as not to attract any more attention than necessary.

Reagan was driving the first vehicle with Dannelle as she gave directions, leading the team through the jungle on what would be called dirt roads. With the directions Dannelle was giving, the team only had to stop twice in order to cross the small rivers that made up part of the road. During these times, the team would have to get out and push the jeeps through the water, to keep from getting stuck in the mud. For the most part, the road was in pretty good shape for traveling on. The only problem they had was making their way up the steep mountain roads. Occasionally, one of the locals would be coming from the opposite direction, and as it was a single lane, everybody would need to get out and help the other driver get around their two vehicles.

After traveling all day, they decided to stop and make camp in a clearing on top of one of the mountain passes. They each took turns standing guard, just in case bandits were in the area. Tony stood guard for the first two hours, listening to the sounds of the jungle, wondering if there was someone or something out there watching them. As he walked around the camp, he saw Dannelle sitting comfortably on a log next to the fire. He decided that if the jungle sounds weren't making her nervous then he didn't have anything to worry about either. Later that night, while he was asleep, the camp was woken up by the scream of a jaguar. Tony got up to go and check on Dannelle and saw that she was still asleep, so he went back to his tent and carefully tucked his gun under his pillow and went back to sleep.

The next morning as the sun rose, everyone was sitting around the fire drinking their coffee to take the chill off the morning. Reagan and Tony were visiting with Dannelle while the others packed up the camp. "How much further is it to the next small town?"

"I'm not sure, where are we now on the map?"

Reagan pointed to their spot on the map, "We're about right here."

She studied the map for a few minutes, trying to find something that she could recognize. Setting the map down, she scanned the terrain around them before finally answering, "I think we should be in the village by nightfall."

"You know that the locals there are probably friends with Gunther.   I'm thinking that we don't want to stay the night in town," Tony said.

"I agree with you. How about we drive around the town and camp on the other side of it.   That way we don't draw any unwanted attention," Reagan replied.

"Dannelle, is there another way around the town that would be accessible with our vehicles?" Tony asked.

"Not that I know of. I think that we may have to leave our vehicles and hike to where Gunther is," Dannelle replied.

"How far is the ranch from the town?" Reagan asked.

"If we stay on the road, we can get to the ranch in the middle of the night. Or if we walk, it would be the middle of the next day." Dannelle said.

"That is, if it doesn't rain or we get eaten first," Tony said, smiling.

"What if we were to leave the vehicles here and hike around the outskirts of the village. Dannelle, is there a better place to park these vehicles without being seen?" Reagan asked, after thinking about it for a minute.

"There is a place, further up the road where my uncle lives. It would be a safe place for your vehicles and that way we don't have to walk as far."

Once the jeeps had been loaded, everybody climbed back in and continued their journey. The dirt road they were traveling on remained good and dry, having no more rivers to cross, they were able to make good time and eventually found her uncle's place. Dannelle left the team there as she and Tony walked into the small town of Goiania, looking for her uncle. She had Tony hide in one of the older empty buildings, "I need you to stay in here while I go and look for my uncle, so that no one will see you and wonder why you are here."

Tony nodded his head in agreement, as he found a place in the shadows to hide. Dannelle headed off towards the town center, stopping occasionally to ask about her uncle. Finding some of the old men seated in the shade of the local cafe she asked, "Have you seen my uncle Pedro around?"

At which that all looked at each other and nodded their heads 'no'.

Tony stood in the shadows of the empty building watching Dannelle as she went from place to place searching for her uncle. One of the younger men in the town stopped and pointed her in the direction of the local mercantile store. She crossed the street and walked into the store and within minutes she came out with, what appeared to be her uncle, walking in the direction where Tony was hiding. Once they were inside the old building Dannelle introduced her uncle to Tony

"Señor Tony, this is my uncle Pedro," then turning to her uncle, "This is the American I was telling you about."

"You are American?   Do you know the President?   I would like to meet him someday. Do you think that you can help me meet him?" Pedro asked, enthusiastically.

Tony, surprised by his questions, didn't know how to reply. Dannelle jumped into the conversation, "Uncle, we need your help."

"What is it you need, little one?"

"Uncle, we need a place to park some vehicles, that will be safe and out of sight. We have parked them at your house for right now."

"That is good, no problem. I will have Miguel, watch over them."

Tony had been watching out the window as Dannelle talked to her uncle and saw the local policeman talking to the young man that had told Dannelle where her uncle was. "I think we have someone looking for us."

The uncle looked out the window and saw the policeman coming in their direction.   Cussing under his breath, he said, "We need to leave right now, so your American friend doesn't get caught."

Sneaking out the back way and into the jungle, the uncle led the three of them back to his house.   When they got there, the uncle had Miguel show the team where to park their jeeps so they wouldn't be seen.

Tony, looking over his shoulder, kept an eye out, just in case the policeman had followed them.   Looking for Reagan, Tony caught his attention and motioned for him to come over where he was.

"What's up, Tony?"   Reagan asked.

"When we were in town, the local policeman took an interest in Dannelle asking around about her uncle's whereabouts.   And I'm worried that he might have followed us here," Tony said, still looking over his shoulder.

Agent Reagan looked around the area and using his hands, signaled to one of the other agents who quickly came over to him. "I think we might have an unwelcome visitor.   I need you to make sure that he doesn't find out that we're here.   Take as many of the others as you need to make sure the area is secure."

The agent turned and pointing his finger to three of the other agents, motioned for them to meet with him, as he headed off into the jungle.

As Tony watched all of this happening with the agents, he was impressed and surprised at how good these guys worked together. "Hey Reagan, where do I sign up so I can be part of this?"   Tony said, smiling as he motioned with his eyes at the other agents.

"If you're really good, go to church on Sunday, maybe, just maybe, I'll put in a good word for you," he chuckled.

"Oh, I am not worthy."

Tony and Agent Reagan walked back over to where Dannelle and her uncle were standing. "How far away are we from Gunther's place?" Reagan asked.

"Maybe a day, if we stay on the road.   Any other way, I am not sure," Dannelle replied.

The uncle, hearing this, looked at Dannelle, "Why do you want to go to the German's place?"

Dannelle didn't know how to answer the question and looked at Tony and Reagan for an answer. "We want to get the German because he is responsible for killing our countrymen and almost starting a war," Reagan answered.

The old man stood there, thinking about what the agent had just said. Looking at Dannelle, then at Tony for confirmation, he shook his head, "I do not like traitors" he said as he walked away.

Reagan walked over to check with the other agents that were standing by their equipment and started talking to them, "We're going to only need two days' worth of supplies to get us up and back from the German's house. Let's try not to take too much if we don't need to, alright?"

One of the agents nodded his head and got busy with the others getting everything together for the next leg of their journey.

Mike Reagan found Tony and Dannelle inside her uncle's house seated around the small wooden table next to the fireplace. He looked over the interior of the house, "Man, what I could do to fix this place up," he said, as he looked for a place to sit down.

Getting out of the sun and into the house, the temperature dropped by about 10 degrees which was a relief for everyone inside. Uncle Pedro had never had this many visitors in his house before, "Miguel, we need some extra food to feed our guests. Go and see what you can find."

"Yes, father. I will go and look."

As they sat there talking amongst themselves, one of the agents who had been working security, came through the door. "We got company headed our way."

"How many and who is it?" Reagan asked, as he stood up.

"One man, he looks to be a cop."

"All of you go outside and wait for me to call you back. Hurry," the uncle said, as he looked around to make sure there was nothing to indicate that anybody was there besides himself and his family.

Mike went outside, "You guys disappear and take the equipment with you."

Tony followed Mike as he headed out of the house following the other agents. He grabbed what was left of the gear, as they headed to the tree line bordering the house to hide. As they sat in the shadows watching for the visitor to come into view, the sweat started to appear on their faces. The bugs finding fresh meat, started showing up to start biting them. From where Tony was, he could see the policeman come up to the door and knock. Dannelle opened the door to see who it was, "May I help you,"

As he stood there looking at Dannelle for a minute she wanted to run and hide from him. She had known this kind of man before and what he was thinking. When he smiled, she could see that most of his teeth were missing and the others were stained by too many cigarettes and wine. As she stood there, she started feeling dirty and wanted to take a bath to clean the filth off of her, especially, after he started smiling at her. Pushing Dannelle aside, he forced his way into the uncle's house and saw him sitting at his table and noticed that the old man didn't even look up at him as he stood there, "What do you want?" he asked.

"I see that your niece has come to visit you.   Is everything okay?"

"Yes, all is well.   She comes from Brasilia for a visit."

"That is good to hear.   Our friend, the Señor Reichman, says that you were his favorite girl while you were there. He told me himself that he wants you to come back."

The policeman was getting upset by the lack of respect that he was getting from the two of them and continued, "He says that you have hurt his feelings by leaving. I hope you did not make him mad by leaving."

"I will never go back there to be his girlfriend, ever again."

"Is that so, well Señor Reichman told me to find you and bring you back. He promised lots of money if I found you," he said, smiling as he pulled his gun out to force her to leave with him.

Uncle Pedro, seeing the gun, stood up to stop her from leaving and was hit in the face by the policeman. Watching her uncle fall to the ground, Dannelle screamed and went to help him. The policeman grabbed her by the arm and held her in place, as she watched her uncle laying there, bleeding on the floor.

The policeman walked over to the uncle, "Please, do not do that again, or else I will have to kill you."

Still fighting him, Dannelle reached up and scratched the policeman's face to which he hit her with his gun, knocking her out. As she went limp, he quickly grabbed her before she fell to the ground. He then threw her over his shoulder and walked out the door and headed back into town.

Tony, hearing Dannelle scream, jumped up to rescue her from the policeman. As he was about to clear the tree line, Mike stood up and motioned for him to stop. Not sure what was going on, he complied and went back to where he had been previously. They continued to sit and wait for Pedro's all clear signal. After another 10 minutes uncle Pedro stumbled out of the house and signaled that it was safe for them to come back in.

"What's up, why did you stop me!" Tony said to Mike, upset that he had told him to stand down,

"Why are we here? What are we here to do?" Mike asked in reply.

"In my book, this isn't right, calling me off like that," he said, realizing that Mike was right.

"Hey, Tony, I'm sorry but right now it's more important that we get Reichman first and then go after the cop. If we had stopped what was going on, chances are Reichman would be gone by the time we got there."

"I know what you're saying is right, but I still don't like it."

"I don't either. Do you understand how many times I've had to make this same decision before now, for the same reasons?"

Unable to answer the question, Tony went outside to cool down and think about what Mike had said.

Mike walked over to where Pedro was being looked at by one of the other agents to see how bad he was hurt. Pedro looked at Mike, "If you get the chance, I want you to hurt our friendly policeman, promise me this."

"Not only will we hurt him, but we'll also bring Dannelle back," Tony said, interrupting the conversation as he walked back into the house.

"We'll bring her back, one way or the other," Mike added.

Beck came into the house and gave the all clear signal to Mike. At this point, Mike sent one of the agents to go get the others. When everyone was gathered together Mike turned to Beck, "Beck, I need you to set up a security watch around the house for the rest of the night."

"Will do, boss," Beck said and went about setting up the security detail.

As the evening wore on, the windows to the house were opened to allow the cool breeze to circulate through the house. There was a stillness in the room where everyone was gathered. Nobody was talking, each of them were deep in their own thoughts. Tony looked around at each of the team members and noticed that all of them looked the same way. He realized that in all of his time being with the FBI agents that he hadn't seen anybody smile except Mike. They were always cool, aloof, and efficient in everything that they did. Speaking only when necessary and always very professional in their actions. For the first time, Tony thought to himself that he was happy about choosing the Navy as a career. He knew that the Seals acted the same way, but they were a breed of their own, not like the other personnel in the Navy. He also understood that Special Forces, and the Green Beret in the Army were the same way.

Miguel showed up later that night carrying some fruit he had picked to eat. Seeing his father with his head all bandaged up, he dropped the fruit and ran over to see for himself that his father was alright and refused to leave his side the rest of the night.

As he walked back into town with his prize, the policeman swore to himself under his breath, complaining about being fat and out of shape. He promised himself that when he was done with the girl, he would start exercising again. He only stopped twice, as he walked the two miles back into town carrying Dannelle. Kicking the door open, he made his way through the jail and put Dannelle into one of the cells, stopping to catch his breath once more before locking the cell door behind him. By now Dannelle was starting to come around and could see that she had been locked up in one of the cells inside the jail. She could see the policeman standing in front of the cell, smiling at her as he rubbed his face where she had scratched him. "You are very lucky that Señor Reichman wants you back in one piece. Otherwise, you would be mine for the night and you would be dead in the morning," he said, laughing as he walked out of the room, closing the door behind him.

Upon hearing this, Dannelle drew herself up into an upright fetal position on the bed with her back against the wall of the cell, wrapping the blanket around her.   She stayed that way until she fell asleep.

Gunther was sitting in his den when the phone rang, "Hello."
"Señor Reichman, this is your friend, I have good news for you. I have found one of your favorite girls and she is sitting in my jail."
"Which one is it?"
"Her name is Dannelle."
"Oh good, is she okay?"
"She is fine.   She is resting in one of my cells.   If you wish, I can bring her out tomorrow."
"That would be fine.   Whatever you do, don't hurt her."
"Señor Reichman, I am sad that you would think I would do that. I will take good care of her.   Good night."
Hanging up the phone, Gunther sat there thinking to himself that he could go get Dannelle tonight and have a most enjoyable evening as she entertained him. He looked at his watch, and being comfortable where he was, he decided to wait for tomorrow.   That would be soon enough for him. Standing up to stretch before heading off to bed, he passed a mirror and stopped to look at himself. Smiling at his reflection, he realized that since being here he had lost about thirty pounds and was starting to feel like he used to when he was younger.   He thoought to himself, *Yes sir, being on the run and living in the jungle agrees with me.*   He took one last look at himself before going upstairs to bed and smiled, knowing that all of the girls would be in his bedroom already asleep.

Chapter XXV

Tony got up early the next morning and decided to go outside for some fresh air. Trying to be as quiet as he could, he opened the door and walked past the agent standing guard just outside the door. He made eye contact with him and nodded his head and the agent nodded his head in return. He hadn't slept very well, simply because of all the noise that came from the jungle during the night. He stood there in the early morning sunlight trying to warm up and relax. Miguel saw Tony standing outside and went out to him and handed him a cup of coffee. He wrapped his hands around the warm cup and took a sip, hoping it would warm him up inside. "Thank you for the coffee," he said, as he smiled at Miguel. Miguel, not fully understanding English, saw Tony's smile and walked away happy.

When he finished drinking his coffee Tony decided to go back to the house. As he got closer, he could hear voices coming from inside. As he got nearer, he could hear Mike talking, "Gunther's house isn't too far from the outskirts of town and Pedro knows where it is and what it looks like."

Wanting to be part of the planning, Tony stepped inside and found a chair to sit on. From his vantage point, Tony could see a rough picture of Gunther's house drawn out on the dirt floor of the room. Mike had all of the agents watching intently as Pedro used a wooden stick to draw the roads to and from the house. "We have one thing in our favor and that's the element of surprise. If we do this right, no one will know we were even there when we kidnap him," Mike said, as he watched Pedro draw the lines on the dirt floor.

Turning to the senior agent, Mike nodded, "Agent Beck will explain the positions and jobs we need to take in order to pull this off, without killing ourselves in the process."

Agent Beck, taking the stick from Pedro, proceeded with his part of the planning. Each agent sat listening to Beck as he explained each of their roles in the operation to get Gunther Reichman out of

Brazil without the Brazilian government finding out he had been taken or, for the lack of better words, kidnapped.

In the meantime, Señor Reichman had gotten used to his freedom there in Brazil and was not so cautious about his coming and goings as he should have been. Having his own bodyguards always around, made up for his lack of caution. He knew, of course, that any Americans coming to the village, would stand out like a sore thumb, especially to the locals. They would, in turn, tell Gunther about the gringos being there for a nominal fee, which would give him enough time to go into hiding, never to be found again.

With all the positions identified, Mike and Tony started discussing the final points about going after Reichman without raising anybody's curiosity. Letting things go the way they had for Dannelle allowed them to keep the element of surprise, which they would need in order to get their man. "Do you think that it's still necessary that we hike through the jungle to get Gunther?" Tony asked.

"I don't see any other way to do this without alerting our friend," Mike replied.

Pedro was listening intently to the discussion going on between the two men, "Pardon me for interrupting your conversation, but I would like to go with you, when you leave tomorrow. Besides, I know a way to go around the town without letting anyone know you are here," he said, holding his head so it didn't hurt so bad.

Mike and Tony stopped talking as Pedro started to explain what he meant, "In my younger days me and my friends would go exploring. One day while doing this, we came across an old campsite that had been used by the drug people. We explored the area thinking we would find treasures and other things. After searching the camp, we came across some bones and guns. We could tell that they had been there for quite a while. We were scared, but being young, we were still curious. So, we continued searching the area, and in doing so we found a trail that led into our little town. As we followed the trail we found that it split into two trails, one part of the trail took us back into our little town and the other part took us away from town, up into the mountains that were on the other side of our town. We followed the second trail and found out that it led to a flat area big enough that you could see the tops of the trees of the jungle below us. Occasionally, we would find trash that somebody had left behind."

"Please continue. Where are these mountains located?" Tony asked.

Pedro, used the stick and drew the trails on the floor. He showed the trail that went into the mountains and ended just north of Gunther's place. Both Tony and Mike looked at the new drawings on the floor, trying to figure out what this meant for their mission. "Do you think it still exists and can you find it?" Mike asked.

"I do not know.   You must remember this was years ago. The last time we went there to the top of the mountains, we could here gunfire."

Tony looked at his watch and saw that it was still early morning. "Do you think that you could show us where this trail was?"

"Yes, I think I still remember where it started."

Tony looked at Mike, "What do you think about a hike this morning?"

"Can I bring some of the guys with us?" he said, smiling.

"It's your party."

At that point, Mike called out to Beck, "You want to go for a walk?"

"Why, what's up?"

"Pedro's agreed to show us a way to get to Gunther's place without having to go through town or the jungle."

"Let me get my camera, and I'll be ready to go." he said, after thinking for a minute.

"Don't forget your weapons, it may be a little hostile with the locals up on the mountain," Mike said.

Within ten minutes, everyone was ready to go.   Each of them carrying a gun for protection and a canteen of water.   Pedro took the lead as they started searching for the trail.   Every so often they stopped to let Pedro get his bearings before taking off again. Pedro would start singing to himself when he knew he was on the right part of the jungle path. Tony was glad when Pedro would stop and check his bearings so that he could catch his breath.   Mike seemed to be doing alright for the first part of the trip, then he started showing signs of being out of breath as well.   Both Mike and Tony were impressed with the fact that Pedro was able to keep going, especially for his age. When Pedro stopped again to get his bearings Tony asked, "Just out of curiosity, how old are you Pedro?"

"Let's just say, I lost interest in the local ladies in town when I turned 70 years old. Those were some good times," Pedro said, as he smiled.

Mike and Tony just sat there, surprised by his response. Beck chuckled to himself, seeing the looks on their faces. At this point, Pedro started looking again for the trail, so the others got up and started following him once again. Within another twenty minutes, Pedro let out a yell, "Aw yes, here is the trail! My memory has served me well."

Mike caught up to Pedro and looked at the trail that lay before them. He could see footprints that had been made recently. Mike grabbed Pedro, "Better let me take point, just in case the trail is booby trapped. Beck, you take the rear. Tony, you watch out for Pedro. And the rest of you keep your eyes peeled."

All of them nodded and took their places in single file. Mike started cautiously walking up the trail, searching for anything that looked out of place. As they followed the trail, they noticed that they were slowly climbing out of the jungle and that it was getting cooler. At one point, Mike signaled with his hand for them to stop, as he could see a trip wire going across the trail. He followed the trip wire with his fingers to a trigger connected to an old-style claymore mine, the same kind that was used in Viet Nam. He cut the trip wire and threw the mine deeper into the jungle so that they could keep moving forward. After walking for another twenty minutes, Pedro stopped and motioned the others to stop, then he put his hand to his ear, indicating that he could hear someone talking up ahead. Moving closer to the voices in a crouched position, Mike and Beck moved further up the trail and disappeared into the deep jungle. A couple of minutes later, Beck came back down the trail to where Tony and Pedro were waiting, "You guys ready to go?" Beck asked.

As they walked up the trail, they could see Mike up ahead signaling them to catch up. When Tony caught up to where Mike was waiting, he asked, "So, what happened?"

"Well we had some small talk with the two men, and we found out that they were Democrats. Doing the right thing, we changed their minds," Mike said, as he handed one of the Ak-47s to Beck and walked on.

Tony stood there for a second, not knowing what to say, except, "I'm glad that voting is by secret ballot."

Mike took the lead again, and the rest of the hike was uneventful. They were able to make good time getting to the top of the mountain. Tony looked at his watch and realized that they had been on the trail for almost five hours. At this point they decided to take a break and catch their breath. Pedro used this time to go off on his own and look around as the others were resting. Within minutes he came back, "The trail you want to take is over there," he said, pointing across the open field.

Checking his compass and watch, Mike made note of the direction and started off again. From this point on, it was downhill and was easier to accomplish. Still walking single file and looking for any kind of booby traps, they found themselves looking at the mountains that Pedro had told them about earlier in the day. Pedro now took the lead and started showing them where Reichman's place was. After clearing one last hill, all of them stopped and looked at the ranch that Gunther called home. Beck took his camera and using a zoom lens, started taking pictures of the layout of the ranch. After he was done taking the pictures, Pedro said, "From here it is only another mile to the house."

Having seen enough, Mike decided to head back to where the others were. Tomorrow would be soon enough for the real job. With the pictures he took, Beck could start tweaking and peaking the operation for the rest of the team. They headed back up the trail in short time and were at the top once again and walking in the direction of the trail that would take them back to Pedro's house. The moon was starting to appear once they found the trail. By now most of them were starting to get tired and started thinking about having something to eat once they got back. They slowly made their way down the trail. When they reached the bottom of the mountain, it was completely dark, almost like being in a tunnel, especially with the jungle canopy blocking out the stars and moon. By midnight they had arrived back at Pedro's house, tired and thirsty and, most of all, hungry. Fortunately, Miguel had some food cooking and it was all ready to serve once they got back. After setting some wooden plates on the table he went to go get the meat that had been cooking over the fire. As he placed some meat on each of their plates, all of them dug in to eat.

"So, do you like what you're eating?" Pedro asked halfway through dinner.

"Yes, is it some kind of chicken?" Beck answered, as the others nodded yes to the question.

"No señors, this is snake meat.   Miguel was very lucky finding it. Sometimes they get to be pretty big, we eat good for a week then."

The three men sat and looked at each, kind of surprised that it actually tasted good, and without blinking an eye, they continued eating. The other agents that had stayed behind knew what it was and had decided to have some MRE's for dinner instead.   They had waited for the three of them to come back, smiling to themselves, as they knew what was being served for dinner.   Thinking that they were going to get something over on their boss.   Mike, for the first time realized that all of his team was inside the house watching the three of them eat.   He looked around at the rest of the team and could see that they were all there, waiting to see what was going to happen as they ate their meal. "I don't want to be a pig; I believe we should let the others have some as well."

All of the agents then stood up to leave. "No, I really think that I should insist on my men trying this," he said glaring at them.

By the time it was lights out, everybody had agreed that snake really did taste like chicken.   In the end, Mike and Tony had the last laugh.

Chapter XXVI

After being in jail all night and not getting much sleep, Dannelle was still half asleep when the policeman came in and banged on the bars with his baton to wake her up.

"Did I wake you?" he asked, laughing at her.

By now she was wide awake and wondering what was going to happen next. He shoved a plate of food through the slot, " I don't want you telling Señor Reichman that I didn't take good care of you, like I promised him," the policeman said, as he sat down to watch her eat.

Taking the plate of food, Dannelle hadn't realized how hungry she was. She sat back down on her bed and started eating her food while watching the policeman the whole time, expecting him to come in and have his way with her. When she had finished, she handed the plate back to him.   He left the room to put it on his desk. The next time he came in, he was carrying a bucket of water and soap, plus some clean clothes for her. "I think it would be nice if you cleaned yourself up and put on these clothes I have for you," he said, as he sat down, all the while smiling so that she could see his teeth.

Taking the bucket of water and the clothes, she stood there waiting for him to leave, "If you don't leave I will tell Gunther you hurt me," she said, hoping it would be enough to get him to leave the room.

The policeman knew that if she said anything to Señor Reichman about him doing anything to her, he wouldn't get his money and there would be hell to pay. No longer smiling now and grumbling under his breath he got up and left the room. She watched him close the door and waited a few minutes before feeling safe enough to wash. Within a few minutes, Dannelle was as clean as she could get using the clothes she had on previously as wash rags. That, and being able to wash her hair with soap, helped rejuvenate her spirit and then having cleaner clothes to wear helped even more.

After banging on the cell door to get the policeman's attention, he came in.   "I'm ready to go back to the hacienda now," she said.

Opening the cell door and waiting for her to pass, he grabbed her by the arm, whispering in her ear so close she could smell his bad breath, "You best not try to escape, if you do, Señor. Reichman may not like what he sees after I catch you."

Ready to throw up because of his breath, she gagged a couple of times. Seeing this, he released her and watched her leave the room and go into the main office. Having regained her composure, the policeman grabbed her again by the arm and led her out the door and to his truck. She sat as far away from him as she could as they drove off, headed to the hacienda and Gunther Reichman.

The next day started way to early or late, depending on how you looked at it, for the whole team.   Tony, when getting up to start his day, had found muscles that he didn't know he had.   Even Mike and Beck were slow to get going.   Pedro laughed at the three of them, "Wait till you get my age, then you will know what it means to be old."

No one replied to Pedro's comment, in fact, as he stood there and laughed at them, they all knew that they were half his age, and he was up and ready to go with them once again, to go get Señor Reichman.   Fact was, he was already to go, as were the other agents, at the crack of dawn.   Finally, getting some coffee and something to eat, they were all ready to hike back up to the top of the mountain.   As everybody put on their gear, Mike called out to them, "Heads up team, on our way up the trail on the mountain we came across a booby trap and some guards watching the trail for their boss. I tell you this just in case they may have set up some more booby traps and brought in other men. There's a possibility that they might be waiting for us this morning. So be aware of what's going on around you at all times. Make sure you use the buddy system everywhere you go. Whatever you do, make sure someone knows where you are. Got it, good. By the way, how was the chicken last night?"

"If anything happens and you run across any men, before you shoot them, ask them who they voted for in America's presidential election," Tony said, smiling, as he tried to get them all to relax.

All of them laughed at the last comments Mike and Tony had made, each of them knew that everything depended on everyone doing their job, otherwise someone could die.   As Mike looked for Pedro, he realized he was gone.   Looking up the trail he could see that he was halfway into the jungle. Tony looked at Mike, "I guess he doesn't get into FBI pep talks."

"We better hurry if we're going to catch him," Mike said, as he started to leave, trying to catch up to Pedro.

Watching Pedro move up the mountain, Tony thought to himself, knowing it wasn't going to be a nice walk in the woods, *"A nice hot bath would sure feel good tonight. And having Ann by my side would really be nice as well."*

By now Mike had caught up to Pedro, and taking the point again, he started looking for the booby traps that may have been put on the trail since last night.   Beck took the six position for the team, while the others kept a wary eye out for anything that didn't seem right. Tony stayed with Pedro to keep an eye on him, as they hiked the trail.   Every so often, Mike would appear and give them all clear signal, letting them know the trail was safe to walk.   After they had been walking for a couple of hours everyone decided to take a break, resting and drinking the water they carried with them. The mosquitoes had found the men and were having a field day.   Every so often you could hear a slap and some cussing to go along with the insect dying.   Most of them were covered in sweat, knowing that it wasn't going to get better anytime soon. Tony looked at the team and noticed that none of them were complaining about the situation they were dealing with.   Each of them acted as if it was just another day coming back from the gym.   Five minutes later, Mike gave the signal, and everybody got to their feet to continue the hike.   They continued to climb higher into the jungle, once they found the mountain the mosquitoes weren't bothering everyone anymore. The cool air was working its magic, forcing the bugs lower into the hotter and more humid part of the jungle.   As they continued their hike, Mike came back down the trail motioning everyone to stop and kneel on the ground.   All of the agents took defensive positions, looking into the jungle, looking for any sign of the bad guys. Mike quietly made his way to his team, "I believe we might have some company up ahead. I guess the other two we took care of last night, were supposed to check in and when they didn't, they sent someone out to look for them."

"How many of them are there?" Beck asked.

"I counted six of them, but I could hear voices coming from the jungle.   I think they found the other two men from yesterday."

"Drug soldiers," Pedro said, as he spit on the ground, showing his utter contempt for them.

"How do you want to handle this, guns or knives?" Beck asked.

"If we take them out, they might send more later and maybe take it out on the village as a way of getting even for the loss of their men," Tony said.

"Good point, our mission is to still go after Gunther. However, that being said, if we take out the drug people along the way, it might save some lives further down the line," Mike said.

"Pedro, do you know where the drug operation is set up," Beck asked.

"I have heard it is one more mountain over from the top we were at last night. I can take you there if you like," Pedro said.

"How far away is it from the top of the flat area?" Mike asked.

"About an hour, we can follow the ridge to get there, we should see their buildings before they see us," Pedro added.

"What are you thinking boss?" Beck asked, as he could see Mike was mulling something over in his head.

"You've seen the house; how hard would it be to get Gunther minus a couple of guys?"

"If I let you have, Tony and Pedro and maybe one of the other agents to go after the drug operation, I think you should be able to handle it alright," Beck replied.

"Tony do you mind going on this other mission with Pedro and one other agent? I have to be with the main force to get Gunther," Mike stated.

Tony looked at Pedro, "What do you think Pedro?"

"I'm ready to go," he replied.

Mike motioned for one of the agents to come over, "There's been a slight change of plans, I need you to go with these guys to take out the drug lab on another mountain top."

Agent Dixon thought about it for a moment and nodded his head in agreement, "When do we start?"

"Just as soon as we take care of these guys up ahead of us," Mike said, smiling.

"Can I help you?" Pedro asked, acting like he was looking forward to it.

"Sure, why not, do you want a gun to use?" Mike asked.

"I don't need no stinking gun," he said, laughing, as he pulled out his knife and showed it to Mike.

Mike and the others were surprised by the size of his knife and couldn't help but laugh at his reply.

"I think I've heard that somewhere else a while back," Tony said.

"I will go after the men in the jungle, okay?" Pedro said, as he got up to go.

Mike nodded his head, "Be my guest."

Within minutes Pedro was gone and couldn't be seen or heard. Mike went back to his team and started to figure a way to get the other soldiers up ahead. Tony, listening to their planning offered, "How about I pretend I'm a tourist hiking alone on the trail and come upon these guys, I let them see me and I start running back down the trail right into you guys?"

All of them sat there thinking about Tony's idea. "Are you sure you want to do this, remember you're an observer on this mission," Mike said.

"I'm getting tired of watching, I want to play," Tony said.

Chapter XXVII

As the truck pulled into the shaded area of the hacienda the policeman got out of his truck and walked around to the other side to let Dannelle out.   It was deja vu all over again for Dannelle. The smell of the air and the surrounding area seemed like a distant memory from days gone by.   She took it all in as she stood there for a moment before being grabbed by the policeman. "Welcome home, Chiquita, I bet you missed it," he said, as they made their way to the front door.

As they stepped up onto the porch, the door opened and there was Gunther standing there waiting for them. Seeing Dannelle once again, he smiled and then gave her a hug, "So, how have things been for you since our last time together."

"I have been well. I see you have lost some weight Señor," she said to him. Thinking in her mind, *"Once a pig always a pig."*

"You flatter me, why don't you go up to your room and get yourself pretty for me."

She walked away and made her way towards the stairs. While both men watched her leave Gunther asked, "Was there any problems with getting her to come?"

"No Señor, all went well. I gave her some clean clothes to wear to come out here to meet you."

"Did you touch her?" Gunther said, with a threatening voice.

"Me, no sir.   I was a perfect gentleman to her."

"I bet you were," Gunther said sarcastically.

"Señor Gunther, how can you doubt me. I'm always a gentleman to your lady friends."

Gunther reached into his pocket and pulled out a wad of money, counted out one hundred dollars and handed it to him.

"Thank you, Señor Gunther, is there anything else I can do for you?" the policeman said, as he quickly put the money in his pocket.

"Not at this time.   By the way, if I ever find out you hurt any of my girls, I will personally kill you myself."

"Señor Gunther, you have me all wrong. I would never harm your girls." the policeman said, caught off guard by his words,

"See that you don't, or I will do as I said.   Now leave,"

The policeman left and as he walked out of the house and drove back to the village, he thought to himself, *"Someday I may kill* Señor *Gunther, just for his money. And live in his house and have his girls all to myself."*

Dannelle opened the door to her old room, walked in and sat down on the bed and started crying. The other girls heard her crying and came in and gathered around her, hoping to make her feel better. After a few minutes, she got up and went into take a real shower and get herself ready for Gunther.   By the time she was cleaned up, it was time for dinner.   As each of the girls came into the dining room, they sat down at their assigned places at the table. Dannelle was to take the seat next to Gunther, this was his way of welcoming her back to the fold.

Miguel, following his father's request, had followed the policeman as he carried Dannelle over his shoulder to see where he was taking her.   All the while being careful not to be seen. Once he knew that he was taking her to the jail he went back home and told Pedro what he had seen. "Miguel, I will be leaving with these men tomorrow morning to go get Gunther.   We will use the old trail that takes you up the mountain.   You know the one I'm talking about?"

"Si papa, I know the trail."

"I need you to watch the jail and come and tell me if the policeman takes your cousin anywhere.   It is very important that you are not seen by anyone."

"Si papa, I will be very careful not to get caught."

Pedro smiled, "I know you will.   Remember that this is very important to Dannelle."

After watching his father leave to go up the trail, he went and got some food, and made his way back into town and found a place where he could watch the jail without being seen from his hiding place.   The next morning, Miguel watched the policeman leave with Dannelle and then saw him come back into town without her.

Making sure that he wasn't seen, he looked around before coming out of his hiding place.   He slipped back into the jungle and looked for the same trail that his father had taken and started following it to find him. He knew this would be a long hike, but he wanted to tell his father what he had seen.

It just so happened that the policeman saw Miguel as he left the place where he had been hiding. Out of curiosity, he wandered over to see what he was doing and followed Miguel as he made his way towards the trail. With a burst of speed, the policeman caught Miguel and took him back to his jail to ask him what he was doing. Miguel was in tears, knowing that the policeman could hurt him if he wanted to.   After refusing to answer the policeman's questions, Miguel was put in the same jail cell that his cousin had been in and was sitting in the corner on the same bed as she had.   The policeman smiled to himself, thinking that it was ironic that another family member was acting the same way as Dannelle had.

"Why are you hiding in the old building on the edge of town?"

"I was climbing around inside looking for something to do."

"Why do I not believe what you say. Oh well, you will tell me what I want to know, sooner or later, my friend."

The policeman took off his belt, opened the cell and walked over to where Miguel was on the jail bed.   From his vantage point Miguel saw that the policeman was starting to smile....

Later that night, Miguel was laying on his stomach, trying not to move because of the bruises and the open cuts on his back from the belt buckle. Through all of the beating Miguel never said a word or even cried. Holding back the tears, he wished his father was here to help him, he would know what to do. Using his blanket as a pillow, he wondered if the policeman would come back in again tonight. The policeman was sitting in his chair, sweating from all of the exertion it took to beat the kid trying to find out what he was doing.   As he sat there trying to catch his breath, he was surprised that Miguel hadn't told him what he wanted to know.   He smiled, thinking that maybe another beating or a night in the jail would eventually open his mouth.   Deciding that he was to worn out to do any more, he locked the door that lead into the cells and went to the cantina.   Hearing the door close behind him, Miguel listened for the front door to close as well. With the policeman gone, he felt safe and was able to let go of his feelings and started to cry.

Chapter XXVIII

Tony, quickly checked to see if his gun was still in his holster. Feeling it there, he pulled the hammer back and adjusted the holster for easier access. "Wish me luck," he said, smiling at Mike.

He then made his way up the trial and started walking towards the men that were looking for the two guards that hadn't checked back in last night.   As he came around a bend in the trail, he saw the six men that Mike had said were there. Sure enough, several of the men were standing guard, and watching for anyone that came along on the trail. Making sure they saw him, Tony placed his hand on his gun under his shirt, then waved at them and then stood there to see what they would do.   All of the men got excited to see an American hiking alone on the trail.   As he got closer to the six men, he waived at them, "Sirs, can you tell me where the drug compound is, so I can buy wholesale?"

Not fully understanding his words, but knowing that all Americans are rich, they started to chase him. When Tony saw them running towards him, he quickly turned around and took off back down the trail. Running downhill he passed the team of agents, yelling, "Here they come!"

"Get ready," Mike whispered as Tony ran by him.

Still running, Tony found a place to get off the trail and hide in the jungle somewhere close to the trail. With his gun ready to fire, he waited for the men to show up.   In about ten seconds, gunfire broke out up ahead of him and within a minute it was over. All six men lay on the ground bleeding.   After checking to make sure that it was clear, Tony got up and went over to where Mike was.   All of the six men were on the ground with only one conscious. Mike was standing over him and watching him as he tried to get away. Mike was surprised that the man was still alive as he had taken a bullet in the chest, "You're going to die here on the trail if you don't answer my questions now."

The wounded man understood what he was saying and through the spasms of pain asked, "What would you like to know?"

"First of all, where's your drug operation at?"

"It is up the trail on the other side of the mountain."

"How far away from here?"

"About a mile from here. Please señor, help me. I'm dying señor."

"Yes, you are.   How many men do you have there?"

"Just workers now, since we are here. Please help me, señor."

"There is nothing I can do for you, by the time we get off the mountain you'll be dead anyway.   Tell me, would you have done the same thing for me and my men if it was us lying on the ground?"

The dying man said nothing to the question.   Realizing he wasn't going to make it, he started praying and just as he said amen, he died. Mike and Tony stood there looking at the dead man. "Isn't it interesting, they find God in their own death, yet think nothing of working for the devil to help people manufacture drugs, with most of the people dying from what they are paid to protect," Mike said.

"Makes you wonder what kind of God they believe in, doesn't it?" Tony replied.

Pedro stood in the shadows of the trees listening, trying to find the other two drug guards.   After a few seconds, he heard one of them cough and could smell the cigarette he was smoking.   Following the smell of the smoke, he carefully made his way through the brush and the trees, looking for where the cough came from. Eventually, he could see both men as they were trying to figure out what to do with the two that had been killed earlier. They were arguing over who was going back to tell their boss about finding the bodies and ask what he wanted done with them. The guard that lost the argument left to go find their boss, while the other one stayed behind to watch over the bodies.   He waited for his partner to leave before going through the pockets of the dead men.   Not finding much, he sat down on a tree stump and made himself comfortable while he waited for the return of his partner.

This was what Pedro had been waiting for, to catch the two men off guard. He carefully looked around the area where the man was sitting.   Seeing a clump of ferns and a tree that offered protection, he slowly made his way there.   As the guard sat there waiting, he began to get sleepy and started to dose.   Pedro, working from the other side of the guard, slowly circled him in the direction of the clump of vegetation. When he finally got there, he sat in the shadows of the brush and waited to see if he had been noticed. After a few minutes he quietly walked up to the guard and stuck a knife into his chest. The guard, surprised by the attack, tried to get up, instead he fell forward onto the ground in front of him. Pedro stood over him and waited for the man to die before dragging him off to where the others were already laying. He wiped the blood off of his knife on the guard's shirt and went back into the dark foliage in search of the other guard.

The second guard heard the shots coming from where his group was located on the trail. He stopped and waited, frozen in place and unsure of what was going on and not knowing what to do. As he listened, he heard voices that he didn't recognize and decided to go back to where his partner was guarding the bodies. On his way back, Pedro met him halfway and catching him unaware, stabbed him. Pedro stood there looking at the man and spoke to him as he lay bleeding to death, "I know you, you're the one that took my son. I guess you won't be coming to our village anymore looking for my other son or anybody else for that matter, will you."

The guard didn't hear the question, but it didn't matter at this point. Pedro looked down on the dead body, thinking out loud, "On your way to Hell, stop in Heaven and say hello to my son for me."

Tony and Mike sat at the top of the trail waiting for Pedro to show up. In a short time, Pedro came up to them with a smile on his face. Looking at him, Mike knew that the two men were dead, "Ready to go on?" Mike asked.

"Ready whenever you are," came the reply from Pedro.

It took the team about another hour of following the trail to make it to the top of the mountain. "Well, here's where we say goodbye for now. Remember, we don't leave until were all together again," Mike said, as shook hands with Tony.

"We'll be back before you get done," Tony said, with a grin as he walked away with Pedro and Agent Dixon.

"You probably will, seeing as how you get the light work for the mission," Mike replied, smiling.

"That's why they pay you the big bucks," Tony yelled back as they were heading over the mountain.

Chapter XXIX

Dannelle had just finished eating the main course for dinner and was sitting there waiting for the desert. Feeling in a good mood, Gunther stood up, raised his glass and cleared his throat, "I'd like to make a toast to our wandering lady who has found her way home to us. May she be glad to be home as much as we are to have her home."

All of the girls stood up and raised their glasses of wine to Dannelle, as did Gunther, who stood there for a moment as they drank their wine and then sat down. Caught off guard with the toast, Dannelle didn't know what to say and feeling trapped, she started crying. She suddenly got up from the table and ran to her room. Some of the girls wanted to follow but Gunther said in a loud voice, "Let her be, she'll be alright. Let's have some dessert."

Dannelle ran into her bedroom and shut the door behind her. She laid on her bed crying, not knowing what to think or do. She despised Gunther, yet at the same time she felt safe with him. He offered a clean house with plenty of food to eat and a warm bed to sleep in. The fact is, she never had it so good. She got up to wash the makeup off her face and get out of her cloths. As she stood there looking in the mirror, for the first time she saw herself as she really was, a prostitute, selling her body so she could live off of a rich man so she wouldn't have to work and still have the nice things in life. Looking a little closer, the light above the mirror magnified the wrinkles that were starting to appear around her eyes. Then she looked at her arms and could see the scars from all the years of drug abuse. As she tried to remember those years of standing on the street hustling for money to buy drugs to feed her addiction it all seemed to be a blur. She also remembered watching some of her friends die either from overdoses or being beat up by the johns.

She realized that her choices in life were physically taking their toll on her body and her soul. She was only twenty-nine years old and felt like a broken down fifty year old. The shock of seeing her body looking the way it did forced her to come to terms with her life. It was at this time that she decided to do something more with her life and take back the control that she had lost to the drugs. Not knowing what to do and knowing that the FBI was coming after Gunther, she thought it best to continue playing the part until it was time to go home to her uncle's place. After cleaning herself up, she went back downstairs to where everyone was sitting out on the pool deck. "I'm so sorry for running away, I didn't realize how much I missed you guys," Dannelle said, as she sat down, trying not to get wet while she played the part.

Gunther was relieved to see Dannelle come out of her room and apologize for her actions. For Gunther all was well, as he watched the girls start to play in the pool. Playing her part, Dannelle walked over and sat on Gunther's lap and started playing with his hair, knowing what the night would bring.

Pedro grew up around these mountains and knew them like the back of his hand. He had hiked all of the mountains that surrounded the village that he called home. Growing up as a young boy every day was an adventure that allowed him to explore the jungle and the mountains looking for treasures that were always just beyond the next mountain. He knew exactly how to get to where the drug operation was being run and where they had their guards posted. He had been up there several times looking for one his sons after he had been forced to work for the drug cartel. On his last visit he had found out that his son had been killed while trying to escape. He had searched the jungle looking for his son so that he could take him home and bury him properly. By the time he found him he decided to bury him there instead of bringing him home. To this day Pedro vowed that he would get even for what they had done to his son.

Having taken out the security guards for the drug operation, he, Tony and Dixon, figured that it would be easy to destroy the compound and save the people working there. Upon reaching the other side of the mountain, they found the trail and started moving down towards the location of the drug operation. Pedro took the lead and the other two followed him. The going was slow at first because the trail had an uphill climb to get around some of the boulders. Once they got around the rocks, the trail started going downhill again.

They found some shade beneath the rocks and stopped to catch their breath. Unable to find some shade for himself, Pedro moved a little further down the trail. Tony had been thinking about the trail that they had been on previously, "I wonder if they booby trapped this side of the mountain like they did the other side."

"That's a good point, to remember. I know if I was wanting to protect my operation from someone, I'd do it," Dixon said, leaning back in the shade of a rock.

Just as he did, he heard a shot ring out and a bullet hit the rock above his head. Everyone scrambled to find cover and looked to see if they could find out where the shot had come from. Using his binoculars, Tony started scanning the ridgeline of the mountain. Cussing to himself, as he couldn't see anything because of the jungle growth. "A man could be standing right next to you and you wouldn't or couldn't see him."

Pedro, hearing the shot and seeing his partners unable to move, went down the mountain and past a rock outcropping to get out of the sight of the shooter. He was looking for the shooter, as well. He waited a few seconds to make sure that the shooter didn't see his movements. Scanning the area below, he waited for a second shot to be fired in an attempt to locate him.

Looking to draw out the shooter to locate him, Tony raised up just enough to see if the shooter would try again. Dixon, being in the worst place for cover, was hoping that when Tony showed himself, he could find another place that would give him more protection. "Give me to the count of three before you make your move," Dixon said to Tony, as he got ready to show himself to the shooter.

Tony looked around and found a spot that would afford more protection when he stood up. Using his fingers, he counted to three, then stood up to give the shooter a target to shoot at. He stood exposed for about two seconds. When the shot was taken, he ducked down behind the rock face as the bullet went right over his shoulder and landed in the dirt behind him. Without standing up, Dixon crawled over into a better place to hide. The shooter, seeing Dixon move, fired again, missing Dixon once more. Hearing the second shot, Pedro looked closely in the direction where he thought the shot had come from, trying to see some movement or flash from the bullet as it left the rifle. When the third shot rang out, Pedro spotted the shooter. Knowing where he was now, he looked up at the others, "Give me a couple of minutes and I'll be right back," he smiled, as he pulled the knife out from under his shirt.

Tony and Dixon watched Pedro go into the jungle and disappear. He found an animal trail and began to follow it, trying not to make any noise as he started searching for the shooter. The shooter was moving as well, trying to get a better shot at the trapped men in the rocks. Tony looked over the top edge of the rock that was protecting him, trying to see where the shooter was and every time, he did this he would hear the rifle report and quickly duck back under cover. Dixon was now looking as well, he was in the best position to watch for the shooter, simply because he could see the trail all the way down the mountain.

Pedro kept moving forward through the jungle stopping to listen then move a little further, always getting closer to where he last saw the shooter. Dixon watched as Pedro moved through the jungle and could tell that he was moving away from the shooter. He looked at Tony, "Hey, can you stand up one more time, for Pedro?"

"Are you out of your mind!?" Tony said, in disbelief.

"Pedro's going in the wrong direction."

"They didn't tell me about this part of the job when I joined the Navy," he said, as he stood up one more time and counted the seconds before getting back behind some protection.

The shooter saw the man stand up and fired once again. This time the bullet hit in front of Tony, missing him completely. Frustrated, the shooter changed his position again. Pedro heard the shot and quickly turned himself around and headed in the opposite direction. Hearing the shooter move through the jungle towards him, Pedro waited for him behind some foliage as he got closer. Finally seeing the shooter, he waited till he walked by him. The shooter wasn't worried about anyone else being in the jungle besides himself and therefore wasn't trying to be quiet. As he walked by Pedro, he grabbed him by the neck with one hand and took his knife and stuck it into his chest. Being unable to get away, Pedro held him in place till he quite moving then dropped him to the ground. It was obvious that he was a guard for the cartel and was there to keep the workers doing their part in the production of the drugs. Pedro looked at him and realized that he was more kid than man, yet he was still old enough to be assigned the job. Taking the shooters gun and bullets, he left the young man where he lay. He found the trail again, and signaled Dixon and Tony to let them know that the threat was gone. Tony and Dixon made their way out of the rocks and finally caught up to where Pedro was waiting by the trail. They saw the rifle that Pedro had on his shoulder. "Let me guess, a trophy for your wall back at the house?" Tony said.

"You never know when this might come in handy again. Besides, the owner doesn't need it anymore," Pedro replied as he headed down the trail.

"The way things are going, he's probably right," Tony said to Dixon.

Tony and Dixon continued to follow him. All three were aware that the rifle fire had probably attracted others that were part of the drug operation. Being more careful where they were walking, it was Pedro who found the first trip wire attached to a claymore mine. After disarming it and throwing it into the jungle, Pedro looked at the other two men, "We must be getting close now. From this point on we will take it very slow."

They were careful to stay on the trail and look for anything that was out of place. Dixon found the second booby trap, more by accident than on purpose. In fact, he almost stepped on it. Fortunately, Tony caught him just as he started to step into the hole. Upon removing the ground cover over the hole, they looked in and they all could see the metal spikes sticking straight up to impale the foot, making it hard to walk. After looking closely at it, Pedro said, "Please do not touch the spikes, they have covered them with poison."

"I've heard of these being used in Viet Nam, but they didn't use poison," Tony said, smiling.

"What did they use?" Dixon asked.

"They used human excrement, very effective and starts to work instantly."

Looking for something long and big enough to destroy the trap, Pedro found what he was looking for and began breaking the spikes inside the hole. Once this was done all three of them poured dirt into the hole to fill it up. After getting the hole completely filled in, they stopped to take a break and catch their breath. All of them found a place in the shade to cool off in. They took a drink from their water containers and rested. Pedro stopped in the middle of a swallow, "Someone is coming, be still."

Everyone froze and waited to see what or who was coming. Tony and Dixon both had their handguns out and ready to shoot. Listening intently, Pedro looked out past the bushes he was hiding in and started to chuckle to himself.   The other two seeing him relax, did the same.   Pedro jumped up to his feet and was gone and was back in several minutes leading a small donkey with him.   He looked around for the other two, "Anybody want to ride?"

Coming out from the shadows, both Tony and Dixon started to smile. "I think the heat is starting to affect our senses," Dixon said.

"Where do you suppose he came from?" Tony asked.

"Probably where we are headed.   They use the donkeys as pack animals to carry the drugs on their backs," Pedro replied.

"We must be very close then," Dixon stated.

"Yes, we are.   In fact, it is just around the bend up ahead," Pedro replied.

"Did you get a look at the setup?" Tony asked.

"Just a little part of it, however, I didn't see any guards around."

"Well then let's go see what's up there," Dixon said, shifting his hat to keep the sun out of his eyes.

"I think it would be best if we separated and came in from three different directions. Just in case somebody could be waiting for us," Tony stated.

All of them agreed that this was a good idea.

As they continued to make their way to where the drugs were being made, they kept watching for more booby traps and also started checking the trees, looking for spotters with guns. Seeing none, they let the donkey lead the way into the group of buildings that was being used to develop the tar from the cocoa plants.

As planned, each of them took a different route going into the area. Pedro came in from the backside of the compound, while Dixon took his in the form of a flanking position, while Tony stayed on the trail. Coming from three different directions into the camp, the chances of surprising someone was on their side. All three of them reached the center of the compound at the same time   after they had checked the buildings that were closest to them as they came in.   They were all surprised that the camp was empty. "All I found were some of the donkeys tied up all together in the shade over there." Tony said, pointing towards what looked like a small barn.

"I cannot believe that everybody would be gone.   Do you see that the pots are still cooking the drugs?" Pedro said, as he continued to look around.

"Maybe we did kill all of the guards.   And seeing that there was no one around   to make them work maybe they just left to go back to their villages," Dixon said.

"Maybe we should check the camp again.   This time we'll do it together," Tony said.

Working together they went through the camp one more time, looking for anybody that may of been hiding.   Pedro, always the one to hear things, stopped in his tracks and motioned for the other two to freeze. Then pointing in the direction where he heard the noise, he slowly made his way towards it. Tony and Dixon fanned out on each side of him and little behind him, waiting for someone to come out of the shadows of the jungle and start firing at them. This time being more careful and taking their lead from Pedro, they slowly made their way to where he was headed. Tony heard a noise also and moved closer in that direction.   Pedro saw a small hut and signaled the other two and waited for them to catch up to him. Tony and Dixon raced up to the small hut and were standing on both sides of the door waiting for Pedro to come and open it.   As Tony looked through the walls of the hut he could see some shadows moving around inside. He used his fingers and pointed to his own eyes first then to Pedro and Dixon, indicating that there was someone inside the hut.   Seeing a open lock in the clasp that kept the door closed, Pedro removed it and swung the door open, stepping aside as he did so. Tony looked inside as did Dixon.   All they could see at first were eyes looking back at them. Tony moved to let the sunlight in and what he saw made him sick.   He looked at Dixon and Pedro, "You need to take care of this, I can't."

Inside the hut were ten people all chained together, aged from ten years old up to fifty. The smell coming from inside indicated that they had been in there for quite some time.   Most of the people had sores that were open and raw and infected. Pedro went in first and speaking in their language he said, "It's okay, we are here to save you, so you can go back to your homes."

Upon hearing this, the people still wouldn't come out. "It's a trick, don't listen to him.   You see their guns?"one of them said.

Understanding their fear, Pedro handed his rifle to Dixon, as he continued to try and convince them, once again, to come out. Dixon stood at the door right behind Pedro.   While he was standing there one of the people inside saw his badge that was attached to his belt.   He pointed to it and told the others, "American Federally," then got up to leave the hut.

The others followed him out and smiled at Dixon, wanting to shake his hand.   Pedro stepped in between the ten people and Dixon, "Where are your guards?   What happened to the other workers?"

"They all gone, back to their villages once they see no guards. We were in hut because we refused to work and some are sick too," said the same one who had spoken before.

"We heard gun shots earlier today.   We figure that the guards had killed someone that does not belong here," said another one in the group.

Tony, feeling better, came over to help his friends take the chains off of the people.   Going through his backpack he found some extra water bottles and gave it to the one that was sick and covered with open sores.

"What do we do now? We don't have the medical supplies needed to help any of these people," Tony said, as he looked at the sick guy.

Pedro thought for a minute before asking the group, "Do you have any medical supplies around?"

One of the men ran off in the direction of one of the buildings. When he came back, he was carrying a bag and handed it to Pedro. He opened it to look inside and could see bandages and tools that a doctor would use and also a bottle of alcohol to sterilize an open wound or anything else that needed it.   Pedro took the alcohol and soaking it in a clean cloth, went over to the old man covered in sores and started cleaning them. The old man gritted his teeth with each wipe of the cloth.   In the meantime, Tony decided to look over the drug operation that had been set up, to see what could be done to destroy it. Dixon was watching Tony as he went around looking things over. He walked over to him, "What are you doing?" he asked out of curiosity.

"I'm looking for something to blow the drug lab into oblivion, want to help?"

"Why not, might make a beautiful fire and explosion."

"I found some of the chemicals over in one of the sheds," Tony said as he pointed to a building that was isolated from the others.

As Pedro worked with the local people getting them squared away to leave, Tony and Dixon were busy placing the chemicals in the right places to blow up the different parts of the lab and destroy the compound. In an hour they had everything set up to destroy the compound. The locals were ready to leave as well after taking anything of value for their own needs. Some of the villagers took the donkeys and started up the trail as they followed Pedro. When all of the villagers were clear of the area and Tony and Dixon were the only ones there, Tony lit the fuse and watched the fire race across the ground headed to one of the fifty gallon drums that had been turned on its side. The first explosion took out the holding tanks and then the drying tables where the drugs were prepped for packaging. The explosion echoed through the valley and finally the shed, holding the left-over chemicals, caught fire and set off another explosion.

By now the jungle around the compound was smoking. Seeing that everything was on fire, Tony and Dixon left to catch up with Pedro who was leading the villagers out of the canyon. Tony, looking at the villagers, could see that none of them were looking back to where they had been. He mentioned this to Dixon, "Would you look back at hell if you didn't need to?" he said, in a matter of fact tone.

"I don't believe I would. Come on, let's go home. Leastwise, to the top of the mountain, anyway."

"We better hurry, before the donkeys, get away and before we get left behind."

Inside a couple of hours as the sun was going down, everyone was settled in for the night on the top of the mountain. Some of the locals that had been rescued decided not wait and headed off in the direction of their village. Even the old man with the open sores went with them, with only a few staying till morning,

As it started to get cold, Tony decided to build a fire and cook up some food for all of them to eat. Pedro, who was seated and looking into the fire, was deep in thought. The memories of his oldest son came back to him as if it was yesterday. Because of this, he didn't see Tony standing there holding out some food for him. Eventually, he looked up and saw Tony there, smiling, with a small plate of food for him. He took the food and replied, "Thank you,"

"You looked like you were deep in thought," Tony said, as he sat down next to him to eat his food.

"I was thinking about my oldest son, who died trying to get away from the drug dealers at the same place we were at today," he said, with tears in his eyes.

Tony was caught off guard with his comment and he sat there not saying another word. Dixon heard the conversation between the two of them, "It was my brother that got killed trying to stay away from the drugs.   He was shot by the ones that wanted him to try the drugs," he said, as he stirred the fire with a stick in his hand.

"Then you understand, my pain as well," Pedro said.

Tony had nothing to say and kept silent, thinking to himself, *"Even the innocent people get hurt,"* while his two friends dealt with their own harsh realities of life.   He remembered his encounter with a young man who had destroyed his life and the lives of the crew aboard the submarines.

Chapter XXX

Dannelle was feeling sleepy after being up all night watching for anything that might indicate that the FBI was there. Around four o'clock in the morning she finally went to bed, thinking *"Maybe tomorrow they'll come."* She grabbed a few pillows as she lay there thinking about everything that had happened to her since she came back. Her mind was still foggy and unable to focus on anything, especially any decisions about how to deal with Gunther. Before too long she was sound asleep, even with the girls moving around and making noise downstairs in the kitchen getting breakfast for themselves, didn't wake her. The girls had seen a change come over their friend. Being aloof, yet still friendly when it was needed. All of them could sense something was different about Dannelle. Even Gunther could feel it. This got him thinking about what happened to her while she was gone and why she came back. When he asked her about it, she would always change the subject or give an answer that didn't really indicate anything. Then she would leave, claiming she had a headache. He was now thinking that maybe she had betrayed him somehow.

Gunther decided to call on the policeman and ask him a few questions. Before leaving the house to visit him, he called all of the girls over to talk to them, that is, except Dannelle. "Girls, is something wrong with Dannelle that I need to know about?"

Their answers were all the same, in that they could tell something was different about her since she had come back. "She doesn't talk to us like she used to."

"All she does is stay up late looking out the window. Like she is waiting for someone or something," another said.

Hearing the last comment confirmed Gunther's suspicions. Not wanting to let on his suspiciouns he told the girlsl, "Please don't tell her that we talked about her. I need to run into town for some things and   I'll be right back," he said, as he went to leave.

He walked out to his truck not knowing what to think or do about what he had learned, got in and drove off, heading into town. When he got there, he parked in front of the jail. The policeman was in his office and could hear someone pull up and park in front. Not expecting anyone, he looked through the window to see who it was and recognized that it was Gunther. He walked over to the door and opened it. "Good afternoon my friend, what brings you here to my humble place of work?"

"I have come to find out what's going on with Dannelle. Did you notice anything strange or suspicious about her when she was with you?"

"No, but as a matter of fact, señor, I have Pedro's son in my jail right now. Maybe he can tell us what you want to know."

Both of them walked back into the jail cell. Gunther was surprised to see the boy lying face down on his belly. Then he saw the bruises and open cuts on his back. He stopped and looked at the policeman, "What did you do?"

"I wanted to know what he was doing in the old building, and he wouldn't tell me. All I know is that he's related to the girl I brought out to you."

"Did you get any answers from him?"

"No, I didn't, but I will sooner or later," he said, with a smile.

"Let me know if he says anything," Gunther said, as he continued looking at the boy.

"I will do that."

As Gunther started thinking about the boy and Dannelle being family, he was starting to see a connection with the old man. But what it was, other than family, still remained uncertain. He drove back to his house thinking that it was interesting that Dannelle showed up when she did. He was curious as to how she got back here to Brazil. Gunther wondered who paid for her trip, maybe it was a wealthy man that was one of her customers. Or could it be someone else with a bigger paycheck that bought her a one-way ticket back to here. He knew it would be just a matter of time before he found out the truth. Until then he would treat her just like one of the girls, he would pretend to care about her as she did him.

Mike could hear the explosion off in the distance and smiled knowing that one part of his job was done. He lay on the ground watching the hacienda from a distance on top of a rise. Using his binoculars, he checked the positions of each of his team to make sure they were all in place and getting set up to go after the German. The guards protecting the German were in place watching and yet not watching. They too had become complacent in their duties. Even the explosion from the drug camp in the mountains didn't alert them that anything was wrong. For this, Mike breathed a sigh of relief and was glad that it hadn't done it.

Beck made his way slowly up the rise and came up behind Mike, "All of our agents are in place, waiting to go."

Mike nodded his head in acknowledgment to Becks comment. "What about the girls, where are they located?"

"They're all in the house taking a nap, and the answer to your next question is that Reichman is in his den reading a book," Beck said, smiling.

Mike smiled, "Someday you are going to be in my place, that is, if you keep this up."

"Heaven forbid, not me. They're going to have to fight me." Beck said, acting as if he had been threatened.

The radio came to life and a voice said, "The target has moved and is going into the kitchen."

Beck picked up the radio, "Roger that." He looked at Mike, "Do we take him now?"

"Where are the guards at," Mike asked.

Beck picked up the radio, "Where are the guards at?"

Several voices came over the radio all saying the same thing, "The guards are still in place."

Mike nodded his head in agreement, "Proceed."

Beck got on the radio, "It's a go. Proceed with the operation."

The guards were taken out first, this required the agents taking them one at a time and tying them up and then gagging them. Then locking them in the barn. Once this was completed the agents came back to their assigned areas to watch for the German.

Gunther was still in the kitchen fixing himself something to eat for lunch. When he was finished, he took his lunch and headed out the back door to sit in the shade of the patio to eat. He walked out and set his food down on the table and stopped for a minute, realizing that he forgot about getting something to drink. He turned around to go back in the house to get it and then stopped. He felt that something didn't look right. As he continued to think about what wasn't right, it dawned on him that none of his guards were around. He went to the front door of the house and looked out the window and didn't see any of his guards at their posts. Quickly realizing something was wrong, he headed back into the den to get his gun from his desk. Making sure that it was loaded, he then headed upstairs to Dannelle's room and woke her up and dragged her out into the hallway by her hair. "What have you done to me, you selfish brat!?"

"What are you talking about? Ow! Your hurting me!" she screamed as they went down the stairs, with Gunther still half dragging her by the hair.

By now all the girls were awake and wondering what all the noise was about, only to find out that Gunther was headed to the kitchen with Dannelle in tow.   At this point Gunther yelled out to the girls, "Don't come into the kitchen!" as he slammed the door behind him.

He and Dannelle then went down into the basement, looking for the door that would lead to a tunnel.   He found the false panel and grabbed the coat hook that opened a small panel to a door that led to a tunnel that would take him out into the jungle to escape. Having already planned for this, he picked up a couple of backpacks loaded with money, food, and some clothes and then continued through the tunnel out into the garden and then the jungle.

Each of the agents entered into the house and went from room to room looking for Gunther.   All they found inside the rooms were the girls, screaming and trying to hide from them.   Beck came in after the door was opened and waited for all the girls to be rounded up.

"Where's Gunther and Dannelle?" he asked when they were all together.

"We don't know," said one of the girls.

"The top floor of the house is clear," said one of the agents who had been upstairs.

Beck nodded his head. "Check the rest of the house.   They must be around here somewhere."

Leaving the room, the agent continued onto the next room which happened to be the kitchen.   Finding no one there, he made his way downstairs into the basement. He started looking around the basement area and found nothing to indicate that someone had been there so he went back upstairs, "We can't find him, sir."

Beck waited for all of his team to check in before making a call to Mike. "We lost him, he's nowhere to be found in the house."

"Are you sure about that?" replied Mike.

"Yes, we've checked the place twice now and even the girls don't know where he went," Beck stated.

Mike was beside himself; the German couldn't have just disappeared into thin air and yet that's what happened. He came down off the mountain and walked into the house and could see that all of the girls were sitting on the couch in the living room.

"Did the girls say anything about their sugar daddy escaping?" he asked, checking in with Beck,

"No, not a word. Besides they're too busy crying from being scared, to say anything," he replied.

Mike decided to walk around the house with Beck, while the other agents kept an eye on the girls. "Did any of the girls say where it was they saw Gunther last?"

"No, but one of the agents heard him yell, 'don't come into the kitchen.   From there no one knows where he went."

Mike thought for a moment before he headed back into the kitchen to start looking around. Seeing the door open to the basement he called Beck to go with him downstairs. They walked around the basement looking for any clues, that would indicate something. Not seeing anything, both of them went back upstairs and started asking the girls, one at a time, about their sugar daddy. After an hour of interviewing the girls, they were still at square one, nobody had any answers.

In the meantime, Gunther and Dannelle were still walking through the jungle getting farther away from the house. As they stopped to take a break and catch their breath, Gunther threw Dannelle to the ground and pulled his gun out and waved it in front of her. "Move and I'll shoot you.   The best part is no one will hear the shot."

Dannelle sat there not daring to make a move, not even saying a word. She knew that the German was angry and would think nothing of killing her and from where she was sitting was surprised that she was still alive. *You can only go to hell once for killing someone, *she thought to herself.

While Gunther was getting his bearings, she looked around and could tell there was nowhere to run or hide for the time being. As she was rubbing her arms where the bruises were starting to show, she looked down and realized that, with all of the commotion going on, she hadn't been able to get any shoes to wear. Her feet were starting to bleed from stepping on all the rocks and under brush as they were making there way through the jungle. Gunther turned and saw her checking her feet and smiled, "Sorry I wasn't able to let you get some shoes. You see, I was in kind of a hurry, when we left the house. Besides, it serves you right for what you've done."

Looking at him, she feigned not hearing the remark. Gunther grabbed her again and forced her to stand, pushing her to go deeper into the jungle, as if he was looking for something. As Dannelle stood up she wanted to cry out because of the shooting pain she felt as she stood on her bare feet. She refused to give into the pain for fear of being shot by Gunther.

Mike sat in the house frustrated, knowing that they had had Reichman right where they wanted him and within minutes he disappeared into thin air. He also knew that to search for him any further would be a waste of time. Not knowing what else to do, he decided that they should go back to the mountain trail and make their way back up to the top to meet up with the others. Having no reason to take the girls with them, they left them at the house to do what they wanted. The team packed up all of their gear and headed back into the jungle, looking for the trail.

With the house all to themselves, the girls decided that it was party time. With the booze flowing and the music playing loud, everyone was having a good time. One of the girls decided to leave the party and take a walk outside to clear her head. As she walked the area around the horse corrals, she could hear someone yelling for help. She began looking for source. She made her way into the barn and opening one of the doors to a horse stall, found the guards all tied up. After she released them they all went into the house. The girls proceeded to explain to the guards what had happened while they were tied up and that Gunther had escaped with Dannelle. The guards, seeing that their employer wasn't around, decided to join the party themselves, with the girls. Figuring that their boss was gone for good. They proceeded to party for the next two days.

In the meantime, Gunther had other plans.   After hiding out in the jungle for the two days, he decided to see if it was clear to head back to his house. He would be taking a chance to get back to some kind of civilization, but anything was better than wandering around in the jungle.   He had spent the two nights in the jungle and, needless to say, he was missing his own bed and some real food instead of having to eat the MRE's.   Gunther felt tired, hungry and, most of all, angry, knowing that Dannelle had set him up.   He grabbed her by the arm once again and pulled her up, even though she was barely able to walk because her feet were cut and bleeding worse than before.   Seeing how much pain she was in, he laughed, "Just think, two more days and we'll be home, or you could die here.   It's your choice."

Dannelle started walking once she realized, by the look in his eyes, that he was serious.   She could hear Gunther laughing as she stumbled along. He knew that it would take two days to get back to the house.   He also figured that in four days the FBI would be tired of waiting for him and would be gone to look elsewhere, thinking that he was somewhere else, hiding in another country.

Both he and Dannelle arrived back at the house in the middle of the night.   Hearing the loud music and people talking, he opened the door and saw his guards with his girls. Not liking what he saw, he threw Dannelle onto the floor and pointed his gun at one of the guards.   He smiled and shot him. The others hearing the gunshot, came into see what was going on.   Seeing their friend on the floor dead and that the boss was back, they were surprised by all of this. Not knowing what to say, they just stood there as he proceeded to shoot them. "You didn't even try to find me, did you!?" he kept asking as he continued pulling the trigger.

When it was all over, all six of the guards were lying on the floor dead.   Gunther ordered several of the girls to take the bodies out of the house and dump them somewhere out of sight.

As they took the bodies out he yelled at the others, "Clean up this mess, before I shoot all of you as well!"

He walked around the house looking at the damage done by the people he thought he could trust.

Dannelle saw the six dead guards laying on the polished rock floor and waited for Gunther to leave so she could find a way to go take care of her feet and get cleaned up. She half crawled up the stairs to the bathroom to start the painful process. As she was working on her feet to get them bandaged, she could hear Gunther talking on the phone to someone in the capitol city. She heard him ask, "Can you send me some men that will be my new guards, to keep me safe."

After asking the question he waited for the reply, then said, "I need them here as soon as possible. And by the way, can you send me someone that does freelance work?"

Again, as he listened to the person on the phone, he smiled, "Thank you. We must do lunch soon," and then hung up the phone.

After thinking for a moment, he picked up the phone again and called the policeman. "Have you learned anything else from the boy?"

"No, Señor Gunther. He has not said a word yet," the policeman replied.

"I want you to do me a favor. I need you to find out where his father is and when you've completed that. I want you to bring the boy to me."

"Si, Señor, I will do this, for you."

"Do not fail me, on this," Gunther said, as he hung up the phone.

Gunther seemed pleased with himself and smiled for the first time in a week. He went upstairs to his own bathroom and looking in the mirror, he was surprised at how he looked. Not shaving for two days and walking through the jungle had taken its toll on him. He decided to take a shower and get cleaned up. The hot water would feel good and would help his sore muscles to loosen up.

After hearing both of the phone calls, Dannelle knew that she must do something or others would be killed in the process. She looked at her swollen feet and sighed, thinking that she wouldn't be much help to anyone right now. All she could do for the time being, was to sit tight while her feet healed, and stay away from Gunther long enough to be able to sneak out and warn the others.

One of the girls came into Dannelle's bedroom and watched her as she bandaged her feet. She went over and sat on the bed next to Dannelle. Seeing her sitting there, Dannelle looked up at her and could see the fear in her eyes. She stopped what she was doing and gave the girl a hug and talked to her, trying to calm her down. After a few minutes the girl ended up taking the bandages from Dannelle and assisted her in wrapping her feet. The two girls ended up falling asleep in Dannelle's room, wondering what the next day would bring.

Miguel was starting to get better now that the bruises were going away, the open sores on his back were starting to scab over, as well. He hadn't seen the policeman for quite a while. In fact, he had wondered what had happened to him. It had been days since he had been locked up. Fortunately, the policeman had made sure that there was someone there to feed him. As he sat on his bunk, he wondered where his father was and why he hadn't showed up yet. Later that night the policeman was back in his office and very upset. Miguel could hear him cussing and yelling as he was throwing things around. Totally frustrated because he could not locate Pedro. As he sat there in his chair catching his breath and wiping the sweat from off his face, a thought come to him to ask the boy where his father was. As he smiled to himself, he thought that maybe he was ready to talk now, knowing that if he didn't, he would be beat again. Getting up from his chair and taking off his belt, he went to the cell where Miguel was sleeping on the bed and opened it. Miguel was awake in an instant, and seeing the belt in the policeman's hand, he knew what was coming. Miguel stood up and tried to run past him. The policeman caught him and threw him back onto the bed. "Where is your father?" he asked, as he raised the belt into the air....

Chapter XXXI

Mike was still cussing under his breath, grumbling to himself about losing the German, as he and his team hiked back to the top of the mountain to meet up with the others. No one said a word about losing Gunther, as each of them were feeling guilty about it. All of them were trying to figure out what went wrong and how they missed him. All of them knew that Gunther was there before they began the operation and yet, when all was said and done, he had disappeared. Where had he gone? And how did he do it?

When they reached the top of the mountain Tony and the others were already there and were happy to see them coming up to the camp. As everybody sat down next to the fire to get some coffee and get warm, Dixon noticed how quiet everyone was. "What happened, did you end up killing Gunther Reichman?"

"No, we somehow lost him, and he took Dannelle with him," Mike said, as he took a cup of coffee from Tony.

"What happened down there?" Tony asked.

"Well, he was there as we thought. But somehow, he found out that we were there and he got spooked and disappeared. Even his girls didn't know where he went," Mike said, as leaned back against a rock and closed his eyes.

Beck continued with the story, "One minute he was in the house, the next minute he was gone, as if he'd never been there at all. The worst of it all is that we never saw him leave the house."

"Well if it's any consolation, we were able to destroy the drug operation and rescue about ten people being held in a old building," Tony said, trying to change the mood.

"That's just great! We were sent here to get one man, we had him, he got away. But the good news is that we destroyed a drug operation and saved some lives," Mike said, sarcastically looking into the fire.

Within seconds, Mike caught himself, realizing what he had said and started to apologize to Tony and the others. "I'm sorry, it's not your fault, that we lost him. I'm sure the ten people you rescued are thankful for what you've done for them. I'm tired and frustrated like the others about losing Gunther."

"You say he was in the house when he disappeared. I take it that you searched the house looking for a clue as to how he got away?" Pedro asked.

"At least ten times. All we know is he went into the basement and was gone," Beck said, feeling just as frustrated as Mike.

"Well, I don't know about you, but I got this feeling he isn't too far away, as we speak," Tony said.

"What makes you say that?" Dixon asked.

"I'd like to think that Gunther likes his comforts to much and isn't one to give them up easily. Besides, I don't think he has a plane to fly away in without being noticed by you guys," Tony said.

"Please continue," Mike responded.

"He's got everything that he needs and wants right there, and starting over, at least to my way of thinking, it's not like him to want to do that," Tony stated.

"Especially, if he thinks that we think he's gone somewhere else," Beck said, with a sly smile on his face.

"Are you saying we should go back down there and see if he returned?" Mike asked.

"What do we have to lose if we go down and check one more time. Besides, it sounds better if we say we checked twice before leaving the area," Beck replied.

Mike sat there for a minute looking at his men. He could see that all of them were willing to give it one more shot. He thought out loud, "Well, what do we got to lose. How about tomorrow we go back down to the house and check it out again to be sure?"

Dannelle's feet were still sore and bleeding a little, yet they were getting better, so much so, she could almost walk normal again. Adriana, the girl that came to her a couple of nights before, refused to leave her side, taking care of her every need, so that she could heal quicker. All was calm in the house, and Gunther seemed to be in a good mood since getting a phone call late last night. He had received word from his friend that his guards were to be there today along with the freelance shooter. Previous to the phone call, he would walk around at night to make sure everything was safe before turning in. The girls were not allowed to be outside of the house, including the pool area. Therefore, they had to entertain themselves by putting puzzles together or play cards amongst themselves.

It was later in the afternoon that the new guards showed up and were ready to go to work. After bringing them into the house and introducing them to the girls, Gunther could tell that some of them had ideas about what they would like to do with them. Seeing this and wanting to nip it in the bud he addressed them. "Just so you men don't get any ideas, girls, will you tell these men what happened to the last guards that failed to do their jobs?"

With all of them looking at the floor, one of girl's said in a hushed tone, "Señor Gunther shot all of them."

Upon hearing this, the men stopped smiling and continued to listen to Gunther as he explained the procedures of guarding the house, the girls, and of course, him.

Gunther could see that these guys would be better guards than the last ones were, simply by the way that they carried themselves. "Are there any questions?" he asked, looking at the guards.

Seeing that there weren't any questions, he continued, "I'll let you guys figure out what your schedules will be for setting up security around the house," he said, as he walked away.

After getting their orders, the guards left the house to do their job. Gunther noticed that the freelance shooter was still seated in the living room and he walked over to him, "I hear you come highly recommended for your skills? I hope you're good enough to go against the FBI agents that are looking for me?"

The shooter looked at him and smiled while nodding his head. Gunther, seeing him smile continued, "I don't know where they are, but I want you kill them all. If you do this, I'll give you 1 million dollars.   But I will need proof that you did your job."

"What would you like me to bring back as proof?"

"Their badges will be enough."

At this point, the shooter got up and walked out the door and went to his truck.   Gunther followed him and watched as he retrieved his rifle and backpack and started walking towards the mountains that were behind the house. As he stood there watching, he wondered if he would be able to do the job, *"I guess we'll know soon enough, it really doesn't matter, either way. If I'm dead, I won't need the money. And if he gets them, I'll continue to enjoy life,"* he said to himself, as he turned and walked back into the house.

Miguel laid passed out on the bed in the cell. The policeman stopped beating the boy thinking that he had killed him. After checking him, he found that the boy was still breathing and had passed out from the pain. He walked back to his desk trying to recover his strength after beating Miguel again. Still no crying and still no words to indicate the whereabouts of his father.

Having left the cell door open, Miguel opened his eyes just a little to see where the policeman was. Pretending to be passed out, Miguel was hoping that the beating would stop. He had, in a sense, played dead in order to scare the policeman. He was still sitting at his desk as Miguel checked again to see what he was doing. The policeman was sweating like a stuck hog and was having a hard time trying to cool down with the office being so warm. He got up and opened the door to let some cool air come in, then looked in on the boy one last time, before sitting down again. Being tired, he closed his eyes for just second, then jerking himself awake once before settling down again. This time the cool air coming into the room, helped him to relax and pretty soon he was sleeping soundly.

Miguel, seeing that the policeman was fast asleep, slowly got up, found his shoes and carefully walked out of the jail and off into the night. Hurting and bleeding from the belt, he stopped occasionally to catch his breath and to ease the pain. He made his way slowly up the trail determined to look for his dad. With it being so dark and with no moonlight to see, he was careful not to trip and fall. Knowing that he was free and able to look for his dad, gave him a second burst of energy that he needed to continue walking throughout the night. He knew that if he kept walking through the night, it would be the next morning when he would arrive at their camp. The satisfaction of knowing he got away from the policeman brought a smile to his face. Fortunately, the policeman wouldn't wake up till the next morning. Which would be more than enough time to find his dad.

The policeman woke up early the next morning to an empty jail. He looked around inside the jail and in each of the cells and couldn't find Miguel anywhere.   His thoughts ran wild, thinking now he was going to be in trouble with the German.   He didn't want to tell Señor Gunther that he had lost the boy because he remembered what he had said about killing him if he failed.   He decided that in order to save his skin he'd better go and look for the boy. This time he was determined to climb the mountain, if necessary, to find him.   He started up the trail to the mountain looking for the boy's footprints to follow.   As he hiked up the mountain, he had found more than just Miguel's footprints along the way.   Surprised by this, he wondered who else was up there on top of the mountain.   He stopped to catch his breath and was cussing at himself for being in such bad shape that he could hardly walk.

By the afternoon, he was exhausted and completely soaked through from sweating and the humidity of the jungle.   He sat down again to rest and stayed there until later in the afternoon. He now started having some soreness in his left arm and began to rub it to keep it from aching anymore.   Finally, after two hours of resting and catching his breath, he started up the trail again.   After taking another two steps he grabbed his chest and fell to his knees. He grabbed one of the vines along the trail for support and tried to pull himself up.   Being unable to do so, he crawled over to one of the larger trees and laid against it and then passed out.   He came to after a few minutes and started thinking that something was terribly wrong with him.   He decided not to go any further up the trail, rolled onto his knees, carefully got up and started going back down the mountain.   Feeling scared, he started walking slowly down the trail, and was now praying that he would get to the village before anything else could go wrong.   As he continued walking it was with labored breathing and having to stop every so often to catch his breath.   He had fallen twice as he hit part of the trail that was tangled with tree roots going across it.   Each time he got up it took all of his strength and the help of the vines and tree limbs that were nearby. Getting up each time required more energy than he had used previously.   It was only out of sheer panic that he was able to push himself to keep going.   He would walk a little bit then stop and lean against a tree to rest then continue on. Each time he stopped his left arm would throb in pain. Completely sweated out, he was now starting to get sick from being dehydrated. It was at this time he saw the village below him and with a burst of energy he managed to keep   going.

Chapter XXXII

Mike was thinking about all that had happened earlier that day, and still couldn't put his finger on what went wrong. He knew Gunther couldn't disappear like that, unless it was something that he had planned before he would need it. But still not having any clue as to where to look for him, is what made it worse. It was still a mystery that would haunt him for quite some time to come, that is, unless he could find him again. He had to hand it to Gunther, he was smarter than he had originally thought. The idea of going back to look for him again was going to make it better, at least he hoped so, when it came to explaining what had happened to his boss. This time the team would be all together instead of splitting up, therefore the chances of finding the German would or should be better.

Dannelle, woke up to hearing men's voices downstairs and found that her roommate was gone. She looked around their room and couldn't find her anywhere. She sat up in bed and moved herself to the edge and put her feet on the floor, expecting to feel pain as she stood up. She was surprised that when she did so, there was very little discomfort. She walked over to the door and slowly opened it to hear what was going on downstairs. The voices of the men got louder, and she could hear Gunther's voice in the middle of it.

She stepped out of her room and into the hall and she saw Adrianna crying as she stood there in the middle of the men down below. As she looked closer, she could see two men holding her in place, "What made you decide to run away?" Gunther asked her.

"I didn't want to get shot by you," she replied.

"Now, why would I shoot you, have you done something wrong?" he asked.

"No Señor, I have done nothing wrong. I remember what you did to those other men is all."

Gunther motioned to the two men holding her to release her and let her go.   As she stood there, Gunther reached out to her and held her for a minute, whispering in her ear, "I'm sorry I scared you.   It was a bad time for me, and I was angry because no one even tried to find me, especially the old guards.   I am not mad at you, so please don't be afraid," he said, as if he was apologizing for his actions.

Adrianna felt better and smiled at him. "Now go play, and we will have no more of this silliness, am I right," he said, smiling.

Adrianna felt better and went upstairs to her room. As she walked up the stairs she saw Dannelle standing there wondering what was going on.   Dannelle motioned for Adrianna to follow her into their room. Closing the door behind them Dannelle asked, "So what happened?"

"I tried to run away from here and was caught by one of the guards in the process," she replied.

"Is everything alright now?"

"Señor Gunther was very understanding about everything and let me go,"

"Next time let me know when you decide to run away, and we will go together.   I happen to know a special way to escape without being caught," Dannelle said, as she thought about where Gunther had taken her when they escaped.

"It's a promise.   I'm headed to the kitchen, do you want anything to eat?"Adrianna asked, as she left the room.

"No thanks, I'll get something later."

Dannelle knew Gunther would kill her and Adrianna if they tried to leave without his permission. The only thing different now was that she knew of his escape tunnel and how to leave without him knowing it.   The question in her mind now was, when to leave.

Gunther looked at his guards as the young girl left them. Waiting for her to be out of ear shot he said, "Next time, kill her if she tries to leave again."

After Gunther left, the leader of the guards nodded his head in agreement and then smiled, thinking to himself, *"Only after I have my way with her first. "*

Gunther was starting to get cagey as he walked around the house. To him, it seemed as if his new life wasn't going the way he wanted it to.   It seemed like everybody was walking on eggshells around him, afraid of saying or doing anything around him for fear of upsetting him.   He walked back into his den and sat down and tried to figure out what to do next to make it like it was before the FBI showed up.   As he continued to think about all that had transpired, he wondered if maybe it was time to find another place to live to avoid all of this.   He remembered that he had been shone two other places besides this one that would have worked.   Maybe it's time to reconsider one of the other places he thought to himself.   As he sat there considering his options, he was hoping that the shooter would collect his million dollars, making the problem go away.   Until then, the girls would just have to get used to him being cranky.   He smiled to himself thinking, *the problems you face when you kill people and steal money and don't want to be found."*

Gunther got up and went over to the window and checked on the guards to see where they were and what they were doing.   Being satisfied that all was well, he found his favorite book and sat down to read.

The shooter picked up the trail that Mike and his team had made when they left Gunther's place.   He could tell the tracks were still somewhat fresh by looking at the impressions made on the ground. He smiled to himself as he followed the tracks and started thinking about the million dollars that was to be his payment and what he would spend it on.   Catching himself not being focused on what he was suppose to be doing, he told himself, *"Remember what happened to your partner when he got careless and started thinking about the money that both of you were going to make when you took out the DEA agent?"*   He stopped in the middle of the trail to listen and get re-focused on his job and what he needed to do to complete it.   He started to survey the area around him as he stood there, trying to see if there were any other indications or clues that would tell him how close he was to his prey. Being unable to find anything he thought, *"I must admit that, with the exception of the tracks, the Americans are very good about not leaving any signs behind that would give them away."* It was this kind of thinking, that would have saved his partner from being killed by the Americanos.   Fortunately for him, his partner had decided to take point and was shot going up another trail just like this one.   Moving at night, who would've thought that the Americans would be tracking them with an infrared optics system on their rifles.   He was lucky to get away by running deeper into jungle than the Americans were willing to go to find him.   He had felt bad about leaving his friend there on the trail, however, under the circumstances, it was too late to help him. Discretion, in this case was the better part of valor, although he still felt guilty about leaving his partner behind.   He came back to reality as he continued his way, now totally focused on what he was doing.   As he looked into the sky, he could see that the sun was setting and realized that it was going to be dark in less than hour. He decided it was a good time to look for a place to bed down for the night and start again tomorrow bright and early.   Upon hearing his stomach growl, he remembered that he hadn't eaten since morning. After rummaging through his backpack he pulled out some candy bars and a hammock.   As he looked around, he found two trees that were big enough to use and tied both ends of the hammock to them. Looking around the area, he found some kindling to build a fire with. Once he got the fire going, and feeling the warmth from it, he sat down and began to eat his candy bars.   Not worrying about the fire giving his position away, he kept it going all night.

As he lay in his hammock, the shooter was half awake and half asleep as he lay above the ground, listening to the noises from the jungle that surrounded him. To avoid detection when he set up camp, he made sure that he was far enough off the trail, so that there would be no surprises during the night.   He lay there smiling to himself, knowing that the next day he would catch the Americanos, get his money for killing them, and retire forever.

Just a few miles away, Mike watched as the sun went down and the moon and the stars started to appear, knowing that tomorrow would be the make or break day for him and his team.   Going after the German had been on his mind the whole time he had been here. Even with the mosquitoes and the humidity, the one and only goal he had was catching Gunther Reichman, either alive or dead.   As he sat by the fire drinking his coffee along with the others, he planned in his mind how he and Beck would setup the team to catch the German once again.

It was at this point that Pedro decided to go scouting around the area where they were camped.   He grabbed the sniper rifle and looked at Mike, "I'll be back shortly, I'm going hunting."

"Can I go with you?" Tony asked, as he grabbed a pair of binoculars to take with him.

"As you wish, my friend," Pedro said, as he started off into the dusk.

"Why are you doing all of this, Pedro?" Tony asked.

"I believe that we should always be on guard with the cartel. I don't think they will be happy once they find out we destroyed their drug operation."

Tony, hearing what Pedro said, nervously started looking around. To him, everything in the shadows was a potential threat.

As they continued to move through the darkness, Pedro stopped and drew a breath, "Do you smell that?"

Tony stopped, trying to catch the smell that had stopped Pedro in his tracks. "No, I don't. Wait a minute, yes, I do smell it now," he said, as the wind shifted a little in their direction.

"We must be very careful from this point on," Pedro said, as he continued walking through the jungle searching for the location of the fire.

Tony was amazed that Pedro could smell the smoke from the fire, whereas he hadn't smelled it all. *Pedro keeps surprising me with his skills. I bet we could learn a lot from this man, if we were to stay here long enough,"* Tony thought to himself.

As the night wore on, they were unable to locate the fire and decided to continue following the trail to Gunther's place. They found a spot to conceal themselves and waited til morning for the rest of the team to show up.

Mike was restless and unable to get comfortable as he slept on the ground, using a rock for a pillow. Aside from being uncomfortable, he was unsure of why he was feeling so restless. He got up from his spot on the ground, looked around and could see one of his men standing guard. He nodded to him and then sat back down next to the fire trying to warm up a little. He was surprised that it was actually cold out here in the jungle at night, then he thought, *"Well, what do you expect for being on top of a mountain?"* He poured himself some coffee, took a drink of it and felt it start to warm his insides. He wondered who had come up with coffee as a drink. If they only knew that the whole world revolved around a cup of coffee to start the day in order to solve all of the problems of the world, they would have given him a medal. He smiled to himself, thinking maybe it was time to consider putting in his papers for retirement, especially if he was able to catch Gunther Reichman. He would be retiring on a high note for his career of twenty-five years of service. As he sat there, he heard some movement coming from the direction of the trail. The agent on guard had heard it too and went to investigate. Mike had his gun drawn and stepped out of the firelight waiting to see what would happen next. Within minutes, the agent came back into the camp and had someone with him. Sensing no real danger, Mike met the two people as they got closer to the fire. At first Mike didn't recognize Miguel. When he did, he stood there in shock for a moment as he looked the boy over. The bruises were very pronounced, and his back was still bleeding from the open wounds. The agent was half carrying Miguel because of how hard the hike had been on him. Grabbing his other arm, Mike assisted the agent to get Miguel to the fire to warm him up and get him something to eat.

It took about five minutes for the other men in the camp to wake up and see that Miguel was sitting there next to the fire, all beat up. "Who did this to you?" Mike asked, as his blood started to boil.

"The policeman, Señor. Where's my papa?" he asked, holding back the tears.

"He's out there looking for more cartel men that might have gotten away," Mike replied.

"What is it that you wanted to tell your papa?" Beck asked.

"The policeman took Dannelle to the Señor Gunther's house. And when he came back, he caught me watching him."

Agent Dixon brought over a first aid kit to start working on Miguel's back, and as he did so, Miguel flinched every so often from the alcohol as it was applied to his wounds. By now everyone was ready to go after the policeman. Agent Dixon walked over to Mike after he was done tending to Miguel. "That poor kid was beat with the buckle end of a belt. I'm surprised that he was able to get to us in his condition."

"I think we need to have some wall to wall counseling with our friend, the policeman," Mike responded.

"Count us in to assist in changing his attitude," one of the team members said, while the others nodded in agreement.

Dannelle was ready to make her escape after getting some breakfast, taking some extra food along with her for her journey into the jungle. Adrianna had done the same thing and was waiting for Dannelle to go once the coast was clear. Watching for the guards, Dannelle waited till they were on the other side of the house. As she was getting ready to leave, she looked over into the jungle, past the patio, and could see her uncle and Tony watching the place. She stepped off of the patio and took one of the beach balls from the pool and threw it out into the backyard. As she walked out to retrieve it, she stopped by the spot where the ball was and waited for Tony and her uncle to make contact.

"So, what's going on here?" Tony asked.

"Gunther is here, and he has a man out in the jungle looking for all of you, to kill you for a million dollars. One more thing, there is a tunnel in the basement that we used to escape from the FBI the last time they were here," she said, as she picked up the beach ball.

"Do you know where this guy is?" Pedro asked.

"He left yesterday carrying the same kind of rifle you have," Dannelle said.

"I want you to stay here till we get back," Tony said, realizing that they had a sniper coming after the team.

"But we want to go with you, we are running away."

"No, it's best that you stay here and let us take care of the sniper first," Pedro said, as both men slipped back into the jungle.

Dannelle picked up the ball, "Yes, uncle, I will do as you say," she said, as she walked back towards the patio.

She looked up towards the roof she saw one of the guards watching her, holding his gun as if he were ready to fire. Pretending not to notice, she brought the ball back to the pool area. Dannelle then went back inside the house looking for Adrianna. When she found her, she whispered, "We need to sit tight and wait a little longer. Something has come up."

Adrianna looked disappointed by her words. Dannelle, seeing this, gave her a hug. "Trust me on this."

"I guess, I really don't have a choice on this do I?" she said, sounding a little upset by the news.

"Not unless you want to go by yourself," Dannelle said, as she walked away from her, feeling somewhat upset by her attitude.

Adrianna realized that Dannelle was upset and knew it was because of her.   She ran after her, "Hey Dannelle, I'm sorry for not being more appreciative or respectful to you.   I'm sorry, will you forgive me?"

Dannelle looked at her, "All is forgiven, you need to trust me on all of this," she said, almost sounding like she was pleading with her.

"I will, I will do as you say."

After hugging each other, Dannelle and Adrianna decided to go up to their room and wait until the FBI arrived.

Chapter XXXIV

The policeman slowly staggered into his office holding his left arm. He sat down once more in his chair and grabbed for the phone and quickly dialed the doctor's office, praying a doctor would be there to take his call for help.   The pain in his arm was still there and his chest felt like a big hammer was working on it and he felt his heart pounding as if it was returning the blows of the hammer that he felt hitting his chest. Unfortunately for him, no one answered the phone.   Now in a shear panic, he got into his vehicle and decided to drive to the hospital not knowing if he would make it or not.

Now aware there was a sniper looking for the team and that the only way to help them was to get word to them, Pedro and Tony knew they had to do something without being shot by the shooter themselves. Pedro was as cool as ice. "Let's go hunting for the shooter," he said, as he looked at Tony,

"Yeah, let's get him before he gets the others," Tony replied.

"My thoughts exactly.   I think the smoke we smelled last night was from the shooter's camp."

They headed back into the jungle and walked carefully as if they were hunting for some big game.   They looked for the trail that would take them to the camp where the FBI agents were.   Hoping that the shooter would somehow show himself, they stopped and listened for anything that was out of place in the jungle. Unbeknownst to the FBI team, they were walking into a trap, unaware that the shooter was waiting for them.

The shooter had gotten up early and after finishing breakfast was back on the trail when he spotted the FBI agents walking in his direction, with his binoculars.   He smiled, knowing that his prey was moving closer to him and quickly scrambled to find a place to shoot from that would give him cover, so he wouldn't be seen when he fired his rifle.   He found an outcropping and climbed into a gap between the rocks and sat there, waiting for his targets to come closer. With the sun behind him, and having an unobstructed view of the trail, he smiled to himself, *This is like shooting fish in a barrel.* "He took two extra clips and his canteen out and took a drink and set it all beside him as he tried to find his targets with his scope.

As they continued walking on the trail, Mike was still feeling uneasy but didn't know why. He decided to stop and rest the team and do a final check on their plan to get the German. They sat in the shade of some trees next to a river out of the heat, to stay cool. Dixon stood up to stretch his legs to get the kinks out when he fell to the ground. A second later the report from the rifle could be heard. Mike, knowing what it was, yelled to the others, "Stay down and find cover! We need to know where that shot came from."

Two of the team grabbed Dixon and pulled him in a little closer to the trees they were using for cover. The shooter didn't see the two men grab his first victim. Mike called out, "Is he alive or what?"

"He's alive, shot just above his heart. It missed his artery, but he needs to be taken to the hospital," said one of the two men that had pulled him to safety.

Watching the man fall, the shooter realized that he had missed his mark. In other words, the man was still alive. Cussing to himself, as he adjusted his scope, he made a promise that the next shot would kill his intended target.

Mike thought about the situation they were in and knew that it would be hopeless to move anyone right now. The shooter would follow and pick them off one at a time if they tried to leave their present positions. Besides, he didn't know if there was more than one shooter that was watching them. Fortunately, they had the jungle for camouflage and water to drink if they needed it.

Pedro and Tony heard the shot that had hit Dixon. They in turn started moving faster knowing that the shooter had the advantage of being setup to take out his targets. Both of the men were hoping he would fire again so that they could find the shooter themselves and take him out.

Mike was looking around the tree he was using for a shield trying to find the shooter. As he did so, another shot rang out with the bullet hitting the tree, just above his head. "Anybody see where the shot came from?" he called out as he hugged the ground.

"He's got us cold; we can't see anything because he's got the sun behind him," one of the agents called out that was on the other side of Mike.

The shooter smiled to himself, knowing that the FBI agents were pinned down, wondering where he was. He sat back against the rock outcropping that he was using for his firing position, grabbed his canteen and took another drink of water from it. He checked his watch and looked at the sun and knew that the men below him would be getting thirsty and would want to move to get out of the heat. The fact was, he wanted them to move so that he could pick them off one at a time.

Hearing the second shot, Pedro and Tony stopped and looked for cover. Tony used his binoculars to look for the shooter knowing that they were close now. The only question they had now, was how close. Scanning the ridgeline Tony saw a flash come from one of the rock outcroppings. He looked a little closer and could see movement now as the shooter took a drink from his canteen. He gave the binoculars to Pedro and pointed to the rocks and where he saw the flash. Pedro started to scan the rocks and within seconds saw some movement also. "How far away do you think he is from us?" Tony asked.

"To far, we need to get closer," Pedro said, as he handed the binoculars back to Tony.

Knowing where the shooter was and what they needed to do to get closer, Pedro headed into the jungle in the direction of the rocks. After walking for a bit, Tony used his field glasses again to search for their target. Not able to locate the shooter because of all the foliage, they didn't know which direction to continue in. It was at this time that the shooter fired one more time to let the men below know he was still there, waiting for them to make a move.

Mike and his team were doing okay where they were at for the time being, yet each of them knew that they needed to find better cover in order to survive. The only option they had was to go deeper into the jungle and get behind the shooter to take him out. However, because Dixon's injuries needed medical attention, at this point they had no other option but to stay where they were and hope that the shooter would get tired of waiting and leave. Mike looked at his watch and realized that it was still morning and knew that their water wouldn't be enough to last the whole day.

Miguel crawled over to Mike, "I know a way into the jungle that will allow us to escape," he said excitedly.

"Can we get Dixon out following the trail?"

"No Señor.   It would be too hard for him."

"We can't leave him behind.   He needs medical attention."

"I think that I will try and find another way out," he said, as he crawled back to where he was situated before.

The shooter, seeing some movement, fired his rifle once more. Mike yelled out, "Someone get a hold of that boy and keep him safe!"

Steve Bishop, one of the other agents, grabbed Miguel and in doing so, got hit in the leg with a bullet by the shooter.   With one hand on the boy and his other hand grabbing his leg, he jumped back behind some cover.   The agent looked at his leg and could see that the shot went clean through, missing the artery.   He wrapped some bandages around the wound and was able to stop the bleeding.   He smiled and gave Mike a thumbs up sign and Mike finally started to breathe again.

With each shot being fired by the shooter, Pedro and Tony were getting closer to him.   Using the binoculars again, Tony could see the shooter clear as day.   Pedro used the scope on his rifle to locate him and found his target.   He smiled, "We need to get a little closer."

Now both men moved slowly through the jungle, making sure not to alert the shooter of their presence and give away their surprise. In another ten minutes, Pedro stopped again and using the scope on his rifle, found the shooter one more time.   Pulling the bolt back on the rifle, he loaded a round into the chamber and lifted the scope up to his eye, waited a second, then fired at the shooter.   The shooter felt the bullet go into his waist and then heard the report of the gun.   He quickly looked around to find out who had shot him and couldn't make out where the bullet had come from.

One of the agents saw the shooter stand up after he had been hit and then turn around. "I see him, he's up there in the rocks.   Sounds like there's another shooter out there," he called out to the others.

Mike, hearing this had forgotten about Pedro and Tony being out there in the jungle.   He smiled to himself, "I guess what's good for the goose is good for the gander as well."

Watching the shooter move from his position and turn around towards the other direction, the agents seized the opportunity and moved from their places of cover to better concealed positions, deeper into the jungle.   Hearing the other shot and seeing the shooter move, all of them were curious as to what was happening on the other side of the rocks.

The shooter realized that if he didn't do something quick to stop the blood flow he would bleed out, in fact, he was already starting to feel faint. He quickly searched through his backpack and found a shirt he could use as a bandage to help stem the flow of blood coming from his wound and wrapped it around his waist. With the bleeding stopped for the moment, he began moving to keep from being shot again, all the while, trying to find the other sniper.

Pedro and Tony watched as the shooter tried to escape, they could also see that he had been hit by Pedro's shot.   The shooter now scared and feeling faint from the loss of blood, had never been hunted by anther sniper like himself.   He quickly moved closer to the edge of the rock outcropping. Tony saw him first, "There he is. About one o'clock, thirty feet over to your right."

Pedro found the shooter again and noticed that he was standing higher up on the edge of the rock outcropping.   He lined him up through his scope and fired again.   Both men watched as the second bullet hit him in the chest. The shooter felt the bullet hit him, knocking the wind out of him.   He dropped his rifle and fell forward, unable to stop himself from falling off of the cliff.   He fell about twenty feet to the jungle floor below, breaking his back in the process. Tony and Pedro quickly made their way to where the body of the shooter landed and checked to make sure that he was dead. They found the man barely alive and in no condition to move.   He was laying on the ground with his body twisted from the impact of hitting the trees when he fell.   Looking at the shooter's body, they could see that second bullet had hit him in the chest where the blood was starting to show. They opened his shirt and could see that the bullet had hit the cross necklace he was wearing. The impact of the bullet hitting the cross and had driven it into his chest, planting it about 2 inches deep into the chest cavity. The impact of the bullet hitting the cross had pushed it through his sternum and had lodged itself into his heart.

Tony watched Pedro kneel down and offer a prayer for the shooter. After the prayer was said, he gave the sign of the cross before getting up and walking away.   As he walked away, both men knew that sometime during the prayer the shooter had died. Afterwards Pedro climbed up the rock outcropping, retrieved the shooter's rifle and supplies and then handed them to Tony, along with the extra bullets.   Both men now walked back with their rifles through the jungle to where Mike and the team were located.

Gunther could hear the gun shots echoing through the mountains and smiled, thinking that the million dollars was very well spent. He had counted five shots figuring that all of them had hit their targets.   Being pleased with himself he took a drink of wine to celebrate.

Mike and the other agents were busy assisting Dixon, getting him ready to move in order to save his life. The other agents had built a patient stretcher, by cutting two poles of the same length and width. They used some of their shirts to slide the poles into the sleeves for Dixon to lay on, so that he could be moved more easily down the mountain. Dixon was awake now and could feel the pain from the bullet, especially as they moved him onto the stretcher. Mike saw that he was conscience, "So how you are feeling?"

"What happened? What's going on?" he asked, gritting his teeth to help with the pain.

"You caught a bullet from someone on the ridge over there," Mike replied.

"How bad is it,"

"We need to get you off the mountain as soon as possible."

"What about the German, what about him?" Dixon asked getting excited as he tried to get off the stretcher and then falling back.

"We'll get him next time, we need to get you to a hospital soon," Mike said, as he quickly tried to calm him down.

"No, we're too close to stop now.   Otherwise, this mission was for nothing, we need to finish what we started," he said, emphatically.

"What about you?" Mike asked.

"What about me?   Dead or alive, it doesn't matter, along as we get the German.   Besides, I've got some comp time coming from this and I wouldn't miss it for the world," he said, smiling.

Mike smiled at Dixon's joke and thought about what he had said, knowing it was the German who had indirectly shot two of his agents. Getting upset, he thought to himself, *'To many people have died because of this one man, he needs to be stopped now. Knowing that the German was at his house, he wouldn't expect the FBI to try again."*

He looked around and started making decisions as to who was going on to finish what they had started and who would be going down the mountain to take Dixon back. One of the agents interrupted his planning, "There are two men walking this way, it looks like Tony and Pedro."

Signaling the two men, Tony and Pedro came over to where Mike was. "How are things going?" Tony asked, seeing Dixon laying on the stretcher.

"Not too good. Two men have been shot, Dixon here got the worst of it. I want to thank you guys for helping us out back there," Mike said, happy to be alive.

Seeing the condition that Dixon was in, Pedro handed his rifle to Tony, "I'll be right back," he said, as he quickly went into the jungle.

Within minutes, he came back with some leaves in his hands. He crushed them up and gave them to Dixon. "Here chew on these, it will help with the pain."

Pedro looked up at Mike. "Cocoa leaves. If you chew on them it helps with the pain."

All of them saw the pain in Dixon's face start to ease as he chewed on the leaves.

Miguel, hearing his father's voice, came running up to him. Seeing his son black and blue with sores from the beating, Pedro grabbed his son by the shoulders. "Who has done this to you?" he asked, already having an idea of who had done it.

"The policeman did papa. He wanted to know where you had gone. But I didn't tell him anything," he said, with pride in his eyes.

"Good for you my son. I'm sorry that you had to go through all of this for your papa," he said, with tears in his eyes starting to show.

Pedro, trying not to hurt Miguel, carefully hugged him for being so brave, and with a determination to find the policeman to settle the score. In a few minutes everyone was ready to go. Tony had already told Mike what Dannelle had said about the German coming back and how they shot the shooter.   At this point Mike had a tough decision to make about his next move. He gathered everyone together, "Men, we have a choice to make and I don't want to make it alone, leastwise without your inputs."

The men all gathered around in a semi-circle listening to their boss. "The way I see it, we have three choices here.   One is to call off the mission and go home and get Dixon to a decent hospital, or two, go get the German and finish our mission."

As he stood there, letting them think it over, he added, "That being said, there's another choice, number three, we can divide up our team and send some of you down the trail with Dixon and the others will go with me to get Gunther."

The first to speak was Pedro, "I have some business to attend to with the policeman.   My son and I will go with Dixon to get him to a hospital."

Tony, looked at Pedro and seeing his eyes, knew exactly what he was going to do to the policeman.   In all actuality, he didn't blame him one bit for what he was about to do. *I'm just glad he's on our side in this,* "he thought to himself.

Steve, who had been shot in the leg raised his hand, "I'll go with Dixon to get my leg looked at just in case there might be an infection developing.   You never know what you might get in this jungle.   I don't want it to create more problems for me."

Mike looked at Tony wanting to know his choice, "In for the penny, in for the pound.   Also, when we were at the house we ran into Dannelle and she told us how Gunther was able to disappear the first time we tried to get him." he stated.

"So, what's his secret?" Mike asked.

"He has an escape tunnel in the basement along the wall," Tony said smiling, thinking how simple yet effective it had been for the German.

"I knew it, I knew it," Beck said out loud.   "I just didn't know where to look for it."

Mike felt a little less frustrated by what Tony had said about a secret tunnel and now was ready to go back and get Gunther one way or the other.

With three people taking Dixon down the mountain trail, that left Mike and the others to go after Gunther.   As they set about making their plans Beck did some quick thinking and came up with a plan as how to use the men to capture the German with no one getting shot in the process. Mike, making sure that Dixon had enough cocoa leaves for the trip back to town, looked at them all, "If were not back by tomorrow morning, come looking for us."

"We'll see you soon," Pedro said, as he and Steve picked up the stretcher and started down the trail.

Mike stood there, saying a silent prayer, asking God to keep them all safe and to keep Dixon alive till they got to the hospital.   Tony walked over to Mike, "You know, Dannelle is still down there.   We need to get going, before it gets to dark."

Mike looked at Tony and nodded yes, picked up his backpack and headed in the direction of the trail that would lead back to Gunther's house. Beck and the other three agents were already moving in single file in front of Tony and Mike.   All of them were determined to stop Gunther once and for all.

The trip back to Gunther's place was all downhill as they followed the trail, making it a quick trip. The agents were determined to get the German, one way or the other.   All of them knew that to many people had died because of this man and he needed to be stopped. Grabbing his gear and following behind Mike, Tony looked at the sun as it started to go down in the west and could see the stars starting to appear.   He looked for the moon and could see that it was going to be a full one tonight.   Chuckling to himself for never being satisfied, he wished it would be cloudy and raining to protect them.   As he looked at the moon again he realized that it was the same moon Ann was looking at.   Because of all the excitement that had been happening he hadn't had a chance to even think about her. He had forgotten how alone he had been and having her in his life filled a void that he hadn't realized was there.   As he thought about everything, and especially her, he made up his mind that when he got home, he would ask Ann to marry him.   Until then it was all about getting Gunther and saving Dannelle.

In the middle of the night, Ann woke up from a dead sleep and started praying for Tony and that everything would be alright for him.   After a few minutes she felt a peaceful feeling come over her.

With the feeling that everything would be alright she fell back
asleep.

Chapter XXXV

Dannelle was sitting on her bed trying to avoid seeing Gunther at all costs. From her perspective, it was all her fault for what happened to Gunther when the FBI tried to catch him the first time. Now that she knew about the escape tunnel, she was trying to find a way to keep Gunther from sneaking out again by using it. She also knew that anything she did would be watched by, not only the guards, but by some of the girls, as well. Thus, making it harder to do anything about the escape tunnel. Adrianna was in the room with her, looking out the window and watching the guards making their rounds. Using her watch, she noticed that they would come around again in fifteen minutes. "Do you realize that the guards make their rounds to the back area of the house every fifteen minutes?"

Dannelle knew this from her own observations that she had made from the same window, since she had started hiding in her room to keep away from Gunther. Every once in a while, Gunther would walk into her room to see if he could catch her off guard trying to escape. Then there were the nights that she would be his for the evening. She would smile and pretend to like him touching her as she would giggle and laugh at the things he would say. Both of them knew they weren't fooling anybody with their act. The only thing that was on Gunther's mind was to keep an eye on her from now on. Dannelle knew this as well, she knew that, if given the right opportunity, Gunther would kill her without a second thought and leave her body in the jungle to rot.

Gunther was in his bedroom with one of the girls and you could hear them laughing together while they drank some champagne. The fact was Gunther was drunk and was having a hard time staying awake. Offering another toast in German, he eventually passed out, leaving the girl to fend for herself. Carefully getting up off the bed, she finished her drink and quietly left the master bedroom. Coming out into the hallway, she rearranged her clothes before anyone saw her. Dannelle silently waited for the girl to walk by before she stepped out into the hallway and headed towards Gunther's room. She looked into the master bedroom and could see that Gunther was sound asleep on his bed. She noticed the empty champagne bottles strewn about the room and she knew that it would be awhile before he would be awake.

Dannelle went back to her room and motioned for Adrianna to come and go with her to the kitchen, "Are you hungry?" she asked.

"Not really. What's going on?" she replied, now curious, wondering why she asked.

"I need you to go with me to find the switch that opens the door to the tunnel."

Making sure the guards patrolling outside couldn't see them in the kitchen as they made their rounds, they went into the basement only to be met by one of the guards there as they made their way down the stairs. Being caught and not having a real good reason for being down there, Adrianna quickly went over to the guard, "Finally we are alone," and kissed him.

The guard went from being suspicious as to why they were there, to being excited about the young lady flirting with him and began kissing her back. Dannelle walked over to the guard, "I have heard that you think my friend is pretty?"

The guard shook his head yes. "I am jealous that you think I'm not pretty as well. I have thought about being with you many times. Now I will let you choose for yourself who is prettier me or my friend here," Dannelle said, as she rubbed his chest.

The guard thought he had died and gone to heaven, having two girls to choose from. Grabbing both, he began kissing Dannelle. "Oh, I see, you can't make up your mind, do you want both of us?" she said coyly.

The guard shook his head yes and continued to kiss the girlfriend. Finally, pulling away from the guard, both of the girls looked at him, "It is too hard to do anything here in the basement, how about we get together tonight after you are finished keeping us safe?" Adrianna said, as she rubbed his chest with her hand. "Ooh, such a man. I can hardly wait," she said, smiling at the guard.

Both girls walked back towards the stairs and then turned and looked at the guard and smiled once more at him. Once they were back in the kitchen and away from the basement door, both girls looked at each other, thinking that was totally unexpected and that they were happy to be able to walk away safe and sound.

"What are we going to do about tonight, with our new friend?" Adrianna asked.

"Let's just hope the FBI gets here sooner than later," Dannelle said, as she and Adrianna walked back up the stairs to her room.

The policeman was scared that while he was driving to the hospital he would pass out and kill himself by driving over a cliff. He stopped every so often when he felt like he was going to pass out from the chest pains and waited until the feeling would go away. Gripping the steering wheel with both hands, he could feel the sweat pouring down his face and into his eyes. He wiped the sweat away from his eyes and started to say a prayer to help him get to the hospital. With what was left of his strength, he forced himself to stay awake for the last two miles of the trip to the hospital. When he finally saw the hospital from the dirt road, he smiled to himself, knowing he was going to make it. He pulled into the parking lot in front of the emergency room entrance and opened the door to his truck and fell out onto the ground. Before passing out again, he yelled out, "Somebody, please help me!"

When he came to, he was resting in a bed in one of the hospital rooms. As he looked around the room, he saw all the medical equipment that was being used in his behalf and could hear a heart monitor beeping. He soon realized that he had an oxygen mask on, as well, to help him breathe. As he breathed in and out, he could tell that his chest still hurt, but just a little bit now. Being fully awake, he watched as a nurse came into the room to look at the I.V. drip in his arm. The nurse saw that he was awake and called for the doctor to come into the room to check on him. In a second the doctor came in and introduced himself, "Hi, I'm doctor Ortega. How are you feeling?" he said, as he used his flashlight to look into the policeman's eyes. "I want you to know that you gave us all quite a scare when you came in earlier today," he said smiling.

Unable to speak, the policeman used his hands to ask, "What happened?"

"You had a small heart attack. Fortunately for you, you will recover from it without surgery. However, you will need to stay here for a couple of days, just for observation, in case something unexpected should happen."

The policemen felt relieved that he would be fine. The doctor saw the look of relief on his patient's face. He picked up the patient's chart, looked it over and was satisfied that all the indicators were reading normal. "You just rest, and I'll check in on you again shortly," he said, as he put the chart back in place at the foot of the bed.

The policeman watched as the doctor left his room and started talking to the nurse at her station. At this point he closed his eyes and was fast asleep.

Pedro struggled to keep the stretcher level as they made their way down the trail, if Miguel hadn't been there, they would have already dropped Dixon a couple times, probably killing him in the process. Miguel kept moving back and forth to help Steve at one end of the stretcher then back to his father's side to help him. They stopped to take a break and catch their breath. Dixon was oblivious to what was going on as he was still chewing the cocoa leaves, he had been given to ease the pain. Pedro looked at him and could see that he was starting to bleed from his wound again. "We need to get that bullet out of him, before he bleeds to death," said Steve, after he looked at him.

"How is your leg doing," Pedro asked.

"It only hurts when I move," he said, smiling.

Pedro could see through Steve's bravado and knew that he was in pain but didn't want to be a burden. Thinking to himself that they still had a long way to go and that Dixon probably wouldn't make it otherwise, he agreed with Steve. After looking around the area, they found a place where they could put the stretcher down without causing to much pain for Dixon. Pedro quickly built a fire while Miguel went to look for some more wood. As they continued to watch Dixon, the bleeding started to get worse and it became obvious that the wound wasn't going to heal on its own. Both men knew that if they didn't get the bullet out of his chest and cauterize the wound, Dixon would soon be dead.

Miguel came back with the extra firewood while Pedro stuck his knife into the coals of the fire to heat it up and get it sterilized. Steve had a first aid kit that contained some alcohol, a small scalpel, some suture thread and needles that would be needed to sew up the wound when it came time. Between the two them, they would operate and do their best to keep Dixon alive. Miguel was given the responsibility to keep Dixon chewing on the cocoa leaves, and keep the fire burning so that the knife would be hot enough to seal the wound.

Steve used the small scalpel to open the wound and cut through the muscle and tissue to find the fragmented bullet. As he was using the scalpel, Dixon let out a scream from the pain and then fainted. Pedro kept Dixon immobile by keeping his shoulders secure. With Dixon passed out from the pain it made Steve's job easier to do while he looked for the pieces of the bullet. Even though he was passed out, Dixon was still reacting to what Steve was doing as he searched for the bullet. After a few tense moments, using his fingers, Steve found the bullet and some of its fragments, as well. He pulled out what he could get to and was able to find the largest piece of the bullet. Using his fingers, he searched for any pieces of bone that might have been shattered by the bullet. When he was finished searching, he took the needle and thread and began sewing up the hole, first the muscle and then the layers of skin. Pedro, using a cloth, assisted in helping to keep the wound clear from the bleeding as Steve finished his part of the operation. All in all, it took about two hours to find the bullet and sew Dixon up. The bleeding started to subside with each suture that was made by Steve. He gave the bottle of alcohol to Miguel, "Pour some of the alcohol onto the wound while your father holds his shoulders down."

Miguel nodded his head, took the alcohol and poured it onto the sealed wound and let it soak for a minute or two before Steve wiped the excess off. Dixon screamed in pain once again in reaction to the alcohol and then laid there quietly as the pain subsided.

By now the blade of Pedro's knife was ready to finish the job. Pedro picked up the knife and had Steve pour the rest of the alcohol onto the blade and laid the knife against the wound and let it sit there for a moment, to cauterize it. The smell of burnt flesh was strong and it was all that they could do stand it while the knife did its job. Dixon reacted to the hot knife by waking up again and then fainting one more time. Pedro took the knife off of the wound. Both men continued to watch the wound to see what would happen next, praying that they were able to stop the bleeding. After a few minutes they could see that the bleeding had stopped. With Miguel's help, they took some of the cocoa leaves that he had crushed and placed them on the wound and then wrapped the wound with bandages from the first aid kit. Still not seeing any bleeding after fifteen minutes, they continued sitting there for a few more minutes to collect their thoughts. All of them were relieved that everything had gone well. Steve took the bullet fragments and put them into a small plastic bag from the first aid kit for later. With Dixon still unconscious, they decided that it was time to continue their journey down the mountain. Fortunately, Dixon stayed that way until they got back into Pedro's village.

Mike and Tony were sitting on top of the hill in the twilight, overlooking the German's house and could see the lights as they turned on in the different rooms of the house. They were waiting for agent Beck, who had been sent down to scout the place, to come back and report. As he looked through his binoculars, Tony could see the guards as they made their patrol around the house and the guard that was sitting on top of the roof. Using a stick, he drew the places where the guards were on the grounds that he had seen. When agent Beck showed up to give his report. Mike showed the layout of where the guards were that had been drawn in the dirt to him. Beck took the stick and pointed to the front of the house, "There's a permanent guard out in front of the house with something covered up right next to him and I'm thinking there may be a couple inside the house as well. I think our friend knows we're still here, at least I think I saw him walking around inside the house with a gun on his hip. Oh yeah, one more thing, there are several girls in the house, as well, I believe they are the same ones as before."

"How many girls did you see?" Tony asked, thinking about Dannelle.

"I counted four girls in there. I believe there are two upstairs in one of the bedrooms. They kept moving the curtains and looking out the window," replied Beck.

"What kind of firepower are the guards carrying?" Mike asked.

"The guards were all carrying automatic rifles. Looks like they're AK-47s, as far as I could tell."

"Any other weapons?"

"No sir.   Although I have to say, it looks like they're expecting us to show," he replied.

"How's that?" Tony asked.

"Well, there's no one outside the house and no one is at the pool. They are all inside," Beck said.

Upon hearing this Mike replied, "I guess we will have to be extra careful then,"

"Maybe the German was hoping the shooter would get us all," Tony said, with the satisfaction of knowing that he had been taken out.

Mike and Beck were studying the map on the ground, when Beck pointed at it with the stick, "If we come from this direction, I think we can take them by surprise."

Mike looked down at Gunther's place through his binoculars and then back at the drawing on the ground, trying to figure if it could be done.   "The only problem is the guard on top of the house.   He's hard to see from the place you want to attack from. From his position he could pick us off.   Needless to say, it wasn't fun the first time we went through it."

"I can take him out from up here, if that will solve the problem," Tony said, in a matter of fact tone.

"You'll have to get closer to take him out.   I think if you can get here, you should be close enough to take the shot and provide cover for us from the guards on the ground when we go in," Beck said, looking at Tony.

"It's a shame we don't know where the entrance to the tunnel is in the jungle," Mike said, feeling slightly frustrated by all of this.

"Dannelle is the only person who knows where it is," Tony replied.

"Maybe, we can get her to help us to get inside the house?" Beck said, looking at Tony.

"Pedro and I got all the way down to the backyard here," Tony said, as he pointed to the drawing on the ground. "Well within eyesight of the guard on the roof.   If what you say is true about having guards in the house, I don't think there's a chance to have her help us without her taking a bullet in the process,"

Nodding his head, Beck said, "Back to plan A then."

"When do we want to do this, it's about eight o'clock now with a full moon," Mike said, checking his watch.

"If we do it now, we'll have the element of surprise on our side. That being said, it may be harder to get to the guards without alarming the German first," Beck replied.

"Plus, I can't provide top cover for you in the dark," Tony said, making his point.

"Then it's settled, we will do it in the daylight, first thing in the morning," Mike said, as he leaned back onto the rock and closed his eyes to sleep.

Taking a cue from their boss, each of them searched for a place nearby to sleep till morning. Not able to build a fire, they would have to deal with a cold camp. Tony reached into his backpack and pulled out some energy bars to fight the grumbling in his stomach and then drank some water to chase it down with. Looking at the rifle and the supplies he inherited from the shooter he counted out the bullets to see how many he had. He searched through the shooters bag and found some extra clips that had bullets in them, as well. He pulled the loaded clips out of the bag and laid them on the ground, he counted five clips holding five bullets each. He realized that he would have enough and then some to do the job. Tony now started looking for a spot to sleep on and finding it, he rolled out his ground cloth and laid on it, he lay there for a second before he closed his eyes wishing Ann was here with him and being glad it wasn't raining after all.

Dannelle and her friend were surprised by the knock on the door to her bedroom and wondered who it could be. She opened the door to see the guard standing there all cleaned up and smiling at her. She had forgotten about their earlier encounter with him in the basement of the house. She had hoped that the FBI would already be there to keep the guard busy. Not knowing what to do now, Dannelle said, "Won't you come in," then looked past her guest around the hallway for Gunther.

Adrianna met the guard as he crossed the room and kissed him, "I've been waiting for you," she said, as she handed him a drink.

Toasting to one another, the guard downed his drink and asked for another. Within seconds the knockout drops started to work. As he felt the effects of the drops, he sat down as Dannelle went to sit on his lap. Adrianna offered him another drink, at this point the guard realized that there was something wrong and began to stand up trying to get to the door, dumping Dannelle onto the floor.   By then the knockout drops went into full effect, causing the guard to pass out and fall face first on top of her.   Dannelle pushed the guard off of her and got up to go look in the hallway to see if anyone had heard the commotion coming from their room. Not seeing anyone, both girls quickly picked him up and put him back into the chair. Dannelle was surprised by this turn of events and was now looking at Adrianna.   Adrianna realized that Dannelle was surprised by what had happened. "I never leave home without this in my hand. Besides, we need it more than the guy I took it off," she said, smiling.

Both of them laughed at her comment, "I wish I had that to use on a couple of my customers," Dannelle continued, "Do we have enough to use it on the others?"

"I'm sorry to say no, there's just enough for my special friends."

Gunther had come to about an hour earlier after being passed out for almost the whole afternoon.   When he woke up, he found his bed empty and with a bottle of champagne in his hand, he got up to go look for the girl that had been there earlier.   He found her downstairs in the living room and walked over to where she was sitting and bent down and said with a smile, "We still have a bottle of champagne to drink."

She smiled at him then giggled.   Then proceeded to stand up and taking his hand, she followed him back upstairs to his room. Closing the door behind them, someone from inside the room turned on the music.

Chapter XXXVI

Pedro had Miguel open the door to his home while he and Steve took Dixon in and placed him on Pedro's bed to let him rest more comfortably. As they looked over the wound, both men could see that there was still no bleeding coming through the bandage. Steve felt around the cauterized area and could feel no pockets of blood pooling which would have indicated internal bleeding. With Dixon still asleep and not bleeding, Pedro and the others were able to relax without being disturbed by anyone. Being home and able to rest, brought a sense of closure for their part of the mission.

While Pedro and Miguel got things ready for their trip to the hospital, Steve stepped out into the darkness of the night and went looking for one of their vehicles that was parked out of sight. Finding one of them, he checked the wheel well looking for the key in the magnetic lock box. He started the SUV up and sat there thinking how foreign it was to be in something modern like this after being in the jungle for so long. He quickly collected his thoughts and put the vehicle into gear and then drove it over to the front of Pedro's house. He got out and opened the tailgate and then pushed the backseat down in order to make room so that Dixon could lay down on the makeshift stretcher.

Both Pedro and Steve carefully carried Dixon on the stretcher to the SUV and placed him into the back of it. Miguel stayed next to him just to keep him from moving around. Pedro got in on the passenger side while Steve got in on driver's side to take him to the hospital.

Driving through the jungle at night was a different experience for Steve and because of it he drove slower in order to keep Dixon still so his wounds wouldn't tear open. After what seemed like hours, Pedro was able to see the lights of the town shining up ahead. Pedro gave directions to Steve so that he could park at the hospital emergency entrance.   Pedro quickly walked through the emergency room doors and within minutes two men followed him out with a gurney to take Dixon inside so he could be looked at by the attending physician. After the doctor began examining Dixon he decided that it would be a waste of his time to do any more than what had already been done, simply because of the work that Pedro and Steve had already done on his wound.   At this point, the doctor decided not to reopen the wound and suggested that the wound should be x-rayed to see if there was something that had been missed by Pedro and Steve.

While they were waiting for the results of the x-rays to come back from the lab, the doctor continued to make his rounds. He stopped at the nurse's station and inquired about the heart attack patient. As they were discussing the patient, Pedro left Steve in Dixon's room waiting for the x-ray results and went to look for Miguel.   As he passed by the nurse's station, he couldn't help but overhear the doctor and the nurse talking about how the last couple of days had been busy with heart attacks and now gunshot wounds.   Pedro wasn't really paying that much attention to the conversation until he heard the word policeman. Now listening a little more closely, he waited for the doctor to say where he had come from.   Unable to hear all of the conversation and not hearing where he came from, Pedro decided to find out for himself, who it was that had a heart attack.   He walked back to Dixon's room and found Steve asleep. He nudged the FBI agent, "I need to see if my old friend is in here," Pedro said, knowing full well he would hopefully find the policeman in the hospital, as well.

Steve nodded his head, "You know where I'll be."

Pedro walked the corridors of the hospital looking into each room. Not finding anyone in the beds, he stopped at a nurse's station, "My cousin was brought in for a heart attack today.   Can you tell me what room he is in?"

The nurse started looking at her computer screen, "What's his name?"

Pedro stood there for a second, not knowing what to say at first. Then quickly thinking said, "Fernando Ortiz.   I know that he works as a federally."

The nurse looked for the name on her computer and was unable to find it, "The only person we have in here for a heart attack is Juan

Sanchez. He is in room 12, down the hall, that way," she said, pointing in the direction of the ICU sign.

Pedro thanked her, "I must be mistaken. Thank you for your time," he said, as he walked back towards the room where Dixon was resting.

When he got back to the room, Pedro saw that Miguel was already there.   Motioning for him to follow him, he took Miguel a little way down the hall before stopping to speak to him. Miguel was all ears as Pedro spoke, "There is a man by the name of Juan Sanchez who had a heart attack and is here in room 12, down that hall," Pedro said, as he pointed towards the ICU unit of the hospital.

"Si papa," Miguel said, as he listened to his father.

"I want you to go to that room and find out who is in there. I think that it maybe the policeman that beat you with a belt. I need you find out for me and then come back and tell me," he said.

Miguel was now ready to go when he heard it might be the policeman. Pedro could see this in the boy's eyes. He grabbed him gently by the arm and continued, "You need to pretend that you are his son who just found out he was in here. Do you hear what I'm saying?"

Miguel, once again, nodded his head yes and then walked towards the ICU nurses' station as if he was on a mission.

Miguel walked up to the nurses station and found that the nurse was away from her desk doing her rounds. As he looked around, there was no one else in the ICU in either direction. He began looking at the numbers on the doors of the patient rooms near the nurse's station and followed the numbers till he was at the door of room 12. He stood there listening for a minute to see if the nurse was in the room. Then peeking inside, he could see the policeman laying on the bed. Even with a oxygen mask on he could tell who it was. As he stood there looking at the man in the bed tears began to fill his eyes and began to fall from them as he remembered the pain from the beatings, he had received from him. The nurse, still on her rounds walked into the room and seeing Miguel standing there came up behind him, "Can I help you?   Where are your parents?"

Caught by surprise, Miguel knew he had to come up with a reason for him to be there. He turned towards the nurse, "He is my papa, is he going to be alright?"

Seeing the tears, she took him back to the nurses station with her arm wrapped around his shoulder trying to comfort him.   She looked for his file on her desk and when she found it she read the report, "He's doing well and will be released tomorrow to go home," she said, smiling at Miguel.

Miguel, wiping the tears away, left the nurses station, thanking her for the good news.   He walked back to where his father was waiting for him and when he saw him he nodded his head yes before going to sit down in a chair.   Pedro smiled and waited for his son to gather himself together so he could talk to him. He was now thinking about what he was going to do to get even for the policeman's brutal acts on his son.   Just as he started to think about it the doctor came in with the x-rays.

"I've finally got the x-rays back; would you like to come out into the hallway and look at them, so we don't disturb the patient?"

Hearing the question, Steve jumped up, "That would be great," as he and Pedro walked out of the room.

The doctor raised the x-rays up to the light so all of them could see. Taking one down and grabbing the next one, the doctor didn't say a word as he was awe struck at what the two had accomplished, by taking the bullet out and stopping the bleeding, and because of it Dixon would live. When they were finished looking at the x-rays, the doctor looked at the two men standing there, "I don't know how you did it, but from what I can tell, you saved this man's life by doing what you did for him. All we need to do is make sure he doesn't get an infection. He'll be here for a couple of days just for observation."

"That is good news, yes indeed," Pedro replied, as he looked at Steve, who was relieved and smiling now.

Knowing that Dixon was going to make it Steve said, "Hey doc, I need you to look at my leg."

"What happened to it?" the doctor asked.

"I was shot through the leg doc.   It's a clean shot, just a hole."

"The doctor was surprised by the agent's nonchalant attitude about being shot and shook his head, "Crazy Americans," as he grabbed a wheelchair for the agent to sit in.

The doctor took Steve to the x-ray room to get pictures of his leg. This gave Pedro a chance to visit with Miguel. "What did you learn?" he asked.

"He is to be released tomorrow to go home,"

"Excellent, we can wait till he gets home before we do anything to him," he said, smiling, thinking of what he could do to him.

Miguel looked up at his dad, "Do we have to do anything to him?"

The question caught Pedro by surprise and at first, he didn't know how to answer it, then he asked, "Why do you ask that?"

"I've been thinking about all of the stuff we've done since the Americanos arrived. We've been very fortunate that no one has died except the bad guys. I wish to stop all of this so that we can go back to being normal again. I'm tired of all the pain that has been caused throughout all of this, mine included," Miguel said, as he looked at his papa.

Pedro saw the tears once again in Miguel's eyes, "How would you like to handle this, seeing as how you were the one that was beat by him?"

"I don't know right now, but I will figure it out shortly," he said, feeling thankful that his dad understood.

"Very well then, I will wait until you are ready," Pedro said, as he looked at his son and smiled to himself thinking how proud he was of him for not wanting revenge as he had.

Both of them sat there while they waited for Steve to be checked by the doctor. Pedro put his arm around his son and just held him till he showed up. Steve walked up slightly limping with a wrap around his leg, indicating that a clean bandage had replaced the old one and rubbing his arm. "Man, I've never had so many shots to keep me healthy before in my life. This hurts more than being shot," he said, as he continued to rub his arm.

Both Pedro and Miguel started laughing at Steve. "Maybe you should have been born here, it's not so bad then," said Pedro with a chuckle.

Checking on Dixon once more and seeing him resting comfortably with antibiotics being fed to him through I.V. tubes, they left to go back to the village and wait for Mike, Tony, and the others to return.

The ride back was quiet and uneventful for them. Upon arriving back at their house, Miguel was already fast asleep in the back of the

SUV.   Pedro carried him into the house and into his room.   Then laying him on his bed he took a blanket and covered him. He stood there with tears in his eyes looking at Miguel for a moment, thinking that his son had become a man almost overnight.   He bent down and kissed him on the forehead and left the room. It was midnight and all of them were tired and ready for bed.   Pedro offered some blankets to Steve before going to his own room to lie down and sleep. The agent found a place to lay down that wouldn't bother his leg to much, near the fire, thinking that he would move the SUV back to its hiding place tomorrow after he got up.   Feeling his leg start to throb, he knew the pain killers were starting to wear off.   He reached into his vest pocket and pulled out some of the cocoa leaves that were meant for Dixon and started chewing on them.   As he lay there, he started to feel better as the cocoa leaves did their magic, within minutes there was no more pain.   As he lay there, he could feel all of the stress begin to leave.   After a few minutes the house was quiet, and they were all asleep.

Chapter XXXVII

Dannelle looked out into the night sky through her bedroom window and heard the Cuckoo Clock start sounding off to let everyone know what time it was. This clock was all that Gunther had to remind him of his homeland. To Dannelle, it was something to behold, as she watched and waited for the Cuckoo bird to make its appearance as it announced the time of day. She was feeling anxious about what was going to happen, all she could do is wait and see what tomorrow would bring for her and Adrianna.

With the help of some of the girls, they had moved the guard that Adrianna had slipped a Mickey to, into the front room and told the other guards where he was, explaining to them that they had found him like this. Fortunately, Gunther was still in his room with the music playing loud enough so that any noise that was created when they moved the guard was covered by it. When this was done, she and Adrianna, went back to their room to call it a night. Before Dannelle went to bed she looked out the window one last time. This time she saw Gunther walking around, looking and listening for anything that was not normal. Having finished the last of the champagne, Gunther had gotten up and left the girl, who was still asleep in his room, to make his nightly rounds. Dannelle was surprised to see him outside and quickly closed the curtains, turned off the light and climbed into her bed and snuggled up next her friend, Adrianna, and fell asleep.

Seeing the bedroom light being turned off, Gunther went off a little farther into the darkness closer to the jungle. As he stood there, he could hear the noises coming from the deeper parts of the jungle and knew that just because the sun went down the jungle was still very much alive, even at night. The creatures that ruled the night were stirring around looking for food in order to survive one more day. He understood the need to survive and, because of that need, he prided himself knowing that he was like one of those creatures in the jungle. The difference was that he, in a sense, felt that he was the king of the jungle. Not being religious in any way, he just thought that if he died, that was all there was. However, that being said, looking into the night sky he still marveled about how big and endless everything was to him. For him, this was the closest thing to believing in a God. He stood there for a moment, taking it all in, and then went back inside to go to bed. The girl that he had left asleep in his bed had now gone back to her room. As he stood there looking at the empty room he was glad that she had gone as he had wanted to be alone tonight. He had grown tired of all that had been happening lately. Even the girls were starting to bore him and he wondered if he should get rid of them and not have any more in the house. Even with the money and the girls he realized that all the girls had wanted was security and they were willing to do anything to get it. Turning his mind off for the night, he took his robe off and threw it across the foot of the bed, crawled into bed and was asleep in a short time.

Unbeknownst to Miguel or Pedro, the policeman saw Miguel enter into his room and stand there looking at him. He knew now that they would be looking for him. Not wanting to be caught off guard by anyone in particular, especially Pedro, he decided to leave the hospital that night. Of course, he would wait for the nurse to make her rounds before leaving the hospital and get the jump on whatever may be coming to him. He pretended to be asleep as he waited for the nurse to leave his room before getting out of bed. After she had left, he went to his door and carefully opened it to see where the nurse had gone and spotted her sitting at her station doing some paperwork. As he moved quietly inside his room, he got himself dressed in the dark so as not to attract the nurse. He then found his keys to his truck and held onto them as he waited for the nurse to leave her station to check on the other patients down the hall. He walked quietly down the hallway and found the door that led to the parking lot. He carefully opened the door, making sure that no one was around and made his way to where his truck was parked and started up the engine, making sure that his headlights were off till he was clear of the of the hospital. He turned them on again once he was on the main road and headed back to the village and to his office. As he came into the village he drove by Pedro's house and saw a vehicle that was a rental. Seeing the SUV parked there only added to the paranoia he was already feeling. When he got to his office, he parked his truck, knowing that tomorrow he would speak to Señor Reichman about someone staying at Pedro's house that was unknown to him. He smiled, knowing that the German would pay him lots of money for the information he had to sell. In the meantime, he closed and locked the door to his office and went into the back area where the jail cells were located, found an empty bed and laid down on it.   He was remembering what the doctor had told him about being careful and not to overdo it because of being weak and tired from the heart attack. The doctor made him realize that it was going to take some time to get back to his idea of being healthy. Still feeling like he had been beat up, he rolled over onto his side to get more comfortable and was fast asleep, knowing that exercise and eating healthy would be the new regimen if he wanted to live.

It was later that night that the nurse came back in to check on him as she did her rounds.   When she noticed that he was not their she called the doctor to let him know that the policeman had gone. Upon hearing this, the doctor shook his head thinking, *"A man that was operated on in the jungle, another with leg wound from a bullet and now the heart attack victim walks out of the hospital without telling anyone. The next time there's a full moon, I'm trading with the other doctor."*

Chapter XXXVIII

Mike and his agents were already awake just as the sun was starting to rise above the mountains. They had already packed their gear and were using their backpacks as something to lean against while they were drinking their coffee, trying to warm up and get going. Agent Beck had brought a couple of Sterno burners with him so that they could have some hot coffee before heading down the trail to Gunther's house. Tony was wide awake and had just completed checking his rifle after adding some oil to the bolt action. He tested the bolt action by going through a few dry runs then loaded one of the clips into his rifle once he was satisfied that the gun would work the way he needed it to. The last thing he wanted to be, was a weak link on the team. He was nervous, and at the same time, excited to be part of what was about to happen. As he looked around at the team, it seemed as if this was just another day at the office. All of them seemed relaxed and as if they were getting ready to go fishing.

"People, you know what's ahead of us this morning. I know all of you have done this type of mission before. That being said, were operating without two of our team here. I need you to remember this and don't do anything crazy and get you or someone on the team killed because you weren't thinking about your situational awareness. Once we leave our comfort area, I want you to think about why we're here and what part you play in this operation," Beck said, looking at the others. He could see that they were already in the zone and ready to go. "Enough said. Remember we have civilians in the house, make sure you're sure of your target before you fire your weapons."

Mike looked at Tony and could tell by the look in his eyes, that he would be fine doing his part of the operation. Seeing that all was ready, Mike nodded to Beck to let him know that he was ready to go. Beck picked up his pack and put it on his back, from here he went about checking each of the other agents' backpacks and weapons making sure everything was secured correctly. Occasionally, cussing at an agent that he had found something wrong with.   None of the agents ever spoke out against Beck because they knew where he was coming from.

For Beck, his thoroughness was based on an incident earlier in his career in the mid-eighties.   It was one of his first experiences as a rookie agent working in the Miami, Florida area.   It was also the same day that two of his mentors were killed during a gun battle in the middle of a busy highway in Miami.   The agents were not fully briefed as what to expect going after the bank robbers.   They were informed that the two bank robbers were trying to get away from the agents in a stolen car.   Beck was asked to stay behind and work with the local police to get more information about the robbers. They left him there at the bank to do so. That was the day that the FBI will remember for quite some time to come. The agents had run the robbers to ground with them having an accident in their stolen car in the middle of the highway.   Eight FBI agents were on one side of the highway and the bank robbers were on the other side.   Each group was looking across the four lanes of the main highway.   Each side started firing at each other while the cars were driving through the fire fight.   In the end, the robbers didn't get away, both of them were killed.   The agents involved in the fight suffered two casualties and three of their agents were seriously wounded as well. In the end, the FBI lost two of their finest agents because of it. Beck had always thought that if he had been there, his two mentors might still be alive.   Promising to himself not to let that happen again, he worked tirelessly learning everything he could from the survivors of the five-minute gunfight and the actual final report on how to handle all kinds of fire fights.   Having learned quite a bit, he was offered a job at Quantico to teach the rookies how to survive and win in a firefight. After five years he went back out onto the streets once again, now working with some of the agents he trained.

Ever since then, Beck was known as a tough meticulous bastard to his teammates.   His reason for being so tough was that he wanted to make sure all of his agents returned home safely.   Since that time, every mission that he had been involved with setting up and running, the agents had always returned home safely.   Because of this, he was respected for his skills and his exceptional ability to do the right thing at the right time through constant situational awareness.

Now moving down, the trail to Gunther's house, all of them were ready to do their job in taking Gunther Reichman back alive or dead. Beck had taken point for the team and all eyes were on him as he cleared the trail in front of them. Mike was behind the agents, watching the other team members as they made their way. Tony was following Mike with his rifle slung on his shoulder with two of the five loaded clips in his vest pocket.

By 7 a.m. all of the agents were in place, having used the darkness of the morning to their advantage. Tony was laying in some tall grass using his scope to find his targets. Every once in a while, he would scan the areas where the agents were trying to get to, making sure there were no surprises for any of them. Two of the agents were coming in from the backyard directly below where Tony was placed. The other two, Beck and Mike, went on into the jungle and were going to come in on the east side of the house. Tony's job was to take out the guard on the roof. The two agents working right below him were to take out the roving guards. Mike and Beck would take out the guard in the front of the house.

Dannelle woke up early and wide awake, not really knowing why after being up so late the night before and could hear the guards talking amongst themselves as they made the changes for the day shift to come on and the night shift to get some rest after they had finished eating. She looked at Adrianna and could tell that she was still sound asleep and would be for at least another hour, maybe two. When she got up, she instinctively went to the bedroom window and looked out. Seeing nothing new, she closed the curtains and started to get herself ready for the day.

Dannelle walked past Gunther's bedroom and could see that he was still sound asleep in his bed. Not wanting to wake him, she went downstairs to get something to eat to tide her over till breakfast was ready. With Gunther still sleeping, she took a chance and went out to sit on the patio and enjoy the coolness of the morning. As she sat there, she never realized how noisy it was in the jungle this time of the morning. After thirty minutes, Dannelle could hear movement inside the house, knowing the cook was busy in the kitchen making breakfast for them. The smell of the food being cooked wafted through the house like a bell going off inside the brains of the people who were still asleep, alarming them that breakfast was cooking.

Everyone was now starting to wake up. After making themselves somewhat presentable, Gunther and the other girls, all came down the stairs and were sitting at the breakfast bar, drinking their coffee while they waited for breakfast. Dannelle stayed out on the patio area savoring every moment of solitude. While she sat there, she caught something moving out of the corner of her eye. Now watching more closely, she could see some movement on the hill in front of her. She   pretended not to notice and carefully continued to watch the shadow, trying to figure out who or what it was.   As she sat there, she was transfixed on the shadow that was still moving a little bit closer to her, only this time, slower. She was excited to think that maybe it was the FBI and they had come to take Gunther and free her from her gilded prison.

When everyone was in place waiting to go after Gunther, Tony quietly pulled back the safety on his rifle waiting for the firefight to start.   The FBI agents below Tony had started to work their way up to the house.   Looking through his scope, Tony found the guard on the roof and waited before having to shoot him.   The guard on the roof top was just starting to get himself squared away for another long day with only an umbrella to keep the sun off of him.   Because he was busy setting it up, he missed seeing the two agents as they snuck over to the fire pit. Then one at a time, each of them made their way to the bushes that surrounded the house.   Both agents were now hid in the green plants that provided shade next to the house.   They pulled their knives out and waited for the guards patrolling the perimeter of the house to come around.   Being set, the agents didn't have long to wait. When the guards came around Dannelle, she stood up and started fixing the dress that she was wearing, pulling up the bottom of her dress revealing more leg than usual.   The two guards stopped and watched her and didn't hear the two agents come up from behind them, as they cut their throats. Then they quickly dragged the two men into the shrubbery next to the house and quietly hid them under the brush as they died. One of the agents looked at Dannelle and signaled his thanks for the diversion.   The guard on the roof, hearing some noise from below, called out, "Hey, what's going on down there?"

Dannelle walked out from under the patio awning and looked up at the guard, "I accidentally dropped my plate of food," she said, smiling up at the guard. "Now I have to go back in and get some more."

Thinking none the worse, the guard asked, "Have you seen the other two men guarding the house this morning?"

"Yeah, they just passed by about a minute ago."

"When you see them again, would you tell them to get me some coffee?"

"Yes, not a problem, I will do that for you," she replied.

The two agents went back to the side of the house and hid again in the shrubbery, waiting for Mike and Beck to take out the guard in the front.

Dannelle, realizing what was going on, stepped back into the house and walked into the kitchen where everyone was gathered together eating breakfast in the nook. She grabbed a plate and helped herself to the bowels of food sitting on the small cart and then sat down next to Adrianna to eat. She could see that Gunther was in rare form this morning as he told stories and cracked jokes to everyone there at the table. Being last to arrive, Dannelle waited for Gunther to say something to her about being late for breakfast but being in such a good mood he said nothing. As she quickly ate her food and drank her juice, she quietly excused herself from the table and went to put her dishes in the sink. She was still expecting Gunther to say something to her as she went back upstairs to her room. Once getting there, she quickly changed from her dress and into some jeans and a shirt to wear. As she came down the stairs in different clothes Adrianna noticed that she was wearing something different. "Why have you changed your clothes?"

"I've decided to go into the barn and look around for something to do. And you know how messy it is in there?"

After thinking for a moment Adrianna said, "Wait I will go with you."

"How about you meet me there when you're ready?" she said smiling.

"Okay, I'll be there in a minute," she replied, as she went upstairs to change her clothes.

By now breakfast was over and Gunther was going upstairs to his room to change out of his robe and pajamas into his regular clothes for a meeting he had scheduled for later that day. As he passed by

Dannelle's room he decided to walk in unannounced. He caught Adrianna coming out of the bathroom wearing pants and a shirt. "Where is Dannelle?" he asked.

"She went into the barn to try and find something to do for today," she replied, wondering why he was asking.

Gunther thought that Dannelle had never been interested in going to the barn before. "What's she planning on doing in there?"

"I really don't know, but I was headed out there myself to join her," she replied.

Not knowing what to make of this, and wondering why she would be interested in going out there he said, "Don't go till I'm ready and I'll go with you,"

Gunther went directly to his room and quickly changed into some work clothes, and grabbed his gun, sticking it into his waistband. Before leaving his room, he looked out his window in the direction of the barn looking for Dannelle. Not seeing her, he closed his bedroom door and went out to meet Adrianna and they walked down the stairs together to go out to the barn.

Tony watched Dannelle leave and go into the barn, and thought to himself, *"At least she is safe now."* Then he saw Gunther come out with a young lady, carrying a gun as they headed towards the barn, at this point he started to panic a little. Not knowing what was going on, he was torn between staying where he was or going after Dannelle to protect her.

Dannelle, now in the hayloft and sitting behind two bales of hay, looked out the upper hay loading entrance thinking that this would be a great place to watch the take down of Gunther by the FBI. She saw Gunther and Adrianna headed towards the barn. Seeing the gun in his waistband of his pants, Dannelle, yelled out to both of them, "Hey guys, what are you doing?"

Caught off guard by her question, Gunther stopped in tracks and stood there while Adrianna kept walking towards the barn. Regaining his composure, he quickly caught up with Dannelle's friend and continued walking towards the barn. By the time, the two of them got to the barn Dannelle met them at the entrance and stood there smiling at them. Gunther not sure what to do asked, "What are you doing in here?"

"I've never been in here before, so I thought it was high time to come and check it out and look to see if there was anything I could find to do," she said smiling.

Gunther didn't know how to reply to this and stood there for a second. He wanted to be upset yet didn't have a reason to be. "Okay, just be careful. I'm going to take a shower now," he said, as he turned to walk away from the two girls back to the house, still trying to maintain control.

When he got back inside the house, he stood there looking out the kitchen window at the barn. Still not sure what was going on, he went up to his room, got himself undressed and turned on the shower and waited for the water to warm up.

Both Tony and the guard up on the roof watched with interest at what just happened. The guard put his weapon down and continued with other things as he waited for his coffee. Tony was relieved when he saw Gunther leaving the barn, knowing that both girls were safe.

Once Gunther was out of sight, Dannelle took Adrianna by the hand and walked back into the barn. Dannelle waited a few minutes, watching to make sure that Gunther wasn't going to return. And then turned to Adrianna, "They're here, the FBI is here," she said, smiling.

Adrianna got excited at the comment, "What do we do now?"

"The first thing we do, is to get to a safe place and away from the bullets," she said, as she took her friend up into the lay loft.

Mike and Beck were in place watching the guard at the front of the house, trying to figure out how to neutralize him so they could secure an entrance into the house. The guard looked at his watch, got up and started looking for the other two guards who were supposed to be making their rounds around the house. He was cussing under his breath at the two guards, thinking they got caught up talking to one of the girls. As he slowly made his way to the backside of the house, the two agents hiding in the bushes, met him and quietly solved his problem of looking for the other two guards. One of the agents coming from the back of the house, signaled to Beck and Mike that the front guard had been disposed of and was now resting with his friends. Mike and Beck, seeing this, carefully made their way up the steps to the front door of the house and opened it. They walked past the living room and into the kitchen and then onto the landing that lead to the basement stairs. While Mike stayed on the landing providing cover for Beck, he carefully and quietly got on his hands and knees and slowly moved down the stairs, looking for a place to hide till he was ready to take the guard out. Finding a dark corner, Beck stood in the shadows against the wall. Once he was in place, he signaled Mike to make some kind of noise to get the guard's attention. Mike, trying to create a diversion, called out to the guard, "Can you tell me where I can find a bathroom, I have to go."

Getting up from his chair, the guard had his rifle in the firing position trying to figure out who it was that asked the question. Beck watched the guard, who was still listening to his radio, slowly walk by him. This gave him the opportunity to come up from behind him and quickly grab him by the head, snapping his neck. Beck waited a minute to make sure that no one heard the scuffle. He then signaled Mike to come down and help him move the body out of sight.

After they hid the body, they both started looking for the switch that opened the entrance to the tunnel that Gunther had used once before to get away. After searching for about ten minutes Beck found the switch that opened the tunnel door. He called out to Mike, "Hey, I think I found the bathroom," chuckling as he said it.

Mike came over to check out what Beck had found. Mike reached in and found a light switch inside the tunnel and turned it on. He motioned for Beck to stay where he was at and then started walking into the tunnel. When he came back, he had a backpack in his hand. "Take a look at what I found."

Beck looked inside the bag and could see bundles of money, some food, and clothes. "Do you think he was going to tell us good-bye before he left?"

"I think you've been doing this to long."

"Hey, I got an idea. How about we push him here, so you can arrest him as he tries to run from us?"

Mike smiled at the idea and nodded his head in agreement.

As they came out of the entrance of the tunnel, Beck toggled the switch on the wall, closing the tunnel and then broke it. He left Mike behind, waiting in the shadows of the basement. He then went out the front door and walked around the house looking for the other agents. After he found them, he called them together, "We want Gunther to know that we're here so that he will make a run for the basement to escape, where our boss will be waiting for him."

All of them shook their heads in agreement and spread out around the house. Once everyone was in place, Beck walked back towards the patio. By now the guard on the roof, who had been waiting for his coffee, realized that something wasn't right. He called down to the guards, complaining about where his coffee was. Unable to see Tony, Beck signaled anyway. Using his hand, he pointed up to the guard on the roof and then slid his finger across his throat. Tony, seeing Beck do this, fired his rifle once and the guard wasn't going to need his coffee after all.

Gunther hearing the shot, was startled by it. He quickly got dressed and headed down the stairs to the kitchen. Seeing no one, he made his way down into the basement and to the entrance of the tunnel. He reached for the switch and when he turned it, it was then that he realized it was broken. He stood there for a moment trying to decide what to do next. Seeing his opportunity, Mike came out of the shadows and hit him from behind, knocking him to the ground and took his gun from him. Mike then cuffed him, picked him up and pushed Gunther in front of him, as they climbed the stairs back into the kitchen.

After hearing the shot, the guards who had been sleeping, came out of their room and started looking for the shooter, going room to room and running into the girls as they did so. After clearing the upstairs part of the house, the guards grabbed one of the girls and using her as a shield, walked behind her as they came down the stairs. The two agents who had been hiding in the living room behind some furniture waited for their chance to get the guards. Beck, watching the two guards as they came down the stairs with the girl in front of them, realized that he didn't have a clear shot, fired his gun into the air trying to attract their attention. Hearing the gunshot, the two guards went in search of the person who fired the shot. As they walked past the front room they did a quick check and continued their search looking for the shooter. The two agents waiting in the front room, shot both guards from behind leaving the girl screaming and now running to get out of the house.

After they captured Gunther, Mike led him out into the backyard and called for all of his men to come meet him. "Gentlemen, this is Gunther Reichman. He's the reason why we've been enjoying the scenery up close and personal in this beautiful country."

Tony, seeing Mike and Beck standing there, came down from his spot and stood with them looking at the man that had caused so much damage to two different countries. "How does it feel knowing that you destroyed so many lives trying to prove that your technology worked?" Tony said, as he hit him.

Reeling from the blow, Gunther fell to the ground and realized that no one would help him get back up. Gunther looked at Tony and said nothing as he continued to look down on the ground in front of him.

"Have you ever read a book called, 'Oh, the Places You'll Go' by Dr. Seuss? Well, you're going to go to Washington, D.C. to meet the U.S. attorneys in the Department of Justice. Then from there, as a bonus, you may be traveling, on an all-expenses paid trip, to Russia to meet new people there, who are definitely waiting to meet you."

Seeing the men surrounding Gunther, Dannelle and Adrianna came out of the barn and walked over to look at Gunther. "How does it feel, knowing you're going to die for what you have done?"

Gunther, hearing her voice looked up at her. "I should have killed you when I had the chance."

"But you didn't," she said, as she slapped him in the face.

The slap was unexpected and almost dropped him to his knees. All of the other men laughed at him as he tried to stand up again.

"You are no different than me. You use people like I do, to get money from them. You may not be a murderer, but you're still trash and a whore and good for nothing else as you keep looking for the next person to take their money," he said smiling, to cover up his embarrassment.

"Go to Hell!" Dannelle said.

"You first."

The statement rang true and it cut Dannelle to the heart. As she walked away, she started to cry. Tony, watching all of this, walked over to where she was standing, "What he has said may be true, but it doesn't have to be that way forever," he said, smiling as he held her.

"Is it possible to change, even me?"

"It all depends on how bad you want the change. It is really up to you."

After all was said and done, Mike and Beck decided to drive back to Pedro's house instead of climbing over the mountain again, and then leave from there to go back to the United States with their prisoner in tow. After they gathered up all of their gear, they found Gunther's truck and loaded him and their gear into the back of it along with the other agents. When they arrived back at the farm everyone was happy to be reunited again. Mike looked around, "Where's Dixon?"

"He's still at the hospital recovering from the surgery we performed on him," Steve replied.

"What happened?"

"You'll need to ask Dixon about it."

To celebrate their catching Gunther Reichman, Tony and Mike decided to treat the team to at least one beer in the cantina. Pedro declined, "I'll stay here and watch Señor Reichman. If you hear a shot, have another beer and then come see what happened."

With that, everyone headed to the cantina to enjoy themselves. Looking at Dannelle and her friend, Tony asked, "Would you like to join us?"

"No, I am ready to stay home for a while."

Adrianna nodded her head in agreement with Dannelle.

As she watched the Americans leave to go to the cantina Dannelle turned to look at Pedro and Miguel. "Would it be alright if I stayed here with you for a while?"

"Why yes, you are welcome to stay for as long as you like," said Pedro.

"What would you like to do now that you are free?" Dannelle asked Adrianna.

"Oh, I don't know, this is all new to me," she said smiling, "Can I stay here for a while to figure it out?"

Pedro was listening to their conversation, he looked at both of them and smiled, "You can stay as long as you like."

As it worked out, Adrianna stayed with Pedro and Miguel for the rest of her life, working the farm with both of them. She ended up taking care of Pedro after Miguel left to go to school, till he passed away.

Miguel came back after he finished his degree in Agribusiness and took over the farm with Adrianna.   He became a representative for that part of the country, and then went on to become the Secretary of Agriculture for Brazil.   A few years later he married Adrianna.

The policeman woke up with a start, thinking that someone was in the jail with him. As he looked around the other cells, he didn't see anything out of place.   Blaming his paranoia on a bad night's sleep, he carefully got up to get himself a shower and some food.   As he was finishing his breakfast, he remembered the job that he had to do first thing.   He had to tell Señor Reichman about the SUV he saw the night before at Pedro's place.   When he finished his breakfast, he got into his truck and drove off in the direction of Gunther's house.   As he drove to the house, he had a feeling that he was being followed, expecting to see the SUV that he had seen earlier at Pedro's place.   He kept looking into his rear-view mirror to see if he was and was surprised to see that no one was following him.   As he made a turn around the bend in the road, he stopped and watched as a young woman was running down the road.   He recognized her as one of Gunther's toys.   Wondering what was going on he backed up and went after the woman.   When he finally caught up to her, he stopped her as she struggled to get away, "What has happened."

"The Americanos are there, and they have killed the guards," she said, crying.

"Did they get Señor Reichman?"

"I don't know.   I ran out of the house after the two guards were killed," she said, as she struggled again to get away from the policeman.

Holding her by the arm, he half carried her with him and put her into his truck.   He made sure that the door was locked on her side of the truck so that she couldn't escape and continued driving towards the house.   Within minutes they arrived at the German's house and found only one of the girls there, sitting in the chair that the guard had used. With his gun drawn, the policeman cautiously walked up to where she was seated. "Where is everybody?" he asked, as he continued to look around.

"Gone, all gone," she replied.

"Where did they go?   Where is Señor Reichman?" he said, after holstering his gun.

"The gringos took him with them."

By now the girl in the truck got out and went to the other girl sitting on the porch and stood by her. Holding her hand, they got up and walked into the house and into the kitchen. The policeman followed them and when he got to the living room, he sat down and smiled to himself, "I guess this house is being confiscated by the police as of right now."

Looking at the two girls who had reappeared, "Would you care to stay here with me?"

The girls looked at each other, knowing they had nowhere else to go, "What would we be doing here?" one of them asked.

"What were you doing for Señor Reichman?"

They   nodded their heads yes in understanding and went upstairs to take a nap. The policeman looked around his new home and walked into the den where he found the cigar box. He opened it, took one of the cigars out and smelled it as if it was a fresh cookie straight out of the oven.   Thinking to himself, *"Nothing but the best for* Señor *Reichman."* Then he lit it up and enjoyed smoking it as he went from room to room exploring his new home. As he went down the stairs to the basement, he found the backpack with the money in it. He looked around and not seeing anyone, grabbed the backpack, took it upstairs and hid it. As he made sure the money was secure, he called the girls to come down and join him in the pool. He sat in the pool, still smoking his cigar, and smiled to himself, knowing this time that Señor Reichman wasn't returning. The girls came over to where the policeman was and started splashing him with water and as they did, he just laughed.

It was only later that Pedro found out that the policeman had moved into the German's house. After finding this out, Pedro waited till the policeman was out of the house with his two girls on a trip somewhere. He went to the house and started looking around and while doing so, he found the place where the policeman kept the money he had found from Gunther. After taking it, he then went into the living room and over to the fireplace, turned on the gas and walked outside. As he stood outside the door of the house, he threw a burning rag into the foyer and watched the house explode, burning to the ground.   He smiled and wished that he could be there to see the look on the policeman's face, knowing he was going back to sleep in the old jail once again, with nothing but the clothes on his back.

Pedro thought to himself, *"Sometimes killing someone isn't the worst thing that could happen to someone that is evil."*

After a few phone calls to Washington from Mike, the Lear jet had landed in a town adjacent to the village where the team was situated. Mike had decided to have everyone leave in the middle of the night to get Gunther to the airport in the SUV's.   This way the townsfolk would be in their beds asleep and would be left wondering what had happened to their dear Gunther, and the other men that were guarding him.

Tony and Mike boarded the flight with their prisoner shackled around the waste and handcuffed, with two of the men from the team watching him. Dixon and Steve boarded last to give the German a chance to get secured.   One of the agents put his seat belt on for him and sat down across from him.   Gunther smiled at the agent, laid his head back on his seat and went to sleep.

They were all still tired from the incident that had occurred at the jail earlier, where they had been keeping Gunther till the plane came to pick them all up.   It almost ended up in a disaster. The locals had found out what had happened to their friend and tried to storm the jail to free him.   Fortunately, Mike had left two agents at the jail to keep guard over their prisoner.   One of the agents fired his gun into the air a couple of times to try and disperse the crowd.   The towns people weren't phased by this at all, they continued trying to break in and get Gunther out of the jail.   This time, someone in the crowd fired at the agents.   Being fire upon, they returned fire by shooting into the crowd and wounding some of the men in the group. The vigilantes realized that the agents were serious about their jobs and left, helping to carry the ones that had been wounded. When the agents came in after the crowd left, they bolted the door and one of the agents went in to check on Gunther and could see the disappointment in his eyes. "I hope you didn't have any ideas about escaping, did you?" the agent said, laughing, seeing the look of frustration in his eyes.

Gunther sat down on his bed, not saying a word.   The policeman was in the cell next to him sitting on his bed, laughing at Gunther, "I don't think you'll be here much longer Señor; I think you may be going to America."

Gunther looked at him, "Leastwise, when I go to jail, I will have clean sheets and warm food.   Where are you going to be?"

"I will be free and out of jail and living in your house," the policeman said, laughing.

Mike had thought it best to have the policeman locked up, just in case he allowed Gunther to escape for some of Gunther's money. Mike used the beating of Miguel as the reason for locking him up, along with sending a report to his superiors, via the U.S. Embassy, explaining what he had done to Miguel.

The flight was nice and gave the men a chance to relax and sleep a little. Tony took his shoes off and stretched out to sleep on one of the reclining seats. When they arrived back in the United States, landing in Phoenix, they were met by some FBI agents from Washington D.C. where Mike handed off their prisoner to them.   From there, the two FBI agents escorted him onto another flight known as Con Air.   Mike and his team stayed the night in Phoenix to clean up before catching a civilian flight back to Washington.   Tony decided to fly back on the same airplane that Gunther was on.   He was surprised at how many felons were on the flight, all of them shackled and handcuffed, wearing white coveralls.   He stayed with the two agents aboard the flight, behind a chain link barrier that separated them from the prisoners.

When the flight landed, one of the agents gave Tony a ride to his car.   As he drove home, Tony realized that his adventure had come to an end.   He called Ann to let her know he was back home and wanted to come over to see her but was to tired and dirty to make the trip. They both agreed to meet the following night.   He changed out of his clothes for the first time in days and headed to the hot tub in his apartment complex, next to the pool.   He turned on all of the jets and sat there for an hour just relaxing, letting his muscles feel the hot water.   At first the water turned brown from all of the dirt he had on him, then the filters in the tub took over and turned the water all clear again. Tony didn't care, he just sat there and closed his eyes and let the hot water do its magic. With his eyes closed he didn't see Ann or hear her get into the hot tub. As she kissed him Tony jumped, surprised that someone had snuck up on him.   Opening his eyes and seeing Ann in her bikini left him speechless.

Later that night, Tony called the Admiral, "Just to let you know, I'm back from my crazy adventure."

"Good, glad to hear it.   How was it?"

"Let's just say, it was real, and it was fun, but it wasn't real fun. The good news is, we caught Mr. Reichman, destroyed a drug operation and some bad guys along the way."

"Take a couple of days off Tony, and then come see me, will you?" the Admiral replied.

"Will do, boss," Tony said, as he hung up the phone.

Feeling refreshed and hungry, he and Ann left his place and drove to a Burger King and ordered himself a double whopper with cheese, fries, a large orange drink, and a milkshake to go.   She of course ordered a salad with all of the fixings.   As he started to eat, he thought he had died and gone to heaven, with hot food and carbonated water.

Tony decided he would drop in on Chance at a later date to catch him up on the latest news and tell he and his wife about his adventures in South America.

He had Ann drive him back to his apartment and they both went in and turned on the T.V.   As it was, he fell asleep on the couch in the middle of the news.   Laying his head on Ann's lap he was fast asleep.   Ann stroked his hair and whispered to him, "I love you Tony and I want to marry you."

Tony barely hearing this replied, "I love you to and I will marry you.   But what do we tell the kids and the Admiral?"

Ann being caught off guard by the question didn't know what to say.   She looked at Tony and he smiled at her and started laughing at the look on her face.   Ann grabbed a throw pillow and hit him with it as he continued to laugh, rolling onto the floor as she started throwing the pillow. Stopping for just a moment she asked, "Did you say that you would marry me?"

"I think I did, what did you hear?" he said smiling.

Ann reached out to him and hugged him, "I'll never let you go, I promise you."

The End

Epilogue

Because of his work with the Navy in finding the USS Dolphin and assisting in finding the location of the bio-weapons, Chance and his team were awarded the highest Civilian Award for Bravery. Because of the classification of their work it was a closed ceremony.

Commander Anthony Jones was promoted to the rank of Captain for the work he did to assist the FBI in finding Gunther Reichman and taking the lead in the investigation in finding a terrorist cell and saving five ships from destruction by locating the bombs that were planted on board the ships. He was re-assigned to the Naval Intelligence section in Washington D.C. as Chief after spending a couple of weeks on his honeymoon with Ann. (The Admiral is still upset at having to find a new secretary.)

Mike Reagan was promoted to Special Agent in Charge in their Anti-terrorism unit for the United States in Washington D.C.

Agent Beck took over Mike's old job, refusing to go back to Quantico to teach.

Agent Dixon went from South America to Bethesda Hospital to finish recovering from being shot. The doctors still talk about the scar on his chest from being operated on in the jungle. When asked if he would like to have it removed, he laughed, "Not on your life. Look what I can tell my grandkids." Agent Dixon went on to become an instructor at Quantico till he fully recovered from his wound. (He still likes to show the rookies his scar and talk about situational awareness.)

The dock worker was found guilty for his part in sabotaging the five U.S. Navy ships and found guilty for the destruction of the USS Dolphin and her crew. He committed suicide in the second year of his life sentence.   His wife and children were never found.

The terrorists were found guilty of attempting a terrorist attack on American soil and for the destruction of the USS Dolphin and her crew and were put in prison in Guantanamo Bay awaiting execution.

Ahmed, accordingly, sits in his cell and stares at the walls while being taken care of by Bashir.   The other two would never come out of their cell out of fear for their lives. They were all eventually executed with the news of their death being broadcast to the world.

The two Mossad agents were given awards for finding and killing the bomber that they had found in Iran and for stopping future bombings.

The CIA disavowed all knowledge that they played any part in the recon in locating the bio-weapons site in Iran.   Dan and John were moved back to their original places in the Middle East and remained quiet about the part that they played in the Terrorist action. With a commendation in their records.

The USS Dolphin and her crew were awarded a Presidential Unit Award posthumously for valor and gallantry.

Gunther Reichman was found guilty of the sinking of the USS Dolphin and her crew.   He's in prison in Florence, Colorado waiting to be moved to Gitmo.   Both Russia and Interpol wanted to prosecute him for the loss of their submarine and crew and the embezzlement of 65 million dollars.   As it was, they agreed with the final verdict of the U.S. court system.   To this day Gunther Reichman has refused to tell anyone where he hid the money and therefore it has never been recovered.

Gunther Reichman's wife and kids were allowed to stay in Germany and reside there for the rest of their lives.   Eventually selling their home and disappearing from everyone afterwards.

Bear Industries fell apart and reorganized into separate corporations, working in their own field of expertise, never to be what they were once again.

Dannelle received a letter from Tony, that had been marked special delivery and brought to her by one of the U.S. Embassy personnel from the capitol of Brazil.   When she opened the letter, she found a note inside along with a money order, "For your new future. Use this money for your education," signed by Tony, Mike, and Beck.

Pedro was allowed to keep Gunther's truck and used it to visit Gunther's house one last time before it burned down.   No one ever found out who started the fire and it was amazing that Pedro's farm now had new equipment to work the fields with.

The policeman was fired and replaced by another police officer and was last seen begging for money for drinks in the local bar. Eventually, he died from another heart attack brought on from excessive drinking and poor eating habits.

* 9 7 8 0 9 9 8 8 0 0 3 8 7 *